A whistle sounded, the train began to chug away, and the air was filled with white smoke.

'Bye.' She waved and waved until the train rounded a bend and Josef could be seen no more.

Jessica collapsed back in her seat. At that moment, all she could think of were Jamie and Dora. Was she fated to go to her grave without ever seeing them again?

Her eyes closed as the hypnotic sound of the train's wheels began to lure her into sleep. She felt awfully odd, she was about to wake up and find that this past year had been nothing but a dream.

'*Au revoir*, Liverpool,' she said, half aloud.

Maureen Lee was born in Bootle and now lives in Colchester, Essex. She is the author of many bestselling novels including *Mother of Pearl*, *Nothing Lasts Forever*, *Martha's Journey* and the three novels in the Pearl Street series, *Lights Out Liverpool*, *Put Out the Fires* and *Through the Storm* are all available from Orion. Her novel *Dancing in the Dark* won the 2000 Parker Romantic Novel of the Year Award. Visit her website at www.maureenlee.co.uk

Have you read them all?
Curl up with a

Maureen Lee

STEPPING STONES

Lizzie O'Brien escapes her dark
Liverpool childhood when she runs
away to London – towards freedom
and a new life. But the past is catching
up with her, threatening to destroy her
dreams . . .

LIGHTS OUT LIVERPOOL

There's a party on Pearl Street, but
a shadow hangs over the festivities:
Britain is on the brink of war. The
community must face hardship and
heartbreak with courage and humour.

PUT OUT THE FIRES

1940 – the cruellest year of war for
Britain's civilians. In Pearl Street, near
Liverpool's docks, families struggle to
cope the best they can.

THROUGH THE STORM

War has taken a terrible toll on Pearl Street, and changed the lives of all who live there. The German bombers have left rubble in their wake and everyone pulls together to come to terms with the loss of loved ones.

LIVERPOOL ANNIE

Just as Annie Harrison settles down to marriage and motherhood, fate deals an unexpected blow. As she struggles to cope, a chance meeting leads to events she has no control over. Could this be Annie's shot at happiness?

DANCING IN THE DARK

When Millie Cameron is asked to sort through her late aunt's possessions, she finds, buried among the photographs, letters and newspaper clippings, a shocking secret . . .

THE GIRL FROM BAREFOOT HOUSE

War tears Josie Flynn from all she knows. Life takes her to Barefoot House as the companion of an elderly woman, and to New York with a new love. But she's soon back in Liverpool, and embarks upon an unlikely career . . .

LACEYS OF LIVERPOOL

Sisters-in-law Alice and Cora Lacey both give birth to boys on one chaotic night in 1940. But Cora's jealousy and resentment prompt her to commit a terrible act with devastating consequences . . .

THE HOUSE BY PRINCES PARK

Ruby O'Hagan's life is transformed when she's asked to look after a large house. It becomes a refuge – not just for Ruby and her family, but for many others, as loves, triumphs, sorrows and friendships are played out.

LIME STREET BLUES

1960s Liverpool, and three families are linked by music. The girls form a successful group, only to split up soon after: Rita to find success as a singer; Marcia to become a mother; and Jeannie to deceive her husband, with far-reaching consequences . . .

QUEEN OF THE MERSEY

Queenie Todd is evacuated to a small town on the Welsh coast with two others when the war begins. At first, the girls have a wonderful time until something happens, so terrifying that it will haunt them for the rest of their lives . . .

THE OLD HOUSE ON THE CORNER

Victoria lives in the old house on the corner. When the land is sold, she finds herself surrounded by new properties. Soon Victoria is drawn into the lives of her neighbours – their loves, lies and secrets.

THE SEPTEMBER GIRLS

Cara and Sybil are both born in the same house on one rainy September night. Years later, at the outbreak of war, they are thrown together when they enlist and are stationed in Malta. It's a time of live-changing repercussions for them both . . .

KITTY AND HER SISTERS

Kitty McCarthy wants a life less ordinary – she doesn't want to get married and raise children in Liverpool like her sisters. An impetuous decision and a chance meeting twenty years later are to have momentous repercussions that will stay with her for ever . . .

THE LEAVING OF LIVERPOOL

Escaping their abusive home in Ireland, sisters Mollie and Annemarie head to Liverpool – and a ship bound for New York. But fate deals a cruel blow and they are separated. Soon, World War II looms – with surprising consequences for the sisters.

MOTHER OF PEARL

Amy Curran was sent to prison for killing her husband. Twenty years later, she's released and reunited with her daughter, Pearl. But Amy is hiding a terrible secret – a tragedy that could tear the family apart . . .

NOTHING LASTS FOREVER

Her marriage failing, Brodie Logan returns to her childhood home, letting out the spare rooms to women with nowhere else to go. Their lives intertwine and friendships develop but then tragedy strikes and the women find that nothing lasts forever . . .

MARTHA'S JOURNEY

1914. To Martha Rossi's horror her underage son has enlisted and is promptly despatched to France, with devastating consequences. Martha embarks on a journey that will give voice to every mother who ever sacrificed a son, taking her right to No. 10's door.

Au Revoir Liverpool

Maureen Lee

An Orion paperback

First published in Great Britain in 2011
by Orion
This paperback edition published in 2011
by Orion Books Ltd,
Orion House, 5 Upper St Martin's Lane,
London WC2H 9EA

An Hachette UK company

A CIP catalogue record for this book
is available from the British Library.

Typeset at The Spartan Press Ltd,
Lymington, Hants

Printed in Great Britain by Clays Ltd,
St Ives Plc

The Orion Publishing Group's policy is to use papers that
are natural, renewable and recyclable products and
made from wood grown in sustainable forests. The logging
and manufacturing processes are expected to conform to
the environmental regulations of the country of origin.

www.orionbooks.co.uk

In memory of my parents,
Hannah and Edward Jordan.

Chapter 1

Liverpool
June 1937

Jessica's mother boasted that, at the age of forty-nine, she could still turn a man's head. 'I wonder if they will still turn when I'm fifty,' she would then say with a coy smile, as if, when the clock struck midnight on her birthday, her lovely face would melt into wrinkles, her startlingly blue eyes fade, and her hair turn grey (an impossibility as it had been grey for several years but dyed a pretty golden blonde). 'I'll become an old woman overnight.'

'Never!' the friends would gasp – it would have been rude not to and so deny that Ethel Farley had the gift of eternal youth. It was the reason why so many of her friends were male and so few female, the latter unprepared to worship at the foot of her shrine.

Earlier that morning, Ethel had married Tom McGrath, a well-known, Liverpool-based barrister, whose sometimes notorious cases were featured in the national press. Tom hadn't stopped to worship, but had swept Ethel off her feet at their first meeting. This time it was she who was doing the worshipping, having fallen madly and genuinely in love for the first time in her life.

'I think your stepfather is adorable,' said Jessica's cousin, Lydia, who was sitting next to her at the wedding breakfast.

'He looks like a gypsy.' Jessica didn't like her mother's second husband and resented him being referred to as any sort of father. He was too dark, too foreign-looking, his hair

1

too thick and curly, his sideboards too long. She considered him rather menacing. Nor did she like the idea of him replacing her real father, who had died five years ago and to whom she had been devoted.

'It's his Irish blood. He's a Celt, not a gypsy. The Celts have been in Ireland since 350BC.' Lydia seemed to know a bit about everything. As girls, she and Jessica had attended the same convent school and been in the same class. Lydia had usually been top in most subjects, whereas Jessica had only been good at Art and English – English Literature that was, not grammar. She had left at sixteen, but Lydia had stayed on, gone to university, and become a school teacher.

Jessica said, 'My real father was Irish and he wasn't dark like that.'

'He wasn't a Celt, that's why, just plain, ordinary Irish.'

The meal was being held in a private room in a small, hideously expensive hotel called The Temple, which was tucked like a secret behind Liverpool Town Hall. Anonymous outside, it was exotic, outlandish even, inside. Lydia added to her reputation of knowing everything by telling Jessica it was a place where well-off people conducted affairs of the heart and men picked up attractive women who were in actual fact high-class prostitutes. Parties were held there that no respectable woman would be seen dead at. 'Though it would be interesting to attend one,' Lydia said thoughtfully, a glint in her eye.

Thirty-three guests had been invited to the wedding, including Tom's twin daughters by his first wife, now sadly deceased, and their husbands, his brother and his brother's wife, and half a dozen other people whose names and relationships to each other Jessica couldn't remember. Also present was Monsignor Rafferty, who had married the couple and was sitting next to the bride.

On her mother's side there was her brother, Uncle Fred, and his wife, Mildred, who were Lydia's parents, and their son, Peter. Bertie, Jessica's husband, was sitting on her other side, and next to him was Gladys, her paternal grandmother, whom she loved dearly. Various unmarried cousins were present, two widowed great-aunts and, last but not least, Ida Collins, Jessica's mother-in-law, whom she loathed. Ida had inveigled an invitation to the wedding, though she had no right to be there.

'She's not a relative of my mother's,' Jessica had complained hotly when Bertie requested she obtain a wedding invitation for Ida.

'She is through you,' Bertie had pointed out.

Jessica hid a shudder of revulsion. 'Not a blood relative.' She'd stopped arguing before Bertie demanded rather than requested an invitation. He always won arguments, wearing her down with the weight of his logic, particularly if they concerned his mother.

They were having breakfast in what was called the 'Indian Room'. On the red, silk-covered walls hung brass swords in jewelled scabbards, carved wooden masks, hideously painted, and loops of coloured rope with little brass bells attached. There were no windows visible. The wooden floor was polished to the colour of old blood. She thought it was almost certainly the room where the unusual parties were held.

The best man, Eddie McGrath, the bridegroom's brother, stood to make a speech. He tapped his spoon against a champagne glass, making a pleasing, mellow sound, and the guests fell silent.

Jokes were made, stories told of Tom when he was a child, then a young man, back in dear old Ireland, the family history relayed in Eddie's gravelly voice with its strong accent. He was older, smaller and narrower than Tom, his features not quite so refined, as if his mother had given birth to him before bringing forth a much-improved version in Tom. As it was, the effort had killed her.

3

The McGrath brothers came from poor farming stock. They'd pulled themselves up by their bootstraps. The motherless boys had been raised by their grandmother, who washed and sewed into the night to pay school fees so her grandsons received a good education. Eddie had worked hard, but Tom had worked harder.

'I paid her back as well as I could,' Eddie said, smiling with a mixture of humility and pride, 'but our Tom here, well, he paid our granny back in spades. Me, I became a mere office Johnny, but Tom turned out to be one of the most famous lawyers in the British Isles.'

Everybody clapped apart from the bride, who picked up the groom's hand and laid it against her lightly powdered, subtly rouged cheek. Jessica considered it an overly sentimental gesture on the part of her mother, a touch embarrassing, but everyone else breathed, 'Aaah!' – apart from Ida Collins, who looked sour. Seeing this, Jessica added her own loud 'Aaah!' lest her mother-in-law think they were of the same opinion or on the same side in any shape, manner or form.

The food eaten – a conventional English breakfast; Jessica had been expecting something more foreign – trays of champagne were carried into the room and Eddie called for a toast to the bride and groom.

'Ethel and Tom!' the room cried with real enthusiasm. On such a day, Jessica thought, her mother must wish with all her heart that she'd been called something pretty and lilting like Rosemary, Cynthia, Madeleine or Talullah. She hated being Ethel; it smacked of woolly hats, cheap handbags and wrinkled stockings, she claimed. 'That's why I called you Jessica,' she told her daughter. 'Shakespeare used it. It rolls so smoothly off the tongue.'

Waiters came in with more champagne and other drinks, along with trays of Turkish delight, glacé fruits, marzipan and assorted chocolates.

'This is a strange wedding altogether,' Lydia mused.

The guests rose from their seats and began to form little groups; the McGraths, the Collinses, the Farleys, the young and the old, the cousins. The youngest was Peter Farley, Lydia's brother, who was twenty-three. The new Mrs McGrath had requested there be no children at her wedding: 'Running round, shouting, spilling things, and generally making a nuisance of their mischievous little selves.'

She had said this with a laugh, but in truth she genuinely disliked children. Jessica could remember her mother's attitude to herself and her brother, William, when they were young. She had disliked any show of childish behaviour. Jessica and William – more commonly known as Will – had been discouraged from laughing out loud, running too fast, playing noisily, any one of which activity could give their mother a headache, though she did enjoy reading them stories. Jessica mainly played with her dolls, making sure they behaved themselves.

It was her father who'd given them piggybacks, played football in the garden, and taken them to the park. She glowered darkly at the man who'd taken his place. Will, who had never met his new stepfather, was a lieutenant in the Royal Navy and currently involved in exercises in another part of the world.

Tom caught her eye and grinned. Jessica turned away, embarrassed. He made her feel uncomfortable. She thought about her own children, missing them. They'd been left with Miss Austin, a retired nurse who lived next door to their house in Sefton Park. In a moment of sheer terror, she imagined five-year-old Dora falling downstairs while Miss Austin had unintentionally fallen asleep, or Jamie, two years older, burning, cutting, scalding or hurting himself in some other horribly painful way, possibly fatal.

'Do you think the children are all right?' she said anxiously to Bertie.

'More all right than they'd be with you, darling,' he

chuckled. He reckoned she was a hopeless mother. Jessica didn't know why. The children thrived, laughed a lot, were happy. She loved them with all her heart and they loved her back. What more did Bertie expect?

Music arrived, coming from a source invisible to the human eye, Al Jolsen singing, 'Oh, how we danced the night we were wed'. The newly married couple began to waltz, Tom whirling her mother around the room so uninhibitedly that people had to step back or be knocked over. Her mother was laughing loudly as her daughter had never been allowed to do, her face flushed, her eyes bright. Tom was smiling, moving faster.

The song ended. Tom picked up his new bride and virtually threw her into the air. 'It's time we boarded our ship,' he shouted, and there was a swift intake of breath.

Afterwards, Lydia said it was because some people recognized that Tom couldn't wait to get her mother to bed: 'It was obvious from the tone of his voice and the look on his face.'

'Why did you know that and I didn't?' Jessica complained, annoyed with herself.

'Because you're so sweet and innocent, Jess,' Lydia said, a trifle tartly. 'Butter wouldn't melt – you know the sort of thing. You'd never think you were a twenty-seven-year-old married woman with two children. By the way, your mother looks terribly smart today. Did she buy that outfit in London?'

'That's what she wants people to think.' She wasn't prepared to lie to Lydia. 'In actual fact, Miss Fleming made it for her. It's a copy of a Chanel model that was on the Paris catwalk only this spring.'

The dress was grey and white georgette with long, full sleeves, a tight belt, and a knee-length, slightly flared skirt. The hat, now removed, was like an upturned saucepan with a huge white organdie bow at the front. Miss Fleming had been making her mother's clothes for years and years. Ethel told people she'd been to London to buy them in Harrods or Selfridges. With her slim figure and ravishing good looks, she showed off the various fashions to their best advantage. Her going-away outfit was a grey three-quarter-length crêpe coat.

Jessica hadn't noticed that her mother had left the room, until she returned wearing the coat and hat and hanging on to Tom's arm. It was midday, time for them to leave. They were sailing first class to New York on the *Queen Mary*, staying a week and returning on an aeroplane, which was very daring. Naturally, her mother had wanted to stay longer, but Tom had a busy schedule. Even in New York, he had business to see to.

They insisted on leaving alone. 'The room's booked for the day,' Tom shouted. 'Have a fine time, why don't you? And order whatever you like.'

They disappeared in a shower of silver confetti and kisses and shouts of 'Good Luck, have a lovely time' and 'Don't do anything I wouldn't do, Tom' from one of the men.

Jessica didn't know why she followed, at a distance, down the stairs and into the foyer, and why she watched through the glass door of the hotel, as Tom helped her mother into the back of a black limousine with a playful slap on her bottom. She still watched, sighing, as the car glided away in the brilliant sunshine – she had forgotten the sun had been shining so brightly when they'd come in.

She had never had the same warm relationship with her mother as Lydia had with Aunt Mildred, but she was fond of her. Since her father had died and William had gone away, Jessica had felt an obligation to look after her fluffy-headed mother, to ensure she didn't come to any harm. Right now, she felt apprehensive seeing her go off with a man she hardly knew. And not just a conventional man, but an outrageous individual, who was bigger and louder and more successful than every other man she knew. She prayed her mother wouldn't come to any harm with this person,

A pleasant, silver-haired gentleman in a dark green uniform approached. 'Are you all right, miss? You look a bit pale.'

'Yes, I'm just . . .' Jessica paused. She couldn't describe

how she felt. Perhaps she'd drunk too much champagne. 'Could I possibly have a cup of tea or coffee?' she asked.

'Of course, miss. Would you like it in the lounge? Tea might be best if you don't quite feel yourself; more settling on the stomach than coffee.'

'Oh, yes. Tea would be lovely. Thank you.' The man reminded her of her gentle, courteous father. The contrast between Gordon Farley and Tom McGrath was stark. Her mother's first husband had been a considerate man, her second was dangerous. She felt slightly sick at the thought and was glad she'd ordered tea rather than the coffee that might have upset her stomach.

'This way, miss.'

The man led her into a quiet dark room filled with brown velvet chairs, and held one while she sat. She was the only person there. 'I'm sorry, it's Mrs, isn't it?' he said apologetically. He must have noticed her wedding ring. 'It's just that you look too young to be married, if you don't mind my saying.'

'I don't mind.' She was used to hearing that. Jessica had none of her mother's charisma. Her eyes were the same blue, her hair a darker, natural blonde; she was exceptionally pretty, but her expression was timid and slightly bemused, as if she were unsure of her place in the world, while her confident, outgoing mother dazzled everyone she met.

She relaxed into the chair, her body ticking away the tension of the last few hours. It was lovely and peaceful here, and when the tea came, she thoroughly enjoyed it.

'Where have you been?' Bertie said irritably when Jessica appeared and announced she was going home. 'You know very well I'm playing cricket this afternoon.' It was an Old Boys' match between his school, St Mary's, and Merchant Taylor's.

'I've been downstairs having tea,' she told him. She'd been

easy enough to find had he really wanted to. Anyway, the match didn't start for another two hours.

'Look,' he said, frowning, 'I think you and Mother should take a taxi home together. She'll help entertain the children until I come home.'

Jessica resisted the urge to scream, '*No!*' at the top of her voice. Since when had she needed help entertaining her own children? 'Lydia is taking me home in her car,' she lied.

Bertie's frown deepened. 'I thought I heard Lydia say she was going shopping.'

'She is; we are.' Jessica hastened to expand the lie lest he suggest Lydia take his mother home with them. 'Dora needs a couple of school blouses from Henderson's. It would be convenient to get them today.'

'Why can't you go another time?'

Why, oh why, was he so often in a bad temper – and only with her?

'If I leave it too late they'll run out of stock,' she said defensively.

'Oh, all right then. I'll be home about six.' He kissed her. 'Bye, darling.'

'Goodbye.' She caught his arm. 'Don't forget to tell your mother she can't come home with me.'

'Why don't you . . .' he began, but Jessica had gone in a flash before he could finish, '. . . tell her yourself.'

'I can't abide her – Ida, that is,' she said when she and Lydia were on their way to Sefton Park in Lydia's little Austin 7.

'Gosh, I didn't know that!' Lydia made a false show of surprise. 'You've been married to Bertie for eight years, yet you've never once mentioned that you disliked his mother.'

'Sorry.' Jessica mentioned it all the time. It made her feel very uncharitable and mean, but she couldn't help it. Mrs Collins was a spiteful woman who was able to wind Bertie, her only child, round her little finger, usually at the expense of

Jessica and even, occasionally, the children. She seemed to resent her son being fond of anyone except herself.

'Out of interest,' Lydia said, 'what do I tell Bertie should he mention our supposed visit to Henderson's? Did we go or not?'

'We went, but they'd sold out of blouses in Dora's size. However, they promised to telephone when new stock arrives.'

Lydia nodded. 'Very good. You are an excellent liar, Jess, extremely convincing.'

'Oh, don't say that! The only person I lie to is Bertie.'

'He's your husband, the last person you should lie to.'

Jessica groaned. 'I know, but it's just that not telling the truth makes life so much easier.' Easier to say when he did the accounts that she'd spent some of the housekeeping on groceries rather than cigarettes or a ticket to a matinée at the cinema – she'd been a few times since Dora had started school in January. He would disapprove of the cigarettes and be horrified at the idea of her going to the pictures on her own. When they'd first married, he'd been timid and easy-going, but had become unnecessarily oppressive over the years, she had no idea why.

Her cousin squeezed her knee. 'Bertie does huff and puff just a bit, but he's frightfully attractive. Being an estate agent is a really good job, and he loves you madly. You're awfully lucky, Jessica.'

'Some people might think so.' Perhaps she had felt lucky once, but no longer. As for Lydia, she was desperate to get married. A fine-looking woman, tall and always fashionably dressed, she had dark brown wavy hair cropped rather mannishly at the back, brown eyes, and aquiline features that tended to look rather haughty and possibly put men off. She needed to meet a strong man, one like Tom McGrath, who wouldn't be deterred by a forceful-looking woman.

Lydia turned into Atlas Road where the Collinses lived in a

modern semi-detached house complete with garage and a leafy garden. Their neighbour, Miss Austin, opened the front door and the children rushed out. They fought with each other to hug their mother the tightest.

'Have you been good?' she asked them.

'As good as gold, Mummy,' Dora assured her. She was blonde and blue-eyed like her mother, while Jamie was a junior version of his cricket-playing, tousle-haired father. Like Bertie, he had a healthy tan after spending so much time out of doors.

'They really have been as good as gold,' Miss Austin told Jessica. 'They're a pleasure to be with. We've been playing cards. I showed them how to play Twenty-One.'

'It's called Blackjack in America,' Jamie informed her.

'That's nice.' Jessica hoped Bertie wouldn't mind his children being taught to play cards.

Lydia had gone to put the kettle on, Miss Austin went home, and the children still clung to their mother as they went indoors. She patted their heads, relieved to find them still alive and in one piece.

'Can we all play Twenty-One?' Jamie pleaded.

'In a minute. Are either of you hungry?'

'Miss Austin made us scrambled eggs and tomatoes for lunch,' Jamie said. 'But,' he added hopefully, 'she didn't give us any pudding.'

Yesterday, Jessica had done loads of baking in readiness for the weekend. She offered them a choice of scones, jam tarts, or fruitcake. They chose the jam tarts, as she guessed they would.

Lydia had made the tea. Jessica poured milk for the children, and the four sat round the table with a plate of slightly burnt jam tarts while Jamie instructed them how to play Twenty-One.

They played for an hour – Jamie showed he had the makings of an ace card player – before Lydia announced it was time she left; she was going to the theatre that evening and had to get changed.

Dora, fed up with cards, took her little pram filled with dolls for a walk around the garden, and Jamie lay on his tummy on the sofa with that week's copy of *Wizard*, which he read from cover to cover at least half a dozen times. Jessica went into the kitchen and began to prepare dinner – lamb chops with mint sauce, mashed potatoes and runner beans, followed by fruitcake, which was not quite as burnt as the tarts.

Bertie would complain the meal was too basic, not exciting enough. 'You have no talent for cooking, Jess,' he had told her numerous times.

Jessica would just shrug and concede she was a hopeless housewife. She detested cooking and cleaning. Her least favourite job of all was hanging washing on the line and having it blow back in her face in the cold weather. On the other hand, she could sew well, knit and embroider beautifully, and made all her own and Dora's clothes, apart from the uniform that the school insisted be purchased from Henderson's. She also enjoyed painting and decorating, an attribute Bertie thought rather odd for a woman.

Leaving the lamb chops in the oven and the potatoes simmering in a pan, she saw Dora was still preoccupied with her dolls and Jamie with his comic. Creeping into the parlour, she closed the door, switched on the gramophone and chose a record from the pile on the shelf underneath.

Minutes later, Al Bowlly's soft, seductive voice began to croon, 'Love is the sweetest thing . . .' Jessica held out her arms to an invisible partner and began to sway around the room, forgetting everything, conscious only of the strange yearning in her breast. 'The moment I saw you . . .' How tenderly he sang. She was no longer in the house in Atlas Road, but somewhere mysterious and romantic, headily perfumed. She could sense her heart beating faster. 'The very thought of you . . .' She could almost believe someone really was thinking about her now, *wanting* to put his arms round her. She stood still for a moment, concentrating, and could feel the arms sliding around her back, stroking her hips.

Jessica groaned just as Dora shouted, 'Mummy, Daddy's home', and she came to with a start, turned off the gramophone and opened the parlour door. Bertie had gone straight into the garden. He came through the back door into the kitchen with their daughter in his arms.

'How did the match go?' she enquired. She felt much too hot and hoped her cheeks weren't noticeably flushed.

'St Mary's won,' he announced with a satisfied grin. His own cheeks were flushed, but he'd been playing cricket, not dancing around the room indulging in impossible dreams.

They ate dinner with Bertie giving a running commentary on the match to an entranced Jamie. He suggested they all went to Sefton Park tomorrow after Mass, and played cricket themselves: 'Daddy and Dora against Mummy and Jamie.'

Jamie hooted his approval and Dora looked pleased. Jessica said she'd make a picnic lunch to take with them. What a perfectly happy family they were!

Later, the children asleep, she and Bertie listened to a John Galsworthy play on the wireless. When it was over, she made cocoa and immersed herself in the latest book borrowed from the Romance Library in the Post Office while Bertie read *The Times* until it was half past ten and time for bed.

Another day over, she thought. There was always something sad about going to bed, knowing she'd never experience that particular day again, feeling as if she'd lost something precious. Behind her, Bertie was checking doors were locked and windows closed.

What was her mother doing now? She imagined a large, brightly lit ballroom on board the ship with an orchestra playing and her beautiful mother dancing with Tom McGrath. She was probably wearing the silver dress Miss Fleming had made. It troubled her that she should envy her mother's obvious happiness.

She undressed quickly, put on her nightdress, and got into bed, edging to the far side, pulling the clothes round her shoulders. Behind her, Bertie was changing into his pyjamas. He went into the bathroom, and Jessica closed her eyes and prayed that when he came back he would think that she'd fallen asleep. She began to breathe deeply and regularly, and didn't budge when he slid into bed beside her.

Then a hand touched her shoulder and he said meekly, 'Do you mind?'

Jessica turned on to her back, wanting to cry, saying nothing, just letting him get on with it, which he did clumsily and noisily, taking ages, or so it seemed.

He finished at last and she turned away, pulling the clothes back round her. She hated it, hated it with all her heart. She would never grow to like it, not if she lived to be a hundred.

Chapter 2

'Can I stay with you, Jess?' William Farley pleaded. 'It wasn't until I came ashore that I remembered Mother had let our old house and I had no idea where she was living with this new chap. And the new chap might not want me staying with them, anyway.'

'I'm sure Tom would love having you, Will,' Jessica assured him, 'but right now he and mother are in New York on their honeymoon. They're flying back on Friday and will live in Tom's place in Calderstones. But,' she added, 'you can stay with us, you know you can, you idiot. There's no need to plead. We have a box room on the second floor, only tiny, but big enough to take a single bed and a chest of drawers.'

'Will Bertie mind?'

'Bertie will love having you as much as Tom would.' Though not as much as she would. Jessica really missed having her brother around. 'You can talk to Bertie about the Navy. He's envious of you leading such an exciting life – his is as dull as dishwater beside yours. He said that if he didn't have me and the children to support, he would have joined the Navy long ago.'

Will looked amused. 'He never mentioned that when we were at school. If I remember rightly, all he ever wanted was an office job. But perhaps,' he continued charitably, 'he didn't like the idea of leaving his mother.'

Bertie and Will had been at St Mary's together. Jessica had

15

met her future husband at a leaving party when the boys were eighteen and she was two years younger. An impressionable girl, she'd considered him impossibly handsome and had fallen crazily in love at first sight.

She looked at Will in his uniform, his long legs stretched out and making the small sitting room seem even smaller. Like their sorely missed father, he was tall and slim with dark ginger hair and an attractive smile. His features, slightly crooked, as if they'd been put together in a hurry, had an irresistible appeal. He was the most popular of men with friends in ports all over the globe. A hopeless letter writer, nobody ever knew where his ship happened to be, and he was apt to turn up out of the blue when they'd imagined him sailing on foreign seas thousands of miles away. Finding her brother on the doorstep was like having the sun come out on a miserably dull day.

'What time do the kids come out of school?' he asked.

'Half past three. I go and fetch them. It's only a short walk away in Princes Park. You can come with me, give them a surprise.' If only he'd chosen a different career and they could have seen him all the time!

'Is it a private school?'

'Yes. It's called St Thomas Moore's Academy for Juniors and Infants. Bertie insisted on it.' He had the children's futures rigidly planned. They would pass the scholarship just like their father and Uncle Will. Jamie would go to St Mary's Grammar, Dora to Notre Dame Convent. Jamie was destined for university; Dora for commercial college.

Jessica hoped neither of her children would take after their mother, who'd failed the scholarship and was as thick as two short planks.

Dora came out of school first. She gave a little scream and threw herself at her uncle. 'Uncle Will, Uncle Will.' Her little face was a picture of delight as she was thrown into the air and caught again in Will's strong arms. The other children looked on, impressed by the tall, striking figure in naval uniform.

As Jamie approached, Will aimed a pretend punch at his stomach and Jamie aimed one back.

'Have you come back to Liverpool for good?' Jamie asked hopefully.

'I'm afraid not, but I'm staying at your house for a whole week.'

Jessica may as well have been invisible as they walked home. The children, having bagged a hand each, skipped alongside the heroic figure of their Uncle Will while he answered their numerous questions as best he could.

No, he didn't sleep in a hammock and, yes, he could row using both oars. His ship didn't have sails and so far nobody had thrown him overboard.

Home again, Jessica made the children's tea and Will went upstairs to unpack. He came down looking almost ordinary, having changed into grey flannels and a check shirt, and carrying presents for everyone.

A book for Jamie, *The Wizard of Oz*. 'It's an American classic,' he said. 'All the kids over there have read it.' A most unusual doll for Dora. 'She's a grown-up!' the little girl marvelled. The doll wore a white beret, a black-and-white check frock, and high-heeled shoes!

'I've got scent for you, sis – Dior something or other; apparently you can't get it in this country – and a tie-pin for Bertie.'

Jessica hugged him. 'You're a lovely chap, Will.' She dabbed the scent behind her ears. 'It's gorgeous,' she assured him.

'I'm starving, sis,' he said pathetically. 'What time's dinner?'

'Not for another two hours. Sit down and I'll make you a sarnie.'

Later, Jamie having gone to read the book somewhere quiet and Dora absorbed in undressing the new doll, Will said wistfully, 'I miss Liverpool, you know, Jess. Sometimes, I feel like packing in the Navy, settling down, getting married and having kids, just like you and Bertie.'

Jessica's heart lifted at the idea of him living nearby, them going out in a foursome. 'Then why don't you?' she urged. 'You've given the Navy eleven years; it's time you had a life of your own.'

'There's more to it than that.' He shrugged, reached in his pocket and brought out a packet of Chesterfield cigarettes and a box of matches.

'Can I have one?' she asked.

'Since when did you start smoking?' he asked, surprised.

'I only smoke now and again – never in the house.' Bertie would smell the smoke and disapprove, as he did of most things she liked. She smoked when she was on her own at the pictures or in restaurants. 'What do you mean, there's more to it than that?'

Will lit the cigarettes. 'I've never liked the idea of being married and in the Navy at the same time, leaving a wife and kids behind. I'd like it even less if there was a war on.'

Jessica gaped. 'But there isn't a war on.'

'There will be, Jess. It's inevitable.' He blew smoke out in a long, steady stream. 'You've heard of this chap, Adolf Hitler, haven't you?'

'I'm not a total ignoramus, Will. Of course I have.'

He grinned. 'I remember a time when you'd never heard of Santa Claus.'

'That's because everyone I knew called him Father Christmas, but you suddenly came up with Santa Claus. Anyway,' she said impatiently, 'I thought we were discussing Adolf Hitler?'

'We were.' Will stubbed out his half-smoked cigarette and straight away lit another. 'Getting a bit too big for his boots, is old Adolf,' he said thoughtfully. 'Friend of mine's brother recently returned from Germany where he was teaching

English. Said there was a pretty gruesome atmosphere there; police, troops on every corner. Needless to say, he's never going back.' His face darkened. 'His landlady had a daughter, only ten, one of those Mongol kids. The authorities only took her away and stuck her in a camp somewhere. She hasn't been seen since. And Jews are having a terrible time, losing their jobs and their businesses. Quite a few have left for France, the States or here. Winston Churchill says our country urgently needs to arm itself in readiness for battle.'

Jessica wasn't about to confess that she had no idea who Winston Churchill was. She continued to smoke, not enjoying it quite so much after listening to her brother. 'It sounds frightful,' she said, 'but if there's going to be a war, which I don't believe for a moment, by the way, why does it stop you from leaving the Navy now?'

'If I left,' he said lightly, 'with my record, I'd be one of the very first to be called up when the war starts.'

'*If* it starts.'

'I think it's more a case of when rather than if, Jess.'

Jessica slowly let the meaning of his words sink in. She got up, stubbed her cigarette out in the sink, heard it sizzle, then took another from the packet on the table. Will lit it for her. 'Chesterfields,' she said. 'Where did they come from?'

'The States,' he said. 'California.'

'I don't believe you. About the stupid war, not the cigarettes.' She shook her head. But what did she know about it? She listened to the news on the wireless, watched it at the pictures, read the occasional newspaper, yet her mind usually switched off if it was anything foreign or political. Adolf Hitler appeared to be a silly little man with a silly little moustache. He looked anything but dangerous.

She was relieved when Dora appeared and demanded help with the new doll. 'I can't get her frock back on, Mummy.'

'Let me do it, sweetheart. It's a tight fit, isn't it?'

She'd refuse to talk about war with Will again, do her best

19

not even to *think* about it. The last one had been pretty horrible. She'd been eight when it finished and could remember it well, all those poor men coming home with limbs missing or badly injured in other ways. The lady living next door to their old house had lost two sons.

Jessica's father had volunteered to fight, but had been rejected on account of the weak lungs that had eventually killed him. And now her brother would be called upon to risk his life, be one of the first to go. Bertie would be called up, too, if not as soon as Will. She thought about Bertie going away, of just her, Jamie and Dora living in the house without him. It was an idea that made her feel quite light-headed because it was so strange, something that she had never, ever imagined would happen.

The children would undoubtedly miss him – but would she?

Lydia burst into the house not long after dinner. 'Where's Will?' she demanded. She was like a young girl again, full of smiles, the haughty look gone. 'When I woke up this morning, I could sense something terrific was going to happen, so I wasn't at all surprised when you called this afternoon, Jess, to say he was home. Where is he?' She danced into the house and down the hallway. 'If he's gone out, I'll kill him.'

'I'm here, Lyd. I'm here.' Will appeared at the top of the stairs and came down two at a time. They met at the bottom and embraced enthusiastically. 'Bertie promised to drive me over to your place later,' Will said.

They'd been such good friends when they were younger that Jessica had often felt jealous. As they grew older, she had imagined them getting married one day, but a girl at school had told her they couldn't.

'The church forbids Catholic cousins to get married,' she'd said. 'Protestants can, but we can't.' At the time Jessica recalled feeling very mixed up about it; half of her wishing Will and

Lydia could get married and the other half against the idea. She still wasn't sure how she felt all these years later.

Lydia had brought wine. Bertie fetched another bottle out of the larder. Jessica opened a tin of assorted biscuits, but all Will could offer was himself.

'But I can be neither eaten nor drunk,' he said regretfully.

'Never mind,' Lydia said. She looked at him soulfully. 'We will just sit at your feet and savour your beauty and your charm.'

At this, Jessica laughed and Bertie pretended to be sick.

Having returned from New York by aeroplane on Friday, Ethel and Tom McGrath treated Saturday as a day of rest and on Sunday opened their house in Larch Avenue, Calderstones, the most expensive and exclusive area in Liverpool, to family and friends. Ethel knew her son Will was home and couldn't wait to see him.

'Gosh!' Will marvelled on Sunday when Bertie drew up outside a pure white single-storey building with Venetian blinds, also white, on the tall windows. 'What on earth would you call that? It looks like a wedding cake. It's a bit different from our old house, and that wasn't exactly a hovel.'

'It's Art Deco,' Bertie explained. Being an estate agent, he was knowledgeable about such things. 'It's built from Satuario marble from Italy and has five bedrooms and four bathrooms. Tom designed it himself and brought over some artisans from Italy to build it. I wouldn't like to hazard how much it cost.'

Jessica had been in the house a few times and disliked it intensely. Privately, she considered it rather vulgar, exactly the sort of showy place that her mother's new husband would want to live in because he was vulgar himself.

'I must not laugh at Mother's house,' Will chanted as they walked along the black-and-white marble-tiled path towards a large and very shiny front door. 'I must not laugh at Mother's house. I must not . . . hello, Mother. I thought marrying a

21

millionaire meant you no longer had to open your own door. Where's the butler?'

'Will, darling.' Ethel McGrath, in brilliant red, with diamonds in her ears and round her neck, and smelling as if she had just bathed in rich perfume, threw her arms round her son. 'Why aren't you wearing your uniform? I did so want Tom to see you dressed as a lieutenant in the Navy. Oh, you are such an outstanding young man. I'm so proud of you. Come and say hello to Tom – he's longing to meet you.'

Will looked over his shoulder at his sister. 'I must not laugh at Mother's house,' he mouthed as he was dragged inside.

'She doesn't make nearly as much fuss of you,' Lydia said as they followed behind.

'There's nothing to show off about me,' Jessica explained.

After having little interest in her children throughout their lives, preferring them to remain seen, but not heard, it had suddenly dawned on their mother that Will, fully grown and wearing a dashing uniform, was someone she could exhibit to her numerous friends. He was paraded in front of them, invited to parties where Ethel, his self-important mother, hung on to his arm.

'It doesn't bother you, does it, Jess?' he'd asked once.

'Not a bit,' she had assured him. 'I'd hate it if she suddenly started making a terrible fuss of me.' By then, she was married to Bertie, and Jamie, the most beautiful baby in the entire universe, had been born. Her mother's preference for Will didn't bother her in the least.

She went into the vast, white hall with Lydia and Bertie – it made her think of a giant bathroom – where Will was being introduced to Tom McGrath. They were shaking hands, both smiling broadly. It was clear they must have decided they liked each other straight away.

At first glance, she couldn't see a soul she recognized, until a wrinkled hand seized her arm.

'Jessie, luv! Where are Jamie and Dora?'

'Gladys!' Gladys Farley, her father's mother, was in her eighties, a small, slight woman with glorious silver hair and light blue eyes. She lived some distance away in Chester. 'They're at home; our neighbour is looking after them.'

For some mysterious reason that Jessica would never understand, sweet-natured Gladys and Ethel, her late son's frivolous and undoubtedly shallow wife, were the best of friends.

Not long after her son had died, Gladys had explained to Jessica why the friendship persisted despite the fact that she was no longer Ethel's mother-in-law. 'In her own way, your mother genuinely loved your father,' she said. 'She isn't capable of showing how she feels about other people – I doubt if she even knows. To be frank, she's too taken up with how she feels about herself. But she's not a bad woman. She made your father very happy and he absolutely adored her.'

Jessica looked across at her mother now. She was holding on to both Tom and Will, her face glowing with excitement. 'The most amazing thing has happened,' Gladys said. 'For the first time in her life your mother has met someone she loves more than she loves herself. Tom McGrath must be a remarkable man.'

Jessica nodded. 'Oh, I'm sure he is, Gran. But I also think he's terribly vulgar.'

'Vulgarity doesn't stop a person from being remarkable,' her grandmother said sagely. She winked. 'Or attractive.'

'Oh, Gran. You don't fancy him, do you?' Jessica was mildly shocked.

'He can tickle my fancy any time he likes,' Gran said, shocking Jessica even more. 'Tell you one thing, though. I wouldn't be surprised if he didn't break her heart one day.'

Bertie said, 'I wish I'd thought to invite Mother. She would have enjoyed looking round the house.'

'I thought she spent Sundays in church with the Friends of Mary Magdalene,' Jessica said.

'Do you have to be so spiteful?' Bertie said crossly.

'Spiteful!' She had no idea what he meant. She was glad Lydia had gone to speak to her parents and Will had disappeared.

'Who's being spiteful?' Her mother linked Bertie's arm and Tom put his hand on Jessica's shoulder.

'Hello, there,' he said warmly, looking down at her with his twinkling brown eyes. His hand felt warm, too; big and strong and warm. To her horror she had a quite unexpected sensation in her tummy that threatened to overwhelm her, and her legs felt as if they were about to give way.

'Hello.' She could hardly hear her own voice for the thunder rolling in her ears.

'I asked who was being spiteful,' her mother reminded them.

'Only a man in Bertie's office,' Jessica lied, amazed that she could think clearly while in such a confused state. What was happening to her? 'I've never met him.' Bertie would definitely come out the worst if she told the truth; she hoped he would be grateful for the lie. 'Did you enjoy your honeymoon?' she asked her mother and Tom.

'We had a wonderful time,' Tom said loudly – Jessica doubted if he could speak any other way. His Irish accent was more pronounced than she remembered.

'New York is marvellous,' her mother cooed. 'Mind you, we hardly moved out of Manhattan – Tom intends opening an office there. If I hadn't married him, I would have loved to work there myself.'

'Doing what?' Tom turned his twinkling gaze on to his wife. 'You can't type and you know nothing about the law.'

Ethel pouted charmingly. 'I could make the tea, darling.'

'That reminds me,' Tom turned back to Jessica, 'you'll never guess what my secretary has done.'

'I've no idea,' she stammered.

'Only gone and joined the Army!'

'The Army!' Jessica, Bertie and Ethel said together. A woman in the Army! They'd never heard of such a thing.

'She's convinced that any minute now Germany will start a war in Europe and she wants to be ready to fight.' His laugh was like a burst of thunder. 'Though I'm sure women won't be allowed anywhere near the battlefield. Anyway, Jessica,' her shoulders were painfully squeezed, 'I've got a big case starting shortly and your mother tells me you can type. I wondered if you would be willing to work in my office a few hours a day until I have found a new secretary?'

'She can't,' Bertie said shortly. Jessica could tell he was inwardly livid at what must seem to him an outrageous suggestion. 'There's the children to look after and housework to do. Jessica has no time for other work. Anyway,' he continued, 'it's a long time since she did any typing. She's probably forgotten how.'

'I would have thought typing was a bit like riding a bike,' Tom said mildly. 'Once you learn, you never forget.'

Ethel jabbed her son-in-law in the ribs with her elbow, so hard that he gasped for breath. 'And it's Jessica's decision whether or not she works for Tom, Bertie, not yours. Perhaps you haven't noticed, but it's no longer the Victorian era. Nowadays, women are considered equal to men.'

Bertie went red and mumbled something incomprehensible. Jessica was glad when her mother and Tom wandered off to talk to someone else, the question of her helping in Tom's office left undecided. She was even more glad when Lydia turned up, then Will, and they could go home and relieve Miss Austin of the children. It had been an extremely disturbing afternoon altogether, and she was glad that it was over.

After the children had been put to bed, Bertie and Will announced they were going for a drink. Jessica persuaded Lydia to go with them. She wanted time to herself, to think about the afternoon and what it had meant.

Nothing, she supposed, after they'd gone. She'd been in a bit of a state, that's all, and that's why Tom's arm, the weight of it, had sent such pleasant shivers up and down her spine. And she was dreading Will going away again, wondering how many months it would be before he returned.

She sighed and went into the parlour where she put an Al Bowlly record on the gramophone, but felt too tired to dance. Instead, she lay on the settee, eyes closed, letting the music wrap round her like a soft, warm blanket. She imagined invisible arms caressing her, imaginary lips press hard against her own, while a passionate voice whispered endearments in her ear.

It wasn't until she recognized the voice as belonging to her mother's husband that she leaped to her feet, rushed into the kitchen and hurriedly made tea.

Chapter 3

Monday was Will's last day in Liverpool. He was spending it with Henry Chapman, his best friend from school, who'd moved across the water to Secombe and become an artist.

'A portrait painter,' Will explained. 'He's got this incredible studio overlooking the Mersey where he lives and works, and is still waiting for his first commission. He sent me a photo of the studio, but I'm dying to see the real thing.'

The second Monday in the month was the day that Bertie did the household accounts. After the children had gone to bed, he produced his cheque book, bank statements and a shiny black ledger, and stationed himself at the kitchen table while Jessica fetched the old biscuit tin in which she kept receipts. She emptied them in a heap in front of him and he tut-tutted.

'I do wish you would keep them together neatly, darling. I'll give you some paperclips, if you like. It's so much more efficient than leaving them in a jumble in that silly tin. Now, if you would kindly sort them out, most recent at the back, while I attend to my own affairs.'

There was silence in the kitchen while Bertie ticked things off and added things up, his lips tight with concentration. Jessica noticed, not for the first time, how small and effeminate his hands were, about half the size of Tom McGrath's. The thought made her feel unnaturally hot. She ran her fingers through her hair as a distraction just in case Bertie was able to read her mind.

Will returned, and Bertie told him to make himself comfortable in the sitting room. 'We're busy out here, old chap. Won't be long, though. Jessica will make you something to eat as soon as we've finished.'

His own accounts done, Bertie began to examine the household receipts, entering the figures in the accounts book: so much for milk, so much for groceries, the butcher, the baker, and so on. Jamie's shoes had been repaired and Dora had needed three-quarter-length white socks, Jessica had bought stockings from Henderson's and borrowed books from the Post Office library at a penny a time. She'd also bought eight ounces of yellow wool and a pair of size ten knitting needles.

Bertie looked questioningly at his wife. 'I thought you already had size ten needles?'

'One broke.'

'I see. How much is left in your purse?'

'Eight and threepence ha'penny.'

He quickly did a calculation. 'You appear to be missing nearly seven shillings, Jessica. There are no receipts for vegetables. I think it's about time you started using a different greengrocer than Plunkett's, one that's not still stuck in the Dark Ages and has something called a till that issues receipts. I mean,' he said distractedly, 'how much of the missing seven shillings was spent on vegetables?'

'Plunkett's is really cheap,' Jessica said. She sighed. 'I'm sorry, Bertie, but I have no head for figures.'

'Then it's about time you acquired one,' he said pettishly.

'*I'll* make up the missing seven shillings,' William said from the next room. He appeared in the doorway and laid a ten-shilling note on the table. 'Keep the extra three, Bertie; it will help in case *my sister* is short again next month.' He laid stress on 'my sister', as if wanting to emphasize their relationship and let Bertie know he didn't think much of Jessica being treated like a thick-witted housekeeper who couldn't add up.

Bertie jumped to his feet, red-faced. 'There is no need for this.' He picked up the note and tried to give it back, but William backed away, ignoring Bertie and saying to Jessica, 'Goodnight, sis. I think I'll turn in. I have to leave early in the morning.'

'But Will, don't you even want a cup of tea? Shall I bring some up to your room?'

He bent and kissed her cheek. 'That's a lovely idea. In a few minutes, eh?'

Jessica put the kettle on. 'Would you like some tea?' she asked her husband.

'No, thank you.' He looked extremely discomfited. 'I don't think your brother has very good manners,' he said stiffly.

'He was just helping me out.'

'There was no need to help you out. What did he think I was going to do about the missing money? Fine you? Lecture you?'

'There wasn't any money missing, Bertie. I spent it on vegetables and little things like tram fares. Would you like me to start keeping the tickets? I might have bought a newspaper one day or ice creams for the children on our way home from school.'

'Then all you have to do is keep a note of these things, Jessica. I'll put a blank sheet of paper in the tin and you can do it from now on.' He laughed ironically. 'I find it hard to believe you helped your father with his accounts.'

'I typed them out, that's all.'

The water boiled and she made the tea, pouring two cups and putting them on a tray along with a plate of ginger biscuits. Bertie frowned when he noticed the two cups, realizing she intended to stay upstairs and drink the tea with Will. But he didn't remark on it.

★

29

Will was sitting, fully dressed, on the bed. He patted the space beside him. 'Shut the door first,' he said.

Jessica put the tray on top of the chest of drawers. She handed him his tea, took her own, put the biscuits on the bed between them, then sat down.

'How long has this been going on?' he demanded. 'This accounts stuff, Bertie treating you as if you were a stupid child? I felt like barging in and giving him a bloody nose, odious creature. I never liked him at school. I've never told you before, but I was more than a bit put out when you met him at that party and it turned out you actually fancied the bugger. I should have objected to you getting married straight away.'

'I wouldn't have taken any notice. He was so sweet and gentle.' He'd given the impression of loving her very much. Perhaps it had been true then – perhaps he still loved her. If so, he had a funny way of showing it. What was the saying? Familiarity breeds contempt. A fitting description for how he felt about her nowadays – apart from in bed, that was. She shuddered at the memory.

William had drunk his tea and was now gorging on ginger biscuits. 'What happened to the money Dad left us, Jess?' he asked, his mouth full of biscuit. 'A thousand quid each. Mine's still in the bank, untouched. Where's yours?'

Jessica blushed, knowing that the answer would make him more angry than he already was. 'We paid off the mortgage with some of it. It saved paying loads of interest.'

'And what did *we* do with the rest?'

'Bought the car. There's about a hundred pounds left in the bank.'

'So you're telling me,' William said in a voice thick with suppressed rage, 'that you paid for both the house and the car, yet that loathsome individual downstairs questions you about buying a new pair of knitting needles and disputes the price of vegetables?'

'Actually, Will,' she said in a small voice, 'not all the money went on vegetables, but on cigarettes and tickets for the pictures, and coffee in the Kardomah in Bold Street.' She didn't tell him that the receipt for the stockings had been found on the floor in Henderson's – Bertie hadn't noticed the size shown was larger than she wore. She hadn't broken a knitting needle, either.

Will laughed. 'You've been fiddling the household bills! But you shouldn't have to. And why did you claim to be no good with figures? Dad used to praise you to the skies, said you had an aptitude for them.'

'Only after he'd explained them to me. At school, I was hopeless.'

'From now on, you must stand up for yourself more, sis.' Will put his hand on the back of her neck and squeezed it gently. 'Stop letting him bully you. I wish I were staying a bit longer. I'd have a few words with that precious husband of yours.'

Jessica rose early, at six o'clock. Downstairs, she opened the kitchen door and could smell a mixture of earth and grass and the flowers about to uncurl their petals for the day. It was going to be glorious, she could tell; the sun already warm in a cloudless blue sky, lighting up the kitchen like the brightest of electric lights.

She woke Will, went back downstairs and made an omelette for his breakfast. Later, she stood on the step in her dressing gown and waved at his tall, uniformed figure until he disappeared round a corner.

He was gone and she had no idea when she would see him again. She clasped her hands together and pressed them against her breast to suppress the ache. Will was the only person in the world, the children apart, who loved her for herself. Her father was dead and she doubted if her mother ever gave her more than a passing thought.

Bertie came down with a frozen face and went to work,

31

pretending not to notice that Will had left without saying goodbye. She wondered how long it would be before he decided to stop sulking.

She took the children to school – Dora in tears because Uncle Will had gone away.

'But, love, you knew he was going,' Jessica reminded her. 'He said goodbye to you yesterday.'

'I didn't think he really meant it,' Dora sniffed.

'Uncle Will would never say anything he didn't mean,' Jamie said primly, sounding a bit too much like his father for Jessica's liking.

She bought the *Daily Post* on her way home. Tom McGrath had mentioned he had a big case starting this week and she wondered if there was anything in the paper about it. She'd look as soon as she'd tidied up.

While taking the bedding off Will's bed, she found a half-full packet of Chesterfields with a book of matches inside, and a plain black sock. She kissed the sock, despite it smelling a bit, and put the cigarettes in her pinafore pocket. She made the other beds, washed and dried the dishes, brushed the kitchen floor, though only the parts that could be seen, put the kettle on for tea, and prepared to read the paper.

She found details of the case on page three. It was called Donovan versus The Crown, and Thomas McGrath was listed as Barrister for the Defence.

Mary Anne Donovan was sixteen years old and had been a live-in servant in the house of Edward Charles Gregory, aged fifty-three, from Walton Vale for three years. Within her first month, her employer had forced his way into her bed. Over time, Mary Anne had borne him two male children. A year ago, she had been expecting a third, when her employer had been found dead in her bed, long after she herself had vacated it. He had been stabbed at least twenty-five times. Mary Anne had been arrested and charged with murder, which she denied. While in prison, she'd given birth to a third male child.

It seemed terribly unfair, Jessica thought. Mr Gregory should have been sent to prison for sleeping with a thirteen-year-old girl against her will. If he had, he wouldn't have been there for Mary Anne to murder. She hoped Tom McGrath would get her off.

She crossed her legs and was aware of the cigarettes in her pocket. What an unexpected treat. Smiling, she took the packet out, removed one, and lit it. It wasn't until Will had come home the week before that she'd smoked in the house. There was something exceptionally pleasurable about it. Now that Will had gone, she'd have to sprinkle lavender water about the place to disguise the smell. She drew in the smoke, blew it out with a happy sigh, and flicked the ash in the saucer. It made her feel relaxed and light-headed.

What she required now was music. She carried the tea into the parlour, the cigarette in her mouth partially blinding her with smoke. With Al Bowlly singing the haunting 'Pennies from Heaven', possibly her very favourite song of all, she sank into an armchair, hugging a cushion with her left arm. Putting the tea down, she took another puff of the cigarette and blissfully closed her eyes.

'Is this all you have to do?' a sharp voice demanded.

Jessica nearly jumped out of her skin. Her mother-in-law, Ida Collins, was staring down at her with such an angry look on her face you'd think Jessica was doing something utterly disgusting – she couldn't think of anything bad enough to warrant such an outraged expression. How could such a plain woman have brought such a handsome son into the world? she wondered for the umpteenth time.

'I'm only smoking,' she said artlessly. Smoking wasn't a crime. You couldn't be sent to prison for it. 'Will left his cigarettes behind so I thought I'd try one.'

Ida scowled. 'Don't you have housework to do?'

Jessica looked dreamily at her mother-in-law. She breathed smoke into her lungs and released it slowly in a long, narrow stream. Ida took a startled step backwards as if worried the smoke might reach and kill her. 'The housework is done,' Jessica said. 'When I finish this cigarette I intend to go shopping.'

'Has William gone back to sea?' Ida didn't wait for an answer. 'I really wanted to see him. It's why I came. He's such a nice young man and was very kind to Bertie when they were at school together.'

'He left early this morning,' Jessica informed her. Ida Collins couldn't have been more different from Ethel. Bertie, Ida's only child, had been born during the menopause. Not long afterwards she was left a widow with a child to bring up alone. Now in her early seventies, drab and shapeless, her lined face reflected the bitterness she felt at the way life had treated her. She wasn't an easy woman to like, let alone love.

'Nobody thought to tell me he was in Liverpool until Bertie mentioned it on Sunday after Mass,' Ida said resentfully. 'By then, it was too late; he had more important people to see and places to go. Why wasn't I invited to tea or something while he was here?'

'I didn't know how much you liked Will, or I would have asked you.' It was up to Bertie to see to his own mother, surely.

'Like hell you would,' the woman virtually spat. She got up from the settee and stamped into the kitchen.

Jessica gasped. She pushed herself out of the chair and followed unsteadily, wishing she'd thought to lock the back door so her mother-in-law couldn't have got in. But why should she have to lock her own back door? How dare Ida walk into her house, confront her in the parlour and accuse her of neglecting the housework.

In the kitchen, her mother-in-law was seated at the table in the same place, on the same chair, as her son had sat the night

34

before doing his damned accounts. To Jessica's horror, tears were pouring down Ida's cheeks. 'I'm sorry,' she stammered, though had no idea what she was apologizing for. 'Would you like a handkerchief?' She was pretty sure she didn't have an ironed one.

Ida shook her head. 'I want to die,' she moaned.

'Oh, dear,' Jessica said inadequately. She sat opposite the woman and reached for her hands. 'Don't cry,' she murmured.

Ida snatched her hands away. 'Don't you dare tell me not to cry,' she shouted. 'What would you know about it? You, with your posh house and posh furniture. You have no idea what it's like to live on a pittance, to plead with this charity and that charity for money to buy shoes for your child.'

'I can only guess what it must have been like for you, Ida.' Jessica had no idea how to deal with the situation and felt like crying herself. 'All I can do is sympathize.'

The woman's eyes were wild. 'I don't want your sympathy.'

'Then what do you want, Ida?' In the parlour, Al Bowlly was singing 'Au Revoir, But Not Goodbye'.

Ida looked frantically from right to left, as if whatever it was she wanted might appear out of thin air. 'I don't know,' she said in a ragged voice. 'I don't know.'

'Would you like us to go into town and have lunch?' Jessica suggested. It would be horrible, but she was willing to put up with it.

'No, no, of course not, you stupid bitch.'

'If that's the case . . .' Jessica went into the hall, grabbed her white jacket and straw hat, collected her bag from the living room, and left the house, '. . . I'll go to lunch by myself.'

She sat upstairs on the tram and smoked one of Will's cigarettes – the matchbook came from a bar in San Francisco, she saw. It helped calm her nerves after the encounter with her mother-in-law which she'd found deeply upsetting. It was almost as if the woman hated her. She'd always been a bit odd, but never as bad as today.

No doubt Bertie would be informed about what had happened, the story slanted in such a way that it was all her fault; that she'd been smoking, neglecting the housework, and had made Ida cry. Jessica groaned and was wondering how she would defend herself when she noticed the tram was passing the King's Cinema in London Road. *Anna Karenina* was on, with Greta Garbo and Frederic March. She'd been longing to see it ever since the trailer had been shown at the City Picture House in Lime Street.

Jessica rang the bell, raced downstairs, and jumped off the tram. She hurried back to the cinema and saw the programme was about to start. After handing over her one and threepence, she went upstairs, entered the empty balcony and sat in the front row.

It was a while before the cinema darkened. The news came on showing the marriage in France of the Duke of Windsor to Wallis Simpson, followed by film of the fighting in the Spanish Civil War. Jessica closed her eyes and kept them closed – she couldn't stand seeing dead bodies. She still didn't open them during a report from Russia about some awful person called Joseph Stalin, who was having people murdered all over the place.

The picture started. Russia again, but long before Stalin had appeared on the scene. There were gracious houses, women in crinolines, and soldiers wearing uniforms more suitable for the theatre rather than for battle.

Oh, but it was so sad, so heartbreakingly romantic. Poor Anna, madly in love with Count Vronsky, refused a divorce by her cold, unloving husband, left completely alone at the end. Jessica could feel her anguish. She forgot to smoke and couldn't stop crying all the way through, sometimes loudly, though it didn't matter. The balcony was as empty when the picture ended as it had been when it began.

She was still dabbing her eyes on the tram on the way back to Sefton Park, having forgotten about the drama that had occurred in her own home only that morning. Fortunately, there was no sign of her mother-in-law when she went inside.

The cup of tea she'd been drinking when Ida had burst in was on the floor in the parlour, a cigarette stubbed out on the saucer. Jessica picked up the things and took them back to the kitchen. The house looked and felt strange, as if it had changed drastically since the morning. 'I don't belong here any more,' Jessica whispered. 'If only things were different.'

She was glad when it was time to collect Jamie and Dora from school. It would bring her down to earth. There were times when she worried that being their mother was the only hold she had left on reality.

Lydia arrived while the children were having their tea. She looked awfully tired. She'd had a horrid day at school.

'I had a horrid morning,' Jessica told her. 'But the afternoon was sheer bliss.' She described *Anna Karenina*, and Lydia said she'd go and see it at the weekend.

'You know how much I love a good romance.' She stretched her arms languorously. 'Frederic March is one of my favourite leading men, though he can't hold a candle to Joel McCrea.'

'Me, I like Clark Gable best,' Jessica declared.

'With moustache or without?'

'Oh, definitely with. In a minute, love,' she said to Jamie, who was clamouring to play Twenty-One. He'd become obsessed with the game, whereas Dora had gone off it completely and preferred to play with her dolls. 'Go and read the book Uncle Will brought, while me and Auntie Lydia have a little chat.'

'It was just school,' Lydia said after Jamie had gone. She

37

shrugged. 'The children are OK, poor little things, but the parents want their heads banging together. There's a little girl in my class, Roseanna, seven. Summer or winter, she never wears knickers. Her clothes are filthy and, I'm not joking, Jess, she stinks to high heaven. Well,' she continued, her voice getting angrier and angrier, 'this morning she only turns up with a deep cut on her forehead, blood pouring down her face, crying her heart out. Turns out her father did it, just gave her a casual punch as she left for school. One of the teachers took her to hospital, and the doctor called the police, who went to see the father. No one has any idea what's going to happen next. I mean, will the father be sent to prison? Or will he just get a rap on the knuckles and be told not to do it again? Either way, what sort of future can Roseanna expect?'

'Does she have a mother?' Jessica asked.

'The mother's expecting her ninth baby any minute and moved in with her sister weeks ago "for safety's sake".' Lydia rolled her eyes in disgust. 'Only six of the nine babies were born alive due to the father's propensity to give his wife a good kicking from time to time.'

'Oh, Lydia, that's awful!' Jessica's earlier encounter with her mother-in-law was so mild in comparison that she was annoyed with herself for getting in such a tuck about it.

Lydia sighed. 'Sometimes, I wish I taught in the sort of school Jamie and Dora go to, where the parents are like you and Bertie and the children don't smell.'

'You're doing far more good where you are,' Jessica told her firmly. 'Oh, there you are, Jamie.' Her son came into the room with a pack of cards and a hopeful look on his face. 'All right, love; we'll play Twenty-One now.'

'I thought you had something to tell me,' Lydia said, 'apart from that marvellous picture.'

'It was nothing, really,' Jessica assured her. 'Nothing to worry about at all.'

★

Bertie came home, having earned a bonus on the sale of a house that had been on the market for months. He had recovered from the sulks he'd had that morning and acted quite normally, promising to buy the children presents and take Jessica to dinner at the weekend. Clearly his mother hadn't contacted him to complain about this morning. Perhaps she never would. Perhaps she was concerned that Jessica might complain to Bertie about *her*.

The next morning, Jessica felt much happier in herself, if not with the rest of the world where there were children like Roseanna, wars were being fought, people being murdered and no doubt all sorts of other horrors taking place that she knew nothing about.

She remembered she still had about half a dozen of Will's cigarettes left. Once the children were at school, the house-work done, and the side door bolted, she sat in the garden smoking – it was another perfect day – and wondering whether to see *Anna Karenina* again.

Somewhere, a bell was ringing. It took a while for her to realize it was the bell on her own front door. She had a visitor!

Tom McGrath was standing outside with a large cardboard box in his arms. 'Where shall I put this?' he enquired.

Jessica stared at him blankly. 'Put what?'

'The typewriter.' He gave the box a little shake. 'I asked if you would do a bit of typing for me, remember? My sec-retary's left and I have this big case starting tomorrow. Now, Jess, me darling girl, will you please tell me where to put this bloody thing before I drop it on me feet.'

Chapter 4

'But . . .' Jessica stammered, 'Bertie said . . .'

Tom held up his hand. 'Your mother said I wasn't to listen to any "buts", Jess,' he said cheerfully. 'I am merely following her orders.'

Jessica persisted. 'Bertie's dead set against me working.'

'Your mother also told me to take no notice of anything Bertie has to say. Jess,' he implored, 'this typewriter weighs a ton. If it drops on me feet I may never walk again and I'll sue you to high heaven. Just in case you've forgotten, I'm a man trained in the law of the land, and I have a reputation for always winning.'

There seemed to be no use arguing. 'This way.' She led him into the parlour and pulled a leaf out of the table, wincing when Tom lifted the typewriter out of the box and put it down with a thud. His iron-grey, perfectly tailored suit and formal striped tie were slightly at odds with his dark, laughing eyes and the black hair that was a fraction too long, curling as it did onto the collar of the dazzling white shirt that there was no question whatsoever of her mother having washed. She reminded herself that there'd been a time when she hadn't liked him, but perhaps she'd been deceiving herself.

'There's paper in the box,' he said, 'letterheads, a box of flimsy and a folder with a couple of dozen letters in addressed to McGrath, Gordon & Willetts, as well as notes explaining how to reply. Someone'll do the envelopes back at the office.

Someone else will be along in the morning and collect what you've already done and bring more. You'll get through this lot in a jiffy, love. Your dear ould mam tells me you're a first-class typist.'

Jessica was surprised and not a little bit flattered that her 'dear ould mam' had apparently been singing her praises for the first time in her life. 'Are the letters about Mary Anne Donovan?' she asked. 'I read about her in the paper yesterday.'

'Two young ladies in the office will be dealing with the paperwork for the trial.' He laid his big hand on the type-writer. 'This is day-to-day stuff, but we don't want to get too far behind with it.'

'I hope Mary Anne gets off,' Jessica said timidly. 'Even if she did kill that awful Mr Gregory, she deserves to get off. I'm only surprised she didn't kill him sooner. *I* would have.'

He looked at her in astonishment. 'What an outrageous thing to say, Jessica Collins! You look like an angel, refuse to take a job without your dear husband's permission, yet claim yourself willing to commit murder in that sweet, innocent voice. You're a very contradictory lady and no mistake.'

Jessica felt herself blush. 'Well,' she said, 'he deserved to die, didn't he?'

'It's a pity you couldn't come to the trial, girl,' he said, suddenly sober. 'There are two sides to every story and the right side is rarely the one featured in the press.'

'I still hope she gets off,' Jessica said stubbornly.

'So do I, Jess.' With that, Tom McGrath grasped her face in both hands and planted a warm kiss on her forehead. 'I'll let meself out,' he said, and did just that, closing the front door with such a bang that the entire house reverberated.

Jessica had no idea how long she sat there, listening to the house settle, still feeling Tom's hands pressed against her cheeks, his lips touching her forehead. She knew there was nothing romantic or suggestive about his behaviour. She was

41

now his stepdaughter, a member of his family. He had been just as demonstrative with his real daughters, Mary and Caitlin, two delightful young women who'd come over from Ireland with their husbands and children for his wedding to Jessica's mother.

She wished she didn't have to share him with so many other people; nieces and nephews, grandchildren, a brother and his brother's wife, Amelia. She remembered how tender Tom had been with Amelia, who hadn't long to live, her body stricken as it was with a rare cancer that doctors didn't know how to treat.

After a while, she got up and examined the letters she had to do; quite simple ones dealing with problems like somebody's tree interfering with the garden of a neighbour, a car damaged but the insurer refusing to pay compensation, noise from a factory, three letters to do with house purchases, two concerning divorce. All quite trite on the surface, but desperately important to the people concerned.

It was ages since she'd used a typewriter. This one was a Remington, new by the look of it, all the silver bits glittering. She practised typing for a while. Soon she was back to her old, rapid speed without making a single error.

'I'm not nearly as stupid as you think I am, Bertie,' she said loudly to the empty room.

Next morning, a young man from McGrath, Gordon & Willetts with a too-big collar and too-short trousers turned up to collect yesterday's letters and bring more. His name was Jack Adams, he told her, grinning widely as if the name were a joke. As he was using the tram as transport, there was time for him to have the cup of tea she offered him and three rounds of toast heaped with strawberry jam.

'How did the case go in court yesterday?' Jessica asked. It was impossible not to grin back.

'Yesterday, it were the Crown presenting their case. I'm not sure when it'll be our turn. Hope she gets off,' he mused. 'Fine-looking girl like that. It'd be a shame to see her hanged by the neck until she was dead.'

'Oh, they wouldn't hang her, surely?' Jessica cried. 'She's not old enough.'

'Wouldn't they?' he said vaguely. 'Then I wouldn't like to see her rot in jail, either.'

Jessica refilled his cup. She appreciated getting information right from the horse's mouth – well, almost. 'Who's looking after her three little boys?'

'Mrs Gregory, the victim's missus. Mind you, Mary Anne's ma has been trying to get them off her for months, ever since Mary Anne carried out the dreadful deed. Can't stand each other, them two women.'

'I'm not surprised,' Jessica said.

Next day, just before lunch, Jessica's mother came to see her, a most unusual event. Since she'd married Bertie eight years ago, she could count her mother's visits on the fingers of one hand.

'How are you getting on with Tom's letters?' she enquired when they were seated in the parlour. Her slim legs were gleaming in the finest of silk stockings. She wore a lilac linen dress with a pleated skirt and a white straw hat with a floppy silk rose on the side. Her shoes, bag and gloves were also white. She looked as if she was on her way to London to have tea at Buckingham Palace.

'Fine,' Jessica told her. 'I've already finished today's.' She pointed at the typewriter, which was still exactly where Tom had put it.

'Tom said last night the ones you've done so far are perfect. You know, darling, Tom would be happy to give you a little part-time job in his office; mornings, say, from ten till one. The money would pay for holidays – you and Bertie have never had a holiday, have you?' She shook her head sadly.

'And it really is time you bought yourself some pretty clothes, Jessica. That frock looks the sort girls would wear in an orphanage.'

Jessica looked down at her brown-and-cream check frock. It was made of thick cotton that didn't crease easily, nor did it show the dirt. 'I quite like it,' she said.

As if her mother had guessed her thoughts and disapproved of them, she said, 'Another thing you could do with the extra money is get a woman in to do the washing and the heavy work, like scrubbing floors and cleaning the inside windows. You know, darling,' she said boastfully, 'never in my entire life have I scrubbed a single floor.'

'I couldn't bear to let someone else do the heavy work,' Jessica said with a shudder. 'Fancy expecting some poor woman – it's bound to be a woman, and she's bound to be poor – to clean for me. What would I do with myself while she was on her hands and knees scrubbing things?'

'Sit down, paint your nails, and thank your lucky stars. It's what I do.' She looked suspiciously at her daughter. 'I do believe you have socialist tendencies, Jessica.'

'I have no idea what they are, Mother.'

It would seem her mother wasn't sure, either. 'Believing all people are equal,' she said, vaguely waving her hand.

'You're right.' Jessica nodded. 'That's exactly what I do believe.'

Later, her mother took her to lunch at George Henry Lee's. 'Our Will thinks you should get out more,' she said in the taxi on the way there. 'He wrote to me – he's still in Portsmouth, you know – and said Bertie keeps you short of money. That's disgusting! And Tom claims you look anxious and need to be taken out of yourself.'

'I'm perfectly all right,' Jessica protested. She knew that she wasn't, but there was nothing anyone could do about it.

'Then why do all these people say you're not?'

Jessica didn't point out there were only two people. Her mother was in the sort of mood during which nothing she said could be denied. She was glad when the conversation turned to the trial.

'Tom said there's going to be a big surprise.' Her mother lowered her voice so the taxi driver couldn't hear. 'It'll happen quite soon, maybe on Monday.'

'What is it?'

'Tom won't tell me.' She turned to her daughter and laughed. She looked so beautiful, so young and gay, that Jessica gasped. 'Oh, he's such an irritating, interesting, *fascinating* man, darling. I do feel sorry for you being married to Bertie, who is such a terrible bore. Oh, and Will said you must stop letting him browbeat you. He also said he would have written to you himself about it, but was worried Bertie might get his hands on the letter and it would make him cross.'

That night, Bertie proved conclusively what a terrible bore he was by objecting strongly to the presence of the typewriter in the house. It had been there for three days, but he'd had no reason to enter the parlour until the third, when he found the typewriter perched on the table.

'What's that doing here?' he demanded.

'Tom brought it,' Jessica said as casually as she could, as if it happened every day that someone came to the house with a typewriter.

'Have you been *working* for him?' His forehead creased into a thunderous scowl.

'Yes. I'm doing it as a favour for Tom. His secretary has joined the Forces, leaving him in a bit of a hole. He has this big case on, you see.'

'I know,' Bertie snapped. 'I was there, wasn't I, when he told us about it? If I remember rightly, I said I didn't want you to have anything to do with it. You have enough to do as it is. I think—'

'Oh, do be quiet, Bertie,' Jessica said, her patience snapping. 'I don't care what you think.' She'd been simmering all afternoon. He *did* browbeat her, but what made her angry was the thought of people noticing. 'I'm doing it for Tom, who happens to be my stepfather, and you have no right to stop me.' He opened his mouth to answer, but she wasn't prepared to let him. 'I have no intention of discussing it with you further, Bertie.'

She swept out of the room and went upstairs to read to Dora, who'd not long been put to bed. Jamie came in to listen while his mother read a story from *The Yellow Fairy Book* by Enid Blyton, by which time Dora was asleep and Jamie went to bed himself. Jessica followed.

'I've nearly finished *The Wizard of Oz* for the second time,' he informed her as she folded back the bedclothes for him to get in.

'I must read it myself one of these days,' she remarked.

'Can I read it to you, Mummy?' he asked eagerly.

'Of course, love.' He settled back against the propped-up pillow, the book on his knee, and she kissed his cheek. 'I'm already looking forward to it.'

Downstairs, Bertie was in the sitting room reading the paper. Jessica went into the kitchen and dried the dishes. She wondered if she hadn't had children, would she have stayed with Bertie? It was one thing to promise to stay with someone through sickness and in health, for richer and for poorer, but what about sticking by a person who sulked at the least little thing and treated you as if he owned you? And browbeat you and left you short of money.

She stayed in the kitchen, cleaning drawers and tidying cupboards, until long after Bertie had gone to bed. He'd wished her a surly 'Good night'.

It was almost midnight before she went up to bed herself, treading lightly on the stairs and giving the third one from the top a miss because it creaked.

In the bedroom, she took off her clothes without making any sound at all, apart from the faintest whisper of crêpe de Chine from her nightdress when she put it on, then slid into bed, keeping well away from her sleeping husband, not even bothering to tuck the clothes around her for fear of waking him.

Her eyes were closed, she felt relaxed and was preparing to drift into sleep herself, when a hand touched her shoulder.

'Do you mind?'

She was turned over; he was ready for her. Sometimes she wondered if she would die in the middle of it. Was it like this for all women? When would it stop, not just for now, but for ever?

After a while, it did stop. But only for now.

It was Friday and Jack Adams turned up to collect what Jessica had done the day before. 'I won't be back again till Monday,' he said, 'so the boss isn't in a hurry for any of these.' He put the folder of new work on the kitchen table.

She quizzed him about what had happened in court the day before.

'Not much,' he admitted. 'It seems the prosecution have built a watertight case. No one thinks Mary Anne has a chance of getting off, except the boss, that is, who doesn't seem a bit worried.'

Jessica wondered what sort of trick Tom had up his sleeve. Now no one would know until next week.

In the afternoon, she went to see *Anna Karenina* again. Will's cigarettes had all been smoked so she bought ten Capstan in the foyer. Once again she was alone in the balcony, able to sob her heart out without a soul to hear.

What sort of emotions did Anna feel when Vronsky refused to have anything more to do with her? Of course, Anna wasn't real, but Greta Garbo was and she was conveying to the cinema audience a great, overwhelming sadness, a love so desperate and unreciprocated that she wanted to kill herself.

Jessica had never felt like that. She loved her children more than anything else on earth, but Anna's love for her Count was a different love altogether, and she would never feel that way about Bertie.

I'll miss it, whatever it is, she thought sadly. There'll always be a big, black hole in my life. Its course is set and there's no possibility of it changing from the way it is now. Perhaps Bertie feels the same. Perhaps there's something lacking for him and I'm not the person who can provide it.

She felt sad all weekend, sorry for Bertie and sorry for herself. She was glad when he went to Wigan to see a cricket match on Saturday afternoon, taking Jamie with him. Jessica and Dora went by tram to the Pier Head and caught the ferry to New Brighton where they built sandcastles, made little moats and rivers, ate ice cream and generally had a lovely time.

On Sunday, it was their turn to visit Bertie's mother in Anfield, never a pleasant experience. This time, Mrs Collins managed to upset both children by insisting they eat the rice pudding that they loathed.

'Eat it! Eat it!' she snapped, tapping the dish with her fingernail.

Dora turned her head and buried it in her mother's shoulder, while Jamie sat rigid in his chair, his lips clamped together.

'Neither of them like rice pudding, Mrs Collins,' Jessica reminded her for what must have been the hundredth time. She was convinced the woman only made it knowing there'd be a scene and Bertie would be on her side, even against his own children. She put her arm on the table in front of the children, as if to protect them from the rice pudding.

'It's good for them,' her mother-in-law insisted. 'It has an egg in it and it's made with fresh milk.'

'It's not good for them if they don't like it,' Jessica pointed out.

'Do as your grandma says,' Bertie commanded.

Dora started to cry. Jessica ate a spoonful of rice pudding and was nearly sick. 'Ugh! The milk's sour or the egg's bad, one or the other. I'm sorry, Mrs Collins, but no one's eating this – unless you fancy eating it yourself.'

'Did you need to humiliate her like that?' Bertie asked after the children had gone to bed. There was an unspoken agreement not to argue in front of them.

'By letting Jamie and Dora eat her damned rice pudding? They could easily have been sick.'

'Don't swear!'

Jessica sighed. Nothing would change. Their lives would continue like this until one of them died.

Jack Adams came to collect the letters, but didn't bring any new ones. 'Everyone's too excited to sort out what to do. Mary Anne's trial will be over today. Before the boss left for the court, he was walking around like the cat that ate the cream.'

'You mean Tom? Mr McGrath?'

'That's right, missis. The other bosses, Mr Gordon and Mr Willetts, are as old as the hills and we hardly ever see 'em.'

When Jack left, Jessica felt gripped by the same excitement. She desperately wanted Mary Anne to be found innocent. What was she to do with herself today? Mondays, she usually did the washing. Today, though, she wasn't in the mood. She wasn't in the mood to go to the pictures, either.

She went upstairs and changed into the pale green fitted suit and Juliet cap she'd made for her mother's wedding, and put up her hair for a change using a silver slide. She looked at herself in the mirror. It was the nearest she would ever get to looking glamorous.

49

'Where do you suggest we go today?' she asked her reflection.

But all the reflection did was ask the same question at the same time.

'I know, I'll go to The Temple, the hotel where Mother and Tom got married, and have a pot of tea and a cigarette in the lounge.' Should some man take her for a high-class prostitute, then he would be sent packing. She was merely a housewife having a break while out shopping.

Jessica felt a surge of excitement. It was a lovely day again and she almost ran to catch the tram, but when she reached the tram stop, she decided to wait for a taxi instead.

Today, she didn't want to mingle with the poor people who would get on the tram on its way into town; children without shoes, women wearing rags, men who were much too thin to be healthy. She'd sooner avoid the sad, haggard faces, the ones so full of despair that you suspected the owner would sooner be dead than alive. She felt pity for these people – if she had enough money she would change their lives for ever – it was just that today she didn't feel like mixing with them.

She told the driver to drop her off at Henderson's where she wanted to buy a new lipstick – bright red for a change; she usually wore pink. She remembered Harris Coleman, the estate agent where Bertie worked, wasn't too far away from the hotel. In that case, when she came out of the shop, she'd catch another taxi directly to The Temple entrance. She'd think up explanations for where the money had gone before it was time for Bertie to do the accounts.

The lipstick was bought and applied in front of the mirror on the counter. 'It looks the gear on you, dear,' said the middle-aged assistant. 'Brightens up your face no end.'

There were a few people in the comfortable lounge with its dark walls and brown velvet chairs; men and woman, some together, some alone. The curtains were almost closed, allowing in little daylight. Pink and cream shaded lamps here and there provided subdued illumination.

She was hoping the waiter who had reminded of her father would take her order, but it was a much younger man who approached.

'A pot of tea, please. Do you sell cigarettes?' she asked.

The man smiled, as if it was a silly question. 'Of course, madam. What sort?'

She was going to say 'Capstan', but had a feeling they were a cheap brand. 'Do you have Chesterfields?'

'Yes, madam.' He seemed to have only been gone seconds, when he was back with her order.

This really was bliss. Jessica poured tea and lit a cigarette with a match out of the little book provided. On a normal Monday – well, today *was* normal, it was she who had decided her part in it would be different – she would have had most of the washing on the line by now, with perhaps a few odds and ends still to go through the mangle. As soon as it had been done, she would put the washing things away, sit down at the kitchen table and have lunch. Usually, she made a sandwich and read the newspaper or a few pages of her current novel.

She'd tell Bertie she'd felt unwell for most of the day, that she'd had to drag herself out of bed to fetch the children home and make dinner. And she'd make omelettes for the meal, omelettes with a little bit of salad. She'd say she'd do the washing tomorrow.

Jessica stretched out her legs and sighed. It would be easy to fall asleep in the quiet, smoky atmosphere of the lounge. How awful if she did and burnt a hole with the cigarette in one of the lovely chairs! A man in a horrid green suit came and sat in a chair a few feet away and began to open a newspaper. He caught Jessica's eye and she quickly looked away.

There was a noise as a crowd of people entered the reception area; lots of laughter and loud voices, all male.

'Where's Maurice?' a man called.

'He left long before we did,' another man replied. 'He'll have been here a while by now.'

The man in the green suit began to fold his paper. He got to his feet and was picking up his briefcase when a voice cried, 'Ah, Maurice, there you are?'

'Tom! We can speak as friends at last.'

'I hope you haven't been waiting long. We were trapped by the press when we tried to leave the court.'

'I've been here only a few minutes.'

To Jessica's astonishment, the newcomer was her stepfather, who was enthusiastically shaking the hand of the green-suited man. She did her level best to sink into the chair, to disappear, but failed miserably.

'Jessica!' Tom gasped seconds later when he turned and couldn't fail to see her. 'What on earth are you doing here?'

What *was* she doing there? Jessica didn't know. 'Smoking,' she replied.

Tom threw back his head and laughed heartily. 'Can't you do that at home?'

'It's not the same,' she said. 'Anyway, what are *you* doing here? I thought you were supposed to be in court.'

'I'm here because this is *our* hotel.' He spread his arms as if to encompass the whole building. 'It belongs to McGrath, Gordon & Willetts. It's where we have conferences and where witnesses stay when they come to testify in one of our cases. It's where, at five o'clock this afternoon, we are having a press conference attended by reporters from all over the country, because, my dear,' he seized her hands and pulled her to her feet, 'Mary Anne Donovan was found not guilty of killing her employer. Instead, Edward Gregory's wife will be standing trial for his murder some time next year.' He looked at her jubilantly and Jessica didn't think she'd ever seen anybody look as happy as Tom McGrath did now.

'You see, Jess, we'd found Mrs Gregory's fingerprints on

the knife that killed her husband. The police were so convinced of Mary Anne's guilt they didn't bother to test for prints.'

'I'm so glad.' She couldn't have been more pleased about anything.

'Just a minute, Jess. I'll see to Maurice, he's our fingerprint expert.' He turned away, grasped the arm of the green-suited man and led him towards the noise in reception. 'We have our own private bar upstairs,' she heard him say, 'where you can drown yourself in champagne. There's food there, too. I won't be long.'

He returned with two glasses of champagne and handed her one. 'To Mary Anne,' he said, touching her glass with his. 'I thought about you in court. I knew how much you wanted Mary Anne to be found not guilty. But you got one thing terribly wrong, you know.'

'What was that?'

'Mary Anne and Edward Gregory were in love, despite the difference in their ages. He's the last person in the world she would have killed. She'll be here for the press conference later. Perhaps you could stay and meet her?'

'I couldn't possibly. I have to be back in time to collect Jamie and Dora from school.' She sighed. 'I'd love to, though.'

A man came towards them waving a bottle. 'More champagne, people? Tom, old chap, you look depressingly sober. Let me refill your glass. And you, too, young lady.'

'I'm in a state of agreeable insobriety,' Tom claimed, nevertheless holding out his glass to be refilled.

Jessica didn't refuse, either. The day, which had already been a little out of the ordinary, was turning out to be one of the most extraordinary she had ever known.

The sounds of merriment were beginning to fade as Tom's colleagues made their way upstairs. The lounge was completely quiet. When Jessica spoke, she whispered, 'I'm so

53

pleased for you, Tom.' It must have been the champagne that made her reach up and touch his face in what could only be described as an affectionate gesture.

Whispering wasn't in Tom McGrath's nature. 'Jessica, girl.' He grabbed her hand and kissed it. She gave him her other hand to kiss, too.

For what seemed a long, long while they stood staring at each other. Time stopped and the world ceased turning on its axis. Jessica's heart beat so strongly and so loudly she imagined it had grown big enough to occupy her entire body.

'Come with me, darlin',' said Tom McGrath.

He led her to the corner of the room where there was a door she hadn't noticed. When the door was opened, it turned out to be a tiny lift just big enough for two. Tom pressed a button, the lift moved, and stopped on a quiet corridor, where he led her into a room whose main feature was a large bed with black satin covers. He picked her up in a single swoop and carried her to it.

'I've been wanting to do this, darlin', from the first time I set eyes on you,' he said, as he laid her none too gently on the bed and began to kiss her passionately.

Chapter 5

On Tuesday, Jessica did the washing more diligently than she had ever done before. She scrubbed stains that normally she would have ignored, folded things neatly before passing them through the mangle so they would dry less creased, and pegged them more carefully on the line for the same reason.

Yesterday, Bertie had been unexpectedly nice when she explained she'd felt too unwell to do housework. He'd accepted omelette for his dinner without a murmur, though he had always claimed omelettes made more of a snack than a proper meal. That morning, he'd even brought her tea in bed for the very first time.

Perhaps she should be sick more often, she thought wryly. When she was well, which was most of the time, he gave the impression of not liking her all that much.

The washing was finished by midday. With a sense of satisfaction, she stood for a while and watched it blowing on the line, then went indoors and made a sandwich and a pot of tea. She remembered the cigarettes she'd bought in The Temple the day before. She'd only smoked two. She found them at the bottom of her handbag and lit one with a match from the little book with the hotel name on the cover.

She didn't feel any shame for what had happened. Neither, she suspected, did Tom. It would never happen again, she wouldn't allow it, and felt sure he didn't want an affair.

Oh, but it had been so wonderful, so idyllic and perfect that

55

she would never forget it until her dying day. Tom's hands, his lips, doing undreamt-of things, touching her in places . . . Jessica shivered at the memory. She felt like a proper woman at last.

After picking up Jamie and Dora, she called in at the butcher's and bought a pound of steak and kidney for a pie, Bertie's favourite meal. One of the reasons she rarely made it was because she couldn't bear to touch offal of any sort. Animal flesh was bad enough, but organs! She managed to slice the kidneys into pieces without actually looking at them.

Bertie sniffed appreciatively when he came in. 'I hope that tastes as nice as it smells,' he commented.

'I can't guarantee it,' Jessica warned him.

He laughed at her acknowledgment that she was a hopeless cook, and Jessica wondered if somehow they'd turned a corner – or if she had. On Monday, through actions, not words, she'd learned something that laid bare the faults in her marriage. Something very important was missing from her life, but now she understood and was prepared to live the rest of her life without it.

The pie wasn't at all bad. 'Your pastry is coming along,' Bertie said encouragingly, 'and I think your gravy is already there.'

It was his turn to read to the children. Jessica was drying the dishes when he came into the kitchen to announce that Dora was asleep and Jamie was absorbed in *Wizard*. 'By the way,' he went on, 'at work today, George Kettle swore blind he saw you coming out of that hotel in town yesterday, you know the one where your mother had her wedding reception. I can't remember the name.'

'Neither can I.' Jessica felt as if the meal she'd just eaten had come back into her throat.

'I told him that was nonsense; that you'd spent most of the day in bed because you didn't feel well.'

Jessica nodded furiously. 'That's right. Tell George he's talking rubbish.'

'I already have, darling.'

Jessica spent all night and the following day trying to convince herself that once Bertie had told George Kettle he'd made a mistake, that his wife had been nowhere near The Temple hotel on Monday, he was hardly likely to go back and try to prove he was right.

Who would he ask? One of the waiters? The man behind the reception desk? *What* would he ask? Did you notice a young woman with blue eyes and blonde wavy hair in this hotel on Monday at about lunchtime?

Even if one of them said, 'yes', there were thousands of women answering that description in Liverpool.

She was quite safe. But did she care if she was safe? Not really. She was still in a state of euphoria and had yet to come down to earth.

'George took that photo with him, the one of you that I keep on my desk, you know the one taken at our wedding?' Bertie said in a flat voice. 'It was my idea he take it because he kept insisting he'd seen you and I wanted to prove him wrong once and for all. He showed it to a waiter, who recognized you straight away, said you went upstairs with one of the legal chaps who own the hotel or something. He described the chap and it sounded very much like Tom McGrath. Apparently, he couldn't see either of you in the upstairs bar so you must have gone into one of the bedrooms. He took you for one of the prostitutes who frequent the place, though he hadn't done so initially. "She looked much too nice," he said.'

Jessica considered denying everything, but she honestly didn't think she'd get away with it.

★

57

For days, Bertie went around looking shocked and miserable. He barely spoke. Jessica was as nice to him as possible, conscious that she had let him down. They talked about it one night and she promised she would never do it again.

'How would you feel if I was unfaithful to you?' he asked.

She thought a while before saying, 'To tell the truth, I don't think I'd mind.'

That hurt, she could see it in his eyes, but he shouldn't have asked the question if he couldn't accept the answer.

It wasn't until more than a week later that he became angry. 'George Kettle thinks I ought to go and see a solicitor,' he said hotly when he came home.

'What about?' Jessica asked.

'About you, about what you did.'

'But how will a solicitor help? I've already promised never to do it again.'

'Infidelity, whether it be once or a hundred times, is grounds for divorce,' he said stiffly.

'But Catholics can't get divorced,' she pointed out. There was a nervous sensation in her tummy; she hadn't been expecting anything like this.

'Not in the eyes of the Church, maybe, but they can in the eyes of the law. Tom will confirm that,' he added spitefully. 'He's a lawyer.' He frowned. 'Tom,' he murmured, 'Tom.' It was as if he'd forgotten the part her stepfather had played in the affair. 'I wonder what your mother will have to say if she finds out.'

With each day he grew angrier. It was as if someone at Harris Coleman – George Kettle, Jessica assumed – was egging him on, stressing how appallingly he'd been treated by his harlot of a wife.

'Cuckolded', that was the word. Just saying it in her head made Jessica feel ashamed. She hadn't intended to hurt Bertie. She'd expected making love with Tom to remain their secret for all time – and if it hadn't been for George Kettle and his persistence it would have.

Oh, *God*! She felt herself go cold inside. Say her mother *did* find out! Jessica would feel terrible, really terrible, and her mother would feel totally betrayed, not just by her husband, but by her daughter, too. There was something sinful about it, like a crime, incestuous even. Lydia would find out and she'd tell Auntie Mildred and Uncle Fred and Peter. And Will, she'd tell Will. And Bertie was sure to tell his mother.

Pretty soon, everyone would know and Jessica wouldn't be able to hold her head up any more.

A few days later Bertie suggested they separate. 'I can't live with you any longer knowing that you've slept with another man,' he said harshly. 'I think we should lead our own lives from now on.'

'Do you really think so?' She wished she hadn't hurt him quite so much.

'Yes, I do. I'm afraid I no longer feel anything for you. There's no love left.'

'Will you go and live with your mother?' she asked. It was awful, but she really didn't mind if he left. Her father's money had paid for the house so it belonged to her as well as the car, though Bertie could keep the car. There was still about a hundred pounds in the bank that belonged to her, and she could get a job of some sort – though not with Tom's firm as her mother had suggested. 'You can come and see the children as often as you want,' she said generously.

Bertie smiled. It wasn't a very nice smile. In fact, it was full of an emotion that could well have been hate. His eyes glittered and, with a sickly feeling, she could tell he was about to exact his revenge for the humiliation she had heaped upon him. 'Oh, it's not me who's going to leave, darling, it's you,' he said in a quiet voice. 'My solicitor has explained everything. You are the person who has committed the wrong, not me. I would like you and your belongings out of this house by the end of the week. And *you* can't see the children as often as you want, but only on Saturday afternoons between two o'clock and four.'

Jessica jumped to her feet. 'You can't be serious. Jamie and Dora are *my* children, this is *my* house, *my* car. The money in the bank belongs to me; at least, most of it does.' A small amount from his wages had been saved over the years.

'Mummy?' Jamie was at the top of the stairs. 'Why are you and Daddy shouting?'

'We're just discussing something important, sweetheart.' Jessica had gone into the hall and was looking up at him, her son, in his rumpled pyjamas, rubbing his eyes. She felt as if a wild animal was tearing at her stomach, pulling it apart. How could she possibly exist if she only saw him and Dora for two hours a week? 'Go back to bed now, Jamie, there's a dear.'

She waited until he had gone before returning to the sitting room where she quietly closed the door. Bertie grinned when she went in. 'You can't do this to me,' she said shakily.

'I can and I will.' He looked horribly pleased. 'I suggest that tomorrow you consult a solicitor yourself and you'll find that I am perfectly within my rights. And don't expect him to treat you nicely, darling. After the way you've behaved, you'll be given very short shrift.'

Jessica was waiting outside the Our Lady of Perpetual Light infant school in the city centre when the bell rang to announce it was dinner-time. Pupils poured into the playground; and galloped off in the direction of their homes. Most were poorly dressed – some without shoes, some filthy – but they were possessed with a liveliness of spirit and an energy that Jessica had never noticed in her own children.

She sighed and went into the building, which smelled horribly, the principal stench being urine even though the lavatories were outside. She found her cousin, Lydia, in the corridor talking to another teacher.

'I have to speak to you,' she said in a choked voice.

A surprised Lydia excused herself and led Jessica outside to a place behind the school building where it was quiet.

'What on earth's the matter?' she asked. 'You look awful. Have you been crying?'

Jessica had been crying non-stop all morning and most of the night. She nodded and managed to stammer a garbled explanation for coming, ending with, 'I need to consult a solicitor, but Bertie said they'll all hate me. Will you come with me, Lyd? I couldn't stand it if they were horrible to me.'

Looking totally astounded, Lydia walked away a few feet. 'Holy Mary, Mother of God,' she said in a loud voice. She came back, seized Jessica by the shoulders, and gave her a good shake. 'I can hardly believe it! What a thing to do! And with Tom McGrath, of all people. I remember at the wedding you said you didn't like him.' For a moment, she appeared lost for words. 'There's a pub over the road, let's go and have a drink.'

She pulled Jessica out of the playground, across the road, and into the pub, which had not long opened. There were only three other customers present, all men. 'Give us some money,' she said. 'I haven't brought my bag with me.'

A few minutes later, Jessica was staring glumly at a gin and orange and Lydia was supping lemonade. 'Bloody men,' she said unexpectedly, 'they're all the same. They can be unfaithful as much as they like, but just let their wives do it and it becomes the crime of the century.'

'Will you come with me to see a solicitor?' Jessica asked timidly.

'There's no need. You don't have to see a man. Remember Honor Brunswick from school? She was in the year before us. *She's* a solicitor. Her office is in Quaker's Alley in town. Give her a ring when you get home. She'll probably be able to fit you in tomorrow morning.'

Honor Brunswick's office was on the first floor of an ancient building with beams on the walls and a sloping ceiling. She was a dainty, dark-haired woman with a tiny, pointed face who reminded Jessica of the child film star, Shirley Temple. She wore a plain white blouse and a grey pinstriped skirt. A matching jacket was hanging behind the door. A girl who looked no more than fifteen was typing briskly in a small side room where Jessica had been asked to wait.

For a woman so overwhelmingly feminine, Honor Brunswick had a remarkably deep voice. Jessica could only vaguely remember her from school and they'd certainly never spoken to each other – she wouldn't have forgotten the voice.

'How can I help, Mrs Collins?' she asked when they were seated cosily opposite each other in front of an empty fireplace. Her desk was on the other side of the room. 'Or would you prefer we were Jessica and Honor?'

'First names are fine with me.' Jessica confirmed. She honestly didn't care.

At Honor's request, she haltingly relayed what had happened in The Temple hotel and Bertie's subsequent demand that she leave the house and only see the children for two hours on a Saturday. 'I mean, can he do that?'

'Before I answer, I'd like to ask you a few questions.' She scribbled something in the notebook on her knee. 'Has your husband ever committed adultery?'

Jessica almost laughed for the first time in weeks. 'Of course not.'

'How can you be so sure?' Honor was looking at her with amusement. 'Men are devious creatures.'

'Well, let's say I doubt it very much.' Jessica blushed. 'He's not particularly good at it,' she said awkwardly.

'And is this the first time you have had an adulterous relationship with another man?'

It sounded awful, put like that. 'Yes, and it wasn't exactly a relationship. It lasted only about fifteen minutes.'

'Long enough for your husband to want to throw you out of the house,' Honor reminded her. 'What about money? Do you have an income of your own?'

'No.'

'Do you live in a rented property or is it being bought on a mortgage?'

'We own it,' Jessica explained. 'My father died five years ago and left me a thousand pounds. We finished the mortgage and Bertie bought a car. There's still some left in the bank, about a hundred pounds, I think.'

'Do you have a joint bank account, Jessica?' the solicitor asked.

'No, it's in Bertie's name. He always sees to the money side of things.'

Honor half closed her eyes. 'I dread asking this question, but is the house in both your names or just Bertie's?'

'Just Bertie's,' Jessica replied.

Honor's reaction to this was similar to Lydia's the day before when Jessica had bared her soul. She shook her head in astonishment. 'Sometimes women amaze me,' she gasped. 'You've been married to Bertie for eight years. You clearly don't much care for him, yet you have quite willingly put every single penny of your father's inheritance in his name. The house, the car, the bank account, everything, while you are left with nothing, apart from clothes and possibly a bit of jewellery.' She frowned impatiently. 'If I had my way the marriage vows should include financial advice: "All monies and property to be held jointly."'

Jessica felt herself go cold. 'Does that mean I'm not entitled to anything?'

Honor shrugged. 'Absolutely nothing! You have committed adultery – who was the man, by the way? Was it an acquaintance of your husband's, a friend? If he was, that would only make matters worse. If the case went to court, judges strongly disapprove of women who sleep with their husband's mates.'

Jessica swallowed nervously. She'd deliberately avoided revealing the identity of the man she'd made love with. 'It was my stepfather,' she whispered. 'My mother only married him a few months ago.'

'I see.' The woman managed to hide any further surprise she might have felt. 'Well, I'm afraid, Jessica, that you haven't a leg to stand on.' She shrugged. 'All you can do is go along with your husband's wishes and, when it comes to financial support, rely on his generosity.'

If only you could go back and undo things. If only she hadn't gone to The Temple hotel that day. If only Tom McGrath hadn't been there. 'What if I ran away with the children?' Jessica asked. She would go mad without her children. What point would there be in life without them?

'I couldn't possibly advise you to do such a thing,' Honor said in her deep, confident voice, which immediately softened. 'But it's what I'd do if someone tried to take my daughter away from me. Have you enough money – that you can easily get your hands on, that is?'

'I haven't any money,' Jessica said wretchedly.

'Nothing you can pawn?'

'My wedding ring, some gold earrings, a gold cross and chain.'

'And where would you go? Where would you stay?' the solicitor asked kindly.

'I have no idea.' Under different circumstances, she could have asked her mother for money and taken the children to live in Manchester or even London. Bertie would never have found them. Jessica stood and discovered her legs were shaking badly. She saw no reason for staying another minute. 'Thank you for the advice,' she said politely. 'How much do I owe you?'

'I'll send a bill to your address, but the chances are you won't be there so it doesn't matter.'

'Thank you again.'

Did her mother know? Jessica wondered. She was in the Kardomah café in Bold Street toying with her coffee. She'd hardly given her mother a thought, which was unbelievably selfish. 'I should tell her,' Jessica thought. 'Before someone else does, like Bertie or his mother.'

But her mother was bound to know by now. It was almost a month since Jessica had met Tom in the hotel. Perhaps she should go and apologize. But how on earth could you apologize for something like that? Say, 'I'm sorry, Mother, but I made love with your husband.' It felt far worse betraying her mother than it did Bertie. In fact, if Bertie hadn't turned on her the way he had, she wouldn't have cared a hoot about sleeping with another man.

She stirred her coffee and a woman on the next table said, 'You'll wear a hole in the cup if you do that for much longer.'

'I'm sorry.' Jessica put the spoon on the saucer with a bang.

'Drink it,' the woman said. 'That might help. Would you like a cigarette? Your nerves are quite obviously in tatters.'

'I've got some in my bag, thank you. I'd forgotten all about them. I only started smoking recently, you see.' She took a half-used packet of Senior Service out of her bag – to Jessica, all the brands tasted exactly the same – and lit one. 'That's better.' She sort of smiled at the woman, who was collecting her things together and preparing to leave.

'I hope your troubles don't completely overwhelm you, dear,' she said putting a threepenny bit on the table.

'They already have,' Jessica whispered after she'd gone. She had no alternative; the only person she could turn to was her mother. And she would have to tell her about Tom, too, before someone else did, someone who wouldn't do it so gently, someone who might even take pleasure in it.

She caught a tram to her mother's house – or some distance away. Vulgar things like tramcars weren't allowed anywhere near Larch Avenue where most of the inhabitants had their own cars or used taxis.

A woman in a grey cotton frock and a white pinafore answered the door. This must be her mother's new house-keeper who lived on the premises. Jessica asked if she could see Mrs McGrath.

'Who shall I tell her is calling?'

'Her daughter.' She could have sworn an odd expression passed over the woman's face.

'Jessica!' Her mother emerged from one of the doors in the hall. 'I thought I recognized your voice. Come in, darling. This is my little sitting room.' She turned to the woman. 'Will you kindly bring us tea for two, Mrs Black?'

'Yes, madam.'

The sitting room was painted an intense scarlet and the delicate, spindly furniture was mainly white. Her mother seated herself in one of the elegant chairs upholstered in white-and-red striped satin, indicating to her daughter to sit on one the same. It was like being in Alice's Wonderland, Jessica thought.

'Are you going somewhere?' she asked. Her mother wore a black taffeta dress with a white organdie frill round the neck and cuffs, and a black patent leather belt encircling her narrow waist.

She waved her hands. An engagement ring that Jessica hadn't known she had sparkled expensively on the third finger of her left hand. 'I'm off to have lunch at the Adelphi with Tom and the editor of some terribly posh magazine,' she said dramatically. 'They're writing an article about him and want to know from me what it's like being married to such a successful man. So I haven't got long, darling. If you're here to apologize for sleeping with my husband, do get it over with quickly so we can move on to other things.'

Jessica wished she could die, there and then, pass away in her mother's lovely room and have nothing to worry about any more. She even closed her eyes and prepared for death, prayed for it, because she was so desperately unhappy that not even the thought of her children made her want to stay alive.

But death wasn't willing to get her out of the hole she was in. Through dry lips, she murmured, 'I'm sorry.'

'I'm sure you are, darling, and I know darn well that you didn't lead Tom on. You haven't got it in you. But when I compared my lovely husband to your miserable one,' she drawled, 'I wasn't hinting that you should have an affair with him.' Jessica noticed her hands were shaking when she picked up a scent spray; she wasn't as calm as she pretended.

Jessica felt the urge to throw herself at her mother's feet and beg forgiveness, but it wasn't the sort of gesture that would have been appreciated. Instead, she said, 'Bertie's throwing me out, Mum, I'm only being allowed to see Jamie and Dora once a week.' She couldn't remember when she'd last called her mother 'Mum'.

'Oh, that loathsome, inadequate excuse for a man,' her mother said scathingly. 'I told Tom, I said to him, he wouldn't have found you so easy to seduce had you been married to a proper man.'

She could hardly believe her ears. 'You've discussed it with Tom?'

Her mother laughed. 'It was him who told me. "Sorry, darling," he said, "but I've seduced your daughter." I wanted to tear his eyes out, but you don't do something like that to a man like Tom McGrath.' Her eyes shone with passion. She looked ever so slightly mad. 'I'd forgive him anything. I'd stand by him if he committed murder – or worse.'

'I see.' Jessica felt faint. She couldn't stand much more of this. The world had gone crazy.

67

'Anyway, are you going to let Bertie throw you out and take away your children?' Her mother had reverted to a matter-of-fact tone that didn't sound all that real.

'I've been to see a solicitor and she said he has a right to do both.' Jessica felt so weary that it was difficult to get the words out. 'I was thinking of taking the children away before Friday when he said I must leave.' Today was Wednesday.

'And where will you take them?'

'I don't know. Manchester, perhaps, or London. I'll find somewhere to live then get a job.' She couldn't wait to get away and start life again. Next time she wouldn't make any mistakes.

'Do you remember your father's cousin, Frances Bell?' her mother asked. 'She used to come and stay with us. She hasn't been since he died.'

'Of course I remember her.' She was an immensely tall woman with jet-black hair and a loud laugh. She'd never married.

'She'll look after you until you find somewhere of your own to live. We still write to each other from time to time. She lives in London – 107 Barnet Road, Islington. I'll give her a call tonight and say to expect you.' She wandered over to a white-framed mirror on the wall and examined her beauti-fully coiffured blonde hair, fluffing it out, tweaking it here and there. Jessica wondered if Tom knew it was dyed. Turning suddenly, she said, 'Now, Jess, have you any money?'

It was the second time she'd been asked that today. 'A bit.'

'You'll need more than a bit. I'll give you what I've got in the house.' She went over to a small white desk, pulled open a drawer and took out a sheaf of ten-shilling notes. 'There's ten pounds there,' she said. 'I've also got a few pounds in my handbag.' She pressed something on the wall above the desk. Mrs Black's footsteps could be heard, hurrying, presumably, from the kitchen. She knocked and came into the room.

'Yes, madam?'

'Will you find my black bead handbag for me, please? I can't remember where I left it. Also,' her smile was like a ray of sunshine on a dull day; Mrs Black visibly melted in front of it, 'may I borrow all the money you have in the house? I'll call in the bank this afternoon and pay you back as soon as I get home. I forgot to tell you, Jessica,' she said when Mrs Black had gone and the smile had vanished, 'Tom and I are going to Edinburgh tomorrow for a few days. He's seeing people about a new case he's been asked to take on, while I do some shopping.'

'I hope you have a nice time,' Jessica said wearily. She couldn't imagine doing normal things like shopping again. She began to make plans. Tomorrow, she wouldn't take the children to school. After Bertie had gone to work, she'd pack their clothes as well as her own and make her way to Lime Street station, having first found out the time of the trains. It all seemed very easy, yet at the same time supremely difficult.

Mrs Black had returned with just under three pounds in notes and coins, and was requested to telephone for a taxi. Her mother was fretting to be gone and Jessica asked for a lift into town. She'd promised to let Lydia know how she'd got on with Honor Brunswick.

In the taxi, her mother described the clothes she intended to buy in Edinburgh, the jewellery. 'And I desperately need a new handbag, preferably blue – not quite navy, but almost.' She half closed her eyes, as if visualizing the exact shade of blue she wanted. Jessica realized she was no longer at the forefront of her mother's mind.

'Bye, darling.' She scarcely looked up when Jessica thanked her profusely for everything while climbing out of the taxi. 'Think nothing of it,' she said distantly. 'Oh, there's just one thing. I'm glad you're going away, Jessica. I shall miss the children, but I'd sooner you and I didn't see each other again for a very long time.' Her lovely blue eyes were hard and unforgiving.

'All right, Mother,' Jessica said humbly, but the taxi door had already been shut and her mother didn't hear.

Lydia was in the playground supervising the children. 'The bell will go in about ten minutes,' she said when her cousin arrived.

'I've had a very busy morning.' Jessica described her meeting with the solicitor followed by the visit to her mother. 'It's going to be all right,' she said. 'I shall leave tomorrow morning. Once we're settled, I'll write and let you know how we're getting on.'

'It sounds awfully extreme, Jess,' Lydia said dubiously. 'So very final.'

'It can't be helped, can it? It's either doing something final and extreme, or giving in to Bertie.'

Chapter 6

The next morning, Bertie didn't leave for the office at his usual time. 'I'm taking a few hours off,' he said without explaining why. 'I'll go later.'

Jessica quietly panicked. She was left with no choice but to take Jamie and Dora to school as she did every morning. It was their last day before breaking up for the summer holiday. Coming home, she walked slowly in the hope Bertie would have left by the time she got there. She went into the park and smoked a cigarette while wondering how to cope with the changed circumstances.

Once Bertie had gone, she would just have to return to school and offer some excuse for taking the children out again. Someone was ill, her mother, she would claim. It meant they would be catching a later train than planned, but that didn't particularly matter.

'Damn!' she muttered when she turned into Atlas Road and saw Bertie had merely driven the car out of the garage into the drive where it was now parked. There was no sign of Bertie himself. She walked towards the house, her stomach on fire, convinced now that something was wrong.

'I'm in here,' he shouted from the parlour when she let herself in. 'Jessica, sit down, please,' he said when she appeared. He nodded towards an armchair and seated himself on a hard chair in the bay window where there was a little half-round table on which papers had been spread – typed papers, Jessica was able to see. The typewriter was still there.

'I want to describe something to you,' Bertie began gravely. He wore his office uniform; pin-striped trousers, black waist-coat, white shirt. The shirt wasn't as white or as beautifully pressed as the ones Tom McGrath wore, because Bertie's had been washed and ironed by Jessica while Tom's had been professionally laundered. And unlike Tom, who was a fine figure of a man, Bertie was youthfully slim, boyishly pale. Jessica had been terribly impressed by his rather hungry, poetic good looks when they'd first met.

'Describe what?' she asked now.

'A situation that hasn't happened, but could happen; it all depends on you.'

She shrugged a signal to go ahead, having no idea what he was talking about.

'I would like you to imagine that I had decided to divorce you.'

At this, Jessica jumped and Bertie smiled, as if he had enjoyed giving her a shock. 'But I thought we were just separating?' she stammered.

'As I said before, it all depends on you, darling. All I ask that you do now is use your imagination – for example, imagine my application for divorce is being heard in court where I will claim that you had intercourse with Tom McGrath, your stepfather.' He spoke with mock earnestness, the suggestion of a smile still on his face. 'The waiter at the hotel will confirm that you both drank champagne and entered a bedroom together where you stayed for fifteen or twenty minutes.'

Jessica sat very still and tried to keep her face impassive.

'Now, Jessica,' Bertie continued, 'imagine something else – the headlines in the newspapers when they get hold of that titbit. "Daughter sleeps with mother's new husband," ' he said dramatically like the voice in the cinema announcing a trailer, even raising his hands some distance apart as if he was displaying a newspaper with the headline shown. 'And Tom's famous enough to turn it into an affair of national interest – international even; hasn't he now got an office in New York? The divorce will be granted and you will be ordered to quit this house – I've seen a solicitor, darling, and that's what he told me; I'm not making it up.' He shuffled the papers on the table as if studying the details there, then looked at her, wide-eyed and impossibly sincere. She could tell he was enjoying himself and wondered if all this time he'd disliked her as much as she'd disliked him?

'I didn't think you were making it up,' she said stiffly. She was panicking again, worse than before. She was finding it hard to breathe, though did her best not to let it show. She ached for a cigarette. What would this do to her mother who loved Tom so much?

Bertie said, as if he could read her thoughts, though it wasn't her mother he was thinking of, 'Imagine – we're still imagining, Jess – what this will do to Jamie and Dora? The children at school are bound to find out and they'll be taunted with it. Some parents will be so disgusted they won't invite them to parties any more. They'll be desperately unhappy and find it hard to love their dear mother because she's the one who is the cause of their unhappiness. They'll grow up with the knowledge that she's a whore.'

'Stop, Bertie,' she whispered, 'stop.' His words were tearing her apart.

'Not yet, darling,' he whispered back. 'I won't stop until I've finished. Imagine again how much better it would be for everyone, our children, your mother, me, even Tom – not that I give a damn about him – if you weren't here?'

'What do you mean, if I wasn't here?' She was getting tired of this. He was playing with her like a cat with a mouse. She put both hands on her cheeks as if trying to hold her head together for fear it would explode. 'Please stop, Bertie,' she pleaded.

He lost his temper. 'I'll stop when I'm ready,' he snapped. 'What I'm getting round to is I don't want you having anything to do with the children again. You're a bad influence on them. I want you out of their lives for ever – and mine.'

'But you said I could see them every Saturday!' Jessica said timidly.

'That was before I discovered you intended taking them away.' He was shouting now, literally spitting with rage. 'You didn't care that *I* would never see them again, did you? My children are my life. I love them more than anything on earth.'

He got up and came towards her, fist raised. Jessica cowered, but it was the chimney breast he hit not her. 'The nerve of it,' he spat, 'the cheek. You sleep with another man, then attempt to steal my children. I would have been left with nothing, but what do you care?'

Jessica didn't answer. He was right to be angry. He wasn't a wicked man and she would have been treating him abominably had she taken the children away. 'I'm sorry,' she lied. She found it impossible to feel sympathy for him.

'It's a bit late to be sorry.' He returned to the chair and sat down heavily. 'Had I not discovered what you were up to, you would have been on your way to Lime Street station by now. Already on a train, perhaps.'

How did he discover what she was up to? It had only just entered her head. Only her mother and Lydia knew of her plans. Her mother would never have said anything. She disliked Bertie intensely.

Lydia! Lydia had told him. She must have telephoned him at the office. Why?

'So,' Bertie said, 'what's it to be, Jess? Are you going to leave us in peace, or am I to sue for divorce and start a scandal? If it's the latter, all I have to do is pick up the telephone and instruct my solicitor to set things in motion. Oh, I know I'll look a bit of an idiot to some people, but most will be right behind me, wishing me well.' He waved one of the sheets of paper at her. 'This is the letter from my solicitor with his advice. Oh, and there's something else he suggested. He comments that you have acted strangely, that The Temple hotel is a haunt of prostitutes, that committing adultery with your stepfather isn't exactly the act of a normal, rational woman. He thinks that you are unhinged and it would be easy for me to have you committed to a mental asylum.'

'Bertie!' she gasped. 'Surely you wouldn't do anything like that.'

He giggled. 'Probably not. After all, you are still the mother of my children. But I still want you gone, Jessica, and soon. I'll collect Jamie and Dora from school and tell them you've been taken ill. You'll stay ill for a matter of months, and then you'll die and we'll all mourn you. You will never see the children again. If you're not willing to agree to that, then, as I said before, I shall tell my solicitor to proceed with the divorce.'

There was silence in the room for several minutes while Jessica tried to sort out her thoughts. She knew he meant every word, that if she didn't leave the house, he would divorce her and chaos would ensue. The publicity would desperately wound the children, possibly destroy her mother's marriage, ruin Tom's career. If she went away, the children would be hurt, but they would never stop loving their mother.

'When do you want me to go?' she asked.

'Now,' he said. 'I have no intention of throwing you out onto the streets and have rented a room for you in a house on the other side of Liverpool, a place called Bootle. In the course of time, you might like to think seriously about moving further away so there is no chance that you and the children will meet. I have already packed your things and will take you there this minute.'

An hour later, Bertie had taken her to the house in Bootle and showed her the room, then driven away – to the office, she presumed. Jessica hardly looked at the room, merely aware that it was large with a high ceiling and big bay window. The furniture was old-fashioned but clean.

The first thing she did was count how much money she had. Over twenty pounds, she discovered, nearly all from her mother, some from Mrs Black and a pound or so of her own. It still wasn't too late to take the children to London; she didn't care how unfair it was on Bertie. She looked at her watch; nearly quarter-past eleven. Lunchtime at school was twelve till one. It was a long journey from this side of Liverpool to the other, but she should manage it in a taxi.

Jessica went outside and discovered she was on a busy main road and there was a park opposite. She had to walk for quite some time before she saw a taxi. She waved it down and asked the driver to take her to Sir Thomas Moore's Academy in Sefton Park. Bertie needn't think he'd got the better of her. Commit her to an asylum, if you please! He'd conceded he wouldn't do it, but merely to threaten it was enough.

Two mothers were waiting outside the school to take their children home for lunch, though this was frowned upon by the headmistress, who preferred pupils ate on the premises. It helped them socialize with the other children, and they were taught table manners.

'Would you mind waiting while I fetch my children?' she asked the taxi driver. 'The bell will go soon.'

She climbed out of the vehicle just as the bell rang. Two small children emerged and were taken away by their mothers. Jessica went inside the lovely old building that had once been a convent. She walked swiftly towards the hall that served as a dining room when necessary. Children were collecting the food on trays from the kitchen. Jessica looked for Jamie and Dora, but could see no sign of them. A young teacher who'd just started, Miss Hegarty, was in charge and came over. Jessica explained she'd come to collect her children. She was about to add that their grandmother was ill, when Miss Hegarty broke in.

'A lady came for them about an hour ago, Mrs Collins. She said she was your cousin and that you were ill.'

'You mean they're not here?'

The teacher looked at her as if she were stupid. 'As I said, your cousin has already collected them.'

Jessica ran outside to where the taxi was still waiting and jumped inside. 'Will you take me to seventeen Atlas Road, please.'

'Have your kids done a bunk?' the taxi driver asked. 'Little buggers. Mine are just the same, always playing truant.'

Jessica didn't answer. The taxi driver rambled on about kids needing a good hiding now and again to keep them in line, while she waited anxiously for him to turn into Atlas Road.

When he did, she could hardly believe her eyes. The curtains were drawn on number seventeen, Bertie's car had gone, and there was a 'For Sale' board outside. Her heart did a somersault.

'Stop, please!'

The taxi drew to a halt. 'Whatever you want, missus.' The driver was beginning to sound bored. Jessica got out, telling him she wouldn't be a minute, and cautiously approached the house. It seemed unlikely anyone was in.

She still had the house keys in her bag. Unlocking the door, she went inside. The place felt curiously empty. All the furniture was there, but other things weren't. There weren't any coats hanging in the hall, apart from her own blue winter one. Bertie's umbrella had gone, though it wasn't raining. When she went into the kitchen, the larder and the food safe were empty.

A piece of paper lay on the kitchen table, one of the foolscap sheets that Bertie had been shuffling around earlier. Jessica picked it up.

'If you are reading this, darling,' it said, 'then you are even stupider than I thought. Do you really think I wouldn't guess you would still try to steal my children?'

With a cry of terror, Jessica ran upstairs. Jamie's room was bereft of books and the clothes had gone out of the chest of drawers and wardrobe. It was the same with Dora. Her dolls were no longer propped up at the foot of her bed and her clothes had also been removed.

Her children had gone; Bertie had taken them. Some people would say it was no more than she deserved.

Jessica lay on the bed in the place where she now lived, scarcely moving for three whole days apart from using the lavatory at the top of the stairs and going out just once to buy milk and tea – and cigarettes. She smoked until her throat felt sore and she coughed so much it made it worse.

She discovered she lived in Stanley Road in Bootle and there were plenty of shops in the area. The taxi driver had taken her to where he'd picked her up, then driven slowly back along the road in the hope she would recognize the house she'd come from. All Jessica could remember was that it was a tall house, at least three storeys, and her room on the ground floor had a bay window. There was a long line of such houses, all identical. The driver realized something terrible had happened and was being kind, though she hadn't liked him at first.

Eventually, she recognized the striped hatbox that she'd placed on the table in the window. Jessica had never used it, she didn't have enough hats, but Bertie must have packed it with things. Later she discovered it was full of underclothes.

She'd paid the driver and entered the house. The front door was unlocked, as was the door to her room.

Where had Bertie gone with Jamie and Dora? It was the thought most dominant in her mind throughout the days and the sleepless nights that followed. Were they in another part of Liverpool? Another part of the country? Or had he taken them abroad? She remembered him once saying he thought Canada would be a good place to live.

The bed was comfortable, but the spring made creaking noises when she moved. She lay and imagined her children crying because they missed their mummy. What had Bertie told them? That she'd died? That she was too ill to come with them? She cried until her eyes felt sore as well as her throat, and her heart ached because she wanted her children so much. She had lost her reason for living.

While she lay on the creaking bed, she imagined what she would have been doing during the day had she been at home; taking the children to school, bringing them home again, washing dishes, preparing meals, listening to the wireless with Bertie. Sometimes, half asleep, she would come to with a start, thinking she had something important to do or had left a meal cooking in the oven, but straight away would realize she had absolutely nothing like that to worry about. It made her feel she was no longer part of the human race.

Who would have thought that Bertie, so mild and inadequate, would have wreaked such a savage revenge on the wife who had deceived him? She felt sure other women must have done far worse, yet not lost their children.

There were times when she blamed Tom McGrath. She was young and naive, inexperienced, and he had taken advantage. But he hadn't dragged her into that bedroom. She'd gone willingly and had enjoyed every minute.

On the fourth day, she woke up to the sound of church bells. It must be Sunday. Stanley Road was quieter than usual. Not so many tramcars went by.

Jessica sat up. For the first time, she examined the room, the heavy red curtains on the wide bay window, the light oak chest of drawers that matched the wardrobe, and a two-seater settee covered with flowered chintz. There was a small sink unit in one of the corners with dishes on shelves underneath, a single gas ring on which she'd been making tea, and a table about a yard square with two chairs tucked under. Well, it meant she could accommodate a visitor should she ever have one. Or perhaps this was a room for two people! The bed on which she lay was a double. A small gas fire stood rather forlornly in the vast marble fireplace.

At least Bertie had found her a respectable room in a respectable house. It was only fair seeing as he would get the money – *her* money – from the sale of the house in Atlas Road. She hadn't heard any undue noise during the short time she'd been there. She wondered how much a week's rent cost and for how long he had paid.

Jessica eased herself off the bed and walked unsteadily towards the sink. She boiled water for tea, made it in a cup, then carefully transferred it to another cup while trying to hold back the tea leaves. A few kitchen things had been provided, but not enough. She must get a teapot and a strainer.

Did buying a teapot and a strainer mean she intended staying in the room?

What alternative did she have? She had to live somewhere. She couldn't stay with her mother – or Lydia, who had a flat with two bedrooms over a musical instrument shop in Upper Parliament Street.

Outside, children were singing. She looked out. A couple were walking past with four children, two boys and two girls. The boys seemed to be involved in a mild wrestling match, while the girls walked, ladylike, hand in hand. 'As I was going to Strawberry Fair singing, singing, buttercups and daisies . . .' they were singing.

Jessica felt as if a knife had been plunged into her stomach and was being viciously twisted and turned, creating such agony that she wanted to scream, '*I want my children back. Oh, Lord, please let me have my children!*'

She threw herself on to the settee and wept until she felt so thoroughly exhausted that she could weep no more.

Never, in her entire life, had she missed Mass. Even in the Catholic nursing home where she'd had the children, a small room had been turned into a chapel.

Her clothes, still in the suitcase in which they'd been folded four days before, were horribly creased. Somehow, they would have to be ironed. She put them on the hangers already in the wardrobe or folded them for the chest of drawers.

The green crocheted suit she'd made for her mother's wedding wasn't as creased as the rest. She washed herself all over with a flannel then put the suit on – she recalled removing it for Tom McGrath the last time she'd worn it. She pulled a comb through her knotted hair, plonked a straw hat with a bent brim on top of the mess, picked up her handbag, and set off for Mass.

The nearest Catholic church, she discovered by asking, was St James's on Marsh Lane. It felt peaceful there. The rituals were familiar, the hymns she knew by heart. She genuflected, stood, knelt, sang, prayed, crossed herself, and it brought some order to her tangled brain. On the way out, she rubbed holy water on to her hot forehead and remembered there was something important she had to do.

She went out and caught a tram into town, then another that took her to Upper Parliament Street. Minutes later, she was knocking on the door of Lydia's flat and could hear her cousin descending the linoleum-covered stairs.

'Jessica!' Lydia gasped.

The words were scarcely out of her mouth before she was flung backwards, ending up sitting at the bottom of the stairs holding the cheek which her cousin Jessica had just slapped with considerable force.

'Bitch!' Jessica spat. 'Traitor! I thought you were my friend.' She had been born three months after her cousin. They'd started school together, taken their First Holy

Communion together, been Confirmed, played in each other's houses, gone to parties, pantomimes and concerts. When they were older, they'd gone to the pictures together at weekends when Lydia came home from university. They'd seen *The Jazz Singer*, the first film with sound. On the way home they'd sung, 'Mammy, how I love ya, how I love ya, my dear old Mammy.'

'I *am* your friend,' Lydia managed to say. 'I always will be your friend, but that doesn't mean I could stand back and allow you to take Bertie's children away so that he would never see them again.'

Jessica had never been so angry in her life before – she hadn't thought herself capable of such anger. 'Allow! *Allow*!' she screamed. A woman over the road had stopped to watch. 'Who are you to *allow* anything concerning me and my children? I confided in you and you betrayed me, you let me down.' She started to cry. 'Now it's *me* who has no children. Bertie's taken them and I don't know where they are.'

'He refused to tell me where he was going with them,' Lydia said weakly.

'Has he given up his job?'

'I have no idea. All you have to do is ring up the firm and ask.'

Jessica resolved she would do that first thing in the morning. She should have done it before, but hadn't been thinking straight. 'I have to go now,' she said.

'Jess!' Lydia struggled to her feet and held out her hand. 'We can't just stop seeing each other. Let me have your address and I'll visit when all this blows over. You might feel different about things in another few weeks.'

Jessica ignored the hand. She said, 'It shows how little you know about anything that you think me capable of getting over losing my children in a few weeks. I'll *never* get over it, *never* – and I never want to see you again for as long as I live.'

★

Later, wandering in the park opposite the house in Stanley Road, she got no pleasure from the sunshine that made the salty air sparkle like diamonds, or the children playing hide and seek in the leafy bushes, or the couples in their Sunday clothes strolling arm in arm. Nothing could lift her spirits, not even the memory of the slap she'd given Lydia.

As she crossed the road to go home, she saw a young woman with a little boy about to enter the house. She waited a few minutes before entering herself, not in the mood to meet someone new and have to introduce herself. Once inside, she could hear the child chattering as he and the woman went upstairs.

'Will me dad be upstairs waiting for us, Lena?'

'No, luv. I've told you, your dad's gone to Heaven. He's looking down on us right this minute to make sure we're both all right, like.'

Jessica looked up and could see the woman's hand moving along the banister. The sound of the toddler's footsteps made her want to cry. She wished she hadn't hung back, that she had spoken to the girl. Still, there was plenty of time. They'd come face to face one of these days.

She went into her room, boiled water for tea and drank it sitting on the settee, looking out of the window at the people in the park and the passing tramcars. She lit a cigarette and idly blew smoke into the air. A smoke circle formed and floated down towards her, getting bigger and bigger, fainter and fainter until it disappeared.

If only *she* could disappear so easily and painlessly. But she had to stay alive because one day, no matter how long it might take, she was determined to find her beloved children.

Chapter 7

Jessica wrote to her mother, but didn't reveal her address. Despite everything, her mother might want to know if she was all right. She did the same when she wrote to her grandmother, knowing Gladys would strongly disapprove of her granddaughter's behaviour.

When she wrote to her brother, though, Jessica told him everything that had happened and where she was living now. Will would still love her, no matter what she had done, and there had to be at least one person in the world apart from Bertie who knew where she lived. As it was, she felt that to have reached the age of twenty-seven without having made a single friend she could rely on in a crisis, and only one relative to correspond with, indicated what a terrible failure she had been as a human being.

Her telephone call to Harris Coleman resulted in the discovery that, as she'd half expected, Bertie was no longer with the company.

'He left all of a sudden without saying where he was going,' Miss Bassett, the receptionist, said. 'Is that you, Mrs Collins?'

Jessica hastily put the receiver down – she had to call from boxes now, feeding in pennies. The house where she lived didn't have a telephone.

She had no idea how to find Bertie. Even if she telephoned every estate agent in the land, they would be unlikely to give her information about one of their employees without asking the employee first. Anyway, he might have started work in a different type of office – and it was even possible he was no longer in England. Apart from once enthusing about Canada as a good place to live, his mother came from Wales. Maybe that was where he'd taken Jamie and Dora. He had aunts and uncles there that he had never met. Was his mother still around? she wondered. Once again she cursed herself for not having thought of that before. She was being very slow these days.

There and then she made her way to Anfield where his mother lived – but no longer, she found, after knocking on the front door. The only response came from a neighbour who emerged from the adjacent house.

'Mrs Collins? She just disappeared a week or so ago,' she told Jessica. 'Horrible woman, she was. Not a bit friendly. Did you know her well?'

'Hardly at all,' Jessica replied, burning with anger and re- sentment at the idea that her hated mother-in-law might be looking after her children.

They were never out of her mind. She saw them all the time, particularly in the park where they were usually on a path some distance ahead, disappearing around hedges as she got closer, darting behind bushes, jumping off the swings, just before she could reach them. She heard them playing in the hall where she lived, laughing, calling to each other, shouting for their mummy. When she opened the door, they would race upstairs and all she glimpsed was the heel of a shoe or the flounce of a skirt, then there would be silence.

She realized she was on the point of madness. She went to see Honor Brunswick and told her what had happened.

'How can I track them down?' she asked.

'One way would be to pretend to buy the house,' Honor said. 'Whoever buys it will be given full details of the seller. You would have to withdraw at the last minute – though Bertie might hide behind a bank or solicitor so his details don't appear on the sale documents. Anyway, that could prove quite expensive. Another way of tracing him is to engage a private detective, though that would be expensive, too. And you have to be careful who you go to.'

'Why?' Jessica asked.

Honor looked grave. 'There's some who'll take your money – and keep on taking it – yet they'll know there isn't a snowball's chance in hell of finding where Bertie and your children have gone. I'll give you the name of one I've heard is trustworthy, though have never used – Albert James. His office is in Eccleston Chambers in Water Street. He'll do things like check the list of passengers on ships, but you will appreciate there are an awful lot of ships leaving an awful lot of ports in the British Isles every day of the week. Then Bertie might have gone by train or driven to wherever he's living now with the children. I wish you luck, Jessica, but you'll need it.'

Albert James told her bluntly she was wasting her time. 'And money,' he said gruffly. He was an immensely tall, well-built man who never smiled. A broken nose and swollen ears indicated he was likely to have been a boxer in his youth.

Jessica was about to leave, not wanting to waste his time either, when he gave an enormous shrug.

'I'll do what I can,' he offered, almost grudgingly, 'but your husband and children could have gone anywhere in the world, Mrs Collins, India, South Africa, Rhodesia – there's plenty of Brits in those sort of places. An educated white man can earn twice what he'd get in his own country, not to mention living in a superior property waited on by servants, and, as long as he doesn't go too far into the wilds, there'll be decent schools for his kids. There's also America and Canada, not with the same advantages, but more civilized. And there's a chance your husband and children might never have left these shores and have settled in the far north of Scotland.' He put his elbows on the desk and looked at her curiously. 'Out of interest, Mrs Collins, what do you intend to do if your family is located?'

'Well, I . . .' Jessica stopped. She hadn't thought that far ahead. Bertie wasn't likely to invite her to join them. The children would have been told she was ill, had deserted them, even that she was dead. 'I would just like to know where they are,' she said eventually, 'no matter where it is.' She'd deal with the knowledge once she'd got it.

He asked for five pounds to begin his investigations. 'Though it won't get me very far,' he said.

Having already spent a quarter of her funds, Jessica realized she would have to find a job. Soon, she would be required to pay rent. She needed things like more bedding, for instance, more dishes, a lamp of some sort – it had taken a little while for her to discover the room was lit by gas when all she'd ever known was electricity. The central light was miserably dim when it grew dark, and she dreaded what it would be like in winter. Even worse was the idea that she would still be there in winter. And it was time she started eating properly, meat and vegetables rather than the cheap pies and cakes she bought daily which were doing her no good at all, not to mention so many cigarettes.

The thought of looking for employment was terrifying. She'd never been for a job interview in her life and the only person she'd ever worked for was her father – and Tom, just for a few days. What if the firm who offered her a job asked for a reference? Who would she give?

Would she ever be able to cope with life on her own?

Perhaps she had been dreaming she had a job because it was a typewriter that woke her; not the sound of it, but the memory of the one that Tom McGrath had brought to the house in Atlas Road for her to do his letters. The day she'd left the house the typewriter had still been on the table in the parlour where Tom himself had placed it only a few weeks before. It was brand-new, he'd said. She'd kept expecting someone from McGrath, Gordon & Willetts to come for it, but no one had. Perhaps Tom had forgotten all about it, or, in view of what had happened, was too embarrassed to send someone to collect it. She recalled that she'd never received payment for the typing she had done, though it hadn't been much. Had anyone been to the house since it became empty? she wondered. They would have had to ask Harris Coleman for the keys.

She fell back asleep, still thinking about the typewriter, and when she woke, it was the first thing that came to mind.

Pleased to have something to do for a change, something with a purpose, Jessica leaped out of bed. Fifteen minutes later she was sitting upstairs on a tramcar on its way to the Pier Head. There, she caught another tram going to Sefton Park on the south side of Liverpool – Bootle was in the north.

The house in Atlas Road was still for sale! Jessica hurried towards it, the key in her hand. For some reason, her heart was beating rapidly. Stupid really, because if the typewriter wasn't there it didn't matter. Why should she care?

But the typewriter *was* there, sitting solidly on the table along with a box of McGrath, Gordon & Willetts' headed notepaper, two pencils, several sheets of carbon paper, and a typewriter rubber.

Jessica sat on the chair in front of the glittering black and silver machine. 'What am I going to do with you?' she asked, but didn't get a reply.

Out of interest, she went around the house, giving it more careful scrutiny than she'd done the first time she'd looked. Nothing had changed. Her winter coat was still hanging in the hall. There were two slightly battered pans and a frying pan in the kitchen, a glass vase and a check tablecloth in the cupboard under the sink, half a dozen books in the living room as well as the little red rug she'd made while expecting Jamie.

Her best bedding was in the drawer at the bottom of the wardrobe in her and Bertie's room – it had, quite literally, been part of her bottom drawer. She remembered the joy and the pleasure she'd got from embroidering the sheets herself, sewing the lace on the pillow slips. She took it downstairs, resolving not to enter the children's rooms or she would cry. Everything was piled in a heap at the bottom of the stairs with her coat on top.

It was then that she noticed the gramophone. It wouldn't have entered Bertie's head to take it. He never played it, didn't own a single record, didn't really like music of any sort. There was enough space for it where she lived now. She *had* to take it with her, she just *had* to!

Would everything fit in a taxi? And how would she call one? The phone was bound to have been cut off, just as the water had when she'd tried to run it earlier. She had no idea where the nearest telephone box was.

She picked up the receiver, dialled O, and the operator answered, 'Number please?'

'Five-one-five,' Jessica gasped, taken by surprise. It was the number of the taxi firm she'd always used. When she got through, she asked if the taxi could possibly accommodate a typewriter, a gramophone, and sundry other bits and pieces.

'Well, I'll do me best, luv,' the driver said. 'Give us your address and I'll be with you in a mo.'

For less than a minute, Jessica actually forgot how utterly miserable she was, and rubbed her hands together gleefully. Two truly marvellous things had happened today – finding all this wonderful stuff and the telephone working. Good things and bad things usually went in threes, or so people said. That meant that another wonderful thing would happen before the day was out.

She came down to earth. More likely it would be some-thing horrible, she thought cynically. She'd had more than

89

enough luck for one day. She'd like to bet it would be a long time before she had any more.

The taxi was approaching the house in Stanley Road. In the back, Jessica nursed the gramophone on her knee, holding it tightly – the records were still in the slots underneath and she didn't want them to fall out. The typewriter was on the seat next to the driver and everything else was wrapped in her winter coat, making a huge, clunking parcel.

'Here we are,' the driver sang when he stopped. 'Hold on back there, luv, and I'll give you a hand out.'

But Jessica was so eager to go indoors and play some records that she wasn't prepared to wait. She opened the taxi door, swung one leg on to the pavement, nudging the gramophone, which lost its balance and slowly headed towards the ground.

Jessica screamed and a grey-haired man who happened to be passing shot forward and managed to catch the gramophone in his arms. The taxi driver tut-tutted and took it from him. He carried it to the doorstep, then put the typewriter down beside it.

'Shall I give you a hand inside with everything, luv?' he asked.

'It's all right, thank you. I'll do it,' the grey-haired gentleman offered.

'Are you sure, mate?' The driver was less than half the age of the other man.

'Quite sure.'

Jessica paid the driver, tipping him a whole sixpence because he'd been so nice and helpful.

He departed, pleased, and it was then that the third wonderful thing happened.

'Hello, Jessica,' the grey-haired gentleman said. 'How lovely to see you!'

Josef Davidson was a widower and had been one of her accountant father's first regular clients. He'd come in the days when Gordon Farley's office had been in a room in his house, sometimes bringing with him his only child, Sara.

The two girls – at ten, Sara was a year older than Jessica – had become friends. They'd had tea in each other's houses, swapped books and confidences, plaited each other's hair, and gone to dancing lessons together at weekends – ballet and tap. Jessica was hopeless at both, galloping around the stage like a carthorse, or so she thought. She'd left after a few weeks, but Sara had continued and six years later had gone to live in London with the intention of making a career on the stage. They'd corresponded, but only for a short while. Jessica couldn't remember whether it was due to her or Sara that they'd stopped writing to each other.

Now alone in his house in Penny Lane, his wife dead and his daughter having left home, Josef left the area to live with his widowed sister in a place called Seaforth, miles away from Sefton Park, but only a short walk from Bootle. He'd acquired a more convenient accountant and Jessica hadn't seen him for many years.

'How is Sara?' she enquired now. 'I keep expecting to read that she's in a show in London.'

'Sara is in Paris,' Josef said surprisingly. 'She met a French actor called Louis Cotillard at drama school, married him, and went to live in Paris. They have two little girls: Marie and Françoise.' He spoke with immense pride, but finished by muttering mournfully, 'I hardly ever see them, not even once a year. Sara is too weighed down by housework to get away, and these days I can't afford to travel all the way to France as often as I would like.'

'But what about your shop by Lime Street station?' He'd had a tobacconist's that stocked cigarettes and tobacco from all over the world, as well as all the bits and pieces that went with smoking, such as leather pouches and expensive lighters. It had been well-known in Liverpool.

He spread his hands dramatically, a gesture she remembered

91

from the past. 'The lease expired and the freeholder, seeing how well I had built up the business, demanded four times as much to renew it. Had Sara been here to offer encouragement, I might have paid the increase, or at least looked for another shop and started again, but without her I just couldn't do it.' He sniffed. 'I have been living on my savings ever since.' He rested his hands back on his knees. 'But enough of me, Jessica, what about you? What have you been doing all these years? I saw the announcement in the *Echo* about five years ago that your father had died. I sent a wreath, but didn't attend the funeral. I wasn't well at the time.'

They were sitting in her room, Josef on the settee, and she on a chair beside the table where the typewriter had been put. Outside, tramcars clattered by, and a car sounded its horn. She could hear the sound of feet on the pavement and people talking. For the first time in weeks she felt like an ordinary human being doing something as ordinary as entertaining a visitor.

She got to her feet and lit the gas on the ring to make more tea. She had known this question was bound to be asked and had already surreptitiously taken off her wedding ring and slid it under the pillow on the bed. It was her intention to tell Josef a different story from the real one, the story she would tell everyone from now on. What had she been doing all these years? he'd asked.

'Nothing much,' she said casually. 'Earlier this year, my mother re-married and went to live in Calderstones, leaving me with nowhere to live.'

Josef looked shocked. Jessica recalled how fond he'd been of her mother, and hastily explained that she hadn't been thrown out or anything awful like that, but had felt in the way. 'I thought I'd like to live somewhere different for a change, so came here.'

'And what is the typewriter for?'

What *was* the typewriter for? She wondered what his

reaction would be if she'd told him she'd just felt like stealing it? 'I'm thinking of starting my own business,' she lied, though had no idea where the lie had come from.

'What sort of business?'

Jessica hadn't a clue. She laughed and told him as much. 'Perhaps I'll think of something.'

'So, you are still Miss Farley. I thought you would be married like Sara and have acquired a family by now,' he said.

'Our lives have gone in two very different ways,' she pointed out, and he agreed.

'I wish Sara hadn't married so young and hastily, and to an actor. Louis is a very unconventional person,' he said regretfully. 'I can tell from Sara's letters that she isn't happy in Paris.'

No one could have been more conventional than Bertie, but Jessica hadn't been happy, either.

Josef left after arranging to meet her for coffee in Morgan's restaurant in Strand Road on Monday morning at half past ten. 'We can talk about old times, when life was good and there was a reason for smiling.'

She watched through the window as he slowly walked away. There'd been a time when she'd assumed he was about the same age as her father, who would still be in his fifties had he been alive. Now, Josef looked much older, a mere shadow of the man she used to know. He'd been born in a city somewhere in Russia with an unpronounceable name, narrowly escaping with his life during the revolution. He still retained the regal look of the count or the duke that Sara had claimed he was.

Jessica sighed and turned away, intent on doing the thing she'd been yearning to do ever since she'd got back from Sefton Park: listen to one of her records, preferably Al Bowlly.

She wandered around the room searching for an electric socket when she remembered – there was no electricity in the entire house.

'Damn and blast!' She kicked the table leg and managed not to burst into tears.

It was odd, but she felt better after denying the most important part of her life: marrying Bertie and having two children. She'd been worrying how she would explain herself to people. Now she wouldn't have to lie and pretend to be a widow; nobody would ask if she had children. She was Jessica Farley who'd never been married and that was the story of her life so far. It was still a lie, but easier to tell than the truth.

It was what she told Lena, the young woman she'd seen going into the house with a little boy whose name turned out to be Calum. Lena, aged eighteen, was in fact the child's aunt.

'His mam died in childbirth,' she explained, 'then didn't his da, in other words me brother, Reggie, go and get himself killed when the boiler exploded on his ship. I'm waiting for compensation off the insurance company and I'll get us a place of our own as soon as it comes.'

She went on to say that her parents had died young and she and her brother had been raised in an orphanage, so Calum was the only person she had left in the world. 'And all he has is me,' she finished. In the meantime, she lived in an attic room on the third floor that was barely twelve feet square and was like an oven in the summer. To support herself and Calum, she worked as a cleaner, taking the little boy with her. She was a lovely girl with grey, long-lashed eyes and blonde curls, and reminded Jessica of her favourite childhood doll.

She was impressed by the girl's fortitude and good humour, and wished she'd shown a bit more of both in her old, secret life. Instead, she'd just smoked herself silly and made a complete mess of everything.

It was Lena who told her about gramophones that you could wind up.

'Wind up?' Jessica said, flabbergasted.

'With a handle,' Lena explained further. She loaned Jessica

Calum's pushchair so she could take her electric gramophone to Mo's second-hand shop in Marsh Lane and ask him to swap it for a wind-up one. 'It's to his advantage, isn't it?' she said earnestly. 'He'll sell your one for much more than the old-fashioned sort.'

'I suppose he will,' Jessica conceded. An old-fashioned, wind-up gramophone was better than none at all.

She took it to Mo's the next day and returned with a wind-up model and a small battery wireless she'd got half-price.

Now she could have music or news at any time of the day or night. At Mo's, she'd bought a painting of orange and yellow chrysanthemums, a genuine original, not very well done, but the paint was laid thickly on and the flowers looked real when she stood the picture on the mantelpiece.

After a month, the room began to feel like a sort of home. She missed her children, always would. There were days when she cried for hours, unable to stop until all her strength had been used up and she could cry no more. It was then that she would pray to die instead. But she mustn't have wanted to die enough because eventually she would crawl off the bed, make tea, and smoke a cigarette.

She didn't miss Bertie. His presence had been like a dark shadow over her life, criticizing her every move, her choice of clothes, her cooking. Now the shadow had been lifted and she had short periods when she felt liberated, free to do anything she pleased. Free to sit up in bed late into the night reading a book, or doing the same thing early in the morning, accompanied both times by mugs of tea or cocoa and the inevitable cigarette. After living twenty-seven years of her life without touching cigarettes, now she was smoking like a chimney.

Gas light came from something called a mantel, not a bulb as with electricity. Lena had showed her how to use it; how to pull a chain to adjust it from very bright to dim, so Jessica had no problem reading books, though had been startled very late one night when the room suddenly went black.

'You need to put a penny in the meter, queen,' Mrs Quigley, the caretaker, said the next morning. She lived in the basement, a short, wedge-shaped woman with unnaturally white skin and hair dyed the blackest of black. She seemed to smoke even more than Jessica and always had a fag – as she called it – attached to her bottom lip. 'I usually put in half a dozen pennies at a time, save being taken unawares when I'm in the middle of doing something important like darning his lordship's socks.' His lordship was her husband who worked on the docks.

'Where is the meter?' Jessica asked.

'In the hallway, queen. It's the one with an A chalked on, seeing as how you're in room A, like. The gas man comes to empty 'em once a month.'

When Jessica looked, the letters went from A to G. She'd seen other tenants going in and out. A young man lived in the room above hers. He rose each morning at the crack of dawn and the floorboards creaked when he walked to and fro. He always closed the front door quietly when he left for work at about half-past seven.

A middle-aged woman, Miss Stringer, lived on the second floor. Coming home from work, her tired footsteps could be heard getting slower and slower until she reached her room. Lena and Calum lived in room G on the top floor. Jessica had no idea who were in the other rooms.

A letter had arrived for her from a property company, Sillicot Homes, to say the rent was twenty-eight shillings a month payable on the first, or seven and sixpence a week. She could either pay in person at their office in Marsh Lane, or give the money to the rent collector who came on Saturday mornings. She decided to pay in person as it was slightly cheaper.

She'd sent Albert James another five pounds so he could

continue to try to track down Bertie and the children: it meant she had little more than five pounds left of the money she'd brought with her. She really would have to obtain more money by finding a job as soon as possible. As far as she knew, there were two ways of doing this; writing after a job advertised in the *Echo* or visiting a place called the Labour Exchange.

Next day, after everyone had gone to work, Jessica went upstairs and had a bath in the communal bathroom. The water came out in a trickle and wasn't very warm. Afterwards she put on her green crocheted costume, combed her hair properly – some of the knots had been there for ages – and took herself to the Labour Exchange in Stanley Road.

Chapter 8

Christmas was approaching. With the curtains drawn, the light and fire turned on, Jessica's room felt cosy and warm, but the only place she wanted to be was Atlas Road with her children. Some nights when she went to bed she drew back the curtains so she could see the brightly lit trams speeding past, the passengers unaware they were being watched.

The last time she'd been to Atlas Road the 'for sale' sign had been removed, though no one was living there. She didn't go inside, but made up her mind never to visit the house again, and put her keys through the letterbox. Another family might be living there when Christmas came and for all the Christmases to come.

She bought Jamie a *Magnet* annual and read it from cover to cover. When eventually she gave it to him, they could discuss the adventures of Harry Wharton and Billy Bunter and the other pupils of Greyfriars together.

For Dora she had bought a doll with eyes that closed when she was laid down and opened when picked up. She had christened it Marjorie because it was a name that Dora loved. Gradually, she was making Marjorie a wardrobe of the most exquisite clothes that a doll had ever had. She bought little scraps of material from the Singer sewing machine shop on Walton Road and odd balls of wool. The clothes were knitted, sewn, crocheted and embroidered with love and the utmost care. She imagined her little girl putting Marjorie to bed in her white cotton nightie, taking her for a walk dressed in the dark green velvet cloak with a hood lined with bright red satin.

Quite a few tears were spilled over the tiny garments while Jessica worked into the night, and on the pages of Jamie's book, because she had no idea when she would give her children their presents. It wouldn't be *this* Christmas. She couldn't help but wonder if Jamie would still be reading *Magnet* when next she saw him, or if Dora would be playing with dolls. How old would they be before she saw them again, *if* she ever saw them again? They were hardly likely to come looking for their mother if Bertie had told them she was dead.

She had anticipated being alone on Christmas Day and had got quite used to the idea, but it had turned out it wasn't to be. As Lena had already told her, she and Calum only had each other.

Jessica had invited them to dinner as soon as she realized they would be stuck all day in the little third-floor room. It would have been desperately mean to have left them on their own. Then Angus Roberts, the charming young Scotsman who lived in the room above and was employed as a trainee manager with the Gas Board, told her he couldn't possibly get to and from his family in a place called Kingussie in northern-most Scotland in the two days' holiday he'd been allowed. So Jessica had asked him to dinner, too.

The other residents in the house had relatives to visit. Mr Duckworth, who sold Magnifique carpet cleaners door to door, had a wife in Manchester who he saw every weekend, and Miss Stringer, the most incommunicative of souls, worked in a hospital and had a mother living in the depths of the Lancashire countryside. Mrs Quigley the caretaker and her husband were spending the day with one of their numerous children. Mr Hewitt was a steward on a ship and wasn't seen all that much. He would be away over Christmas, he informed Jessica.

'In the South of France,' he told her, flashing the shiny white teeth that contrasted sharply with his black, silky moustache. 'Wish you could be there with me, darling,' he added, winking. He was a terrible flirt.

'I'm afraid I shall be working,' Jessica told him stiffly. She was incapable of flirting back.

Since September, she had been employed as a shorthand-typist in the Estates and Planning department of a partially built factory on Kirkby Trading Estate. It meant catching a bus to Walton Vale, then a tram as far as Fazakerly. At the terminus, a single-decker bus would be waiting to take the twenty or so workers to the factory where, eventually, munitions would be made for the war that many people seemed to think was inevitable. Why else would they be building a factory to make guns and bombs with which to attack Germany? The twenty workers would one day increase to more than a thousand.

When Jessica started, only the shell had been built. There would eventually be a press shop, a machine shop, a tool room, drawing office, dozens of other conventional offices, a canteen for the workers, another for management, a kitchen, a clinic, a dentist and a doctor, and lavatories all over the place.

'No one will ever be caught short,' claimed Mick Taylor, the person in charge of this complicated project. His title was Clerk of Works.

There was a plan of the proposed building on the wall of Jessica's office. It was being erected far more quickly than a conventional building using a system of hardwood panels popular in Denmark with a concrete floor and an asbestos roof. But a foundation had to be laid, drains to be dug, electricity installed, telephone lines connected. Then the machinery had to be bought – the lathes and milling machines – a variety of tools, not to mention the typewriters and drawing office equipment, the desks and chairs and, for some rooms, carpets.

Jessica had got the job through the Labour Exchange where she'd registered as Miss Jessica Farley. During the first few weeks, she had been terrified, expecting people to find fault with her work, knowing she would burst into tears if they did. But everyone had been very kind and Mick was the nicest boss in the world. Not once had he criticised her work. It wasn't that he was doing her any favours, she realized after a while. He didn't find faults because there were none to find. Her father had always told her she was a 'jolly good little worker', and he'd meant it.

And it was infinitely preferable to working in a stuffy little office in a creaky old building in the city. Kirkby consisted mainly of green fields, and the air smelled fresh and invigorating. Jessica brought sandwiches for lunch and, until winter set in, had eaten them sitting on a hill outside the soon-to-be factory, which had been dubbed Kirkby Castle.

By Christmas, the interior walls had been erected, the windows installed and doors fitted. In the not-too-distant future, the machinery would start to arrive.

Only one other woman worked there, Sally Conway, who made the tea and kept the place clean. A widow in her forties, she was keen to become friends and had cut Jessica's hair short one lunch-time.

'I can't tell if it makes you look younger or older,' she remarked when it was done.

Jessica thanked her and said she didn't care how young or old she looked. She'd just wanted hair that was easy to manage.

She had always loved Christmas. Every year she'd bought more and more decorations, a bigger tree than the year before, too much food, too many cards, presents for people who really didn't expect one. Bertie said she made them embarrassed. 'They feel awful because they haven't bought anything for you,' he said sourly one year.

'Oh, but I don't mind if I don't get a present back.'

'Maybe not, but they do. Honestly, Jessica,' he'd said once, 'you're like a child. The most innocuous things please you.'

Then, as now, Jessica could see no harm in that.

This year, she had bought a handful of cards, knitted Lena a matching hat and scarf, and got a wind-up train for Calum. For Josef Davidson, whom she met regularly, she had bought a set of pale grey stationery on which he could write to his daughter, Sara, in Paris.

She had thought that would be the extent of festive purchases, but at Kirkby Castle each day she would find two or three Christmas cards on her desk, as well as little parcels containing scented soap, a make-up bag, boxes of handkerchiefs, a diary with a white leather cover – that was from Mick – a scarf, a jar of bath salts, and even a framed photograph of Clark Gable for whom she'd once expressed a liking.

Sally gave her a lovely pair of pearl stud earrings surrounded by tiny diamonds. 'They're not real pearls, or real diamonds,' she assured Jessica when she opened the box.

'Thank goodness!' Jessica gasped. 'If they'd been real, I couldn't have afforded the insurance.' She recalled her father had once bought her mother of pearl earrings. When she'd lost one, all hell was let loose, but it hadn't been found.

On the Saturday before Christmas, she went to town and bought a load of presents to give back, as well as a supply of emergency gifts in case she was given more. On impulse, she also bought a dozen balloons, a dozen lengths of tinsel, and a long-playing record of Bing Crosby singing Christmas carols.

Back home, she found an airmail letter from her brother, Will, had been pushed underneath her door. He was coming home at Christmas, but not until Boxing Day.

'Hooray!' she shouted at the empty room, waving the letter in the air.

The fact that she was actually looking forward to Christmas

both confused and upset her. She couldn't understand how she could be anticipating anything with pleasure while she was so unhappy inside. In a crazy sort of way, she would almost have preferred to have had an unpleasant job, lived in a place she hated, not have met Josef again, and for Will not to be coming home. It would have more suited her mood rather than the relentless friendliness and goodwill with which she was surrounded. She didn't have time to mope and brood and feel depressed.

But that could only be a good thing, a more sensible part of her insisted. For goodness' sake, girl, grow up and thank your blessings, even if there aren't all that many of them, she told herself sternly.

It was quite a task preparing Christmas dinner on a single gas ring. Jessica had boiled the chicken the day before and would serve it cold with sautéed potatoes, tinned peas and Bisto gravy. Lena had bought a dozen mince pies from the bakers and Angus's mother had sent two homemade Christmas puddings all the way from Kingussie. She had also sent Jessica a card and a present, a truly gorgeous mohair scarf knitted in a tartan pattern.

'Thank you, dear Jessica, for looking after my baby over Christmas,' the card read. Angus blushed when she showed it him.

'Mothers!' he said, rolling his suspiciously moist eyes. 'This is my first Christmas away from home and I expect she'll miss me. I'm the youngest,' he added unnecessarily.

It was a dull day, the sky full of dark grey clouds that raced by as if they were in a desperate hurry to get somewhere. Only a few trams rolled past, most surprisingly full. Music could be heard coming from the pub on the corner, but in Jessica's room they had their own music – Bing Crosby singing 'Silent Night'.

It's a good job we like each other, Jessica thought, when the three adults and one small child sat round the tiny table, knees pressed against each other, elbows poking. She had never felt so proud of a meal before. To have heated the peas, made the gravy, and sautéed the potatoes all on the same ring using the same pan, while keeping everything warm, was something of an achievement.

In Angus's room, one of the puddings was simmering away, and any minute now, Jessica would make custard. She prayed she wouldn't burn it – she usually did no matter how violently it was stirred.

Angus, a lovely young man with bright red hair, couldn't take his eyes off Lena, who looked terribly pretty in a navy-blue linen frock with a sailor collar that she'd got from Paddy's Market. It was obvious he had a crush on her.

Calum had his new train on the table and attempted to share his dinner with it, but the train positively refused to eat a thing.

Dinner over, they pulled a cracker each. Jessica swapped her whistle with Calum's pink hairslide, and Angus insisted on sliding the emerald ring out of his cracker on to the third finger of Lena's small, well-worn hand.

Angus smiled at her adoringly, but Lena didn't appear to notice. When he fetched the pudding, he brought with him two bottles of Irn Bru, a bright orange drink special to Scotland that he swore had all sorts of healthy qualities.

'It will put muscles on your muscles,' he told them confidently.

Jessica and Lena assured him they had no desire for muscles in the first place.

'Is it alcoholic?' Lena asked.

'No, but it's possible to convince yourself it is,' Angus said with a wink.

Jessica managed not to burn the custard, the pudding was delicious, and afterwards they pretended to get drunk on Irn

Bru. Angus joined in with Bing Crosby – the record was on for the fourth time – singing 'Christmas is coming'.

'The goose is getting fat,' he warbled. Everyone joined in, and the effect was enjoyably rowdy. It wasn't until the carol had finished that the sound of someone knocking on the door could be heard.

Jessica answered and found her brother on the step. 'Will!' she cried delightedly. She threw her arms round his neck and dragged him inside. 'I wasn't expecting you until tomorrow. We're having a party. We're all drunk on Irn Bru.'

She introduced him to Lena and Angus, and to Calum, too. The little boy looked shyly up at the tall, uniformed figure. When Will sat down, he managed to crawl on to his knee where he perched contentedly.

Jessica made tea and produced the mince pies. She had told Will in her letters that she wanted to be known as a single woman without children with him her only relative, and hoped he would remember. He had no luggage apart from a small haversack, and she assumed he'd been to see their mother with whom he would no doubt be staying while he was home.

His arrival had brought them all down to earth. After a while, Angus announced that before it got too dark he was going in search of a telephone box to call his family in Scotland. 'I've got a whole half-crown's worth of pennies,' he announced.

Lena lifted a sleepy Calum off Will's knee and took him upstairs for a nap. Jessica insisted they all return later. 'I'll make sandwiches with the rest of the chicken, and there's another pudding to eat.'

Will delved in to the haversack and produced a Christmas cake and a box of chocolates. 'Bought in New York,' he announced.

'I'll be back,' Angus promised. 'In fact, I wouldn't miss it for worlds. This has been a much better Christmas than I expected. Thank you, Jessica. When I tell Ma, she'll probably knit you another scarf.' He kissed her bashfully on the cheek.

Lena promised to return the minute Calum woke up. 'I wouldn't miss it for worlds, either.'

'Well,' Will said when only he and Jessica were left, 'I'm flabbergasted.' He removed his navy-blue pullover, saying he felt too hot. 'I expected to find you wallowing in the Slough of Despond. Instead, I find a party going on and you apparently drunk to the eyeballs on Irn Bru.'

'It's not intoxicating,' Jessica assured him.

'Anything's intoxicating if you're in the right sort of mood.'

'Oh, Will!' She sat down at the table and buried her face in her hands, though didn't cry. 'I've been thinking about Jamie and Dora all day. Where are they? Have they had a nice dinner? Is Bertie's mother with them? Yet I've enjoyed myself, too. I'm like two different people,' she wailed. 'I can't understand myself, I really can't.'

Will sat and put his arm round her shoulders. 'You're strong, that's why, Jess. I never dreamed you would be so strong. I thought you'd buckle under, go to pieces, but you've coped incredibly well.'

Jessica lifted her head. 'Have you been to see Mother?' she asked.

Will laughed. 'Well, I saw a glimpse of her. She'd invited half of Liverpool to Christmas dinner – the most important half. She waved to me and I ate a quick dinner in the breakfast room, served by a very nice lady called Mrs Brown. I left a message to say I'd be back later.'

'It's Mrs Black. She lent Mother money to give to me.' She wondered if her mother was missing her and the children over Christmas, if by now she had been forgiven.

'Tell you who was there today,' William said. 'Lydia. She and I had a long talk.'

'Lydia can—' Jessica began, when there was a popping

sound, and both the fire and the light went out. Outside, it was half dark, but the lamps in Stanley Road were already lit, providing enough illumination to see by. Jessica turned off the gas, picked up the jar of coins she kept on the mantelpiece beside the painting of chrysanthemums, and took it into the hall where she put a dozen pennies into the meter. Back in the room, she lit both the fire and the gas lamp with a match and closed the curtains.

'There!' she said.

She saw that Will was watching her with amusement. 'It was Bertie who used to do that sort of thing in Atlas Road. You're coming on, Jess, growing up.'

'We didn't have a penny meter in Atlas Road,' she reminded him. 'A man would come and read the meters, and Bertie would send cheques.'

'Even so, you're a real heroine the way you've adapted to the changed circumstances.'

'*Tragic* circumstances,' she emphasized. 'Anyway, about Lydia, she can go and jump in the lake. If it wasn't for her, I wouldn't be living here, but in London with Jamie and Dora. Would you like more tea?'

'I'd love more tea but, Jess, what about Bertie?'

'What about Bertie?' she asked belligerently as she ran water into the kettle.

'Apart from being a complete ass – as I witnessed for myself last time I was at your house – he was a pretty harmless sort of chap. It hardly seems fair that he should be deprived of his children when it was you who was in the wrong.'

Jessica was standing over the kettle waiting for it to boil. She felt outraged. 'Are you on Bertie's side?'

Will had transferred to the settee, his long legs stretched out. The last time she'd seen him so relaxed was in Atlas Road and she'd been leading a perfectly ordinary life. 'Of course I'm not on Bertie's side,' he said easily. 'I'll always be on your side, sis, whatever you get up to. But I wish I'd been home when it happened, or Dad had been alive. All you and Bertie needed was a good talking-to.'

'If I'd insisted on staying, he was going to divorce me,' Jessica told him. 'It would have been in all the papers, Tom would have been disgraced – I mean, having had an . . . an affair with his stepdaughter,' she could feel herself blushing, 'and it would have killed Mother. It would even have affected the children.'

'And make Bertie look an even bigger ass than he already was. No man in his right mind would willingly do such a thing. He was having you on, Jess. You should have just stuck around and he'd eventually have got over it.'

'I needed a friend to talk to,' Jessica said bitterly. 'And I thought Lydia was my friend, but she betrayed me.'

Will shrugged. 'She's sorry.'

'Not half as sorry as I am. Because of her I lost my children.'

'She asked for your address so she can come and see you.'

Jessica stamped her foot so hard it hurt. 'Don't you dare give it to her. I never want to see her again as long as I live.'

The front door of the house opened and closed. Angus shouted, 'I'm back', and ran upstairs. Light footsteps could be heard slowly coming down. A small voice said, 'Will the big man still be there?'

'Yes, love. His name is Will,' Lena replied.

Will said, 'Are Lena and Angus engaged? I noticed she was wearing a ring.'

Jessica snorted. 'Now who's being an ass? It came out of a Christmas cracker. It's probably worth less than a farthing.'

'I'm not an expert on precious stones,' Will said in a hurt voice. 'She's very pretty, Lena.'

She looked at him in surprise. 'Do you fancy her? She's much too young for you.'

'I'm twenty-nine, not exactly approaching my dotage.' He sounded even more hurt. 'What's she, eighteen, nineteen?'

'Eighteen.'

'I'm not even old enough to be her father.' There was a tap on the door and he leaped to his feet. 'I'll let her in.'

So much energy and gaiety had been expended earlier in the day that later on the atmosphere was rather subdued. Jessica put her Al Bowlly records on the gramophone, and they lazed around, talking quietly, Angus describing what it was like living in Kingussie. 'It's the most beautiful place on earth, at the foot of the Cairngorm mountains and on the banks of the River Spey,' he said dreamily. Under the gas light, his red hair looked as if it were on fire. 'My parents run a small hotel. I didn't want to leave, but I knew I had to. If I stayed too long, perhaps got married, then I would never have got away. I wanted to see what the rest of the world was like before I settled down. I won't be with the Gas Board for ever.'

'It sounds lovely.' Lena's big blue eyes were like stars. 'I'd love to go there one day.'

'I'll take you,' Angus said quickly. 'In the summer, maybe. Calum would love it.'

'We'll see.' Lena smiled, but Jessica just knew somehow that she would never visit Kingussie. She went on to tell them how much she detested cleaning people's houses. 'When I was young,' she said solemnly, as if she was old now, 'I wanted to work in a flower shop – I didn't know it was called a florist's then. Mam promised, hand on heart, that she would make sure I did. But, all of a sudden, as if a curse had been put on us, Mam died of a heart attack. Months later, Dad died, too. I was only five, and Reggie, me brother, seven, and we were put in an orphanage. Reggie hadn't been out for long when he married Muriel, who died having him.' She nodded at Calum, who responded with a smile, having no idea what she was talking about. 'Then didn't our Reggie go and get killed on his ship, so there's only the two of us left and I'm too busy cleaning to think about working in a flower shop.'

'But that's terrible,' Will said wrathfully. 'You should get an allowance off the State.'

'Oh, yes, and pigs might fly,' Lena said sarcastically. 'Me and Calum will be all right once we get compensation off the shipping company.'

Later Will described what it was like being in the Navy, the strange life he led on the ship when there were times when you desperately wanted to be alone, but it wasn't possible. 'Some ports like Hamburg and Marseilles you can't wait to get away from; others you never want to leave.' He loved Buenos Aires and Vancouver. 'As for New York, one of these days I might well jump ship and stay there.'

'Would everyone like another cup of tea?' Jessica asked brightly just in case she was expected to contribute towards the conversation.

Will arrived early the next morning. 'How do you fancy going to the matinée at the Empire this afternoon to see *Aladdin* he asked Jessica, who hadn't expected him until the afternoon. 'Appropriately for Boxing Day, I've got a box.'

'How on earth did you manage that?' Jessica knew from past experience how difficult it was to get tickets for a panto-mime on Boxing Day. You had to book months in advance.

'Someone gave them to Tom McGrath and he gave them to me.'

'I'd love to go. Are you going to ask—'

Will didn't wait for her to finish. 'Lena and Calum, yes. And Angus; we can't leave him out.'

'Did Tom want to know who you were taking?'

'He didn't ask.'

'Does Lydia know you've got them?'

'Well, *I* certainly didn't tell her,' Will said patiently. 'Are you coming or not?'

'Of course I'm coming.'

Jessica sat at the back of the box and didn't leave at either of

the intervals, worried she might come face to face with someone she knew.

Will sat with Calum on his knee and Lena beside him, the
perfect little family, she thought with a touch of jealousy.
She'd never had to share her brother with another woman
before, apart from Lydia, who didn't really count because she
was his cousin. She moved her chair closer to Angus so he
wouldn't feel left out.

The show was an extravaganza of wonderful dancing, glorious singing and the most beautiful costumes. It would have
made a perfect end to an unexpectedly enjoyable Christmas if
it hadn't been for the meal at the George Hotel opposite that
finished the holiday perfectly.

Jessica had another day's holiday before returning to Kirkby
Castle where she found she had a new boss. Mick had left and
she now worked for Talbot Stewart, the personnel officer. It
was his task to engage the staff required for when the factory
opened in mid-March. Half-page advertisements were
inserted in newspapers all over the country; others went into
local papers requesting accommodation. To the delight of the
owners, bed and breakfast establishments were booked for at
least a year ahead.

And Harvey Cope arrived from Muswell Hill in London
to sort out the electricity, falling head over heels in love with
Jessica the first moment that they met, and completing dis-
rupting the pretend life that she had created for herself.

Chapter 9

On New Year's Eve Jessica went to tea with Josef Davidson and his sister, Ruth, in their small terraced house in Seaforth. Ruth, whom she had never met before, turned out to be a tall, drooping, sad-faced woman whose black crêpe blouse and hobble skirt were about twenty years out of date. The string of pearls and long matching earrings she wore had turned yellow with age. Her iron-grey hair had been set in rigid waves and was covered with a hairnet.

The house smelled of mothballs and was like a museum, darkly furnished, with every surface covered with ornaments and faded photographs.

'I hope you don't mind, but the food is kosher,' Ruth said when they sat down to eat.

'Kosher?' Jessica had heard the word before, but had no idea what it meant.

'Food that conforms to the rules of the Jewish religion,' Josef explained.

'But why?' Jessica was puzzled. 'You're not Jewish, are you?'

'We are,' Ruth said crossly. 'But for some reason Josef likes to keep the fact a secret.'

'I just don't think it's anyone's business but our own,' Josef said mildly. 'Jessica is a Catholic, but it's not tattooed on her forehead.'

'Nor is being Jewish tattooed on mine, Josef. But it is what we *are*. Personally, I think you are ashamed of our religion.'

Jessica was beginning to feel embarrassed. She was later to discover that Ruth and Josef quarrelled all the time. After a tea consisting of salmon sandwiches and trifle, she relayed how things were progressing at Kirkby Castle. 'We've reached the stage of advertising for staff from all over the country.'

'What sort of staff?' Josef asked.

'Just about every sort,' Jessica told him, 'from engineers and office workers to cooks and cleaners. The wages are at least a pound a week more than average.'

Josef's eyes gleamed. 'Would they be wanting clerks and letter writers, that sort of thing?'

'Oh, absolutely that sort of thing,' Jessica assured him.

'And would they laugh if they received an application from a person of my age?'

Jessica didn't know his age, but reckoned he was about sixty. 'They definitely wouldn't laugh. I'll let you into a little secret, shall I?' She lowered her voice as if someone from Kirkby Castle was in the parlour listening. 'They prefer to take on older people. You see, if a war starts, young people, particularly the men, will be called up and replacements will have to be found. It's more convenient to take on older staff now.'

Ruth was listening, clearly outraged. She glared at Josef. 'And if you go out to work, brother, what am I supposed to do all day in this house on my own?' she demanded angrily.

'You were already living on your own when I moved in, my dear sister,' Josef said smoothly, 'so you can continue to do whatever you were doing then. Or you could apply for a job yourself!'

'I'm sorry about that,' Josef said later when he walked Jessica to Seaforth station. 'It was as much my fault as it was Ruth's. We never cease to rub each other up the wrong way. The thing we argue about most is our Jewishness. Although I cannot deny I am a Jew, I do not practise my religion and Sara was brought up to be the same. I don't want to take any part in the ceremonies and holy days. Whenever I do, it is only to please Ruth, otherwise she will acquaint me with the rough edge of her tongue.'

'It was a very pleasant evening,' Jessica assured him, though it wasn't true; she hadn't enjoyed it a bit.

They had reached the station where they wished each other a Happy New Year and shook hands. Josef said as soon as he got back, he would write a letter of application on his new notepaper for a job at Kirkby Castle. Jessica had already given him the address. 'Let's hope 1938 brings some good luck for a change,' he said drily.

Her room in the house in Stanley Road felt cold when Jessica went in. She lit the gas mantel and the fire. In a minute she'd go upstairs and collect Lena and Calum. They'd planned to listen to music until the New Year came in. It was more comfortable in Jessica's room and they could watch the fireworks in the park over the road when the bells tolled at midnight.

She sat down for a moment to get her breath back – it was a long walk from Bootle station. The house was silent. The residents were either out or being very quiet. Angus had gone to a pub in town with friends from work.

Last year, Jamie had been allowed to stay up to see in the New Year. She'd been surprised that he managed to remain awake for so long. Her mother-in-law usually stayed with them till gone midnight when Bertie would take her home in the car.

She returned to the present. She'd never dreamed – well, why should she? – that the year which had begun so hopefully, as new years nearly always do, would end in such an unnatural and unexpected way.

Jessica sighed. If she stayed here much longer, she'd sink into the Slough of Despond, as Will had thought she might. She wondered what the Slough of Despond was like and imagined it being a bottomless pool of thick mud into which you just slid down and down until you'd swallowed so much of it that you couldn't breathe any more.

She shuddered at the thought, jumped to her feet, and went upstairs, walking quietly just in case some people had deliberately gone to bed in order to miss the arrival of the New Year, something she could quite understand. She knocked on Lena's door.

'Come in,' said a male voice.

Surprised, Jessica opened the door of the tiny, claustrophobic room and found her brother, wearing corduroy trousers and an Aran jumper and looking very much at home, occupying the only chair. Lena was sitting with her feet on the bed beside a sleeping Calum. She and Will looked as if they'd known each other for ever.

Lena said, 'He rang the bell once, so I knew it was for you. When I answered the door I told him you'd gone to tea with your friend in Seaforth and he asked if he could stay and wait.' She blushed prettily. 'Of course I said yes.'

'Did he now!' Will had been told she was going out. He'd deliberately arrived early in the hope of seeing Lena, which was understandable. As Will's sister, Jessica would come a firm second after any woman he was in love with, though she was concerned Lena was too young for him. He needed someone more sophisticated – someone like Lydia, but who wasn't his cousin. Their mother would eat a girl like Lena for breakfast.

She said, 'Shall I go down and make tea? There's loads of Christmas cake left. Calum can sleep on my bed.'

'You go ahead,' Will said. 'We'll be down in a minute.'

There was something significant about the 'we'll', as if it was already acknowledged that they were a couple. Jessica felt dizzy with astonishment and dismay at the rapidity of events. A week ago, her brother had been a confirmed bachelor who'd once told her he had no intention of getting married while the country was at war. She pushed her hand through her hair in a troubled gesture. The country wasn't at war, but the signs were that it soon would be. Maybe Will still didn't intend to get married, and his feelings for Lena were just a flash in the pan. Or, if they did get married, it wouldn't be until the war, which had yet to start, was over.

The door opened and Will came in with a sleeping Calum in his arms. He looked just as handsome in casual clothes as he did in uniform. I'm getting ahead of myself, Jessica thought. Maybe he just admires Lena. After all, she's a lovely girl, not just in looks, but in personality, too. It's marvellous the way she's taken on Calum. Another woman might have shrugged off the responsibility of her brother's child and let Calum go into an orphanage.

The New Year arrived, as she had anticipated, with the ringing of bells and the sound of fireworks. When they stopped, Will picked up a still-sleeping Calum to take him back upstairs, and Lena kissed Jessica and wished her a Happy New Year.

'I don't know why, but I've got a feeling that 1938 is going to be a really good year for me and Calum,' she said.

'I do hope so.' Jessica gave her a hug.

She was scraping crumbs of Christmas cake off the plate to eat, when Will returned. He threw himself on to the settee. 'You always used to do that,' he said.

'Do what?'

'Eat the last of the cake, whatever sort we had.'

'I hope you don't expect me to say I'm sorry.' She stuffed the last few crumbs in her mouth. 'As for you, you always got a funny look on your face when you'd done something wrong like broken a dish or spilled ink on the best carpet.' She rubbed her hands together and the last of the crumbs fell on the floor. 'You've got it now – the look, that is.'

Will took a packet of cigarettes out of his pocket, drew one out with his lips, then tossed the packet to his sister. 'A few minutes ago I asked Lena to marry me and she accepted. There's nothing wrong about that.'

Jessica's response was a groan. She lit the cigarette and didn't speak. Stanley Road sounded as busy now as it did during the day, though with rather more singing, 'Auld Lang Syne' being the favourite, and some First World War songs. There was plenty of traffic, including trams. She wondered how long the drivers and conductors had been working and what time it would be when they got home.

Her brother was looking at her with amusement. 'I would have thought congratulations were in order, not a grunt.'

'It was a groan, not a grunt. Anyway, shut up a minute while I think about it.'

But Will wasn't prepared to shut up for a second, let alone a minute. 'Lena and I are the only ones who need to think about it. I want you to be happy for me, sis, but if you disapprove, then it's just too bad. We're getting married by special licence in Brome Terrace register office at midday on Monday. You can come, if you like, be our bridesmaid.'

'That hardly gives me time to buy a new frock.' She didn't have an even faintly decent hat.

'I thought, if I looked after Calum tomorrow, you could take Lena into town and help her buy a new outfit? You can buy yourself something at the same time.'

'But I have to go to work,' Jessica protested.

'It's Saturday,' Will pointed out.

'Oh, all right.' How could she possibly refuse? 'It's all very sudden. Is Mother coming to the wedding?'

'What! Are you kidding?' Will gasped. 'She'll want to take over, insist on it being held in a church, try and turn it into a society affair. I'd end up not getting married for months. I'd prefer to keep Lena a secret from our frightful mother for the time being. You've never mentioned her to Lena, have you?'

'I've told Lena hardly anything about myself, only that I have a brother in the Navy called Will.'

'There's another thing . . .' Will paused and looked uncomfortable. 'I'm not going to force myself on Lena, or anything like that. I'll wait until she's ready.'

Jessica wondered how he would know.

'Do you mind?' Lena asked next day when Jessica congratulated her on her forthcoming marriage.

'I think it's absolutely wonderful,' Jessica said as sincerely as she was able. She hoped Will wasn't being too impetuous and Lena's head wasn't stuck in the clouds. How many eighteen-year-olds in her position could have resisted a proposal of marriage from a handsome sailor who clearly wasn't short of money? Very few, if any, Jessica imagined. She had been two years younger than Lena when she'd met Bertie, and probably would have married him there and then had he proposed. All she could hope was that her brother and Lena would be considerably happier than she and Bertie had been.

Lena insisted on buying her wedding outfit from Paddy's Market. 'Will can buy my clothes once we're married, but until then I insist on paying for them meself,' she said firmly.

'But you'll be married by the day after tomorrow,' Jessica reminded her.

'I don't care,' Lena said stubbornly.

'Then where *is* Paddy's Market?' Jessica had never been near the place, though it was too famous not to have heard of. She'd always bought her very unremarkable clothes from George Henry Lee's or Henderson's. She imagined clothes from markets being full of fleas and smelling horribly.

Paddy's Market was a place where two contrasting worlds met, where the poor and the relatively well-off rubbed shoulders. The poor were after clothes for coppers for themselves and their children, clothes that might have had half a dozen previous owners. For the relatively well-off, a visit to a market was an enjoyable day out when they might well pick up a real bargain.

Some of the stalls sold clothes only fit for cutting up for dusters, but others displayed good-quality items with the occasional well-known label. Lena acquired an off-white tweed swagger coat, an orange velvet frock for underneath, and a rather strange-shaped white felt hat with an orange feather. Jessica offered to lend her a white handbag and gloves, so all that was left to buy were shoes. A pair of hardly worn fawn ankle boots proved ideal.

'Why don't you buy something while you're here, Jessica?' Lena suggested.

'Well . . .' She'd noticed a smart tan woollen costume with a fur collar and cuffs that was her size and priced at a mere fifteen shillings and sixpence.

After she'd bought it, she put Lena on the tram to Bootle, then went into town and bought a hat from C&A Modes. The world would have to be ending before she would wear a hat that had rested on another woman's head. C&A was a shop she'd never been in before, but needs must when the devil drives, as her grandmother was fond of saying. Jessica still wasn't quite sure what it meant.

She had expected to be the only guest at the wedding and was surprised when Will, in a smart grey suit, arrived with a best man who turned out to be Harry Chapman, his artist friend from across the water.

It was a simple, touching ceremony that Jessica had trouble accepting was actually taking place. She held Calum's hand throughout, then passed him to Lena when she had officially become Mrs William Farley. As on Boxing Day, the small party went for a meal at the George Hotel in Lime Street.

'They already look the perfect little family,' Harry

Chapman said when the newly married couple were seated at the table with Calum between them. The little boy kept glancing from his aunt to the strange man who had just become his father, aware that something very important had happened, but unsure what it was.

'I hope they always stay that way,' Jessica said.

She caught a tram home. At some point in the journey – she still wasn't sure what the districts were called – the tram slowed down and passed a woman who was standing on the pavement waiting to cross the road, and holding Jessica's daughter, Dora, by the hand!

Jessica's heart missed a beat. She got shakily to her feet and stumbled towards the rear of the tram, which had picked up speed and was going so fast she couldn't possibly have jumped off. She could still see the woman and the little girl, though they were getting rapidly smaller. In fact, it was obvious even from this distance that the girl was too young to be Dora. How could she have made such a stupid mistake? She returned disconsolately to her seat.

The incident cast a dark shadow on what was left of the day. She lay in her room with the light off until it was time to go to bed. She felt too unhappy to even listen to music that she normally found soothing. Will, Lena and Calum were staying at the George for the next two nights until Will's leave came to an end on Wednesday. Tomorrow, it was his intention to search for a better home for his little family to live – and for himself to stay when he came home on leave.

Jessica couldn't help but feel glad for Lena, yet would miss her being upstairs. She'd miss Calum, too. Often he would sit on her knee while she read Enid Blyton's *Sunny Stories* that she'd bought especially for him. In a way, Calum slightly – only slightly – made up for the lack of her own children.

She began to cry until the tears became a flood and the pillow was soaked. She cried because she could see no future for herself. Her life was over and she couldn't see a reason for living any more.

Harvey Cope, known as 'Harve', was a Cockney born within the sound of Bow bells. He spoke very fast in an up and down melodic voice, and had the loudest and most infectious laugh that Jessica had ever heard. His curly hair and his eyes were as black as coal, and he cut a rather rakish figure in his black trousers and black leather waistcoat worn over an always colourful, open-necked shirt.

Harve Cope, Fred Cooper and Malcolm Swift had come from London to Kirkby Castle to sort out the electricity, to separate the bunches of wires that came spurting through walls and ceilings, bury them in channels, and connect them to switches, power points, light fittings and various items of machinery.

Jessica met Harve in the unromantic setting of one of the ladies' lavatories. It was only a few days since Lena and Will had got married and she was still feeling low. Harve was on a ladder pulling wires through the ceiling when Jessica went in to spend a penny.

'Oh, gosh, I'm sorry,' she gasped, though had no reason to be.

'Bloody hell!' Harve jumped off the ladder – she didn't know his name then, only that he was one of the three electricians who'd recently arrived to work there. 'I forgot to put the "Out of Order" notice on the door. I'm even more sorry than you are, darlin'. I'll come back later.' He made for the door and Jessica did the same. They bumped into each other when they both reached for the handle and his warm hand rested on top of hers.

'I'll go somewhere else,' Jessica stammered.

'It's all right, darlin', I'll wait outside.'

Jessica wasn't prepared to have a strange man waiting outside while she went to the lavatory. She turned the knob and

Harve's hand at the same time, and went in search of another lavatory, cautiously opening the door of the first she came to in case one of the other electricians were inside.

Harve came to her office about an hour later. 'Ah, so this is where you work! Your name's Jessica, so I've been told.'

'Yes.' She felt nervous all of a sudden.

'I'm Harve,' he said. 'Is it all right if I call you Jessica?'

'Absolutely fine.' She wasn't sure why she nodded her head quite so furiously.

He regarded her seriously for quite a few seconds. 'Would you like . . . I mean, how about us going for a drink together one of these nights? Or would you prefer the flicks?'

'The flicks?'

'The pictures. How about *Fury* with Spencer Tracey? It's on at this picture house called the Palace near where I live.'

'Where do you live?'

'Bootle. We've got digs there. Where do you live, Jessica?'

'I live in Bootle, too.'

'That's convenient.' His dark eyes started to dance. 'We could go to the flicks *and* a drink.'

'All right.' She was never able to explain what got into her. She'd had no experience with men apart from Bertie, the only one she'd ever been out with – she didn't count Tom McGrath. But there was something irresistible about Harve Cope. It wasn't long before she realized he felt the same about her.

On their first night at the Palace cinema in Marsh Lane where they saw *Fury*, she was conscious the entire time of his shoulder pressing against hers. She was aware of his breathing above her own, his long hands folded on his knees, his fingernails cut very short, his soapy, chemical smell – he must wash with that green carbolic stuff. She was convinced she could sense the beating of his heart through their touching shoulders.

Afterwards, they went for a drink in a crowded pub that had

sawdust on the floor and a man playing an out-of-tune piano at a furious rate while another man held a glass of frothy beer against his lips so he could drink and play at the same time.

Jessica laughed. When she was with Harve, she laughed a lot. It was almost possible to believe that life could be fun.

Later on, he walked her home and shook her hand at the front door of the house in Stanley Road. She didn't ask him in as she didn't want to appear forward.

That weekend, they went to the pictures again, this time to see Charles Boyer in *The Garden of Allah*. They sat in the back row and Harve held her hand. When he took her home, she asked him in for a cup of tea.

'Or coffee or cocoa,' she added.

'Oh, tea, please. I'd really love a cuppa.'

After he'd finished the tea, he kissed her once on the lips. She would have liked him to kiss her twice or even a dozen times, but after one he announced he was going home.

She got the impression he was holding himself back, that the next time they went to the pictures he would put his arm round her and, if he came back to her room, he would kiss her more than once. She really didn't mind. For the first time in many months she wasn't consumed with thoughts of Jamie and Dora for every minute of every day, though at the times when she did think about them she felt guilty, as if she was letting them down by thinking of something else – someone else. In other words, Harve Cope.

Chapter 10

Josef Davidson went to Kirkby Castle for interview and was offered a job as a storekeeper. He accepted on the spot and took Jessica to dinner as a way of showing his gratitude.

'I should have done it before, found myself work,' he said over the meal in La Porte Rouge, a newly opened French restaurant in Bold Street. 'But I convinced myself I was too old to work again, that people would laugh if someone like me turned up for an interview. But Mr Stewart, the personnel officer, actually seemed quite pleased to see me.'

The waiter, who had a strong Liverpool accent, not at all in keeping with the restaurant's name, came to remove their dinner plates and take their order for dessert.

'Mr Stewart told me about you,' Jessica said when the man had gone. 'He said you're exactly the sort of responsible, trustworthy person he wants. He wished he could get staff like you for the entire factory.'

'Did he really?' Josef flushed like a schoolboy. 'How fortunate I was to be passing your house in Stanley Road that day when the taxi drew up and you and your gramophone virtually fell out.' He smiled at her fondly.

'I was fortunate, too,' she reminded him. His steadfast presence had helped her through the terrible time when she'd just lost her children.

'Are you completely happy in your job, Jessica?' he asked.

'I love it,' she assured him. 'Why do you ask?'

'When we first met, before you started work there, you seemed very lost. I got the impression that you were a forlorn, very sad young woman.'

'I found moving away from home upsetting.' Jessica wrinkled her nose. She'd been more devastated than upset, and would have preferred it if Josef hadn't brought the matter up, but then he knew nothing of the real circumstances.

'My Sara,' he said, worriedly shaking his grey head, 'has never been happy living in Paris. I've told you before. She works much too hard and her husband, Louis, is a decent enough chap, but has no regard for her feelings or her health. All his attention is focused on that theatre of his.'

Jessica had imagined the theatre being very grand, like the Empire or the Royal Court in Liverpool, but when she mentioned this to Josef, he shook his head. 'It seats no more than about thirty, but Louis thinks of little else, even though it makes hardly any money.' Joseph sighed. 'He and Sara barely scrape a living.'

Jessica clicked her tongue. 'I'm so sorry,' she said sympathetically, though wondered why Josef had chosen to tell her this now.

'I desperately wish she would come back home before this wretched war begins,' he went on. 'She is a British Jew. If Germany invades France and she is discovered, she could end up in one of these wicked camps I keep reading about where they throw the people they disapprove of; Communists, Socialists, perverts, criminals, the mentally ill and the Jews. Marie and Frannie could well suffer the same fate.'

Jessica reached across the table and touched his hand. 'I seriously doubt that will come to pass,' she said softly.

'I think it will,' he replied in an anguished voice. 'All the signs are pointing to it. Hitler is a demagogue who wants to rule the world. Taking over Europe will merely be the first of his conquests. I have written to Sara numerous times and asked – demanded – that she come back, but she takes no notice.

She lacks all spirit. She doesn't care what happens to her or her children.'

'What do you intend to do about it, Josef?' She suspected that he'd been leading up to her asking that question.

'I would very much like to go to Paris and make sure she returns,' he said. 'Not now, not yet, but later when war becomes a certainty. But I know she won't listen to me who she considers an old fool. She is very stubborn, my Sara. She's more likely to listen to *you*, a friend. I will pay your fare, naturally, and give you enough to live on while you're there, as well as enough money for you, Sara and the children to get home. I can afford to now I have a job.'

'But I have *my* job,' Jessica protested. She felt sorry for Sara, and Josef, but felt she was entitled to put herself first.

'I know. I wouldn't dream of suggesting that you leave your job, but if, one day, you feel inclined to, please think about what I said tonight.'

The waiter arrived with Jessica's trifle and Josef's apple pie, and the matter of his daughter wasn't raised again until another half-year had gone by.

Jessica and Harve slept together for the first time on Good Friday. Harve, Fred and Malcolm were working every day over the holiday in the rush to get Kirkby Castle up and running and producing munitions.

Jessica hadn't forgotten that 17 April was Dora's sixth birthday, but she hadn't realized that was the date until it was announced that morning on the BBC News. From then on, to the exclusion of everything else, she visualized her daughter opening her presents after breakfast, which had been the routine when they'd lived in Atlas Road, seeing her little face light up when she found yet another doll in one of the parcels. Dora genuinely loved her dolls; she worried about their welfare, made sure they were warmly dressed in winter and put to bed early every night in the nighties ironed with the toy iron that held no heat, but which she was convinced pressed her dollies' clothes just as well as a real one.

Jessica took Marjorie, the doll for which she'd made such an exquisite wardrobe before Christmas, out of the cupboard where she had rested ever since, and nursed her all morning, singing a lullaby in a creaky voice while tears poured down her cheeks.

At midday, a little bit of common sense prevailed and she realized she couldn't very well spend an entire day behaving so mawkishly. She got dressed and went to see Lena and Calum, who now lived in a comfortable little flat over a milliner's shop in South Road, Waterloo.

But Lena and Calum were out. Thinking they were likely to have just gone for a walk on the sands at the bottom of the road, Jessica waited but they didn't return. It turned out Lena had taken the little boy to the fairground in Southport.

Back home again, Marjorie was lying on the bed looking bored without an owner. Jessica put her back in the cupboard, made a pot of tea, and smoked three cigarettes without a pause between them, lighting the new ones from the stub of the one before.

She sat in the window, drinking tea and smoking the rest of the afternoon away. As it was Good Friday, the shops and offices were closed, and there was less traffic than usual on the road. At about six o'clock, an old black car drew up outside and she recognized it as the one Harve shared with Fred and Malcom; they'd come from London in it together. Harve climbed out of the back and walked towards the house, jaunty in his check lumber jacket and corduroy cap. Jessica gave a little cry and ran into the hallway to let him in.

He was reaching for the bell when she opened the door. Perhaps there was something about her face that told him how desperately pleased she was to see him. Perhaps he just as desperately had wanted to see her.

'I've been thinking about you all day, darlin',' he said

thickly. 'You look even prettier than I remembered. I couldn't wait another hour and a half before we met.'

'I'm glad you didn't.' Jessica held out her arms, and Harve scooped her up and carried her into the room where he laid her tenderly on the bed and began to remove her clothes, kissing her breasts when he released them from the pink brocade brassiere, burying his head in her stomach after he'd pulled down her skirt. He stared at her naked body as if it was the most wondrous thing in the world, then hurriedly removed his own clothes before lying beside her, kissing her as she'd never been kissed before.

'Hurry up,' she mumbled. She couldn't wait for him to be inside her.

And suddenly he was. And it was glorious, unbelievably glorious. Jessica wanted it never to stop, but suddenly it ended in a spasm of sheer delight and she collapsed back on the bed, exhausted, while Harve collapsed beside her.

'Bloody hell!' he gasped.

Jessica said nothing, just buried her face in his neck, where it fitted perfectly, and tried to get her breath back. They lay in silence for a while, until Harve said in an even voice, 'You've done that before. I could tell by the way you said "hurry up", as well as other things. I don't know why, I thought you'd be a virgin.'

'Are *you*?' Jessica asked. Her mouth was against his ear. He smelled of perspiration and the plaster he'd been drilling for most of the day.

'No.' There was a strain of anger in the word. 'But you, Jessica, you're not the sort I'd expect to have slept around. You *look* like a bloody virgin. You look like butter wouldn't melt in your mouth.'

Someone else had said that to her once, she couldn't re-member who. She sat up and said mildly, because she wasn't the slightest bit upset, 'How dare you suggest I've slept around? That's a horrible thing to say.' She reached for his packet of Senior Service and the lighter that he'd put on the bedside table.

'Oh, I'm sorry, darlin'.' He pulled her back against him. 'I'm being unfair, ain't I? I don't know why the man thinks he can have it off with any woman that's going, but his girlfriend has to be as pure as snow.'

She lit a cigarette. 'Where are all these pure-as-snow women supposed to come from if men insist on sleeping with so many?'

Harve laughed, but she could tell it was a false laugh. He wasn't very pleased to find she'd slept with at least one other man. In the past, she had learned that the best way to deal with any unpleasantness and embarrassment was to tell a lie, as long as it didn't hurt anyone.

She said, 'I had a fiancé once, but he died.' Hopefully he wouldn't mind her having slept with a fiancé.

'Oh, darlin'!' He lit a cigarette for himself and they leaned companionably against the bed headboard. 'What happened?' he asked, kissing her ear.

'He was an engineer on a ship, but was killed when the boiler exploded.' It was what had happened to Lena's brother.

'What was his name?'

'Harold Porter,' she said easily. 'Everyone called him Harry. We were going to get married the following Christmas – it was 1935 – but everything had to be cancelled.' She looked up at him. 'Do you mind terribly if we don't talk about him any more? It doesn't feel right when I'm in bed with another man.'

'The name Harold Porter will never be mentioned again, darlin', at least not by me.'

It was as if they were courting, the way they gradually got to know each other, taking pleasure in the growing familiarity between them, Jessica being shown photographs of Harve's huge family – he had a great-grandmother called Hilda –

discovering unexpected things about him, such as his aversion to potatoes in any form, the fact he was a Communist, his fear of thunder, his love of cats – particularly ginger ones – and his addiction to Everton Mints which he'd only just acquired.

It was so different from when she'd started courting Bertie; months had passed before he kissed her. Looking back, it had been a very limp first kiss. Their relationship was very serious and neither of them laughed much. The first night of their marriage had been a disaster, but Jessica, naive and inexperienced, hadn't recognized it at the time. She'd thought everybody's first nights were the same and the limp kisses were only normal. Her mother hadn't talked to her about it, given her advice, told her what to expect. Looking back now, she realized Bertie had been a hopeless lover.

Early in May, Kirkby Castle went into production. Newcomers referred to it, mundanely, as Kirkby Munitions. Not every department opened at the same time. The canteen began making meals at bargain prices, the First Aid room opened mornings only until a qualified nurse could be acquired for the afternoons, desks in the various offices were gradually being filled, and the engineering section began producing shell casings and small parts for aeroplanes, while waiting for the explosives that would be loaded in a small structure half a mile away from the main building. The reason for the distance was in case there was an explosion.

Instead of one small bus, now half a dozen double-deckers waited at the tram terminus in Fazakerley to take people to work. There were other pick-up points for people coming from Ormskirk and Southport. The staff car park was nearly full, though the use of cars was expected to fall drastically once the war started and petrol was rationed.

In June, Fred Cooper and Malcolm Swift returned to London, their job done, but Harve stayed in Kirkby to be the resident electrician.

'You look after him now,' Fred said sternly to Jessica when he and Malcolm came to say goodbye. 'Don't hurt the lad. You'd have a long way to go before you'd meet a nicer geezer than Harvey Cope.'

'I wouldn't dream of hurting him,' Jessica protested. But could she absolutely guarantee that?

There was no possibility of them getting married. Not that Harve had asked. She reckoned he would want nothing more to do with her if he knew the truth, that she was already a married woman whose husband had left, taking their children with him when he discovered she had slept with another man, a man who just happened to be married to her mother.

It sounded awful, terrible, the stuff of cheap novels. She could never, never tell Harve about her past. She loved him too much to hurt him. 'I love you, Harve,' she said aloud.

There! She'd said it, admitted it, if only to herself. She was in love with Harvey Cope, but all it meant was that, in one way or another, she would eventually lose him, just as she had lost the children she loved.

A few days later, she applied for a passport. If things got too awkward, then she knew what she could do.

The war that people feared so much was creeping closer. Adolf Hitler appointed himself War Minister, his country mobilized and marched into the Sudentenland, while France called up its reservists.

Observing some activity in the park across the road, Jessica asked Mrs Quigley what was going on.

'They're going to have an ack-ack battery there,' the caretaker said with a grim smile.

'You mean guns and things?'

'Yes, queen, guns and things.'

It was a hot Saturday afternoon halfway through July. In another few days, it would be exactly a year since she'd left Atlas

Road. Jessica had been into town to buy shoes – Josef kept issuing dire warnings about the shortages there would be once war started.

'Food, clothes, toys, every sort of fuel, anything electrical, they'll all become impossible to buy once the conflict has begun,' he said a trifle portentously. 'The other day Ruth bought herself a new umbrella and some nail scissors.'

The shoes had been advertised in the *Liverpool Echo* the night before. Considerably reduced, they were Clark's, rust-coloured suede with a narrow heel from T.J. Hughes's, an inexpensive shop like C&A Modes that she was inclined to frequent nowadays, rather than the classy places where she used to shop. After buying them, she had treated herself to coffee and a cream cake in the Kardomah accompanied by two cigarettes.

She'd hardy been home a minute and was about to try on the shoes again, when the doorbell rang once, meaning that it was for her. She knew it wasn't Harve because he usually played a tune on it, 'Yankee Doodle Dandy'. She hoped it was Lena and Calum – Will was due home soon, and both were so excited they could hardly keep still.

But it wasn't Lena who stood outside, but another woman, whom she had no wish to see.

'Hello, Jessica,' said Lydia. 'I saw you in town and followed you home. I caught the same tram and waited for you to come downstairs. I hope you don't mind.'

'Of course I mind,' Jessica snapped. 'Didn't I tell you I never wanted to see you again?'

'That was nearly a year ago. I've been worried about you; we all are.'

Did it mean that now Lydia was going to tell her mother and Tom where she was, as well as her own mother and father and all their other relatives? Was she about to be deluged with visitors? She stood back to let her cousin in, feeling as if she didn't have much choice.

'This is a nice big room,' Lydia remarked when she entered what was now Jessica's home. 'You've made it look very pretty. I like your painting.' She pointed at the glossy sun-flowers.

'It *is* a nice room,' Jessica conceded, 'but not nearly as nice as the ones in our house in Atlas Road where I'd still be living if it wasn't for you.'

Lydia sat on the bed. She looked pale and tired, not at all well. 'I don't think you realize just how cruel it would have been to run away from Bertie taking the children with you. You knew how much he loved them.'

'I'm their mother,' Jessica said angrily. 'Did you think I didn't love them, too?' She stood by the window, too edgy to sit down.

'Of course I didn't. But I wasn't expecting *him* to run away, was I?' She pursed her lips. 'You merely got a taste of your own medicine. Bertie turned the tables so it was you who suffered instead of him.'

'Did you follow me home just to tell me that? If you did, then I suggest you leave immediately.' Jessica opened the door for Lydia to go, but she didn't budge from the bed. 'I didn't give a damn about Bertie suffering,' Jessica continued. 'You didn't live with him; you didn't know what he was like. As for Jamie and Dora, I've missed them more than words can say, but I haven't missed Bertie a bit.' She took the cigarettes out of her bag and lit one. 'I can't believe I put up with him for so long. I should have left years before.' She took a quick puff and blew the smoke out in an angry stream.

'You look different,' Lydia said, 'more wide awake, not so dreamy.' She nodded at the cigarettes. 'Can I have one of those?'

Jessica handed her the pack and the lighter. She wasn't interested in Lydia's opinion of her. Yet when they'd been best friends, they'd had plenty of arguments that occasionally turned to rows. Lydia, who was much cleverer and had a quicker mind, usually won, and they always made up after-wards. Despite the unpleasant things they'd just said to each other, and the awful thing Lydia had done in the past, Jessica wondered if it was the time for making up now.

She was trying to think of how to go about it, when Lydia said wearily, 'I'm sorry. You know I would never deliberately hurt you. I thought by telling Bertie it would mean you and the children would stay at home, he'd forget about what hap-pened with Tom McGrath, and eventually everything would be all right again. I've really missed you, Jess,' she finished tearfully. 'Shall we shake little fingers like we used to do?'

'Only when we were very young,' Jessica said quickly. The thought of doing it now made her want to giggle. She lost all interest in making peace with her cousin.

Lydia sighed. 'Have you any idea where Bertie and the children are?'

'No. I was about to ask you if you'd heard anything.' About once a month she sent Albert James, the private detective, five pounds for a further search, but he could still find no trace of her family.

'I think Tom made some enquiries, but came to a dead end.'

'How are Tom and my mother?' She thought frequently about her mother, less about Tom.

Lydia slipped off her shoes, swung her feet on to the bed, and lifted the pillow until it was behind her head. 'I hope you don't mind if I make myself comfortable. Tom and your mother?' She shrugged. 'Things haven't been the same be-tween them since the thing happened with Tom and you. I don't think she can forgive him.'

Jessica recalled her mother saying nothing could possibly change her love for Tom. 'I'm sorry about that,' she said. She really meant it, deeply regretting what she and Tom had done that day. It had changed her own world in an unimaginable way.

Lydia shrugged again. 'It's Tom's own fault; he should have known better.' She chewed her nails, something Jessica had never known her do before. To her astonishment, her cousin's eyes were full of unshed tears. 'Has Will been home since Christmas?' she asked.

'He hasn't, no, but he will be soon.'

'Last Christmas, I'd been so looking forward to seeing him, but he spent hardly any time at your mother's and none at all with me, apart from us having a little talk.' Her voice shook. 'Was he with you much?'

'Quite a bit. And I know he went a few times to see that artist friend of his who lives over the water, Harry Chapman.'

To her consternation, Lydia burst into tears. 'I haven't had a letter from him in months – we used to write to each other all the time. Do you think he's met someone else, Jess?'

'He might have done,' Jessica said cautiously, unwilling to break the news that Will had indeed met someone else and, what was more, had married her. It was up to Will to do that. Her brother can't have realized how much he meant to Lydia.

She thought she ought to remind Lydia that she and Will were cousins, but when she did Lydia merely snorted and began to wipe her eyes. 'As far as I'm aware, the Catholic religion is the only one that bans marriage between cousins. D'you really think it would stop Will and me from getting married?'

'Did you discuss marriage?' Jessica asked, still cautious.

'No, but we both knew it would happen one day. It was understood.'

'Will's nearly thirty and you're twenty-seven, no, twenty-eight.' Lydia had had a birthday in May. Soon, Jessica would turn twenty-eight, too. 'If you were going to get married, why didn't you do it years ago?' Jessica wished she hadn't gone to town that day, that Lydia hadn't seen her and followed her home. Everything was getting terribly complicated. It had always been obvious that her brother and her cousin were fond of one other, but she'd never suspected that Lydia was genuinely in love.

'Will said to me once he didn't want to settle down until he finished his time in the Navy,' Lydia assured her.

Jessica didn't like pointing out that he'd said the same thing to her, so it could hardly be considered a proposal of marriage.

In the basement downstairs, the chiming clock Mr and Mrs Quigley had got for their Silver Wedding struck five. Jessica was expecting Harve at six, but he could well come earlier. She didn't want him and Lydia coming face to face, preferring the different strands of her life be kept entirely separate. In fact, it was essential.

'I'm going out soon,' she said. 'You'll have to excuse me while I get ready.'

Lydia's face fell. 'I thought we could do something to-gether, like go to the theatre? There's a Somerset Maugham play on at the Royal Court. In fact,' she said eagerly, 'now we've met, why don't we start going to the pictures and the theatre again? I've missed you. Surely you must have missed me, too?'

'Oh, yes,' Jessica lied. 'But I've made new friends and I'm seeing one tonight.'

'Where are you going?'

'To Southport for dinner.'

'That's nice.' Lydia opened her handbag, took out a compact and began to powder her face. 'Did you say earlier that Will is coming home?'

Jessica wished she hadn't. 'I'm expecting him at the end of this month. Right now, he's on his way back from Australia.'

'Australia!' She laughed, but it was more like a bark. 'The other side of the world, eh? I hope this time he's home he remembers to pay me a visit.'

'I'm sure he will,' Jessica said lamely. By now, she thought Lydia was behaving very oddly, and was anxious for her to leave. Her heart dropped at the thought that she might have to

136

find somewhere else to live if she didn't want to see her cousin again.

She removed her cotton frock, splashed her face, rubbed underneath her arms with a flannel, and put on the linen skirt and lemon blouse she'd ironed that morning. Throughout, Lydia watched, frowning slightly, as if she wasn't very pleased about things.

'How's school going?' Jessica asked.

'I've left,' Lydia said abruptly. 'It got too much for me. I gave up my flat and I'm back living with Mum and Dad.'

'I'm sorry about that.' The minute she saw Will she would demand he put Lydia straight. He was a gentle soul and would be alarmed to know how much he'd hurt her.

'What do you do with yourself during the day, Jessica?'

'I had to get a job, didn't I? I'm a secretary in a . . . factory, an engineering factory.' She didn't say where it was.

'My, you *have* changed. You've never had a proper job before.'

Jessica didn't answer. The Quigleys' clock had just struck half-past five. She quickly dabbed powder on her nose, painted her lips a delicate pale pink, and ran a comb through her short curly hair.

'I'll have to be going now,' she said.

'Is there a lavatory in this place?'

'It's upstairs, second door on the left.' Jessica went into the hallway and locked the door of her room and waited for her cousin to return. She took ages in the lavatory and eventually appeared, dragging her feet as she came downstairs, looking so desperately miserable that Jessica almost wished she wasn't seeing Harve and could go to the theatre with Lydia instead. The feeling didn't last long. Remembering who was responsible for her losing her children and living in this house, her world falling apart, she hardened her heart. Lydia was only getting what she deserved.

Outside, Jessica pointed where to catch the tram back to

town. She was embarrassed when Lydia clung to her, pleading that they see each other again.

'I'll write to you and arrange something,' she promised.

A tramcar was coming. Lydia and the tram arrived at the stop together and she climbed on.

'Hello, darlin'.' Jessica jumped as Harve's arms slid round her waist from behind. 'Who's that you were with?'

'A cousin.'

The tram went by. Lydia was sitting by the window. Her jaw fell when she saw Jessica and Harvey together. Her face turned to watch, twisted in what looked very much like hatred. She said something, but Jessica would never know what it was.

'You never mentioned having a cousin before,' Harve said.

'She's a very distant cousin.'

Over those few July days, for the second time in Jessica's life, everything changed. Her cousin, Lydia, had come back into her life; over dinner in Southport, Harve proposed marriage and suggested they do it straight away; and at work on Monday, while opening the post, she found a letter from Mary Austin, who'd lived next door in Atlas Road, applying for the job of part-time nurse in the First Aid room.

At first, Jessica felt tempted to throw the letter away. No one would ever know. Miss Austin would merely think she hadn't got the job and her application had gone unacknowledged. But that didn't seem fair. The woman had loved Jamie and Dora, and they'd loved her back. She must have been hurt when the Collinses had left without even saying goodbye. The letter was placed in a filing basket to be answered.

She didn't know what to do about Harve, who refused to take no for an answer. Why wouldn't she marry him? Did his breath smell? Was it his Cockney accent? Was she prejudiced against electricians? Why did she insist on saying no, when the obvious answer was yes?

Why, why, why?

He would go down on one knee in pubs and restaurants and propose in a loud voice for the umpteenth time. He'd sing to her, 'We'll gather lilacs in the spring again . . .'

'Ah, go on, luv, marry the poor bugger,' a voice would sometimes cry.

Josef Davidson was overjoyed when Jessica told him she would go to Paris, stay with Sara, and do her utmost to persuade her to return to Liverpool before the war started. She gave in her notice at work and asked that she leave quietly without any fuss. She advised Mrs Quigley she would be vacating her room in the near future, told Lena she was going away for a while, wrote to her mother and sent a card to Lydia saying the same thing. She would write to Will from Paris.

And she wrote to Harve, a long, sad letter, telling him everything because, after much thought, she reckoned that was the best, least cruel way. She wasn't refusing to marry him; she couldn't because she was already married with two children. She told him about Tom McGrath, her stepfather. She would post the letter on the day that she left England for Paris.

'I do love you, Harve,' she wrote, wiping her eyes before the tears she was shedding dropped on to the paper. 'I love you with all my heart. I would marry you like a shot if I were free.'

She'd sooner he be disenchanted than she just go away without any explanation, leaving him to always wonder why she'd gone.

They went out the night she left Kirkby Castle, to see Mickey Rooney in *Love Finds Andy Hardy*. It was a comedy that normally she would have loved, but, for her, their last hours together were bittersweet and she kept wanting to cry.

'Why are you so unhappy, darlin'?' Harve asked when they were back in her room and had made love for the final time.

'If you married me, I'd make sure you wouldn't be unhappy again for the rest of your life.'

Next morning, she posted the letter, packed her suitcase, and said goodbye to Mrs Quigley, bequeathing her the *Magnet* annual she'd bought for Jamie, Dora's doll and the typewriter that she'd gone to all the trouble of stealing yet never used again. Outside, she waited for Josef to arrive in the taxi that was to take them to Lime Street station.

'Goodbye, Jessica.' She was leaning out of the window and Josef was holding her hand as the train prepared to leave. 'I can never thank you enough for what you are doing for me and Sara. She is longing to see you. It was the first time I can remember her sounding happy in a letter.'

She squeezed his hand. 'I'll write as soon as I can,' she promised.

A whistle sounded, the train began to chug away, and the air was filled with white smoke.

'Bye.' She waved and waved until the train rounded a bend and Josef could be seen no more.

Jessica collapsed back in her seat. At that moment, all she could think of were Jamie and Dora. Was she fated to go to her grave without ever seeing them again?

Her eyes closed as the hypnotic sound of the train's wheels began to lure her into sleep. She felt awfully odd, she was about to wake up and find that this past year had been nothing but a dream.

'*Au revoir*, Liverpool,' she said, half aloud.

Chapter 11

Paris
December 1938

Paris was full of contrasting smells, particularly in the mornings. From one direction, the whiff of sewers and other unpleasant odours was prevalent, though not as strongly on this crisp winter day as in the clammy heat of summer. Turn a different way and there'd be a hint of expensive oils and fragrances worn the previous night by opera and ballet aficionados and the nightclub set.

The smell changed yet again when Jessica entered Les Halles, a huge glass and metal structure, like a greenhouse, crammed with stalls of fresh fruit and vegetables. Here, the sharp, pungent scents were those of the countryside. Every stall had sprays of holly for sale in honour of Christmas only a few days away. Voices sounded hollow and resonant in the vastness.

This time last year, Jessica recalled, she had lived alone in Stanley Road, Bootle. The year before, it was Atlas Road in Sefton Park with her husband and children. Who would have thought this year would see her in Paris with her old friend Sara Davidson, now Sara Cotillard, who had changed considerably since they'd last met.

'Madame, madame!' Vegetables were being pushed underneath her nose by eager sellers, as well as exotic fruit and flowers from hot foreign climes. She pushed everything away, knowing exactly what she wanted; two leeks, two large onions, potatoes, tomatoes and mushrooms, which she'd buy from the stall run by the lady with one arm. She also wanted a chicken big enough to make a casserole for three adults and two children which she'd get from M. Auteil who owned the butchers in rue de la Grande Truanderie where she lived, and bread from the *boulangerie* in the same street – the narrowest in Paris, she'd been told, being merely ten feet wide. Sara said the name meant Street of the Great Beggar – 'or it might be thief.'

Before returning home, Jessica went to the nearby La Caverne for a coffee. It was a dark, brooding restaurant full of smoke from a live coal fire that had badly stained the walls and ceiling. She patronized it because the *café crème* came with a little jug of thick, buttery cream and the patrons were generally surly and unfriendly. It meant that no one would speak to her; she could sit and ponder in complete peace, something she could never do in the Cotillards' where, even at this early hour, Sara could well be screaming at Louis over something or other.

Louis never screamed back, just regarded her with a sort of bemused expression that only made Sara scream louder because what she wanted was a fight and Louis wasn't prepared to cooperate. She upset her youngest daughter, Marie, who began to scream, too. Even at eight, Marie's shrill yells could outdo her mother by a few decibels. Françoise, known as Frannie, two years older, would demand in a loud voice that everyone be quiet. To avoid the bedlam, Jessica would go for a walk or up to her bedroom, depending on the weather or what time of day it was.

The man sitting opposite in La Caverne was reading *Le Figaro*. There was a photograph of Neville Chamberlain, the British Prime Minister, on the front page. He had been in talks with his French counterpart, Edouard Daladier. Jessica was about to read what they'd said to each other, when the man rattled the paper in annoyance and turned the page. She ignored his thunderous glare and stared ahead, her thoughts returning to the Cotillard household.

She had written to Josef Davidson, Sara's father, a few times, describing his daughter's situation as tactfully as she could. It wouldn't do to say everything was sweetness and light, but if she told the truth, Josef would have got in a panic, given up his new job and travelled to Paris on the next ferry to sort out his daughter's life.

When Jessica had last seen Sara Davidson, she had been sixteen, a pretty girl with long brown hair, brown eyes and an impish sense of humour.

Now she was twenty-nine, though looked much older, and her hair was chopped untidily short. Her brown eyes were hopeless and tired, and she was deeply unhappy most of the time.

Golden-haired Louis was as handsome as a god. Jessica wondered if his attitude of beatific patience had been acquired as a way of coping with his neurotic wife, or if it was his apparent indifference to her feelings that had sent Sara over the edge in the first place. Perhaps his patience had snapped a long time ago and he no longer cared.

The couple rented two adjoining seventeenth-century fourth floor properties in rue de la Grand Truanderie. They lived in one and the other had been converted half a century before into a tiny theatre. The third-storey floor had been removed and five rows of serried benches, each seating six adults, had been erected on the floor below. A stage and back stage area had somehow been squeezed in. The dressing rooms were in the attic.

The downstairs front room opened on to the street, acting as a foyer for the theatre where tickets were bought, programmes collected and refreshments bought, although, until recently, none of these things was available. The audience had been getting in for free.

The foyer was Sara's responsibility, but she claimed to have neither the time nor the inclination to do anything about it.

Evenings, she would be totally exhausted, her nerves in pieces after another gruelling and unnerving day.

Louis didn't appear to notice that the family was getting deeper and deeper into debt. As long as there was a theatre where his plays, and the plays of his friends, could be performed, he was content. One day, a well-known producer would be among the audience and a play, hopefully his, would be transferred to the Comédie-Française or the Palais-Royal or some other major theatre.

It had been a while before Jessica comprehended the extent of the Cotillards' problems. Marie and Frannie had been missing school because their mother had no will to do the shopping. Meals were late, the house was filthy. Louis was no help. He sat in the theatre for most of the day writing yet more plays. His friends came to see him and, through the thin walls, they could be heard arguing and laughing, having fun, while Sara tore her hair out and screamed that it wasn't fair.

Jessica began to do the shopping, using her own money because she wasn't willing to ask the shops for tick – it was possible tick was unheard of in Paris. She insisted Sara help when she scrubbed the floors, encouraged the girls to tidy their rooms. She handwrote tickets and stationed herself in the foyer well before the performance was about to begin, selling them for 23 francs, the British equivalent of half a crown. It only required an audience of thirty for the theatre to be full. The takings soared to 630 francs a week, a small fortune.

It was ironic, she thought, the way she had reformed the Cotillards' lives when she wouldn't have been in Paris had she not made such an utter mess of her own.

Debts were paid off, new furniture bought for the apartment, and new curtains for the theatre. Two small bikes had been purchased and were hidden in the men's dressing room – Christmas presents for the girls. Louis was able to pay the actors a few francs or take them for a meal now and then.

The man reading the paper folded it and pushed it in

Jessica's direction. '*Pour vous, mademoiselle,*' he muttered. He must have noticed she wasn't wearing a wedding ring.

'*Merci beaucoup, monsieur.*' Jessica smiled at this unexpectedly generous gesture.

'*Vous n'êtes pas Française?*' He could tell from the few words that she wasn't French.

'English.' She had been taught French at school and had been surprised by how much she could remember – and how quickly she'd learned more. She mustn't have been as thick as she thought. She could already manage better than Sara, who spoke a mangled version of French and English that hardly anyone could understand.

The man stood, put on his hat, a cream homburg, and gave a little bow. 'Good day, miss.'

'Good day.' She nodded. She hadn't noticed before how good-looking he was; thirtyish, brown-eyed, a broad, strong face. He was also quite tall, she saw, as he walked out of the restaurant carrying an expensive brown coat over his arm. She thought of Harve and briefly of Tom McGrath. She missed having a man in her life, but didn't want to get involved in a relationship. She wouldn't be there for long and didn't want to hurt someone else in the way she'd hurt Harve, or risk being hurt herself.

She still thought about her children, thought about them the minute she woke up each morning, in the minutes before she fell asleep at night, and during the hours in between, wondering where they were, what they were doing. Did they think as often about their mother? How long would it be before they forgot her altogether?

In the foyer of the *Petit Théâtre*, Louis could be seen in discussion with a young man who had recently written a play for the theatre. Suddenly, they began to laugh so much they could hardly stand up. In the house next door, Sara was fast asleep at the kitchen table, her head in her arms.

The room was long, dark and depressing, extending from the front of the house to the back, with a beamed ceiling that was much too low, and a deep brown sink that never looked clean, no matter how hard it was scrubbed. The wooden table was just as frustrating, positively refusing to shine after a really energetic polishing. There was a living room and half a dozen bedrooms upstairs, but the Cotillards spent most of their time in the kitchen.

Shelves covered the walls, exposing an array of battered pans and chipped bowls. Too many insects used the kitchen as their home for Jessica's liking. There was no sign of the girls. Jessica remembered yesterday had been their final day at school until the next term started in the New Year. Marie must be having a lie-in and Frannie absorbed in a book.

Sara raised her head and yawned when she sensed Jessica's presence. 'Where have you been?' she asked sleepily.

'Shopping.' Jessica put the bag on the table as evidence. 'I'll wash the chicken in a minute and you can disembowel it.' It was bad enough having any sort of contact with dead animals, but plucking them and cutting out their innards was beyond her. In Liverpool, she'd bought fowl already plucked and gutted, and cut up meat with her eyes closed.

'What are we having today?' Sara asked with interest. She bore no resentment for the fact that Jessica had taken control not just of the kitchen, but the rest of the house and the theatre, too.

'Chicken casserole.' Jessica sat down with a sigh. 'Is there any coffee made?'

'There's some on the stove. Oh, but we have no milk!'

'I've bought milk *and* cream.' She began to empty the contents of the shopping bag on to the table. Sara went to collect the coffee. It would be thick and strong and taste like tar, but Jessica didn't mind as long as there was cream to lace it. 'It's a lovely day out,' she said. 'Cold, but nice and crisp.

Shall we take the girls somewhere this afternoon – a park, maybe, or one of the big shops?'

Sara's face lit up. She seemed to be in an exceptionally good mood this morning. Without the usual scowls and frowns, she looked quite pretty. Small and neat with thick glossy hair, she reminded Jessica of a Victorian doll. 'Oh, yes!' she said as she filled two tin mugs with coffee and put them on the table. 'A big shop – what about Samaritaine?'

'We could have lunch there,' Jessica suggested. 'There's enough money, isn't there?'

'Loads!' Sara hugged herself. 'Oh, Jessica. I'm so pleased you came to live with us. Though I can't for the life of me understand why. What on earth did Papa say to make you give up your life in Liverpool to be with us?'

'Who in their right mind would turn down a stay in Paris if it was offered to them on a plate?' Jessica responded. 'And I won't be giving my old life up for long, will I? Your father wants me to make sure you're back in England with the girls before the war starts.'

By now, most people had accepted that war was inevitable. Only the other day, the Italian Parliament had been replaced by a Fascist Chamber that had immediately renounced the 1935 agreement the country had made with France. 'I'm sure it won't be long before you, me and the girls are back in good old Liverpool,' she finished. Louis hadn't said if he was coming with them.

Sara made a face. 'I'm not sure how I feel about leaving. I could well love Paris if things here were different. If we were just a normal family and Louis didn't own that frightful theatre.'

Jessica sipped the coffee. 'You might feel more positive about getting out of France with the children if war was imminent.'

'I suppose I would.' Sara stared thoughtfully at her friend. 'I'm glad you're here. I resented you at first. I wondered what

Papa was up to, but I've changed my mind. Now, I don't know what I'd've done without you. I think me and Louis were on the road to hell; you came just in time.'

Jessica, embarrassed, tried to think of what to say, but Sara continued. 'You know, you're not a bit like I remember. All those years ago when we were friends, you gave the impression you wouldn't have said boo to a goose, but now you're terribly sure of yourself. Louis will be eternally grateful for the way you've transformed his theatre, and the girls love you. Jessica Farley, you will remain my friend for ever. I can't understand why some nice man didn't snap you up years ago.'

Marie was an adorable little girl; sensitive, obedient, helpful with the housework, affectionate with her father, and good at school. She was also uncommonly pretty with a heart-shaped face, a small, perfect nose and eyes the colour of milk chocolate. At bedtime, her mother would wind strips of cloth in her long brown hair to make ringlets.

Her sister, Frannie, was none of these things, but Jessica couldn't help liking her best. Frannie was the odd one out in the Cotillard family. Quiet and fiercely independent, she had more intelligence than her mother, father and sister put together. She was also insensitive, disobedient, anything but adorable, and was invariably to be seen with her head buried in a book, sometimes a very adult one. She would have done much better at school than Marie, except she was only willing to learn what she wanted to know. The thrilling history of the French royal families was one thing; Frannie devoured every book she could find, as well as those on the Italian Mafia, Hollywood films, the First World War and other things she found of real interest. But the agricultural output of her country was something else altogether; Frannie wasn't even faintly interested in the tonnage of wheat produced or the quantities of cattle. She was brilliant at maths when she could

be bothered, but showed no real interest in anything concerning figures.

Yet she was a fascinating child. She and Jessica had quite
long discussions on a variety of topics. Why had the Duke of
Windsor given up the throne for Wallis Simpson when she
wasn't even faintly pretty? Frannie wanted to know.

'He probably thinks she is the most beautiful woman in the
world,' Jessica said in reply. 'Or maybe he didn't care how she
looked because he loved her so much.'

The debate had gone on for days, as did the one about Jack
the Ripper. Frannie was convinced she could have solved the
murders had she been alive at the time.

They'd hardly been in Samaritaine a minute when Frannie and
her mother became embroiled in an argument. Sara wanted
the girls to have new dresses for Christmas, but her daughter
preferred a book.

'You can't wear a book!' her mother snapped.

'I already have loads of dresses, Mama,' the girl insisted. She
and Marie spoke French or English when they talked to their
mother, Jessica had never discovered just why one language
was chosen rather than the other.

'Has it escaped your notice, darling,' Sara said patiently,
'that you are a little girl and little girls *grow*? You are many
inches bigger this Christmas than you were last year. The
dresses you have now are getting too small. You need more.
Do you want the little boys to see your knickers?'

Marie raised her head, her face almost hidden beneath a
mountain of ringlets. 'Are we getting more than one dress?'
she said hopefully. Her mother ignored her for once.

Frannie's haughty face took on a look of disgust. 'I am not a
little girl, Mama,' she said coldly, 'I am ten, and at school I do
not mix with *little* boys.'

Jessica didn't feel like an argument. It was one o'clock on
a lovely day in Paris. So far, everything had gone well. That

morning, the washing had been done and was hanging on a line in the kitchen, a chicken casserole for tea was cooking slowly in the oven, they were about to spend money they could actually afford to spend, then have lunch in the restaurant on the fifth floor. She didn't want the day spoiled by an argument about clothes.

'Why don't we all go and look at the girls' dresses now,' she said to Sara. 'Buy one for Frannie — if she sees one she likes, that is,' she added tactfully, 'then she and I will go down to the book department in the basement, and you and Marie can stay upstairs and take your time looking at dresses?'

This seemed to meet with everyone's satisfaction and from then on the afternoon continued without a trace of unpleasantness. Frannie's dress was plain blue with a Peter Pan collar and long sleeves. She insisted on it being too big in the hope it would be another year before she had to have another. Marie appeared with two dresses both fussily detailed with loads of embroidery and tucking. Each had a giant sash.

'I *hate* sashes,' was all Frannie had to say when she saw them. She was nursing her books, a collection of Katherine Mansfield's short stories, and *Murder at the Vicarage* by Agatha Christie.

After lunch, they did more shopping, buying Christmas presents for each other and for Louis. Jessica had already sent cards and presents to Liverpool. Her brother Will was coming home and Lena was expecting a baby who would be born in May. Josef had told her that Harvey Cope had gone back to London. Everything was changing there.

When they left the big shop, she stared at the starlit sky of Paris. Here was a different world, alien and exotic, nothing like Liverpool.

The family had been home for nearly two hours when Sara decided it was time for tea. The chicken casserole in the oven smelled delicious. The table was set, the girls were called, Jessica opened the door at the bottom of the stairs that led to the theatre and shouted for Louis.

'*J'arrive*,' Louis shouted back.

Everyone was seated by the time the food was carried from the oven to the table. Sara, wearing thick gloves, was frowning. The reason for the frown was made obvious when she removed the lid from the iron dish and it was revealed to be almost empty.

'I wondered why it was so light,' she croaked, her face red with rage.

What remained of the food was stuck to the bottom of the dish. It would be a hard job getting it clean.

Marie burst into tears. 'I'm hungry,' she sobbed.

Jessica managed to grab the dish seconds before Sara brought it down on Louis's head. 'Bastard!' she screamed.

'Ouch!' Jessica yelled, having forgotten the dish had come straight from the oven. She ran to the tap and poured cold water over her burnt hands.

'*Tu es un cochon, Papa*,' Frannie shouted. 'A horrible, horrible pig.'

'I didn't know it was for our tea,' Louis mumbled. 'Claud and Patric were hungry.'

'So you thought I had made chicken casserole for you and your friends? You think I am fool enough to make a meal for men I've never even heard of? Am I cook to the whole of bloody Paris?' Sara flung the dish into the sink. It made such a terrible noise that Marie began to cry again.

'The house will fall down,' she wailed.

'We were hungry,' Louis repeated, little realizing he was only making things worse. He looked genuinely ashamed.

'Well, bastard, now *I* am hungry, your girls are hungry, Jessica is hungry. We are all hungry, but you, you cannot possibly be hungry because you and your friends have eaten a casserole made for five people between you.'

'I think we should go out to dinner,' Jessica said, hoping her head wouldn't be bitten off. Sara was liable to throw caution and good manners to the winds when she was angry.

'Please, Mama, let's go out,' Maria pleaded.

Everybody sat and watched Sara as she gradually simmered down. Her breathing slowed, her shoulders sagged as her neck became less rigid and her lips became less tight, her eyes no longer looked as if they were emitting sparks.

'All right,' she said, and there was a general sigh of relief.

'If we eat at the Café Edgar across the road, I can keep an eye on the theatre,' Louis said. 'The audience for tonight's play will start arriving soon.'

'Then we most certainly will eat at the Café Edgar,' Sara said sarcastically, 'for we must never lose sight of the theatre.'

Jessica had always loved the theatre. Before she married Bertie, she had gone with Lydia to see many famous stars like Laurence Olivier, Vivien Leigh and John Gielgud at various theatres in Liverpool. And Bertie hadn't been averse to seeing a show on her birthday or on anniversaries.

She found Louis's *Petit Théâtre* fascinating and would have liked to become more involved, help with the costumes and the posters, watch rehearsals, had it not been for the animosity between Sara and her husband. It might have looked as if she was taking sides. It would help improve her French – she'd only understood half of the few plays she'd managed to see so far.

Louis was undoubtedly maddening to live with. He was thoughtless, his mind more preoccupied with his theatre rather than his family. Sara should have married someone like Bertie, someone who went to work at the same time every morning and returned home at the same time at night; a man who had weekends off, brought in the coal and did things like take the children for walks while his wife made the Sunday lunch.

Louis did none of these things and Sara would never get

used to it. There were times when he seemed to forget that he had a wife and children. He was writing scripts in his head or learning the words or working out the best way his latest play should be presented.

He was, in his own way, a remarkable man. But Sara never offered a word of encouragement or approval of his achievements. In an effort to turn him into a more normal husband, she dispatched him on messages and he would go to the wrong place or buy the wrong thing, or come back having met a friend and completely forgotten he'd been sent on an errand by his wife in the first place.

In the Café Edgar, Jessica and the Cotillards ate the food in silence apart from when speaking to the waiter. Martin, owner and maître d' of the restaurant, had welcomed them with a charming smile that was wasted on Sara, who bit his head off. They were the only customers at such an early hour. Louis remained subdued, Sara was still quietly fuming, the girls looked fed up, and Jessica's bandaged hands were hurting badly. More than anything, she wanted to be in her own room reading a book or just thinking.

Suddenly, Sara banged the table with her knife. Everybody, including Martin and the waiter, jumped. 'I have an announcement to make,' she said in a loud voice. 'I'm having a baby. The doctor says it's due to arrive in the middle of June.'

'Oh, Mama!' Marie burst into tears, whether of joy or sadness, Jessica couldn't tell.

Frannie rolled her eyes. '*Au secours!*' she drawled. (It meant 'help'.)

'Congratulations, Sara,' Jessica stammered.

Louis jumped to his feet and left the restaurant, leaving Jessica to pay the bill because Sara hadn't brought her bag.

It's going to be absolutely awful, she thought. Sara's going to be even more bad-tempered and unreasonable than ever. I won't be able to stand it. As soon as Christmas is over, I shall go back to Liverpool.

But there was nothing left for her in Liverpool. She'd go to London instead, get a job, find a flat, join things, make friends.

Sara looked as if she would snort fire any minute, Marie was sobbing her heart out, Frannie would have hated to know how lost and forlorn she looked. Across the street, the lights were on in the theatre and Jessica remembered the tickets she'd made for that night's performance – a play called *Mon Ami* written by Louis – were still in the house.

She realized she would never be more needed than she was here, in Paris with the Cotillards. She added a 10-franc tip to the money for the meal and got slowly to her feet. 'I'm going,' she said tiredly.

Frannie followed behind. She slipped her hand inside Jessica's then withdrew it quickly. 'I forgot your hands were burnt. Do they hurt badly?'

'They're not so bad,' Jessica sighed. 'Not so bad at all.'

Chapter 12

'Good morning.'

The speaker slid into the chair next to Jessica's while she was having coffee in La Caverne. When she looked, she recognized the man who'd given her his newspaper – just before Christmas, she remembered. Now it was April. She'd thought about him a few times since, but had never imagined seeing him again.

'Good morning.' She gave him a brief smile.

'I thought you might not be using this place any more – it's a bit dismal, don't you think?' He wrinkled his nose. 'Not good for anyone with a bad chest; all this smoke!'

'Do you have a bad chest?'

'As far as I know, my chest is perfectly healthy.' He thumped it and it made a hollow sound.

Jessica couldn't resist smiling. 'I come here because people generally never talk to me. I come to relax and think.' The smile turned into a laugh. 'Sorry if that sounds rude.'

The man laughed, too. 'It does, rather.' He held out his hand. 'Sam Deveraux, interpreter at the Canadian Embassy.'

So he was Canadian. She shook his hand. He had a nice firm grip. 'Jessica Farley.' She had no idea how to describe herself. 'Cook, nursemaid, theatre assistant, oh, and all sorts of other things . . .' Her voice trailed away.

He looked impressed. 'The ones you've mentioned so far sound interesting, in particular the theatre assistant.'

She explained what it involved. 'I write out the tickets and the programmes and provide refreshments in the interval.' She often wished she had the typewriter she'd stolen from her old house and had passed on to Mrs Quigley in Stanley Road, having never used it once in its new home. It would have saved a lot of time with the programmes. As for the tickets, all she wrote was the title of the play and the author; she could produce the required thirty in no time. 'Your job sounds interesting, too.'

He shook his head. His dark hair was very thick and slightly wavy. His eyes were brown with little gold shreds. 'It's as boring as hell,' he said flatly.

'How many languages do you speak?'

'Five fluently, three not so bad.'

Jessica reached for the shopping, mainly vegetables, from beneath the table. She had a feeling that Sam Deveraux was about to ask her out. It was a very nice thought; she liked him, and would have preferred not to turn him down, but she didn't want to get involved with a man. Soon she would be returning to England and she genuinely didn't have the time for a relationship outside the house. What was more, after Harve, it seemed wrong to lead a man on when she couldn't marry him.

'I have to be going,' she said. 'I have loads to do today.' It was true.

He picked up the bag for her. 'Will you be here tomorrow?' he asked hopefully.

'I usually shop every other day,' she told him. She wouldn't be coming to La Caverne again. It was a shame because she loved the coffee. She hurried away, waving. 'Goodbye,' she said in a rush.

'*Au revoir*,' Sam Deveraux called. His voice followed her out of the café. 'I would have come before, but I've been away since before Christmas.'

Jessica turned and waved again with her free hand, but

didn't speak. She wondered where he'd been? Canada, maybe. Her ability to attract men had taken her by surprise. A number of Louis's theatre friends had invited her out. Back in Liverpool, Harve had fallen in love with her – and she with him, she reminded herself. And of course there was Tom McGrath . . .

Bertie was the first man she'd gone out with – the only man, until Harve. She'd felt extraordinarily flattered, never dreaming that other men might have wanted to date her, too.

There was a spring in her step as she made her way home, stopping to buy two pounds of beef for a stew, milk and cream, and a couple of long, crusty loaves. The *boucher* asked if she would like the meat chopped up.

Jessica made a horrible face. '*S'il vous plaît, Monsieur Auteil,*' she said with a shudder.

The *boucher* laughed out loud, grabbed the chunk of bloody flesh, and attacked it with a hatchet. He was putting on the fervour for Jessica's benefit. He couldn't comprehend her dislike of dead animals and this was his way of making fun of it.

Jessica arrived home to find the girls had left for school, Louis was nowhere to be seen and was probably in the theatre, and Sara was still in bed.

Since the night in the Café Edgar when she announced she was expecting a baby, Sara must have decided to endure a frail, delicate pregnancy. Jessica was convinced she was, like the *boucher*, putting it on. She rose at midday with loads of sighs and a little rest in between putting on each item of clothing, then came downstairs clutching the banister, her lips curved in a brave smile. Jessica remembered she was training to be an actress when she'd met Louis.

'How do you feel this morning?' Jessica would ask.

'I'm bearing up,' Sara would reply gamely.

'You look well.'

She hated to be told that. 'Appearances can be deceptive,' she usually said, or sometimes she said nothing at all.

Irritating though Sara's brilliant acting could be, it was preferable to her endless fits of bad temper. And better for the unborn baby, too, otherwise the poor little mite would be in a continual state of nervous tension as it lay curled up in its mother's raging womb.

Afternoons, the women went for a stroll along the banks of the River Seine or window-shopped in one of the big leafy boulevards, stopping for coffee on the way home.

It was an enjoyable life. After tea, Sara would retire to the lounge on the first floor where she would listen to the wireless or read a book. Jessica would station herself in the theatre foyer until that night's performance began. Then she would bolt the door on the inside – it couldn't be locked properly in case someone wanted to get out – and help the girls with their homework, her command of the French language increasing all the time.

'You sound almost like a native,' Louis had said more than once.

Louis spent more time in the house and less in the theatre since Sara had gone through her astonishing change of personality. He talked to his daughters more, discussed the theatre with Jessica – not the artistic side of things, but the practical. He seemed to think she was an expert on running things.

'Sell wine?' he queried when Jessica suggested it.

'Before the play starts and during the intervals,' Jessica confirmed. 'We could sell it by the glass. That's what they did when I used to go to the theatre in Liverpool.'

'I knew they did it in big theatres, but I never thought of doing it in mine. What if people can't afford it?' he said worriedly.

'Then they can't have it.'

'But that hardly seems fair,' he protested. Jessica could see nothing unfair about it, but Louis went on, 'I don't like the idea of some people having wine and others not. It's not my idea of a just society and I'm not prepared to let it happen in my theatre. People paying to get in is one thing,' he said earnestly, 'after all, I have a family to keep, but making money when I don't need to is quite another.'

'Then why don't we ask them to give what they can afford? If they can't pay anything, then they can have the wine free. It'll just make for a nicer atmosphere if people can enjoy a drink between acts.' If insufficient money came in to cover the cost of the wine, then she'd put a stop to it.

Louis beamed. 'You're full of good ideas, Jessica.'

He came into the kitchen while she was unpacking the shopping on the morning she met Sam Deveraux for the second time.

'Bad news, I'm afraid,' he said gloomily.

'Is Sara unwell?' Jessica asked quickly.

'No. Great Britain is calling up men of twenty and twenty-one. I just heard it on the radio.'

Jessica carried the bloody parcel of beef to the meat safe while doing her best not to look at it. 'What for?'

Louis shrugged. 'To train as soldiers, I expect. What else would they want them for?'

'Oh, dear!' Jessica said inadequately. Hitler was forever invading one country, annexing another, building up his army to the extent that it could take on the entire world, or so it appeared to her. 'Yesterday, Sara said she was going to ask if you would be coming with us to England once the war begins.'

Louis frowned angrily. 'She did ask, and I said no.'

'Can't you bring yourself to leave the theatre?' She assumed that must be the reason he wouldn't leave.

'It's nothing to do with the theatre.' He looked even angrier. 'I'm not prepared to desert my country when it's in a state of war. I shall fight for it one way or another, not hide away in England.' Unexpectedly, he grinned. 'Naturally, Sara disapproves, but fortunately she's too weak to have hysterics.'

Jessica thought they should be grateful for small mercies, but didn't say so, despite it being true. She didn't want to appear critical of her friend. 'I'll go and wake her up,' she said instead.

She poured a glass of milk and took it upstairs. Sara was awake and staring out of the window. 'It looks nice outside,' she remarked.

'It's a lovely spring day,' Jessica sang. 'Though a bit nippy.'

Sara pushed herself to a sitting position on the bed. 'You sound happy.'

'Do I?' She was half-happy. She would never be truly, wholeheartedly happy again until she found her children. And how could anybody be really happy when the world was about to plunge into a war which, if it was anything like the last one, would be hell on earth, at least for the troops, if not ordinary people. No, it was meeting Sam Deveraux that had cheered her, despite knowing there was no chance they would meet again.

'Are you and Louis having an affair? Is that why you're so happy?'

What a *nerve*! Jessica banged the milk down on the bedside table so hard that it spilled. 'Honestly, Sara, you really are the end. Do you really think you can say things like that to people when there's no earthly reason at all?'

Sara actually had the cheek to sound annoyed. 'Well, he didn't sleep with me last night,' she said belligerently.

'He didn't sleep with me, either!' Afterwards, Jessica couldn't remember a time when she had so completely lost her temper. Not even with Bertie had she ever felt so cross. 'Louis probably slept in the theatre,' she said in a voice tight with fury. 'If you recall, just lately you've been complaining you need more room in bed. He was just being kind and gentlemanly. What a lousy opinion you must have of your husband and me.'

Sara began to cry. She often did when she realized she'd lost an argument or had spoken out of turn to the extent of causing real hurt. She wiped her eyes on the sheet while sobbing through it. 'I'm sorry, Jessica,' she said piteously, 'but you don't realize what it's like having a baby. Your mind goes completely haywire and you have all sorts of bad thoughts, suspicions and horrible dreams. And I'm so tired all the time, as well as feeling slightly nauseous. And . . . and . . .'

Jessica butted in before Sara could think up more excuses for having accused her of having an affair with Louis. 'I know exactly what having a baby is like,' she said quietly. 'In fact, I've had two – and my husband wasn't remotely as understanding as yours, and I didn't have a friend staying who did all the housework. Yet *my* mind didn't go haywire, I didn't have any bad thoughts or bad dreams. What's more, I wouldn't have dreamed of accusing another woman of having an affair with my husband.'

Without waiting for Sara's reaction, she slammed out of the room, ran downstairs, grabbed her handbag off the sideboard and her coat out of the hall, shouted 'ta-ra' to an astonished Louis, and left the house.

Her bad temper disappeared when she stepped outside, quite literally swept away by the fresh, tangy air. She strode along the boulevard de Sébastopol. The girls were already out, waiting for customers in doorways and on corners, shivering in their thin clothes. Such sights had shocked her to the core when she'd first come to Paris. Back in Liverpool, she had never knowingly set eyes on a prostitute, but Bertie had claimed that she, his wife, had been taken for one in The Temple hotel the day she'd gone upstairs with Tom McGrath. It meant she had something in common with these girls.

Apart from the places that sold food, shops in the city didn't open until between ten o'clock and noon. Most shutters were either up or were being slowly removed by yawning staff. There were few sightseers around.

She crossed the rue de Rivoli and walked along the river-bank until she came to the bridge that led to Notre-Dame, the magnificent cathedral whose first stone was laid in the twelfth century. There were plenty of tourists here. Louis said an uncommonly large number had come to admire the beauties of Paris before there was a chance of them being bombed to smithereens by the Luftwaffe.

Jessica entered the massive church, still overawed by its size and the sound of distant voices; this must have been well over her hundredth visit. Mass was being said at one of the small altars on the periphery. She genuflected, lit a candle and knelt to pray, but was hindered by thoughts instead. At first, the thoughts were of her children. It was eighteen months since she'd seen them. She tried to imagine how much they would have changed since then, but it was impossible. They would be taller, naturally. Dora's hair might have been left to grow longer. What size shoes did Jamie take these days? His feet had been growing at a rapid rate. Thinking of them now did not induce an influx of tears. She didn't know whether she had hardened to her loss or got used to it. But she would never get over it.

She prayed for Sara, for her baby to arrive safely, and for it to be a girl. Sara wanted another girl, Marguerite. 'I shall call her Margie – or would Rita be better?' Louis was allowed no say in the matter. She couldn't abide boys: 'Tough, rough little creatures. They kick you to death before they're even born.'

Jamie had kicked Jessica, who hadn't minded. She'd just laid her hands on her stomach and enjoyed the activities of her first baby inside her womb. She'd been really angry with Sara for saying she didn't know what it was like to be pregnant, so angry that she told her she had children and a husband. Sara would be aching to know further details. Well, she could go on aching, because she wasn't going to be told a single word, though, knowing Sara, she was probably too concerned with herself to have noticed what Jessica had said.

She remembered that she was supposed to praying for Sara, not having an imaginary argument. She said three Our Fathers and three Hail Marys and left the church. Back in the rue de Rivoli, she sat on one of the chairs outside a restaurant and ordered coffee. When it came, she lit a cigarette. She'd cut down drastically on smoking since coming to Paris – Sara didn't like it and considered it bad for the children.

For almost an hour, she sat and watched the world go by, enjoying the freedom of doing absolutely nothing and having no one to please but herself. Just now, she wasn't in the mood to go back home and face a possibly contrite Sara, and an apologetic Louis. The children would sense something had happened when they came home from school, that there'd been a row.

She left the restaurant and was strolling further along the rue de Rivoli when she noticed a cinema down a side street. The picture showing was *Anna Karenina*. It would almost certainly be in English with French subtitles. Even if it had been dubbed into French she would understand most of it.

This time, the film didn't reduce her to tears as it had on the other occasions she'd seen it. She actually felt quite impatient with Anna for falling in love with such a horrid individual as Vronsky. Anna's husband was played by Basil Rathbone, a Liverpudlian like herself. She warmed towards the tall, gaunt actor in a way she hadn't done before. In Liverpool, his family had a street called after them in the Wavertree area.

When she came out of the cinema, a wind had sprung up, the sun had disappeared and it felt colder. She turned left, then left again, feeling that if she continued she would eventually come to the rue de la Grand Truanderie and home. But, to her dismay, after a while she found herself completely lost. She could easily have stopped and asked the way, but she'd been living in Paris for more than six months and it was time she knew the way herself.

Anyway, what was she, a 29-year-old woman, doing wandering alone in a foreign country where the only person she knew was her unpleasant friend, Sara? She shivered, wanting to cry, wanting her children to hold and kiss and talk to, rushing blindly now, up and down strange streets whose names she didn't recognize, growing more and more desperate.

Eventually she arrived at the boulevard de Sébastopol, bursting into it, seeing the *magasin de chaussures* on the corner where she always admired the contents of the window, the beautiful shoes she'd never seen the likes of before.

She stopped dead and waited until she'd got her breath back, before making her way sedately back to the house where she happened to be living now, but didn't belong.

The Cotillards were in the kitchen, all four of them sitting round the table eating. Someone, either Sara or Louis, had made the beef stew. The HP sauce Jessica had managed to track down for herself in a little grocers that sold English food, was on the table in front of a knife and fork and a wooden place mat – *her* place, Jessica realized. It had been set because she was expected back any minute.

Sara got to her feet and came towards her. 'Are you all right?' Her stomach was absolutely huge. Jessica was suddenly struck by just how big she had grown. It was almost as if she'd increased massively in size since that morning. 'I'm sorry,' she whispered.

'I'm fine,' Jessica lied. Or was she lying? The odd feelings she'd been having had fallen from her like a cloak.

Louis put a plate of stew in her place. 'It tastes good,' he said.

'In Liverpool, we call this scouse,' Jessica commented. She sat down and reached for the sauce bottle.

The girls grinned at her from across the table. 'I've got a composition to do for my homework,' Frannie said in French. 'What is "*composition*" in English?'

'Composition is an English word, too. Or you could say essay. What is it about?'

'What I would like to be when I grow up.'

'And what *would* you like to be when you grow up?' her father asked.

'I'd like to be all sorts of things,' Frannie said seriously, 'but most of all I'd like to be a soldier.'

'Do you have women soldiers in France?' Jessica asked. Tom McGrath's secretary had joined the Army, she remembered.

Louis said France did, but couldn't remember what they were called. Jessica tucked into her meal. By the time she had finished, she felt thoroughly at home again and it seemed like a perfectly ordinary day. Sara didn't mention anything about Jessica's husband and children. The angry words had gone completely over her head.

As Louis and his writing friends could not possibly have kept the *Petit Théâtre* supplied with a never-ending succession of new plays – there was a fresh programme every fortnight – inevitably it became necessary for old plays to be performed. This week it was *La Lettre*, written by the British author and playwright W. Somerset Maugham, a play that Jessica had seen many years before at the Royal Court in Liverpool and was anxious to see again.

She was in the brightly lit foyer of the tiny theatre dispensing free programmes and tickets at 23 francs a time, welcoming new faces with a smile, shaking hands with the people she already knew, when a familiar figure walked in, though not one she'd seen before in the theatre.

'Good evening, Miss Farley,' Sam Deveraux said with a little bow as he removed his black slouch hat. He actually wore a dress suit, the shirt brilliantly white, and looked desperately handsome as well as completely out of place among the rest of the audience, some of whom were quite scruffily dressed, the women included.

Jessica gasped. 'How did you know where the theatre was?'

'It would seem this is the smallest theatre in Paris,' he said seriously, though his lips twitched in a half-smile. 'Somebody at the embassy knew exactly where you were.'

She hadn't realized the theatre was so well known. 'Would you like some wine?' she asked. 'It's ten francs a glass – if you can afford it.'

'He bowed again. 'Yes, please, and yes, I can afford it.'

'It will take the roof off your mouth and the enamel off your teeth,' she promised.

'I don't mind.' This time he gave in to a smile. 'Where do I leave my hat?'

'On your knee. Excuse me.' She turned away to deal with the new people who'd just come in.

Instead of entering the theatre, Sam Deveraux waited in the foyer until all the tickets had been sold and Jessica had bolted the door. He had attracted much interest in his grand clothes. 'Isn't he a famous Hollywood actor?' one woman had remarked to her partner. 'I'm sure we saw him in a film with Carole Lombard.'

'You'll have to squeeze on to the end of a bench,' Jessica told him.

'I don't mind that, either.' He was extremely easygoing. 'May I please have more wine?'

She refilled his glass, telling him he was a glutton for punishment.

'Do you intend to watch the play?' he enquired.

'I do, actually. I saw it years ago in Liverpool and I'd like to see what it's like in French, not that I'll understand every word.'

'I noticed a rather nice restaurant across the road.' He

nodded through the window at the Café Edgar. 'Why don't I explain the bits you don't understand afterwards over supper?'

'Why not?' What harm would it do? As soon as Sara's baby was born, she and Jessica would return to Liverpool along with the girls. There wouldn't be time to become emotionally involved with Sam Deveraux.

Chapter 13

Sara's baby was born at home in the middle of June. She had a boy, Joseph, named after her father, though spelled the English way.

Jessica's heart had sunk when the midwife announced the baby was a boy, knowing how much Sara had wanted a girl and half-expecting her to burst into tears or complain bitterly it was Louis's fault. But she seemed perfectly happy with her little fat baby when Jessica and the girls went in to see her after the midwife had gone.

'Isn't he beautiful?' she said happily, as if a boy had always been her first choice. 'Will you be his godmother, Jessica?'

'It would be a privilege.'

A few days later, a letter came from Will to say that Lena had also given birth to a boy: 'We're calling him Daniel, not for any particular reason, but because we both like the name, as does Calum, who we felt had a right to be consulted. Once Lena is on her feet again, I am taking her and the boys to meet Mother. It's unfair to keep her in ignorance any longer, and now we are an established family hopefully she will find it easier to accept us and not try to interfere.'

Jessica had become aunt to Daniel and godmother to Joseph within the space of a few days.

A few weeks later, she approached Sara about returning to Liverpool. They were taking Joseph for a walk in his giant second-hand pram and had stopped for a rest in the gardens of the Palais Royal. Sara lifted up the baby, threw him over her shoulder, where he settled like a little old man with fluffy yellow hair, and began to rub his back in case he had any wind left after breakfast.

'But I'm not sure if I want to leave Paris,' she said, making a face. 'I've grown to love it here while you've been living with us. I'm sure we'll all be quite safe if there's a war.'

'I won't feel safe, not at all,' Jessica protested. 'I'm English, one of the enemy. If the Germans invade France, I'll be arrested and sent to a prison camp or something. And the same goes for you.' She shook her head. 'I have no intention of staying in Paris.'

'I'm English but married to a Frenchman,' Sara argued. 'Doesn't that make me French? And Germany invade France! Whatever gave you that idea?'

'It's the whole point of war, Sara, powerful countries taking over countries not so powerful in order to make their own empire bigger and even more powerful. What's more,' Jessica went on, 'your father's really worried about you.' Sara would argue with Death that it wasn't the right time for her to die. 'That's why he wanted me to come to Paris, to make sure you left before the war began.' She watched a tiny boy chase a pigeon, frowning indignantly at the bird when it flew away. It was such an innocent and charming sight that it was hard to believe something as cruel and murderous as war was expected any minute.

In readiness for the expected air raids, public buildings had been hidden behind mounds of sand bags, sirens had been installed to warn the population of approaching planes, shelters built. Josef and Will's letters confirmed it was the same back in England.

'There's a trembling anticipation in the air,' Josef had written, his prose much more dramatic than Will's. 'We lie in bed at night expecting the worst.'

'It won't be any safer in Liverpool than it is here,' Sara continued to argue. 'And at least here I have my own residence. In Liverpool, I'd be living in a tiny house with Papa and Aunt Ruth. She'll complain about the children – I know that for certain because she used to complain about me when I was little and we didn't even live under the same roof. And,' she continued indignantly, 'I was an exceptionally well-behaved child, whereas Françoise is a little bitch and Joseph does cry rather a lot.' Joseph burped, but she continued to rub his back as if it gave her something to do.

'But what if Paris is bombed?' Jessica asked.

'Is there the faintest chance on earth that Liverpool won't be, what with the docks virtually on everybody's doorstep? Frankly, I'd feel much safer from the bombing living here.'

Jessica had wanted to avoid the issue of religion if she could, but it was the final bullet in the gun that would hopefully persuade Sara to take herself and her children to the country of her birth.

'You're Jewish, Sara,' she said bluntly. 'Your children are half-Jewish. Hitler hates Jews. Surely you are aware of that? There are concentration camps in Germany, Jews are forced to wear yellow stars on their sleeves, they have been ordered to leave their jobs and their possessions have been commandeered. And when Germany invaded Austria, they were treated appallingly, made to scrub the streets while the rest of the population looked on and laughed.'

But Sara even had an answer to this. Since leaving Liverpool, she informed Jessica, she had virtually forgotten she was Jewish. She hadn't been near a synagogue, or observed any special Jewish days for years and years. 'The children are Catholic like Louis – well, you know that. Joseph was baptised in St Eustache.'

Jessica was finding it hard to keep her temper. 'The Germans won't be interested in any of that,' she said patiently, 'only in the fact that you are Jewish. They will ask for your papers and it will be on your birth certificate – at least, I think it will.' She wasn't wholly sure. If someone was married to a Catholic, had Catholic children, perhaps the fact that they were Jewish would go unnoticed. But Sara was also English, which could well be regarded as a good enough reason to be sent to a camp, no matter who she happened to be married to. Jessica had started the conversation feeling pretty sure of herself, but by now felt totally at a loss.

Sara put Joseph back into his pram and they made their way home. Halfway there, she remarked casually, 'Nicole Auteil, the butcher's wife, was Jewish. She was born in Rostov in Russia. Unfortunately, she died in childbirth about four years ago. She was ever so sweet.'

Jessica felt herself go cold inside. 'Were you two friends?' she asked.

'Good friends, yes.'

'Did you have many good friends who were Jewish?'

'A few.' Sara shrugged indifferently. 'We all had small children and used to meet in the Tuilleries when the weather was nice. I only went because of Nicole and stopped when she died; I found it boring and Frannie used to bite the other children. One of the women sometimes comes with her husband to the theatre.'

Jessica sighed. She didn't feel like continuing with the argument just now, but very soon she would tell Sara that it was imperative she leave France as early as possible. How many people in Paris knew she was Jewish? Once the Germans arrived, it wouldn't be safe for her, or her children, to live in the city any more.

When they got home, Jessica found Sam Deveraux waiting for her. He often visited during the day when he was short of work at the embassy, which seemed to be most days. He'd been in the theatre with Louis, but came into the house when he heard her arrive with Sara and the baby.

'Hi, there,' he said, popping his head round the kitchen door.

'Hello.' Jessica liked his informality and easygoing manner. Nothing made him lose his temper apart from any mention of Adolf Hitler. Sara really liked him and welcomed him into her home on his ever-increasing visits.

'Hello, Sam,' she said cheerily as she removed Joseph's knitted bonnet and thick cardigan.

Sam came in and chucked the baby underneath his double chin. 'He must have grown another inch since I last saw him,' he remarked. He had taken off his suit jacket and tie, and looked healthy and handsome in his open-necked white shirt.

'You only saw Joseph yesterday afternoon,' Jessica reminded him. 'If he grows at that rate, he'll be six feet tall by the time he's two.'

Jessica's shoulders were squeezed and the top of her head kissed. Although they saw each other most days, a casual kiss, a squeeze of her hand, an occasional hug, was the limit of her intimate contact with Sam Deveraux, which suited her perfectly and no doubt suited him. They got on well together and agreed on most things. In the very near future, Sam would return to Canada and Jessica to Liverpool. They would never see each other again and that suited her perfectly, too – and no doubt him.

That evening, she wrote to Josef Davidson and asked if it was possible for him to rent a bigger house in Liverpool.

'Sara is worried that living in Ruth's house will be too cramped. She is also concerned that Ruth will find the children rather tiresome,' she wrote. She remembered the unpleasant atmosphere a few years ago when she'd had tea at the house. It had been New Year's Eve, she remembered. She wouldn't have fancied living in the same house as Ruth either, even without children.

'I am having trouble persuading Sara to leave Paris,' she

continued. 'I think it would help if she knew she was returning to a house big enough for herself and the children.'

She finished the letter, put it in an envelope and addressed it. She'd buy a stamp tomorrow, not the usual half a dozen, just the one, in case there was a chance she wouldn't need to write any more letters to Liverpool.

It was like living on a knife edge, like waiting for an axe to fall every single day. Sara was driving them all crazy. Even Sam Deveraux, who didn't really know her all that well, felt impatient with her.

'Any minute now, most of our staff, me included, will fly back to Canada,' he told Jessica, 'but a few are returning to London by train and ferry. I can arrange for extra seats for you, Sara and the children, but I'll need to know soon. Every form of transport is going to be crowded with people trying to leave France.' As Canada was part of the British Commonwealth, their embassy would close at the same time as Britain's. The American embassy would remain open for as long as that country remained uninvolved in the war.

Louis pleaded with his wife to pack her own and their children's belongings and make her way to Liverpool – or somewhere else, if she preferred, as long as it was away from mainland Europe. 'What about Ireland or even the United States? Sam might be able to get you into Canada.'

If Sara decided not to go, Jessica resolved under no circumstances would she stay once war was declared. She had children of her own that she hoped to see again one day and wanted to remain alive for them. As for Sara, she had lost all patience with her. They hardly spoke nowadays. She had a feeling Sara had every intention of going to England, but was enjoying being the focus of attention, keeping them all dangling on a string.

Increasingly desperate letters arrived almost daily from Joseph, who had managed to rent a nice, spacious house in the countryside not far from Kirkby Castle where he worked. Quite a few young men who worked in the factory had been called up, he told her.

Will wrote, sounding anxious, wanting to know when his sister would be coming home: 'And Mother is concerned about you, keeps wondering where you are. Is it all right to tell her you're in Paris, but coming back to this country soon? By the way, she has welcomed Lena and the children into the family with open arms.'

Jessica bought more stamps and wrote to say that it was all right to tell her mother she would be home soon. It was a relief to know she was concerned about her. Perhaps Jessica had been away long enough to be forgiven. When she got home she would go and see her straight away.

Throughout August, Germany issued frequent warnings of its intention to invade Poland, making war a certainty as Britain and France had signed a treaty to protect the country if it was attacked. Pierre Auteil, the son of the butcher, was called up, as well as two of the young actors who appeared regularly in Louis's theatre.

At last, when the month was almost over, Sara began to prepare to leave, and everyone concerned uttered a sigh of relief. Jessica decided to wear her best hat for the journey and only to take the clothes with her that she'd recently bought for when Sam took her out to tea or dinner. She imagined them hanging in her wardrobe until she was an old woman when she would fling open the door to show people. 'These are clothes I bought a long time ago in Paris,' she would say.

It was a hot, sultry morning and the Gare du Nord station was packed solidly with passengers and their friends and relatives who'd come to see them off, all walking briskly in different directions, tripping over or bumping into each other. The atmosphere was bad-tempered and over-wrought, and there was hardly a smile to be seen. Impossibly long queues snaked from the ticket offices, ending somewhere unseen.

Louis, who was carrying the big suitcase containing everything important, got lost almost straight away. It was Jessica who found the platform where a train stood impatiently puffing smoke and waiting to transport them to Calais. She signalled to Sara, who was carrying the baby, to follow. Marie, sobbing silently, was clinging to her mother's skirt and Frannie clutched Jessica's hand when she really needed both to carry her own luggage.

Someone remarked that the first class carriages were at the front, which was a relief because every compartment they'd passed so far had been full to capacity.

'Hurry up!' Sara said from behind.

'I'm hurrying,' Jessica snapped. After dawdling for so many weeks, Sara now seemed in a desperate hurry to board the train when there was still quarter of an hour before it was due to leave.

They had reached carriage B. The girls scrambled on first. 'We're in compartment number six,' Jessica told them. She took Sara's handbag and parcel of baby things for the journey and helped her on to the train before getting on herself. As she struggled along the corridor a familiar scream rent the air which she recognized as coming from Sara.

'What's the matter?' She had arrived at the door of their compartment, longing to sit down. Last night, she'd found it surprisingly painful saying goodbye to Sam Deveraux. Already, she was looking forward to receiving the letter he'd promised to send to her in Liverpool even though she'd thought she wouldn't care if she never saw him again. She badly wanted to sit and think about this, to sort out her feelings.

'Frannie's not here,' Sara screeched. 'Marie said she just went to the other end of the carriage and got off again.'

By now, Marie was crying loudly. 'She said she didn't want to go to Liverpool, that she'd sooner stay in Paris with Papa.'

'And where the hell is Papa with the suitcase?' Sara had only just noticed that Louis wasn't there.

'I'll go and find them both,' Jessica vowed. The sooner she saw the back of the Cotillard family the better. Once they were in Liverpool, it would be a long time before she made any attempt to see them, even Frannie. She put her own small suitcase and her hat on the rack and left the train, clutching only her handbag. There was no sign anywhere of either Louis or his daughter.

She walked back to the ticket barrier. Still no sign. Where Louis was concerned, it seemed advisable to stand still in the hope of him seeing her rather than the other way round. This idea seemed to work because a red-faced, breathless Louis suddenly skidded to a halt in front of her and she directed him towards the train.

'Carriage B,' she shouted after him. 'Compartment six.'

As Frannie had got off the train to avoid going to England, there seemed little sense in merely waiting for her to approach. She had to be found – and soon. Jessica began to rush around the station, shouting her name. She investigated the ladies' toilets, even to the extent of looking under the doors in the hope of seeing a pair of childish feet. She looked behind the newspaper kiosk and the sweet stall, then went outside the station to see if Frannie was hiding there. All she could see were endless taxis drawing up and frantic passengers rushing into the station as if the German Army was following close behind. Jessica returned to the station, frantic herself by now.

She was met with the sound of a loud whistle, a train hooting in reply, and watched in despair as the train containing Sara, two of her children and Jessica's suitcase and her best hat set off on its journey to Calais.

'Jessica!' It was Louis standing some distance away and waving. 'You have missed the train,' he shouted.

'I know,' she shouted back. 'I lost all track of time.' She began to walk towards him and discovered she was limping.

Her heart was beating crazily and she was also perspiring profusely. 'Did you get the suitcase to Sara before they left?'

'Yes,' he panted.

'Did Frannie turn up?' They'd reached each other by now. It was a bit late to think this now, but she should have stayed close to the train. Just imagine if Frannie had merely been tormenting her mother by getting off and had caught it after all.

'No.' Louis grasped her shoulders. 'Sara was so angry; no Frannie, no you, nearly no suitcase.'

'I've missed the train!' Jessica said, almost to herself. Her possessions were on their way to Calais, but not her. What was she supposed to do now?

'Where is Frannie?' Louis ran his fingers through his golden hair.

Jessica didn't care. She reckoned Frannie was somewhere close and was likely to show herself any minute now that the train to Calais had gone. 'I need a coffee and a cigarette,' she said to Louis. 'Frannie will turn up when she's ready.'

Frannie turned up when Jessica and her father were in the restaurant. '*Bonjour*,' she said cheekily.

'Do you realize the enormity of what you've done?' Jessica asked coldly, suppressing her desire to strangle the child in full view.

'I'm sorry.' The little girl's expression completely changed and she burst into tears. 'I honestly didn't mean for you to miss the train, Jessica, but it was no use telling Mama I didn't want to go to Liverpool; she would have just said I was going and that was that. I didn't expect you to come after me. I'm really, really sorry.'

'And so you should be,' Louis said fondly. He had never been known to speak angrily to his daughters, let alone punish them. 'So you wanted to stay with Papa, eh?'

'Yes, Papa.' Frannie crawled on to his knee and began to suck her thumb.

Jessica finished the cigarette, drained the coffee, and asked if they'd mind going home so she could think quietly and peacefully about what to do next. 'I'll pay for a taxi,' she offered.

Would the place ever be the same without Sara sitting at the kitchen table bellowing at everyone in sight? Despite this having got on Jessica's nerves ever since her arrival, she nevertheless missed the sight and sound of her friend when she returned to the unnaturally quiet house. She made coffee and the three of them sat awkwardly round the table, not quite knowing what to say.

'I'll ring Sam in a minute,' Jessica eventually said. Her still unsettled heart gave a little jump at the thought of seeing him again. There was a post office in the boulevard de Sébastopol with a row of telephone boxes inside. 'He might be able to get me on a train tomorrow.' And Frannie, if she agreed to go this time.

'I thought he was leaving today, same as you, but on a plane.' Louis didn't look the slightest bit sad his wife and two of his children were on a train racing towards another country. Jessica wouldn't be surprised if he was pleased that Sara had gone, if not Marie and Joseph.

Early in the afternoon she rang the Canadian embassy. The telephone was answered by a man who spoke good English with a French accent.

'The embassy has virtually closed down,' he told Jessica. 'There is only a skeleton staff left.'

'I was hoping to speak to Mr Deveraux,' she said, though it was probably hopeless.

'I'm afraid I don't know if Mr Deveraux is here or not. The bulk of the staff left for Canada this morning. If he should turn up, who shall I tell him was calling?'

For a moment, she actually forgot what surname she was using. 'Jessica Farley,' she said after a pause.

Sam arrived at tea-time, just as Frannie and Jessica were sitting down to onion soup left in the pot from the day before, with bread and cheese. Louis had disappeared into the theatre and couldn't be found when Frannie had gone to look for him.

'Well, what's all this?' Sam said. 'I could hardly believe it when I called in the embassy to collect my luggage and was informed that you'd telephoned earlier. I thought you'd be halfway to Calais by then.'

She told him what had happened, not caring that Frannie, the person responsible for her missing the train, was sitting at the table looking both ashamed and defiant.

'I don't like Liverpool,' she said in a low voice when Jessica had finished.

'How would you know?' Jessica snapped. 'You've never been there.'

'I just *know*.' With that, Frannie announced she was going to look for her papa again because she was worried about him.

After she'd gone, Jessica turned to Sam. 'I was wondering if you could possibly get me a seat tomorrow,' she asked. 'It wouldn't have to be first class. I don't care how I travel.' If he wasn't able to help, she'd just have to stand in a queue and hope she'd get a ticket when she reached the front. And she didn't know what to do about Frannie – it was up to Louis to sort it out.

Sam's face wore a look of deep concern. 'Lord, Jess, I'm sorry, but there's nothing I can do – except come to the station with you and help you buy a ticket. The embassy has virtually closed down altogether. If I returned now, I'm not sure if I could get back in.'

'But where is your luggage? I thought you were flying home today?'

179

He grinned. 'It's next door in the theatre.'

'What time does your plane take off?'

'It took off five minutes ago,' he said, looking at his watch.

'What!' Jessica leaped to her feet. 'You've missed it.'

Sam put his hand on her shoulder, lowered her back into the chair and sat in the next one. 'It doesn't matter,' he said easily.

Jessica was struck dumb. Too much was happening. When she'd got up that morning, she'd anticipated being in Liverpool by tonight. To be truthful, she hadn't been looking forward to it with untold delight, but it was how the day was supposed to go. It was against all expectations that she found herself still in Paris.

And now it would seem Sam's plans had also changed, but he didn't seem to care.

'What do you intend to do now?' she asked. 'Why did you change your mind?'

'Finding that you were still here.' He slid his arms round her and pulled her towards him. 'I really missed you last night,' he whispered in her ear, 'though I didn't expect to.'

'I missed you, too,' Jessica whispered back.

He kissed her properly for the very first time, a long, sweet, warm kiss. The kiss was something else that she hadn't expected. This day was turning out to be one of the strangest of her life.

Three days later, on a Sunday, Jessica, Sam and Frannie were listening to the wireless and heard the British Prime Minister, Neville Chamberlain, declare that Germany had refused to retreat from Poland and the two countries were now at war. Later in the day, the French President, Albert Lebrun, did the same.

After the second announcement, Frannie ran in to the

theatre to give her father the news. She and Louis came back a few minutes later. For some reason Louis must have felt compelled to shake hands, first with Jessica, whom he also kissed on both cheeks, then Sam.

'What's happening now?' he asked. The question was directed at them both.

For the last few days, Sam had been living in the house, sleeping in Marie's room. The two men, almost the same age, enjoyed each other's company. Sam said, 'Stay, I suppose, that's if you'll have me. Nothing's going to happen for a long time. I may as well be here as anywhere.'

'I'm glad!' Louis smiled. 'Really glad.' He squeezed Sam's shoulder and kissed Jessica again.

'I'm glad too.' Frannie looked extremely pleased with herself, as though this arrangement was exactly what she had wanted. '*Je suis très, très* happy.'

Sunday was the day the *Petit Théâtre* was normally closed, but people came all the same, as if they felt the need to explain what the war meant for them and listen to others talk about the previous war, the one to end all wars, as it had been called at the time.

Some climbed on to the tiny stage to explain their feelings, to say what a mad, mad world it was that wars were fought at all. 'You'd think we were wild animals, not human beings,' proclaimed a very old man.

A few of the young ones announced that first thing in the morning they would call in at the recruiting office and volunteer to fight. A boy of no more than fourteen swore that if the Germans should ever set foot in his country he would personally kill as many as he could; a grey-haired woman declared passionately that she would help him.

When the time came for them to leave, for the first occasion ever in Louis's theatre, the audience stood to attention and sang the national anthem, the Marsellaise, with all their hearts and souls.

Afterwards, they left the theatre quietly, wondering what lay ahead.

Chapter 14

1940

'*O Romeo, Romeo pourquoi es-tu, Romeo?*' Juliet said in her sweet, girlish voice. It wasn't possible to create a balcony on the small stage, so Juliet spoke from a window cut in the plywood scenery painted to look like an old grey stone wall. The long hair of her blonde wig fell over the sill.

'*Quelle lumière jaillit par cette fenêtre? Voilà l'Orient, et Juliette est le soleil!*' (But, soft, what light through yonder window breaks? It is the east and Juliette is the sun.) Romeo was kneeling on the stage and his bones creaked as he got to his feet.

Nadia and Georges Jourdan had been married for nearly fifty years. Jessica had never heard of them, but Louis said they'd been an institution in the world of French theatre until two years ago when Georges had lost his sight. They had actually offered to appear in Louis's theatre when word had reached them that he was having trouble finding actors. Many of his regular male performers had been called up or had volunteered to fight. Others, women included, had moved to towns and villages in other parts of France to be with their families, or had gone abroad to hopefully find work in America where Broadway as well as Hollywood beckoned.

Two of the remaining actresses were playing male parts in *Romeo and Juliet* – Louis had a part, too. He had already written a play set in a convent with an all-female cast and Sam Deveraux had translated one called *The Women* by Clare

Boothe Luce that had been a hit on the American stage some years before. It was in rehearsal with a group of amateur actors – women were more readily available than men – and due to be performed the week after next when the present play finished its two-week run. The Jourdans would appear again within the month and had yet to decide on the play. They knew so many by heart and had a wide variety to choose from.

War or no war, Louis was determined his little theatre would never close.

No one laughed at the two elderly actors playing characters less than a quarter of their ages. Nadia spoke with the voice of a fourteen-year-old, but the heavy stage make-up had collected in the crevices of her cheeks and round her mouth, making her look even older than her nearly seventy years. Although he was two years his wife's senior, Georges looked younger, was less wrinkled, but his movements were slow and unsure.

There was something terribly touching about this aged Romeo and Juliet, these sparkling stars of the French stage, not quite so lustrous now, but putting all they had into their performances. They could not have acted with more feeling and sensitivity had they been at the Comédie-Français. A star-struck Louis couldn't believe his luck. Not only had the theatre been packed to capacity every night, it would have been possible to have shown the play twice, even three times every day to a crowded house.

Since war had been declared six months before, it was rare that any theatre in the city had much in the way of empty seats. Their country was in mortal danger with the mighty German Army literally on its doorstep, and Parisians felt the need to be with each other. In Louis's little theatre, they sat with their shoulders pressed against each other, taking comfort from the fact that they were all in this together – and helping to keep them all warm.

It was the coldest winter anybody had ever known. Icicles

184

hung outside the windows, animals left outside froze during the night, and vehicles stuck to the icy streets. The air was painful to breathe and emerged in little anguished puffs of white.

The heating for both the theatre and the house came from the kitchen range where the food was cooked and water was heated to be carried through pipes to a radiator in the living room upstairs and the theatre. However, fuel of any sort was difficult to get and the water that ran through the pipes into the radiators and out of the taps was only faintly warm. Louis kept a brick in the oven during the day, then wrapped it in a towel for Frannie to take to bed at night.

It was the cold that had led Jessica and Sam to sleep together. 'Do you fancy having a human hot water bottle tonight?' Sam had said one freezing December night – Christmas had been less than a week away.

It seemed very unromantic, but wasn't unromantic at all when it had happened. It was tender and sweet because they'd been friends before becoming passionate and romantic lovers. Now they slept in each other's arms with Jessica wondering how she, a modest, well-brought-up convent girl, had managed to make love with four different men before reaching the age of thirty. It seemed terribly shocking and even more shocking that she didn't care.

She appreciated being with Sam over Christmas when thinking about her lost children could easily have made her lose her mind. Had Bertie taken them to a place where they'd be safe during the war?

Where *were* they? It would have been easy to tear her hair out with frustration. There were times when she was tormented with grief and a longing to see her children again, though she presented a calm, untroubled face to the world and nobody would ever have known.

Louis, playing the prince, spoke the final words of the play. '*Car jamais aventure ne fut plus douloureuse que celle de Juliette et de son Romeo.*' (For never was there a story of more woe than this of Juliette and her Romeo.)

It was over.

The audience rose to its feet and cheered the two stars when the curtain lifted and they came on hand in hand to take their bow.

Nadia was presented with a single red rose, as she was every night. She accepted graciously, but didn't speak. Both she and Georges looked tired. After they had changed, they would take a taxi back to their apartment on the Quai de la Tournelle in the Latin Quarter. They absolutely refused to let Louis pay either for the taxi or their performance. Jessica got the impression that they admired him as much as he adored them.

After the Jourdans had gone, only a handful of people left the theatre. The rest stayed and began to talk about the play, the weather, the war, and anything else they could think of. At times, the discussions got quite heated. Louis wandered around with a jug of wine, filling up glasses and not getting a franc in return. Had Sara been there, she would have burst a blood vessel.

Jessica and Sam returned to the house next door with Frannie, who had been allowed to stay up because it was Saturday and there was no school the next day. Ostensibly, they left to put Frannie to bed, but in reality because they wanted to go to bed themselves, and not just because it was cold.

For all Frannie's initial bravado, she had eventually confessed that she missed her mother and Marie.

'And Joseph just a little bit. I didn't realize it, but I even miss Mama's screaming,' she told Jessica.

'Do you wish you'd gone to Liverpool now?'

'Oh, no!' The little girl made a horrified face. 'I'd sooner be here with you and Papa and Sam, but it'd be nice if Mama could be here for just one day a week.'

A single letter had managed to reach them a few days after the war had begun. It was from Sara, written in pencil while on the train or the boat across the Channel and posted in Dover, demanding that her daughter be dispatched to Liverpool forthwith accompanied by Jessica who, she hinted, had also deliberately missed the train. On arrival, Frannie would be in receipt of a jolly good hiding.

Jessica imagined the anger passing from her old friend on to the paper. She supposed it would be relatively easy to go home now that the initial rush was over, though there was always the risk the Luftwaffe would bomb the Channel ports or the ferries. The loss of shipping to the curse of U-boats had led to terrible loss of life. Even without this risk, she had no wish to leave France, despite Paris being more dangerous than Liverpool. Paris was a mere drive away from Germany, the two countries separated by something called the Maginot Line, a fortified wall of troops and weaponry that kept the enemy at bay. In order to reach the British Isles, the Germany Army would have to get as far as the French coast then cross the English Channel en masse, no easy task.

But Paris was more exciting; things happened that would never happen in Liverpool. And Sam preferred to stay rather than return to Canada. 'We're living through history, at its hub,' he said once.

'What will we do if Germany invades?' Jessica queried.

'The war might be over before they have the opportunity.' No one thought the war would last very long.

'But what if it isn't over by the time they *do* have the opportunity?' she persisted.

Sam thought before saying, 'Then we'd better ask Louis where we can get false papers made.' Louis knew everything.

'False papers!' It was like being in a film. She couldn't help but wonder what Bertie would say if he knew what his meek, obedient little wife was up to.

'We'd be taking our lives in our hands,' Sam pointed out, sober now.

'I don't care.' There were times when she genuinely didn't give a damn, and times when she thought about her children and cared a great deal. Say if Bertie was called upon to join the Forces. Would he leave the children with his mother? Or would he decide it was time they were returned to their real mother? Had he really told them she was dead?

It was too painful to think about so she thought about something else instead.

She felt guilty for ignoring Sara's repeated demand that Frannie be sent to Liverpool. Yet the girl definitely didn't want to go. What was more, Sara's demand was always accompanied by the threat that Frannie could expect a good hiding when she came, after which she wouldn't be able to sit down for a week. After reading her mother's letters, Frannie merely laughed and showed no inclination to obey. She was old enough to know her own mind, or so she claimed. Jessica could only believe her.

She wrote back and said that she was sorry, but Frannie preferred to stay in Paris, adding, 'She is extremely happy here.' That seemed rather tactless. She tore up the page and wrote, 'She is company for Louis, who is missing you terribly', an outrageous lie. Louis was in his element looking after the theatre and hardly ever mentioned his wife.

One Sunday in March, Jessica and Frannie emerged from St Eustache where they had been to Mass, to find three British soldiers sitting on a wall outside. From the news, she knew there were thousands of British troops in France, but it was the first time she'd come across them in Paris.

She stopped and said, 'Hello.'

They jumped off the wall, clearly pleased to hear an English voice. It turned out they were waiting to be collected by an officer who had brought a dozen of them to Paris the night before for a night on the town. Their names were Big Alfie, Little Alfie and Tommy Dunn, and they had lost all their money playing cards. Well, Big Alfie had; the other two had just been watching and expecting him to win a fortune.

'What time is the officer due?' Jessica asked.

'Two o'clock this afternoon,' Big Alfie replied dolefully. He wasn't all that big, but Little Alfie was exceptionally small. 'It's bloody freezing in Paris. Mind you, it's just as cold at home according to the letters from me missus. She ses she'll have to burn the sideboard if it doesn't warm up soon. There's not a lump of coal or coke to be had anywhere.'

Jessica had heard the same from Will and Josef. She took the three men home and made them omelettes covered with grated cheese and accompanied by sliced tomato and bread. She was no better a cook now than she'd been when living with Bertie, but in Paris only Sara had complained. Now Sara had gone and Jessica's cooking was accepted without criticism. Indeed, sometimes she was complimented on her efforts, particularly her boiled fruitcake.

'Eggs are rationed at home,' Tommy Dunn remarked.

'They are here, too, but these were a gift.' Last night, someone had paid for entrance to the theatre with half a dozen eggs.

Louis and Sam came in and were introduced to the visitors. Wine appeared and Tommy Dunn began to sing, 'It's a long way to Tipperary . . .' and everyone joined in, even Frannie, who didn't know the words and just made them up as she went along.

It was Frannie who noticed when it was half past one, nearly time for the soldiers to be collected and returned to their camp in Chartres. She and Little Alfie, who was only eighteen, boyishly handsome, and only an inch or so taller than she was, promised to write to each other.

Louis took the men to the place de la Republique where

they were to be picked up, Frannie went to her room to start the letter to her new friend, and Jessica sat on Sam's knee.

'I enjoyed that,' she said, kissing his ear.

'So did I.' He kissed her on the lips with rather more passion that she had his ear. 'This isn't going to last for ever, you know,' he warned, 'this rather sleepy, pretend war. What do they call it in England? The "phoney war". One of these days things are likely to get pretty gruesome.'

Things got pretty gruesome two months later in May when the Germans marched into France. They ignored the Maginot Line, which was supposed to protect the country from invasion, and came through Belgium instead.

It was called the Blitzkrieg, the murderous advance of the Germany Army across the countries of Norway, Denmark, Holland and Belgium, accompanied by the horrific bombing and shelling of streams of innocent civilians who were trying to get away, perhaps the cruellest act of all.

The first refugees from Belgium had arrived in Paris in a trickle before the invasion. At first, it was just those fortunate enough to possess some sort of vehicle. Cars swept through the city; from the new and gleaming, to the old and ramshackle, followed by bicycles and exhausted horses pulling tumbrils full of goods and people. Lastly, came the families pushing handcarts or children's prams piled high with their possessions, sometimes with babies or small children on board, the bigger ones trailing wearily behind.

The trickle quickly became a flood as the refugees poured through Paris, on their way to some Never-Never Land where they thought they would be safe. There were soldiers with them, dejected and sad, British and French, their destination Dunkirk where ships were waiting to take them across the Channel to safety.

No one knew that Frannie was standing on corners in various parts of the city, looking for Little Alfie with whom she had fallen in love – and he with her, she said tearfully, showing her father his letters. Louis had discovered her on the corner of the rue de Rivoli and the rue du Renard when she should have been at school.

'Hang school,' Jessica said later when she heard. 'I'll come with you tomorrow.' The next day, she tore a dozen baguettes into chunks, stuffed them with cheese, and took Frannie with her to help hand them out to the refugees or the soldiers, it didn't matter which, who shuffled or marched painfully through the streets. She did this several times a day for several days until the flood returned to a trickle and eventually dried up altogether. During all this time there was no sign of Little Alfie, and Frannie never heard from him again.

The story was told over and over again, about the trek to the port of Dunkirk on the French coast by members of the British and French Expeditionary Forces who'd lost their friends or their regiments in battle, as well as their weapons, bits of their uniforms, and even their shoes. Now they were on their desperate way to board a ship that would take them to England.

More than 300,000 men were rescued by a flotilla of assorted ships, from tiny sailboats to giant ferries, and delivered safely to the other side of the Channel.

'Wars are not won by evacuation,' Winston Churchill, now Prime Minister, said on the wireless one night. Deliverance was not a victory.

A few days later, German troops entered Paris.

'Shall we go and see them?' Frannie looked at Jessica, who looked at Sam.

'I'd sooner not provide them with an audience,' said Sam.

Frannie's face fell; she was disappointed. Sometimes, Jessica forgot she was still a child. Rows of marching troops would make quite a spectacle if you ignored the symbolism, which

Frannie probably would. 'I'll come with you,' she said. 'I'll just comb my hair and change my shoes.'

Oh, but it was a horrible sight, the row after row of stiff-faced troops in their iron helmets marching in line after line, arms swinging, their heavy boots almost deafening as they came down the Champs-Elysées. The sound was menacing, heralding an end to certainties, and the promise of terror to come.

The people lining the streets were mainly silent apart from an old lady in a doorway behind them who was weeping noisily.

'I don't like it,' Frannie whispered. Her big eyes were round and frightened.

'Neither do I.' Jessica was frightened, too. From now on, they would be living in an occupied city. What sort of changes would there be? A curfew had been promised, food rationing was on the cards. It was a bit late now, but she wished she'd sent Frannie to Sara in Liverpool. Even if the girl had received the threatened good hiding, it was better than living under the thumb of the Germans. Even knowing that, the likelihood was that Frannie would have refused to go.

In the *Petit Théâtre* that night, after the performance, the audience rose to their feet and sang the national anthem.

'We're going to sing it every night from now on,' Louis said afterwards. He laughed, rather recklessly, Jessica thought. 'Until we're stopped, that is.'

Later, when it was past midnight, Frannie was in bed, and the three adults were in the kitchen, sitting near the remains of the fire, Louis gave Jessica and Sam the false papers he'd had made for them.

Jessica examined her birth certificate to find she still had the same Christian name, but her surname was now Lavoir.

'Jessica Lavoir,' she said aloud. 'Jessica Lavoir.' She repeated the name more casually, resolving to practise and get used to the strangeness of it so it slipped quite naturally off her tongue. She had also retained the same date of birth, 3 August 1910, and had been born in a town called Reims. Her father's name was Claud Lavoir and her mother Marguerite Balasko. Louis had genuinely been born in Reims and his mother still lived there. Jessica was his cousin who had come to live in the rue de la Grand Truanderie to look after him and his daughter, Françoise, after his wife had left him.

Sam originated from Quebec and was of French descent. The name Samuel Deveraux was quite acceptable, though he had a new passport to show he was born in France, not Canada. He was Jessica's fiancé and worked as a waiter in the Café Edgar. Martin, the owner, would confirm this if asked.

Louis showed them where to hide their passports and any other personal papers so there'd be no chance of them being found if the house was ever searched. The hiding place was under a floorboard in the broom cupboard.

'Searched!' Jessica gasped.

'It's most unlikely, but you never know,' Louis warned. 'We have to be prepared for any *éventualité*. Oh, and Jessica, a German isn't likely to recognize you have an accent, but if a Frenchman does, say you spent some time at a school in England. That should cover it – and have the name of a school ready. Don't ever pause and look worried if you're asked a question you can't answer.'

'I didn't realize I had an accent,' Jessica said. She had thought she spoke French perfectly.

'Well, you have, though it's very charming.' Sam blew her a kiss across the room, and she blew one back.

'Don't I get a kiss, too?' Louis said forlornly.

Kisses were blown at him from both Sam and Jessica, who was forever marvelling about the strangeness of things and the subtle tricks of fate. She had no idea how long the war would last, but she was about to spend it in the company of these two men in a funny little house, which was in the narrowest street in Paris. One of the men she was madly in love with and the other she loved as she would have done a brother – almost as much as she loved Will, her real brother. And, of course, there was a young girl upstairs who they were all responsible for.

The time they would spend together would at least be interesting. She hoped it would be no more than that.

Chapter 15

The Germans troops were behaving like tourists. They saun-
tered around Paris with their cameras, snapping the churches
and the gracious buildings, the elegant, tree-lined avenues and
smart shops. They asked Parisians to take photographs of them
standing bashfully at the foot of the Eiffel Tower or in front of
the Arc de Triomphe where a swastika flag hung. Scrupu-
lously polite, they held open doors for women and patted
small children on their heads.

It was 1941 and summer again when this benign occupation
that had continued for a year began to change. Whether it was
the occupiers who changed, or the French people turning
against the occupation of their country by a foreign power,
Jessica never knew, but all of a sudden there was murder on
the streets of Paris. Shots could be heard in the middle of the
night as well as shouts and screams; footsteps running and
footsteps following. Frenchmen were being shot for no reason
– 'executed' Louis claimed – while German soldiers were
killed and grenades thrown into places where collaborators
and the German hierarchy mixed.

The death toll mounted. A movement had been formed,
referred to as the Resistance, urged on by the French hero,
General de Gaulle, who was living in London. Members were
French as well as other nationalities, many of them Jews, but
all had a single purpose: to wage an internal war against the
increasingly brutal foreign army that controlled France.

The war was taking its toll in other ways. Identity cards had been issued, food was becoming more difficult to acquire even when rationed, fuel near impossible to obtain. There were blackouts, endless curfews. Life was becoming meaner and had less colour. There seemed little reason to smile, though in the smart cafés and theatres, the rich restaurants and bars, life continued more brightly and more lavishly than it had ever done before. The German elite were always present.

And the great city of Paris in the blackout looked spectacularly beautiful when lit only by the moon and the stars.

One night, as the audience sang the Marsellaise at the end of the performance, there was a hammering on the downstairs door of the *Petit Théâtre*. A voice shouted something in German.

Jessica went down and opened the door. Two German soldiers were standing outside. To judge by his immaculate, well-cut uniform, the younger one appeared to be an officer. He barked something at her.

'*Je ne comprends pas*,' she said with a charming smile.

'What is that noise, that song?' the man demanded in reasonable French, not quite so boorishly this time. Perhaps it was the smile that persuaded him to remove his cap. He was a perfect specimen of Aryan manhood with white-blond hair and intense blue eyes.

Jessica smiled again. 'It is the Marsellaise, our national anthem,' she explained in French. 'This is a theatre, tonight's performance has just finished, and it is a ritual that we sing the national anthem at the end of a show. It is the same in a cinema.' She knew full well that the anthem had been banned.

'From now on you must stop. You must never sing that song again.' The officer bowed courteously and managed a slight smile. 'If you wish to sing, I suggest you learn the words of the German national anthem, "Das Deutschlandlied", and sing that instead.'

'Thank you for your advice. Goodnight.'

'Goodnight, madame.' The officer bowed and clicked his heels.

She fluttered her eyelashes and closed the door.

'I quite enjoyed myself,' she told Sam later. 'It was just like a game.'

To her surprise, he grabbed her by the shoulders. 'It's *not* a game, Jess,' he said angrily. 'I wish you would realize that it's deadly serious. Tonight, you might easily have been arrested. Right now, you could be in a police station somewhere.'

'For what reason?'

'They don't need a reason, darling.' He took her in his arms. 'I wish we weren't here,' he whispered. 'I wish now that we hadn't stayed. I'm just idling my time away when I should be in uniform fighting these bastards.'

She hadn't realized he felt like that. 'It's too late now, Sam,' she said. Her arms tightened round his neck. It was *her* fault that he'd stayed. Although Frannie had deliberately missed the train, it was Jessica who'd contacted the Canadian embassy to ask if Sam could get them on another, preventing him from catching his own plane home. 'I don't *really* think it's a game,' she told him. 'It's just that it's easier to cope when you pretend.'

'I understand.' He sighed. 'We've both been pretending. We're a pair of fools, Jess. We should have gone home when we could, and taken Frannie with us.'

Louis was involved in something. As soon as the night's play was over, instead of the audience staying on, as had become the custom, they would be tactfully shooed out until only Louis and his friends were left behind. Long, subdued conversations would follow.

Jessica and Sam had been politely but firmly discouraged from attending these gatherings. The reason for them desperately worried Sam.

'What's Louis up to?' he would mutter as they listened to the muffled sounds coming from next door.

'I've no idea.' Jessica couldn't even try to guess.

'Bloody fools,' Sam said one night. They were sitting up in bed wrapped in each other's arms. Jessica knew that neither of them would sleep until Louis's visitors had gone. 'I'd like to bet he's joined the Resistance and they're plotting something.'

'The Resistance?' she murmured. She slid down the bed under the clothes as if worried someone – Frannie, for instance, in the next room – was listening to *their* conversation. Sam slid down with her until they were both buried beneath the bedclothes. 'But that's terribly dangerous, isn't it?' she said.

'Really dangerous,' Sam growled, 'as well as being entirely useless. A few soldiers killed here, a few there. The war won't be shortened by a single second; yet completely innocent men and women will be slaughtered in reprisal.'

There was silence for a while. It was like being inside a tent, Jessica thought. She had a feeling she'd once slept in a tent in the garden of their old house in Sefton Park when she was a child, but couldn't remember who she'd been with; Will, maybe, or Lydia, or Sara. It seemed so long ago that it was hard to believe it had happened.

'I shouldn't criticize,' Sam said eventually. 'These guys are being really brave. But I honestly don't know what anyone can do that would lead to victory except join the Forces and fight. I'd like to be in the Air Force – British or Canadian, I don't care – and bomb these Fascist monsters out of existence.' There was longing in his voice. 'I can fly a plane. My first job was for a delivery company back in Canada and they taught me to fly.'

'You could try to get back to England through Spain and join up there,' she said encouragingly. She'd heard of people who had managed it, though knew she was wasting her time. Sam would never leave while she was there.

He proved this by raising himself on an elbow and looking down at her. 'Do you seriously think I'd leave you here on your own?' he said angrily.

'I wouldn't be on my own,' she said. 'There's Frannie and Louis.'

'There's no one who'd look after you like I would. And Frannie needs looking after herself. Louis lives in a different world from most people and can't be relied upon to protect anyone, not even himself – it's probably hazardous for us to be living in the same house,' he snorted. 'Christ knows what sort of plans he and his friends are hatching.' He lifted the bed-clothes; the voices in the theatre could still be heard. 'I know a way of shutting them out, at least for a while.' He kissed her long, hard and passionately . . .

'I love you, Jess,' he whispered.

'And I love you, Sam,' she sighed.

By the time they had finished making love and lay on the bed, exhausted, next door was completely silent.

One morning, Jessica became aware that there were people in the theatre. They were doing their best to be quiet, but she could hear movements throughout the day. Stairs would creak, doors would open and close, there was a mumble of voices.

It had always been her habit to go next door and remove the rubbish left from the night before – the crumpled paper bags, lost handkerchiefs, the occasional glove or scarf, and abandoned programmes. Today, she didn't like to carry out these tasks, but not because she was scared. It just didn't seem a good idea to go into the theatre if possible strangers were present. In the end, she approached Louis and asked what was going on. He was sitting writing at the kitchen table. Frannie was at school and Sam had gone in search of fresh fruit and vegetables of which there was a shortage – as there was of most things.

At first, Louis professed to have no idea what she was

talking about, as if during the years that she had lived there he'd never noticed that she tidied up the theatre every single day. Mind you, he was so vague that perhaps he hadn't. Even on Mondays, when the theatre hadn't been used the night before, she brushed the floors and straightened the curtains, often mending them if necessary.

'I asked,' she repeated, 'if it was all right to go next door. I don't like to disturb the people who are there.'

'It's all right,' Louis said offhandedly, 'I'll tidy up today.'

Jessica rolled her eyes impatiently. 'It's not just because I'm curious, Louis, but Sam and I have a right to know what's going on. I hope you're not putting Frannie in danger.' He wouldn't do it deliberately.

He looked annoyed as well as flustered, and ran a hand through his wonderful hair. 'I would never put Frannie – or you and Sam – in danger,' he protested.

'Then who are the people next door who have been creeping around all day? Are they from the Resistance?'

'No. They are merely living there temporarily.'

'Who are they?' she persisted.

'Some chap with his daughter and her fiancé,' Louis said reluctantly. 'They are waiting to be picked up and taken to America.'

'Waiting or hiding?'

'Both.'

'Really?' She sat opposite him at the table, even more interested now. 'Why do they have to hide here? What have they done that they have to hide *anywhere*?'

Louis spread his hands and shrugged. 'They are German Jews,' he said simply. 'From now on, the *Petit Théâtre* will be a staging post and we shall regularly be having people to stay.'

That sounded pretty dangerous to Jessica.

Sam returned and was informed of the current situation. It was decided there and then with Louis that, as far as possible,

Frannie was to be kept ignorant of what was going on. It wouldn't be fair; she was much too young to be trusted with such a secret. If she heard noises, she was to be offered an innocent explanation.

'Like it's a rehearsal,' Louis said.

The next day, he wrote the name and address of his mother, Frannie's grandmother, who lived in Reims, on a postcard and gave it to his daughter, insisting that she carry it with her everywhere.

'Keep it in your bag, in your pocket, anywhere, as long as you always have it on you,' he advised when Frannie came home from school.

'Why, Papa?' she asked. She looked frightened.

'So you'll know where to go if something happens here.'

'What kind of thing?' She was even more frightened.

Louis looked faintly desperate. 'I have no idea, *cherie*, but we are living in an occupied country where absolutely anything can happen; bombs can fall, people can die, disappear.' He shrugged dramatically. 'Anything!'

Unusually for Frannie, she burst into tears. 'I don't want you to die or disappear, Papa.'

Louis pulled her on to his knee. He could be the nicest father in the world when he remembered. 'I have no intention of doing either, *ma petite*.'

'Then why do I have to carry the card everywhere I go?' Frannie sobbed.

'It's just like having an identity card – like Papa does himself. These are strange times, *cherie*. You know that, don't you?'

'Of course I do.' She buried her head in his shoulder. 'I love you, Papa.'

'And I love you, Frannie.'

Jessica and Sam met the people living in the theatre that night after the play was over and Frannie had gone to bed.

'Come with me,' Louis said when everyone had gone.

They followed him into the theatre where he lifted the seat of the middle bench to reveal a large space inside in which a number of candles flickered furiously in the draught. He said something in German and, reaching down, helped three people climb out; a lightly bearded man of about fifty, a much younger man roughly half his age, and a girl of about eighteen. They blinked in the much brighter light of the theatre. All looked considerably dishevelled and weary.

They must have been hiding down there during the play. It had been a hot day and the room smelled strongly of perspiration and cigarette smoke. There were no windows and it was hard to breathe. It was probably the most unhygienic, uncomfortable and unhealthy theatre in the world. The lavatory was in the yard outside and stank to high heaven. It was the only part of the theatre that Jessica couldn't bring herself to clean.

Louis spoke. 'This is Gerhard Schumann and his daughter Helga, and Helga's fiancé, Eric Stern. Neither Gerhard nor Eric can speak French or English, I have only a few words of German, but fortunately Helga is able to speak quite good English.' He smiled benevolently at everyone. 'Jessica and Sam,' he said, pointing to them.

They all nodded. Jessica didn't bother trying to start a conversation. She merely asked Helga if they would like something to eat.

'Please.' She looked relieved. 'We are all starving. All we have eaten today is bread and cheese. It would also be greatly appreciated if we could have a hot drink. My father is desperate for coffee.'

Jessica returned to the house. She cut potatoes into thin slices and fried them on the open fire – the need for hot water necessitated a fire on the warmest of days. She put three plates on the table, bread, a few strips of red pepper, and a chunk of cheese on each followed by the potatoes when they had been fried to a crisp. It wasn't a very appetizing meal, but she didn't think the visitors would turn up their noses at it. That afternoon, Sam had walked a long way before he'd found the peppers.

Louis had brought their guests into the kitchen where they fell upon the food and ate every mouthful.

'That was very good,' Helga said when the plates had been wiped clean. Everyone looked considerably better for the meal. At the other end of the room Sam was making coffee.

Jessica smiled. 'It was the best I could do under the circumstances.'

'Once this war is over,' Helga said, 'I will invite all of you to dinner in America.'

'Louis told me that's where you are going.' She sat down on the bench beside the young woman. 'What part of America?'

'New York. Tomorrow, we are being taken to Marseilles to catch a boat that will take us directly there.' She hugged her knees. 'I cannot wait. I have always wanted to live there. I tried to persuade Papa to leave Germany years ago when Hitler turned upon the Jews, but he was too blind, too cautious. Now it is difficult and dangerous to leave when before it was quite safe.'

Her father seemed to sense what his daughter was saying. He bent his head and muttered something in German. 'He can't stop apologizing,' Helga said. 'Now he feels guilty all the time.' She laughed. 'Serves him right.'

Sam brought the coffee. Jessica hoped the drink, for which he was so desperate, would cheer the older man up a little.

The next morning, the theatre was completely quiet. Their guests had gone during the night. Louis said, 'I hope they get to New York safely.'

Jessica went next door. She spread the sleeping bags over the benches so they would be aired before the next guests arrived. They really should be washed, but there might not be time for them to dry. Louis said new people could come at any time.

Jessica was concerned at how easily Frannie had burst into tears when her father had given her the postcard. She was worried that she hadn't been giving the girl enough attention; that she was too taken up with Sam. Unlike her sister, Frannie never invited girls home from school. It therefore wasn't surprising that she wasn't invited to other girls' houses. She didn't appear to have any friends. She spent most evenings alone in her room reading. She was nearly fourteen and it was about time she had some sort of a social life.

'Would you like to go to the cinema at the weekend?' she asked when Frannie came home that afternoon.

She looked interested. 'What's on?'

'Mainly French films, some German, a few American, one of which is *The Wizard of Oz*.'

Frannie clapped her hands. 'I would *love* to see *The Wizard of Oz*.'

'Then we shall go on Saturday afternoon and have tea afterwards.'

'Can I bring a friend from school?'

'Of course.' Jessica felt both surprised and pleased. 'What's her name?'

'Marcel. He's a boy. He'll pay for himself. His family has loads of money.'

Even more surprised, Jessica said, 'I thought you only had girls at your school?'

'The Germans appropriated Marcel's school for offices. We took some of the senior boys into ours. He can't speak English, but I expect the film will have French subtitles.'

It was rare these days that Jessica moved away from the rue de la Grand Truanderie. It might well be extraordinarily narrow, but she had found everything she needed could be acquired there: food of every description when it was available; several shops selling household necessities, clothes and shoes; a travel agent; two pharmacies; two hotels; an undertaker; and a number of restaurants. Her entire life was mainly lived underneath a narrow strip of sky.

But there wasn't a cinema. On Saturday, a warm, breathless July day, Jessica took Frannie and Marcel Guilborg to see *The Wizard of Oz*. It was on in Saint Germain on the other side of the river and the most convenient way to get there was on the *Métro*.

Three German soldiers were stationed at the entrance of Les Halles *Métro* station, not standing to attention, but laughing and talking loudly to each other. More were present at Mabillon where they got off.

Jessica had half-expected Marcel to be tall, skinny and studious, a bit like Frannie herself, but he turned out to be an exceptionally handsome boy of about sixteen, dark-eyed and dark-haired, with a romantic air about him.

And rather than plain, awkward Frannie being overawed by her charming boyfriend, it was he who was quite obviously enamoured with her, hanging on to her every word, gazing at her with his brown eyes full of something approaching veneration. In the cinema, he attempted to put his arm round her shoulder, but she dug him in the ribs with her elbow and he turned disconsolately away.

For Jessica, it was the wrong film to have come to see. She really should have known better. From the very first scene, she thought how much her own children would have loved it. She visualized Dora and Jamie's reactions all the way through. Jamie would have found the Tin Man, the Scarecrow and the Lion terrifically funny, and Dora would been scared of the flying monkeys. She would almost certainly have asked her mother to make her a pinafore like Dorothy's, and Jamie would have sung 'We're Off to See the Wizard' every night as he tramped upstairs to bed.

Neither Frannie nor Marcel seemed aware of Jessica silently crying her eyes out the whole way through the film. She claimed to have a headache when Frannie noticed her red, swollen face afterwards.

'Oh, but I still want us to have tea,' she assured the girl when she offered to skip the meal and go straight home. 'I'm really hungry,' she lied.

Marcel accompanied them back to the house in rue de la Grand Truanderie. Jessica asked if he would like to come in for a coffee, but Frannie butted in. 'He can't. He has home-work to do, just like I have.'

The young man hung his head and shuffled away, looking very forlorn. He'd hardly said a word the entire afternoon.

Inside, Sam and Louis were in the kitchen playing chess. They both looked up and grunted a welcome.

'You were very rude to Marcel,' Jessica remarked to Frannie. 'I felt really sorry for him.'

Frannie snorted. 'Don't ever feel sorry for *him*, Jessica. He's nothing but a bloody Fascist like his father.'

Sam and Louis raised their heads in astonishment – Frannie had never been known to swear before – and Jessica gasped. 'Then why are you going out with him?'

'I'm not going *out* with him,' Frannie said indignantly, 'I'm *spying* on him. His father is a top official in the *gendarmerie*, and me and this other boy at school, Henri, are trying to work out a plan to have him killed. The father, that is, not Marcel.'

Chapter 16

'Jaysus Mary and Joseph, Frannie!' Jessica sat down with a bump, her hand to her throat, scarcely able to believe what she'd just heard.

Across the room, Louis got to his feet and went slowly towards his daughter. Jessica watched, worried what he might do. Slap her, swear at her, tell her she must never speak to Marcel or her friend Henri again. But he did none of these things, merely took hold of both her hands and said, 'What is Marcel's surname, Frannie?'

'Guilborg,' Frannie replied. 'Marcel Guilborg, Papa. His father is called Charles.'

Louis nodded. 'I've heard of him, the father. He's a collaborator, a top policeman, who has adopted the Boche's filthy ways with enthusiasm. He has his own little torture chamber in the Avenue Foch. Have you been to their house, *cherie*?'

'What *is* this, Louis?' Jessica's shock had turned to anger. 'Why aren't you outraged at what Frannie just said? She's not yet fourteen, for goodness' sake, and she's talking about killing someone. But you, you question her as if you think it's a really good idea.'

'It *is* a really good idea,' Frannie said indignantly. 'Henri and I have been spying on the Guilborg's for weeks. We've been to their house loads of times.'

'You idiot!' Jessica's strangled comment was lost as Louis embraced his daughter and called her a 'grand little thing'.

Jessica glanced at Sam and rolled her eyes, and he rolled his back. She went over to the stove and began to make coffee. For the first time in ages she longed for a cigarette – she hadn't smoked for months.

'You should have invited Marcel in for coffee,' Louis said thoughtfully. 'I could have asked him a thing or two.'

Frannie snorted for the second time in a few minutes. 'And what if he became aware of the people in the theatre? Do we have people staying in the theatre at the moment?' She looked at their surprised faces and smiled sarcastically. 'You must think I'm really stupid.' She tossed her head. 'I'm not deaf, I heard – I *smelled* – the meal being made in the middle of the night as well as people moving around the theatre during the day.'

'I think you are the cleverest young woman on the planet,' her father said admiringly.

'If Sara were here now,' Jessica commented, 'she would be going up in a blue flame. She would be *fuming*.'

There was silence while everyone imagined Sara in one of her worst rages. Then Louis shook himself and said, 'Well, Sara isn't here now, is she?'

'I almost wish she was,' Jessica muttered. 'She'd soon put you and Frannie straight.' She poured the coffee and gave everyone a cup. After a single sip, she discovered it wasn't even warm.

Louis announced that two people were due to arrive to-morrow when it was dark and stay in the theatre overnight. 'Germans again – Otto and Mai Braun, a schoolteacher and his wife. He was arrested for bringing anti-war propaganda into the classroom. He was on his way to an internment camp when friends helped him escape and directed him here.'

'Here?' queried Sam, speaking for the first time. 'When you say "here", do you mean Paris or the theatre?'

'Both,' Louis replied. 'As time goes by, the theatre will

become known as a place where desperate people can stop and stay, even if it's only for a night's rest.'

'But Louis,' Sam said mildly, 'do we really want the place to become well known as anything other than a theatre? What if the Boche discovers we're sheltering fugitives? It could land all of us in trouble, Frannie too.'

Jessica had never known Louis lose his temper before. 'If you don't like the idea, Sam, then you know what to do,' he shouted. 'Fuck off and find somewhere nice and safe to live.' He turned his angry gaze on Jessica. 'You too, Jess. You obviously don't approve of what I'm doing. You and Sam can live out the war in the countryside. If you're lucky, you might never come across a single German.'

'Hold on a minute.' Sam went red and pushed Louis in the chest. 'Have you forgotten why Jessica and I are here? Because your daughter got off the train in the Gare du Nord and Jess had to go and look for her, preventing her from catching the train herself. Then I missed my plane to Vancouver when Jess called on me for help.'

Jessica felt annoyed again, this time with Sam. 'But there was nothing you could do to help, Sam,' she said crossly. 'There was no need for you to miss your plane. I wish you hadn't now.' Though in all honesty, she would have felt bereft without him.

Frannie stamped her foot. 'You're horrible. I hate all of you. I'd go and live with *Grandmère* in Reims, but then I wouldn't see Henri again and I really like him.'

Who was it who missed the bloody train on purpose? Jessica wanted to say, but kept her mouth shut. It would only make matters worse.

'I don't want to live here on my own,' Louis said pathetically, his temper gone.

'I suggest that we have dinner in the Café Edgar after tonight's performance has finished,' Jessica said calmly. 'We can discuss matters there.' Things were unlikely to get heated in public. 'I'll go over now and book a table, shall I?'

'*Très bien*,' Louis grunted. He looked embarrassed.

'That's a really great idea, Jess.' Sam couldn't stay mad for long.

Everyone looked at Frannie. 'Can I have wine?' she asked.

'You can have anything you want, *cherie*,' her father said fondly, patting her head.

It wasn't until well past eleven that they entered the Café Edgar, where the curfew was completely ignored. Martin, who had a lavish handlebar moustache, but not a single, solitary hair on his head, came hurrying towards them and showed them to the table that Jessica had booked earlier. The restaurant was long, narrow and dimly lit. There was only room enough for a row of tables on each side with a restricted passage in between. Their table was at the very back on the far side of the little bar, slightly quieter and more private than the rest. The smell of other people's cigarettes once again made Jessica long for one herself – she'd been aching for one for hours but was determined not to give in to the craving.

They waited until it was time for dessert before discussing the reason they were there. Eating *crème caramel* didn't require the same total dedication as the main meal of *coq au vin* or *steak mignon*, even if the amount of meat was minimal. Louis was the first to speak.

'I want to do something meaningful towards the war,' he said. 'I'm thirty-four, too old to have been called up when war was declared. I should have volunteered, but left it too late. I genuinely didn't think it possible that Germany would invade, but now they have and, like most French men, I find the situation thoroughly objectionable.' He stared at Sam for whom his words seem to be intended. 'Using the theatre as a staging post to help people seems a patriotic and worthwhile thing to do.'

'Yes, but although that makes you feel better about your-self,' Sam argued, 'in the process, you're endangering Jessica and Frannie. And I disagree with what you said about most Frenchmen finding the current situation intolerable. It would appear some of your police are quite happy to do the enemy's bidding. They chase protesters and round up Jews with every bit as much enthusiasm as the invaders. And it's not just the police who have clung on to their influential positions.'

Louis nodded regretfully. 'You're right, Sam. I should have acknowledged that fact.'

'Are you in the Resistance?' Sam asked bluntly and much too loudly.

'Shush!' Jessica put her finger to her lips. She glanced at the customers sitting nearby, but nobody gave the impression of having heard.

'Sorry,' Sam closed his eyes and hunched his shoulders as if trying to make himself invisible.

A waiter approached their table and began to clear the dishes. Jessica ordered coffee.

'I am *not* in the Resistance,' Louis half-whispered when the man had gone, 'but I know people who are. They're the ones I get my instructions from.'

'So it *is* dangerous,' Sam said. 'If you're found out, you'll either be shot or sent to a camp, possibly taking the rest of us with you.'

'I don't mind,' Frannie said stoutly. The only other times she'd been allowed to stay up so late was on New Year's Eve, yet she looked as fresh as a daisy. 'I think Papa is being very brave.'

'No, I'm not, *cherie*,' Louis said distractedly. It was clear he didn't like being reminded he was putting other people in danger, particularly his daughter. 'It's the people I help who are being brave.' He glanced at Sam again. 'My address, the theatre's address, is known to only a handful of other people – as a shelter, that is. I don't even know their full names and they are all upright, highly respected citizens – one is actually of the cloth – who are unlikely to be questioned by the police for any reason.'

Sam looked doubtful. 'I still don't like it, Louis.'

Louis shrugged. 'I'm sorry, Sam, but as I said earlier, you and Jessica can always find somewhere else to live, somewhere safer. As for Frannie, she can go and live in Reims with my mother.'

'I'll do no such thing,' Frannie said, outraged. 'And Papa, you said before, you didn't want to live by yourself.'

Louis groaned. 'I wish I hadn't said that. One minute I'm talking about volunteering to fight, then saying I don't want to live alone. *C'est ridicule.*'

'I'm with Frannie, I don't want to move, either.' Jessica put her hand on top of Sam's. 'What about you, Sam?'

'Like Louis, I didn't expect the invasion to happen so suddenly. Under different circumstances, I would have joined the Forces. But while I'm here, I'm willing to help the people who shelter in the theatre in any way I can.' He shrugged, frowning. 'I just don't like the idea of you and Frannie being put in danger.'

'But you're nothing to do with me, Sam,' Frannie protested. 'As long as Papa doesn't mind, that's all that matters.'

At this, Jessica felt bound to point out that she felt it was her duty to look after Frannie for her mother's sake. 'I know you refused to go to Liverpool, but I feel guilty for not insisting that you did.' She'd been too weak-willed. Had she really wanted to go herself, she could probably have talked the girl round.

'I think,' Louis said gravely, 'that we've known each other long enough for us all to matter to each other.' He turned to Sam. 'I'm sorry I lost my temper earlier, Sam. I'd hate it if you or Jessica went away. As for Frannie here,' he put his arm around his daughter, 'I'd send her to her *Grandmère* but wouldn't trust her to stay, so it would be a waste of time. I suggest we forget today ever happened and remain friends for as long as we all may live.'

Sam raised his glass. 'Here's to us!'

'To us!' the others chorused.

'It's just like *The Three Musketeers*,' Frannie chuckled. 'I'll be D'Artagnan.'

Jessica was glad they were all friends again, but no decisions had been made about anything. The matter of what to do about the theatre had been left dangling in the air.

It was September, about six weeks after the dinner at the Café Edgar, and Jessica was buying croissants in the *boulangerie* where Madame Vierny, the owner, who was eighty if a day, was already serving a male customer who wore a black velvet beret and an artist's smock.

'I have never been so glad to see the back of anyone,' she was saying. She spoke so fast that Jessica always found her French difficult to keep up with. 'I knew that man long before he became chief of police. Ten years ago he arrested my grandson, Georges, for giving a speech in the place du Châtelet. Georges is a Communist,' she said proudly, 'presently fighting the Fascists alongside Tito in Yugoslavia. Being a Communist has never been a crime in this country. But Charles Guilborg dragged Georges off the streets and threw him into prison. Didn't keep him long, though.' She twisted her lips contemptuously. 'We had a lawyer, a Communist himself, and he had my Georges out of prison like a flash of lightning. Guilborg was brought before his superiors and reprimanded – it was in the newspaper at the time. I've got the cutting upstairs if you'd like to see it.'

'Another time, Madame Vierny,' the customer said hastily. 'But, like you, I am not sorry to know that Charles Guilborg is dead. A Frenchman who tortures other Frenchmen is not fit to live.' The man lifted his hat. '*Bonjour, madame. Bonjour.*'

The customer gone, Madame Vierny turned her raddled smile on Jessica. '*Bonjour, mademoiselle.*'

'*Quatre croissants, s'il vous plaît, madame.*' They had a croissant each for breakfast, dipped in coffee as a way of saving butter. 'How did Charles Guilborg die, madame?' she asked.

'He was murdered!' the old woman said ghoulishly. 'Stabbed in his evil heart as he went for his evening walk around the Île Saint-Louis. I wish I'd been there and seen the bastard die.' For a second time Jessica listened to the story of her grandson, Georges the Communist. 'At least now I myself will die in peace.' The old lady smiled triumphantly.

Jessica hurried home. Apart from buying meat in the rue de la Grand Truanderie, she was glad she'd done most of her shopping in Les Halles when she'd first come to Paris. It meant only a few local people knew she was English. She trusted them all to keep the knowledge to themselves, but would have worried had more people known.

When she got in only Sam was in the kitchen. It was barely half past six and Louis and Frannie were still in bed. She told Sam about the murder of the man that Frannie and her friend, Henri, had sworn to kill.

'Damn!' He looked horrified. 'I can't believe Frannie had anything to do with it. At least, I don't want to believe it, but Frannie confessed to have been spying on the guy. I suppose they could have told Louis where he went for a stroll each night.'

'And Louis could have passed the information on to who-ever killed him,' Jessica theorized. She couldn't imagine gentle Louis killing anybody in cold blood.

'There was no mention of the son, Marcel, coming to any harm?'

Jessica shook her head. 'No.' She recalled how enamoured the boy had been with a rudely unresponsive Frannie, and prayed he was all right, other than being upset that his father had died in such a horrible way. It wasn't fair that people should have to pay for the sins of their fathers.

There was a loud knock on the front door and she nearly jumped out of her skin. Every time it happened she expected to find a crowd of German troops outside, come to arrest the entire household. Sam had told her not to be silly. 'If they were here to arrest us, they would break down the door, not politely knock.'

Now he said, 'I'll see who it is.'

Somewhat ominously, it was Henri at the door. They had already been introduced to Henri. Unlike Marcel Guilborg, he was exactly the sort of boyfriend Jessica would have expected Frannie to have – very tall, very thin and very clever. He had a head of thick, dark curls, a grave manner and wire-rimmed spectacles. This morning, however, there was no sign of his usual gravity and he rushed into the kitchen looking elated.

'I've come to see Frannie.'

'She's still in bed,' Jessica said. 'I'll fetch her for you.'

But Frannie must have heard the knock and was on her way downstairs wearing the lilac velveteen dressing gown that had belonged to her mother. It was actually an inch or so too short for her. Her hair, usually tightly pigtailed, was loose and spread over her shoulders in untidy waves. She'd had her fourteenth birthday last week and Jessica was aware for the first time how grown up and almost beautiful she looked.

'*Bonjour*, Henri,' she said calmly.

'Have you heard the news?' Henri asked excitedly.

Frannie didn't answer. She grasped Henri's hand and took him to the living room upstairs, closing the door behind them. From then on nothing could be heard. Jessica and Sam were left in the kitchen staring at each other.

Sam stuffed his hands in his pockets and rolled back and

forth on the balls of his feet. 'Are you thinking what I'm thinking?'

'That they definitely had something to do with yesterday's murder, yes.' Jessica sighed. 'Shall we discuss it with Louis?'

'I think it best we didn't. It might only cause a row.' He stood and stretched his arms. 'I'm sick of Louis and his daughter – and Henri. I feel like going on a long, exhausting walk. Want to come with me?'

Jessica shuddered. 'I daren't. I worry I'll be stopped by the police and they'll be able to tell I have an accent.'

'Just say you went to school in England. That's what we agreed.'

'It sounds suspicious. They might check my papers and find out they're forged.' Jessica poured coffee and said she'd take it to Louis in bed. 'See what his reaction is when I tell him about Charles Guilborg.'

She was back within minutes. 'Louis isn't there,' she said worriedly. 'His bed hasn't been slept in. What are we supposed to make of that?'

Sam didn't know what to make of it, and neither did she. Several more hours were to pass before they did, and the news was grim.

Jessica felt restless and could tell that Sam felt the same. She was glad when Frannie and Henri reappeared and said they were going somewhere.

'Where's "somewhere"?' Jessica asked.

'Erm . . . Henri's house,' Frannie replied.

'Is there a Junior Resistance?' Jessica asked Sam when the youngsters had gone. She sat down and began to chew her nails. Sam didn't answer, just made more coffee.

'I reckon we should go out,' he said after a while. 'We can't just sit here until Louis decides to come home. My nerves are in shreds.'

'And mine are in tatters. Let's go out, then.' She'd just have to risk being stopped by the police. 'Where to?'

'Have you seen Chartres cathedral?'

'I've never gone beyond the outskirts of Paris since I came,' she confessed.

'Then you shall today.'

They left from Montparnasse station for the roughly fifty-mile train journey to Chartres. As all her good clothes had gone to Liverpool without her and she'd never got round to buying more, she was wearing a summer frock and a white cardigan and beret that she'd bought from C&A Modes during the time she'd worked in Kirkby Castle.

'You look nice,' Sam said, kissing her when they were about to leave. He'd put on his lightweight grey suit and a slouch hat, a style he was particularly fond of. Today the colour was pearly grey. She told him it made him look like a criminal in a Hollywood film.

The French countryside sparkled in the September sunshine. At times, the only colours visible were the blue of the sky and the different shades of green of the fields and hedges, the orchards and vineyards. Occasionally, there would be the vivid flash of flowers, a silvery patch of water, a white cloud that crawled like a caterpillar across the sky. They passed tiny shuttered cottages nestling within clumps of trees, and villages that looked as if they belonged in the Middle Ages.

Jessica clutched Sam's hand and began to relax. She hadn't realized just how tense she'd been until she could feel it ebbing away. Her breathing became slower and she felt at peace with the world, though knew it wouldn't last. Before the day was out, they would be back in Paris and her worries would start again. Even now, although she tried hard not to, she kept wondering if Louis was home and if he'd anything to do with Charles Guilborg's murder.

★

Chartres cathedral was a Gothic masterpiece dedicated to Blessed Mary and John the Baptist. It had stood, intact, for almost seven centuries. Jessica walked over stones worn to a curve from the tread of thousands of feet. She stared, entranced, at the glorious stained-glass windows that shone brilliantly in the afternoon sunshine, warming her face.

Tilting back her head to look up, she became dizzy and nearly fell. Sam caught her in his arms and she rested her head on his shoulder. The building, the magnitude of its beauty, the miracle of it, the proof that many hundreds of years ago man was able to create something so remarkable, gave her a feeling of reassurance, a sense of certainty. If this wonderful building had existed for so long, then so would France, so would Europe and the rest of the world. One day, she didn't know when, the evil that was Germany would be destroyed and goodness would be restored.

It was going on for six o'clock when they arrived home. The door to the theatre was open and there were half a dozen young people in the foyer, three boys and three girls. She remembered a teacher from the Elysée de St Anne had turned an Agatha Christie novel into a play and it was being performed by pupils in the top class.

She went inside. 'Is Louis here?' she asked. She could hear footsteps upstairs, more voices.

For what seemed like a full minute, there was dead silence. Then a girl with raven-black hair and beautiful grey eyes burst into tears. 'Ah, mademoiselle,' she cried, 'do you not know?'

Jessica was mystified. 'Know what?'

'Louis and three others have been arrested for the murder of Charles Guilborg, our chief of police. They are all in prison in the Avenue Foch where they were to be tried this very afternoon.' The young people turned to each other in a mutual embrace and more began to cry. The black-haired girl continued. 'The chances are the trial is already over, mademoiselle. They could have been executed by now. Dear Louis might already be dead.'

Chapter 17

Jessica had almost forgotten she and Louis were supposed to be cousins. 'Are you a relative?' the official had growled when she'd arrived at Gestapo headquarters in the Avenue Foch and asked if she could see Louis Cotillard.

'I'm his cousin,' she replied, remembering just in time.

'He's being executed in the morning with the others. The firing squad's due at five o'clock.'

She was too distraught to answer, merely nodding.

The man shoved an open ledger in front of her. 'Sign your name and put your address,' he grunted.

After scribbling something barely legible, she was taken downstairs into a basement room without windows then shown into a smaller room in which the only furniture was a small iron bed, the striped mattress uncovered and badly stained. There was no pillow. A pale Louis, looking abnormally thin, as if he hadn't eaten in weeks, got to his feet and didn't speak until the official locked the door behind him and went away.

'You shouldn't have come,' he said angrily. 'You shouldn't have brought suspicion on yourself by coming to see me.'

'I'm sure by now someone has realized we live in the same house,' she said. Moved to tears, she threw her arms round him. How quickly death could come, she thought, stroking his face. 'Oh, Louis,' she said anguishedly. 'Why did you do it?

What about Frannie? And Sara and your other children in Liverpool? Didn't you think of them?'

'I didn't expect it to happen like this, Jessica.' He sighed and gently pushed her away. They sat together on the bed. 'Michel was supposed to wait until it was dark before he killed the bastard. But I don't know what came over him. He did it when it was still daylight. There were two German officers in a café across the road and they saw what had happened. Michel ran for it, they followed, the gendarmerie took over, and Michel, the damn fool, led them straight to us. We were waiting in a bar in the rue Saint Antoine.'

'Well, I won't be saying any prayers for Michel,' Jessica said bitterly.

Louis smiled; a sweet, forgiving smile. 'He just panicked. We were all on edge. We drew lots for who should do the killing, and Michel lost.'

'You all lost, Louis.'

'You're right, Jess.' He smiled again – how could he possibly bring himself to smile under such circumstances? 'You seem to have always been right, ever since you came to live with us.' He turned to her and cupped her face in both his hands. 'You know, Jess,' he said gruffly, 'in another place, at another time, we could have . . .' he paused. 'You know what I mean?'

'I do, darling.' If she had met him before she'd met Bertie, if he hadn't been married to her friend . . .

His hands left her face. 'Where's Frannie?' he cried. 'Don't let her come to see me, will you? I couldn't bear it. And it wouldn't be fair on her. It's not the sort of situation for a young girl to get mixed up in.'

You should have thought about that before, you stupid idiot, Jessica thought, but didn't say. Oh, Louis! She wanted to weep on his shoulder.

As if he'd read her thoughts, he said, 'I don't want you crying over me, Jess. Once tomorrow's over, I hope you will do your best never to think of me again. And no praying, if you don't mind. I can't stand the idea of people praying for me.'

She shook his arm. 'Oh, Louis, I shall never stop thinking about you and I will say a prayer for you every night for the rest of my life.'

'Jess!' He began to cry himself. 'I don't want to die,' he wept. 'Look after Frannie for me, won't you? And keep the theatre going. Oh, and tell Sara how much I loved and missed her.' He paused. 'If she was here now, she'd kill me. Another thing; let Sam go. He desperately needs to wear a uniform and do his bit.' He began to laugh hysterically.

'Shush.' Jessica stroked his cheek. 'Shush now, darling.'

He stopped laughing and began to sway where he sat. He was falling asleep, she realized. She stood and eased his long body down on to the bed, then sat on the edge, watching him. At first, his eyelids flickered and his lips moved as if he was talking to himself, but after a while his body relaxed and she could tell he was lost in a deep, welcome sleep.

There were footsteps in the corridor outside; the official, probably coming to tell her it was time to go. She kissed the sleeping man softly on his brow, murmuring, 'Goodbye, Louis,' and was ready to leave when the door was unlocked.

'Quietly, please,' she whispered when the official was about to slam the door shut, and the man complied.

Jessica left the building feeling more upset than she had when she'd lost her children. At least with them she'd known that it couldn't possibly be for ever, that one day she was bound to see them again, but Louis – sweet, obliging, forgetful Louis, who'd been a hopeless yet adorable husband, who'd loved his children to distraction even if he did forget they existed from time to time – at five o'clock tomorrow morning he would stand in front of a firing squad made up of men he had never known, and they would shoot him dead.

★

By now, it was half past nine and almost dark. At the theatre, the play had finished, but the young teacher, Jean-Paul, had stayed behind in case Jessica came back with news of Louis.

'Good news?' he asked hopefully.

Jessica shook her head and told him what had happened. Clearly upset, he offered to look after the theatre until she felt able to make a decision about its future. She recalled Louis had asked that she keep the theatre going and felt grateful for Jean-Paul's offer. She gave him a programme of performances planned for the next four weeks, then hurried next door, desperate to see Sam. She wondered if Frannie was home. She hadn't been there when they'd come back from Chartres.

To her intense disappointment there was no Sam and no Frannie when she went indoors. She returned outside, closed the shutters, went back inside and sat twiddling her thumbs, her mind all over the place. How would Sara feel right now if she knew her husband was due to be executed in the morning? She was bound to be upset, but it was hard to guess what her real feelings had been for Louis.

How much longer would she herself remain in France? Jessica wondered. Quite out of the blue she was overwhelmed by a longing to be in Liverpool, visiting familiar places like Lena and Will's little flat in Waterloo that they shared with Calum and Daniel, the new baby.

You never know, Bertie might have decided to forgive her and have come back to Liverpool with Jamie and Dora. A spasm of pain passed through her at the idea that this could have happened, yet she wasn't there. It had never been her intention to leave Liverpool for such a long time.

Until now, she had felt at home in Paris, but it was here where her dear friend Louis had been sentenced to die in the morning, and now it felt alien and unreal. She wrapped her arms across her chest as if trying to protect herself from the wickedness that had overtaken the city she loved, and prayed Louis would remain asleep for most of the night, at least. It was impossible to imagine how he would feel when he woke with the realization of what the morning had in store.

For something to do, she decided to get ready for bed. Upstairs, she discovered the beds hadn't been made. The day had started off badly, she recalled, in the *boulangerie* when Madame Vierny had announced that Charles Guilborg had been murdered and she'd wondered if Frannie had had something to do with it, too.

Please don't let it be Frannie who'd told her papa that Monsieur Guilborg made a habit of strolling around the Île Saint-Louis of an evening, she prayed. The girl would blame herself for the rest of her life.

Her hands shook as she made the beds, beating the pillows as they'd never been beaten before, tucking in the sheets so tightly that it would be a struggle to get them out again. She was making Louis's bed, tears streaming down her cheeks knowing that he would never sleep in it again and she should really be putting the bedding out to be washed, when the front door opened and a voice shouted, 'Jessica.'

Sam was home.

She ran downstairs, straight into his arms. This was where she wanted to be more than any other place on earth. She didn't care where she was, Paris or Liverpool, as long as it was with Sam.

'Where have you been?' she cried.

'Doing my utmost to contact Louis's mother in Reims.' He was out of breath and there was perspiration on his forehead. 'I telephoned the cathedral. I remembered Louis saying once that his mother sometimes played the organ there. Whoever answered the phone promised to get a message to her urging her to come to Paris straight away.'

'How far is Reims?'

'About eighty miles.'

'She'll be devastated, poor woman.' She'd met Louis's mother just once. She'd asked to be called Simone, Jessica recalled. A widow in her fifties, she was a gracious, grey-haired lady with a genuinely kind manner. She had a daughter, too, who lived in Vichy France. Sara, for some reason, had disliked her mother-in-law – not that Sara had ever needed a reason to dislike anyone. Because of this, Frannie and Marie had seen little of their grandmother, though Frannie evidently doted on her. She pulled Sam towards the table and they sat down.

'I've also been to the Avenue Foch,' he continued, 'but they wouldn't let me in to see Louis because I'm not a relative. Did you see him? Oh, darling!' He turned in his chair and pressed her against him, as if the real horror of the situation was only now sinking in. 'They said he's being executed first thing in the morning. And we can't have the body to bury ourselves,' he added bitterly. 'I didn't ask what they intended doing with it.'

'Once he's dead, I don't care what happens to his body, but I suppose his mother would prefer to have him buried in a coffin with a Requiem Mass.' She looked at her watch; nearly eleven o'clock. In another six hours Louis Cotillard would be dead.

'I wonder where the hell Frannie is?' Sam said worriedly. 'It's pretty damned late.' There was a knock on the door and he said in a relieved voice, 'That's probably her now. She must have lost her key. I'll let her in.'

It wasn't Frannie that he showed into the room, but a tall, thin man with curly, slightly receding black hair. Jessica knew who it was straight away.

'I'm Lucien Brun, Henri's father,' he said in English. 'If you're worried about Frannie, she's with us, though in a very upset state – not surprising in view of what's to happen to her father. My wife and I didn't realize there were others at home who would be concerned about her. As soon as she told us, I came immediately to assure you that she's all right, if grieving badly.'

His English contained hardly a trace of accent. He had a gentle, clever face with dark expressive eyes. Casually dressed, his clothes gave the impression of having cost the earth.

Sam nudged a chair forward with his foot. 'Sit down,' he said, and the man complied.

Jessica got up and fetched a bottle of red wine from the pantry. She put it on the table with the corkscrew for Sam to open, then went in search of glasses. It wasn't just that she was looking after their visitor, but she felt like a glass of wine herself and probably Sam would, too. It scared her that Lucien Brun had automatically spoken to them in English. What had made him assume they weren't French? It was only Frannie who could have told him. She must have a word with the girl when she came home. No matter how upset she was about Louis, it was essential that she avoided getting Sam and Jessica into trouble by giving away their true identities. They'd be sent to a concentration camp, at the very least.

Sam had opened the wine and filled the glasses. Jessica drank hers as easily as a glass of water. She refilled her glass – the men had barely sipped theirs.

'Where do you live?' she asked Lucien Brun. It was a silly question considering the circumstances. She wasn't even vaguely interested in the answer. Perhaps it was the wine that she'd drunk much too quickly and was already making her feel dizzy.

'We have an apartment in the Marais, the rue Saint-Gilles,' he replied politely. 'But it's an expensive area and I recently lost my job so it might be necessary for us to move. I taught at the Sorbonne.'

'That's a shame.' She rubbed her eyes and discovered they were wet. Without realizing, she must have been crying.

Their visitor must have noticed. He said kindly, 'I had better be on my way. Esther, that's my wife, will be worried about me. If Frannie's up to it, I'll bring her home in the morning.'

He got to his feet and made for the door, and it was only then that Jessica saw the yellow star on the back of his jacket. He was Jewish. The Germans had made every Jew in Paris wear a yellow star. It had also been ruled that Jews could only travel in the last carriage of the *Métro*, as if they were inferior to the other passengers. It would be the reason he had lost his job at the Sorbonne.

'Oh, Sam,' she wept when Lucien Brun had gone, 'what a horrible world it has become.' It was hard to imagine it ever getting better.

That night, they didn't go to bed, just stayed at the table drinking wine, then coffee, then wine again. The night was quiet. A curfew was in force from 11 o'clock, so from then on there were no late singers, no laughing crowds going home from nightclubs or parties, no footsteps, no voices outside. The Café Edgar closed the blackout curtains and the patrons, mainly local, stayed until it was time to go quietly home. The rue de la Grand Truanderie, narrow and easily missed, was rarely visited by night patrols.

As it neared five o'clock, Jessica and Sam watched the fingers of the old rusty clock ticking the minutes noisily away as they approached the fateful hour. When it happened, Jessica could have sworn she could hear the shots that ended the life of Louis Cotillard.

'You couldn't have heard them from so far away, darling,' Sam assured her.

'I felt them then,' she whispered. 'I felt them in my heart.'

The morning sun had appeared, filtering through the shutters in dazzling strips of light, when Simone Cotillard, Louis's mother, arrived, her eyes red-rimmed and her body aching from head to toe. She had been given a lift, she said, in a ramshackle truck with wooden wheels that normally carried vegetables to market. Every time they'd driven over a bump in the road she had been almost thrown from her seat.

'May I have a short rest, please?' she asked. Her French was soft and lilting, delightful to listen to. 'In Louis's bed if you don't mind. That's the place I really want to be right now.'

Sam was introduced. Jessica kissed her and told her to go upstairs and she'd bring her a cup of warm milk. When she went into the room with the drink, Simone was sitting on the bed nursing her son's pillow as if it were a baby.

'He was always a bold child,' she said, 'afraid of nothing. Not naughty, but too courageous for his own good; climbing trees that were much too high and swimming in ponds that were dangerously deep. But that was twenty or more years ago. I would have thought he'd have got over his boldness by now.' She took the milk gratefully and declined something to eat. 'Later, please, when I have rested.' She looked towards the door, as if she was expecting someone to come in. 'Is Frannie still asleep?'

'Frannie!' Jessica sighed and told her where Frannie was and what she might have been up to. 'Lucien Brun is bringing her home later today.'

The older woman's eyes filled with tears. 'It sounds as if it's a case of like father, like daughter,' she murmured.

Downstairs, Sam had opened the shutters and the room was bright with sunshine. To Jessica's surprise, M. Auteil, the *boucher*, was seated at the table with a glass of wine. He had come to express his condolences for the death of Louis.

'*Il est un homme formidable,*' he said emotionally, holding up his glass.

Not *is*, Jessica thought, *was*, Louis *was* a great man.

M. Auteil was only the first to come. Throughout the day, more and more people came to pay their respects to Louis; old friends, traders in the street, the waiters from the Café Edgar, with Martin, the maitre d' at their head, people who had

attended the *Petit Théâtre* and those who had acted there –
some quite famous names from the French theatre, according
to Sam. At one time there were as many as twenty sitting
round the kitchen table or standing, all lamenting Louis's
death. Sam ordered a dozen bottles of wine. The odd prayer
was said, the occasional speech made, numerous tears shed.

In the middle of the accolades for her son, Simone came in.
'I think I prefer to be in the upstairs living room,' she said after
a while. 'I already know what a wonderful person my Louis
was.'

A few minutes later, Frannie and Henri arrived. Lucien
Brun waved from the door, but didn't come in. Frannie's face
was expressionless. Jessica merely hugged her and whispered,
'Your grandmother is upstairs, love.'

The young couple disappeared – Henri wasn't wearing a
yellow star, she noticed – and people continued to call until it
was time for that night's performance in Louis's little theatre to
start.

When Jean-Paul arrived with his young pupils, ready to per-
form that night's play, the teacher looked at her questioningly.
'Is it all right to go ahead?'

Jessica nodded vigorously. 'Louis asked me to make sure the
theatre was kept going,' she said.

Jean-Paul agreed. 'I think that would be the right thing to
do.'

The theatre was crowded. Jessica had to turn twice as many
people away as were let in. The audience was in a sombre
mood, not ready to watch a thriller, even one based on the
work of such a famous writer, but they laughed and gasped
and applauded, even hissed at the villain, in all the right places.

The cast took only one curtain call, but the audience
showed no sign of leaving. Instead, they turned to each other
and began to talk about the theatre and its proprietor, Louis
Cotillard. There were arguments about their favourite plays,

their favourite actors, how uncomfortable the seats were, how much Louis had contributed to the entertainment, if not of the nation, but at least of Paris.

'*Vive la France!*' one man shouted.

There was an answering shout, '*Vive la France!*'

'God bless Louis Cotillard. May his theatre live for ever.'

'For ever!' the crowd shouted. 'For ever and ever and ever.'

The next day, Jessica put the biggest photo of Louis that she could find on the stage, arranging the numerous flowers that had arrived round it. She left the door to the theatre open, and, as the day progressed, more and more flowers were added until the stage became a carpet of flowers. For the only time she could remember, the theatre smelled fresh and sweet.

The next morning, a policeman came. He wore plain-clothes and spoke French with a German accent. Jessica suspected he was a member of the Gestapo. He questioned them closely about Louis. Had they known what he was planning? Did they know his friends? He asked, politely, if he could search Louis's room, and Simone, just as politely, showed him upstairs.

Sam was out and perhaps the three generations of women – Louis's mother, his cousin and his daughter, all distraught – convinced the man that they were completely innocent in the matter of the murder of Charles Guilborg. He shook hands with all three, even expressed his condolences, and went away.

The months passed quietly, the weather grew colder, and the days got shorter. Christmas came and was celebrated with little fuss, as was the arrival of 1942. The running of the theatre had been left to Jean-Paul. Jessica felt exhausted and much too emotional, bursting into tears over nothing at all. Some nights, in the early hours, she met Simone downstairs. Neither could sleep. Frannie slept, but badly. She could be heard tossing and turning, crying and groaning in her room, and the next morning her young face looked battered, as if she'd been involved in a night-long fist-fight.

It was Henri, she said, who had told Papa that Charles Guilborg went for an evening walk around the Île Saint-Louis. 'But not so that Papa's friend would go and *murder* him. It was me and Henri who planned on murdering him. We'd worked out a foolproof plan.'

It was all too much for Jessica, hearing this girl of fourteen, this *child*, talking quite calmly about murder. When, early in January, Simone talked of going back to Reims, remarking sadly how lonely she would feel without Louis – 'I know I didn't see him all that much, but I knew he was *here*, not all that far away in Paris' – Jessica eagerly asked if she could go with her: 'Just for a few days to get the sights and sounds of Paris out of my head.' It was full of the crack of bullets and marching feet, and pictures in her head of men, women and children wearing yellow stars.

'I would love that, Jessica,' Simone said graciously. 'I do hope that Frannie will agree to come with us.'

At first, Frannie claimed she would prefer to stay in Henri's house, but changed her mind and decided to go to Reims instead. 'It won't be so noisy there. Henri's mother plays the piano most of the time and you can't hear yourself think.'

Sam declined to go with them. 'To tell the truth, I wouldn't mind a rest myself. I might well lock up the house, sleep in late, and listen to the wireless for the rest of the day. I'm fed up *talking* to people.' He grabbed her. 'Apart from you, my darling, Jess. I'll miss you dreadfully.'

They'd hardly been on the train to Reims five minutes when Jessica began to miss Sam. On reflection, the idea of doing nothing but sleep in and listen to the wireless seemed rather appealing.

But once in Reims, she was glad she'd come. It was an ancient city with a magnificent cathedral that had been damaged during the First World War. Simone lived on the outskirts in a small, neat apartment on a cobbled street full of small shops.

'Louis and my daughter, Alice, were raised on a farm about a mile from here,' she told Jessica. 'I gave it up soon after my husband unexpectedly died. It would have been a sacrifice for Louis to stay and look after it. All his life he had wanted to act, do something in the theatre. Once I'd sold the place, he felt it was all right to go to drama school.' She sighed. 'He was in London when he met Sara and they got married.'

'Mama didn't like our theatre,' Frannie said.

'I know, *cherie*.' Simone twisted her lips and said no more.

Everything in the apartment was white. The lace-trimmed tablecloths and napkins looked as if they had been dipped in the virginal snow that covered the streets outside. The dinnerware was eggshell-thin white china. It was like living in a cloud. Church bells woke them of a morning; a lonely owl hooted them to sleep at night.

Jessica spent time alone in the cathedral, though she had no idea what to pray for apart from Louis's soul. Was there any chance of anything good happening, however hard and sincerely she prayed? It felt as if France, as if most of Europe, had been cursed for evermore.

Simone bought Frannie clothes from some of the small smart shops dotted around the city. The girl was showing rather more interest in clothes than she had done in the past; a dark purple jumper with a polo neck was chosen with care, as well as a straight skirt to match and a black cardigan with pearl buttons. All suited Frannie's rather sober taste.

A Singer sewing machine was produced from the hall cupboard. Simone, having bought three yards of black bouclé, proceeded to make her granddaughter a short swagger coat.

Jessica couldn't wait for her to finish. She'd badly missed

232

the sewing machine she'd had in Liverpool, and had bought a length of blue woollen material in a local market to make a winter frock.

The days were taking on a dreamy, unreal quality. There weren't nearly as many enemy soldiers in Reims as there were in Paris. It was actually possible to imagine that peace had broken out.

Despite this, in her heart she was looking forward to returning to the capital – and Sam. She'd only come for a few days but had stayed for almost a week. She would leave soon. Frannie could stay if she preferred.

She got her hands on the sewing machine and was rushing to finish the frock, wondering what Sam would think of it, when he surprised her by turning up in Reims to tell her he was leaving France to join the British Air Force.

'But on one condition,' he added.

'And what's that?' Jessica asked.

'That you stay in Reims with Simone.' He folded his arms and stared at her, as if daring her to say no.

Chapter 18

'But you might be killed!' Jessica stammered. They were in the little white sitting room where he looked big and cumbersome and out of place. Simone and Frannie had gone shopping.

'I could be killed anywhere, Jess,' he said soberly. 'We all could. Louis was killed in Paris. No,' he gestured impatiently, 'I'm doing nothing to help the good side win. Somehow or other, I shall make my way to England and join up.'

'What will happen if I refuse to stay here?' She looked at him intently.

Sam shrugged. 'Then I shall stay with you in Paris,' he said simply.

She couldn't do that to him. It would be desperately selfish. Most women weren't given the choice of whether their men went away or stayed behind; the men were called up and had no say in the matter. And she mustn't forget that one of the last things Louis had said was, 'Let Sam go.'

Jessica stared at her hands for several seconds, without seeing them. Then she nodded. 'I'll stay in Reims,' she promised. 'I like it here.'

His eyes lit up and she hated to see how happy he was to be freed from the burden of caring for her. He glanced around the pretty room. 'You'll be safe here,' he said, as if the lace tablecloth and curtains would provide protection against the Boche. 'Will Frannie stay?' he asked.

'We haven't discussed it, but I reckon she would. She's terribly fond of her grandmother.'

'That's good.' He looked relieved and ran his fingers through his thick hair. He must have been worrying about Frannie. 'Louis would have expected me to make sure she was all right.'

'I shall have to go back to Paris to collect my things.' Jessica got up, went over to the window and looked out. There was a small shoe shop opposite; she'd never seen a single person go in or out during the time she'd been in Reims. She wondered how the owners managed to keep going with so few customers — or none at all. Next door there was a hairdresser who seemed to do more business — Simone had her hair trimmed there. Reims was peaceful, but it was also desperately dull.

'I realize that.' He came behind her and put his arms round her waist, and she leaned back against him. 'I can't imagine life without you.' He buried his face in her hair. 'But . . .'

'. . . you've got more important things to do,' she finished for him. He twisted her round so they were facing. 'I'm sorry, I'm sorry,' she whispered when she saw the misery on his face.

'It's not more important,' he said raggedly. 'It's just that it's necessary. I've got to live with myself for the rest of my life. How am I going to do that if I sit out the war in Paris? I bet my brothers have all joined up by now.'

Jessica imagined the horror of his parents if they had. 'I understand,' she said. 'I understand.'

'I've a question to ask,' he mumbled. 'Will you marry me?'

'Marry you!' There'd never been any suggestion of marriage between them. 'Why are you asking now?'

'Because I'm going away, you idiot.' He squeezed her so hard it hurt. 'It didn't matter before. We were together and that's all I wanted, to be with you. But from now on we shall be living apart and I want you to be officially mine, to wear my ring, to let the world know that you are Mrs Sam Deveraux.' He picked her up and swung her around, then

235

dropped on to one knee, laughing now. 'So, will you marry me, Jessica Farley?'

If only she could! But she couldn't. Not only that, she couldn't tell him why. She couldn't say, 'I can't marry you, Sam, although I would love to. You see, I'm already married and have two wonderful children who I haven't seen for years.' But then she thought of another perfectly legitimate excuse. 'We couldn't possibly do anything official.' She shook her head gravely. 'I'd be too scared to apply for a marriage licence, get married in a church or a register office or what-ever they call them here. We'd be drawing attention to our-selves.'

'I've already thought of that.' He stood and rested his hands on her shoulders. 'Do we really need a licence, Jess? If people really love each other, is it necessary for them to have a piece of paper to confirm it? Anyone can pronounce us man and wife, and that would be good enough for me. What about you?'

Before she could answer, the front door opened and Simone and Frannie came in. Jessica rushed into the hall to meet them. 'Sam and I are getting married,' she cried. 'Aren't we, Sam?'

'Most definitely.' Sam threw his hat into the air. 'Now we are off to buy the ring!'

Sam must have expected her to accept his proposal; he had everything arranged.

On the morning after they'd returned to Paris, he advised her to put on her best dress and be ready to get married in an hour. Anticipating this, the night before, Jessica had stayed up late hemming the skirt of the blue frock she'd made in Reims.

Sara had left behind most of her hats and Simone found a white straw halo hat very similar to the sort that Deanna Durbin had worn in the picture *Three Smart Girls*, Jessica remembered. She'd gone to see it with Lydia. It took a few seconds to recall her cousin's name.

'As long as you don't mind wearing a summer hat in winter,' Simone said.

'I don't mind a bit.' Jessica jammed the hat on her head.

Sam, in his best suit, escorted her into the theatre where the entire staff of the Café Edgar were gathered with Martin at their head. He was holding a piece of paper on which it turned out that Sam had written in his terrible handwriting the words of the wedding service in English.

The waiters' shirts were so white they hurt the eyes and Martin's black evening suit was adorned with a pair of fringed red and gold epaulettes.

He coughed and boomed 'Welcome' when the small wedding procession came in. Holding the paper only a few inches from his nose, he began to read.

'Do yow, Samuel Lyle Deveraux, tak thees woman to be thy awful weeded wife to 'ave and to 'old from thees day forward, for reecher and for poorer, in seekness and in 'ealth, to love and to chereesh, till death do yow part?'

'I do,' Sam said in a strange voice. Jessica could tell he was doing his utmost not to laugh.

Martin turned to her, the bride. 'Do yow, Jessica Mary Farley, tak thees man to be thy awful weeded husband . . .'

Jessica's 'I do', and the act of Sam slipping the ring on her finger, was the signal for the release of the hilarity that they all felt. Even Simone, whose English was poor, had latched on to the merriment of the occasion. Like Frannie, she was laughing and crying at the same time.

Everybody kissed each other, including the waiters, and the excited party made their way from the theatre to the Café Edgar only just across the narrow street where a special table had been set for the newly married couple and their guests.

Despite rationing, quite a feast had been prepared; fruit salad to start with, followed by steak tartare with tiny new potatoes, and *crème caramel* for afters. Martin apologized for the fruit cocktail being tinned. 'It was all we could get,' he said disgustedly.

'I *love* tinned fruit salad,' Jessica assured him, which was true. Jamie and Dora had done so, too, though Bertie had always insisted on it being fresh, complaining when the banana turned brown. 'You should leave putting the banana in until the very last minute,' he would chide.

What a strange thought to have at her wedding to another man! Jessica might have been shocked had she not felt so amused and delighted with the events of the day. She was actually committing bigamy of a sort. She had two husbands!

She turned to Sam. 'I love you,' she said.

'And I love you, darling.'

Martin produced a bottle of champagne. The cork hit the ceiling when it was opened. 'Today is the day,' he said, 'when we all love each other.'

As the day wore on, Jessica's feeling of elation was exchanged for one of fear. Sam was setting off first thing in the morning. One of Louis's contacts had arranged for him to be picked up by a lorry in Orleans and taken to Spain.

She didn't ask what sort of lorry, who would be driving it, how long it would take, and if he was about to walk all the way to Orleans? Then there was Spain, a country every bit as Fascist as Germany, ruled by General Franco, a dictator, who had overturned the legally elected government by force. There'd been a civil war. A young man Will had known in Liverpool had gone to Spain to fight against the Fascists and had lost an arm. How would Sam get from Spain to England? Had the journey by sea already been arranged? She didn't ask any of these questions in case Sam didn't know any of the answers and she would be more fearful than she already was.

'As soon as I arrive in England, I'll try and get word to you,' he had promised.

How on earth would he manage to do that? It was another question she didn't ask.

Later, when it was time for the theatre to open, Jean-Paul announced that his wife was expecting a baby and wanted to move away from Paris.

'To Nantes, where her parents live. I've advertised for a teaching job there, but shall continue looking after the theatre until we leave,' he assured her. 'Though the present programme finishes in six weeks' time and you need to make more bookings.'

'I'll start tomorrow,' Jessica promised. Tomorrow, Sam would be gone and she would be as miserable as sin. Extending the programme for the theatre would be an ideal distraction. Jean-Paul went next door to get things prepared for that night's performance.

Henri arrived straight from school, longing to see Frannie – or so said the expression on his face the minute he set eyes on her. Frannie had been off school for almost a fortnight. Jessica wondered if she should have written to the headmistress. Maybe she could write a note in the morning for the girl to take with her.

In the kitchen, there was dance music on the wireless and wine on the table. Perhaps because there'd been a wedding, Frannie and Henri began to dance. They looked awkward and stiff together, as if they'd never done it before. With an impressive flourish, Martin, who was still there, apparently having forgotten he had a restaurant to run, invited Simone on to the floor. Sam pulled Jessica out of the chair.

'You'll look after yourself in Reims, won't you, Jess?' he whispered. 'Keep your head down, don't do anything rash.'

Her throat ached too much to answer. She clung to him, moving her head against his shoulder, a sort of nod.

'Are your clothes packed ready to leave?'

'Everyone's clothes are packed.' She hardly recognized the strange voice as her own.

'I'm sure you'll all be happier there than in Paris.' He caressed the back of her neck. 'There are too many responsibilities here, too many dangers.'

'I know.'

'I'll never stop thinking of you,' he said huskily. 'You are the love of my life. No matter what happens, I shall never love another woman as much as I love you.'

She woke up, weak with love-making and full of sorrow that Sam had gone. During the night she told him about Bertie and her children, but all he did was kiss her more. The house was silent and it was still as dark as night outside. Sam must have crept out of bed and left without making a sound. In a way, she was glad because she felt convinced that she would have made a scene and tried to prevent him from leaving.

Where was he now? She twisted the thick gold wedding ring round her finger and imagined him just outside Paris, travelling on a bus or trying to beg a lift from an innocuous vehicle taking animals to market or transporting household goods.

After a while, she got out of bed and went downstairs to make coffee – these days tea didn't have the same soothing effect as it had used to. It wasn't long before Simone joined her. She waved her arm around the kitchen.

'Now this is a house without men,' she remarked with a sad smile.

'It happened so suddenly,' Jessica said. Much too suddenly.

'Louis's death was the reason for Sam going.' Simone sighed. 'Later on, I shall go to Reims and collect my things.'

'And I shall unpack mine.' She'd never had any intention of leaving Paris. 'I hated lying to Sam,' she said, 'but he badly wanted to join the fighting and it would have been unfair of me to stop him by insisting we live here. I hope you don't mind my saying that I would have died of boredom in Reims.'

'I don't mind. I always liked the quietness, but feel quite differently now that Louis has gone. I have the urge to turn my life round.' Simone put the bubbling coffee pot on to the table. 'You lied very convincingly,' she said. 'We all did.' It had been necessary for all three women to convince Sam they were returning to Reims.

'Someone told me once that I was an excellent liar.' It wasn't exactly the sort of thing to be proud of. Jessica poured coffee and pushed it towards the other woman. 'Do we have milk?'

'A little in the cupboard. I'll get it.'

'I'm so pleased you're staying,' Jessica said when Simone returned with a small jug of milk.

'Do you mind?' She raised her eyebrows.

'I just said I was pleased, and it's not up to me to mind. You're Louis's mother; you have more right to be here than I have.'

'Don't be ridiculous, Jessica. You've been looking after Louis – and Frannie – all this time. You have every right in the world to be here.'

'Let's say we all have the same right; Frannie, too.' Soon, they would sort out the income from the theatre and arrange their share.

Simone laughed. 'Until Sara comes back. Then I'll be sent packing back to Reims with my tail between my legs and she will reign supreme over everyone and everything.'

Frannie shuffled in, her hair a mess, rubbing her eyes. She looked at her grandmother, then at Jessica. 'So, this is how it will be from now on,' she said. She held out her hands to both women. 'Now *we* are the three musketeers – and Henri can be D'Artagnan.' She clapped her hands to her cheeks. 'What a really stupid thing to say,' she gasped and ran out the room. It wasn't all that long ago that the three musketeers had included her father.

Jessica was about to follow the heartbroken girl, when Simone said, 'I wouldn't, if I were you. Let her get used to how things are in her own way. It's something we'll all have to do.'

Weeks went by. It was March when Jessica found a scrap of paper on the doormat that had been delivered during the night – she had no idea from whom or where it had come from, and wondered how whoever had delivered it had know she was in Paris, not Reims. It was to say that Sam had safely arrived in England and sent his love. She had given him her mother's address to write to, and wondered how long it would be before she would be home to read his letters.

She went to St Eustache where she knelt and conveyed her thanks to God for delivering Sam safely to England, despite thinking he wasn't really much of a God to allow such desperately horrible things to happen in His world.

Their lives were totally influenced by the war. The shortage of things like food and fuel was only part of it, the curfew a mere inconvenience. More serious was the practice of people being taken from the streets and sent to work as slave labour in Germany, and the fact that French Jews were treated abominably.

News of what was happening elsewhere in the world was minimal. Everyone was aware that Germany had invaded Russia – a really big mistake, according to people who knew about such things. After all, Napoleon had done it and his troops were slaughtered. This could be Hitler's undoing, or so everyone hoped.

In the deserts of North Africa the British Eighth Army was fighting the Germans led by General Rommel, the Russian

Army had surrounded the Germans at Stalingrad, the Duke of Kent had been killed in a flying accident.

At the end of the old year, the Japanese Navy had sunk the American Fleet anchored in Pearl Harbor and America had entered the war.

Jessica was having trouble making up a programme for the theatre. Amateur dramatic groups that Louis had used no longer existed. Nadia and Georges Jourdan had gone to live in the countryside. The professional actors that were left were fully employed. In Paris, the theatre remained very popular.

'We could have a concert,' Frannie suggested. '*Grandmère* can play the piano and I could sing.'

'*Can* you sing? If so, I've never heard it.' She knew Simone had played the organ in Reims cathedral. 'Though not when anything important was going on,' she had said.

Frannie tossed her head. 'I have a pleasant light soprano voice, according to Madam de Fleury who takes us for music.'

'Let's hear it, then.'

The three women went into the theatre and Simone began to play scales on the piano. Even Jessica, who had always considered herself to be tone-deaf, was able to recognize the instrument was badly out of tune.

Simone winced. 'This needs tuning.'

'I'll try and find a piano tuner. Frannie, what song are you about to sing?'

' "Night and Day".'

'I'm only used to playing holy music,' Simone complained. 'I've never heard of "Night and Day".'

Frannie began to sing without the benefit of the piano. 'Night and day, you are the one . . .'

Her voice was high and sweet and pleasant to listen to. 'Are you capable of singing like that for two hours?' Jessica asked when she'd finished.

'Of course not,' Frannie snorted.

'Then what do we do for the remaining one hour and fifty-five minutes?'

Frannie shrugged and said she had no idea.

It had given Jessica an idea, though. A music hall! Get other acts – somehow from somewhere: a juggler, a magician, dancers. Oh, and have a talent night – they could offer prizes. Next week it would be Easter – perhaps they could engage a choir. 'Don't worry, Louis,' she whispered. 'I will never let your theatre close, not for a single night.' Except, of course, on Sundays.

On Easter Sunday, they were treated to *déjeuner* – lunch – in the Café Edgar. It would seem that Martin had a crush on Simone and was determined to impress her. Henri was invited – he and Frannie did everything together nowadays.

The meal was similar to Jessica and Sam's wedding break-fast, except it was tinned grapefruit, not fruit salad. It was, however, remarkable for something else. While eating the sweet – *crème caramel* again – Jessica felt horribly nauseous. Nor was she enjoying the wine. What was more, she hadn't had a period in months . . . but this had happened before when Bertie had disappeared with the children and she had put it down to being so terribly upset. She'd been just as upset when Louis was executed and Sam had gone away.

This time, however, she knew the reason – she was pregnant. There'd been the faintest suspicion at the back of her mind, but it had seemed so unlikely she'd refused to acknowledge it. She and Sam had agreed from the start that it would be irresponsible to bring a child into the world while they were living in a foreign country embroiled in a terrible war. But she wasn't quite sure what had happened on the last night she and Sam had spent together. It would seem they'd forgotten to act responsibly. But perhaps a baby would be a good luck charm, making it a certainty that one day she and

244

Sam would meet again and get married properly. She felt sure Bertie would be pleased to see the back of her.

Well, she wasn't going to announce it in front of everybody, just as Sara had done years ago in the very same restaurant. Then, it had been a bad-tempered occasion. But at that moment, the realization that she was expecting Sam's child made Jessica feel like the happiest woman on earth. No, she would reveal her secret tomorrow when only Simone and Frannie were present.

She rested her hands on her stomach and thought about the baby living inside.

Back home, they listened to the wireless until after tea when Frannie and Henri played cards for the rest of the evening, Simone picked up her knitting, and Jessica made notes and tried to work out a programme for the theatre that would last until summer.

At ten o'clock, Henri went home, and soon afterwards Simone and Frannie went to bed. Jessica would have gone, too, but there was still some warmth left in the fire and she wanted to sit and think about the child she was expecting. If only she could get word to Sam.

She was dozing off when she heard the knocking on the front door. Not quite so much a knocking, but a thumping, and there was something urgent about it. Jessica approached the door cautiously.

To her surprise, it was Henri, and the boy was crying uncontrollably. He almost fell into the house.

'Henri, love! What's wrong?' She helped him to his feet, led him into the kitchen, and sat him in front of the still-warm hearth. The boy was shaking, too, most unusual for Henri who, while only sixteen, was normally very grown up and full of confidence.

He clung to Jessica, burying his head in her breast. 'They have taken away my parents, *ma mère et mon père*, and

Delphine, my little sister,' he sobbed. 'When I got home there was no one there. A neighbour told me they'd all been taken.'

'Who by, love?' Jessica asked, though she already knew the answer.

'The Boche,' Henri said in an angry voice. 'Who else could it be but the Boche?'

After a while, the crying gave way to utter weariness and an obvious need to sleep, so she gathered armfuls of bedding out of the airing cupboard, took it into Marie's old room and made the bed, then fetched the brick out of the oven meant for her own bed and put it between the sheets at the foot – the weather wasn't all that cold, but she'd needed a brick to keep warm since Sam had gone away.

Henri had brought nothing with him, so she dug out a pair of Louis's old pyjamas, slippers and a dressing gown. They were all much too big, but it didn't matter.

Downstairs, she took Henri's hand and led him up to Marie's room. 'Get undressed,' she urged, 'while I make you a nice warm drink. I'll be back in a minute.'

She put milk in a pan on top of the slightly glowing coals. What made her think that her baby would be a good luck charm when there was no such thing as good luck nowadays?

It wasn't long since Delphine, Henri's sister, had been a baby herself, but it hadn't stopped her from being brutally removed from her home along with her parents. Jessica's blood ran cold when she thought of the inevitable destination of Henri's family: a concentration camp, where unspeakable things were rumoured to be happening to Jews, young and old. She doubted if Henri would ever see them again. His parents would be relieved that their son hadn't been home.

For the second time that day, she put her hands over her stomach, this time protectively. She feared for her baby. She resolved never, ever to be parted from him or her, to never,

ever let her baby out of her sight. She would not lose this child as she had lost her others.

The next day, Simone went round to where Henri's family had lived and was told that quite a few Jewish families had been rounded up.

'Is the boy with you?' a woman asked.

'I've never met him,' Simone had replied. 'She seemed such a nice woman,' she said to Jessica later. 'But I didn't want her to know where Henri was.' She sighed. 'In other words, I didn't trust her.'

All day, Henri followed Jessica around like a puppy. Frannie was upset. 'I'm his girlfriend, why doesn't he turn to me?' she said tearfully.

'Because he's lost his mother, love,' Jessica explained. 'Right now, I'm the nearest thing to a mother in his life.' She would be there for Henri as long as he needed her.

Chapter 19

The pain woke her. It was as if her stomach was being ripped apart. It made it worse that she was much too hot. She kicked the sheet away from her feet, creating a brief, welcome draught. Six months ago, in the midst of the freezing winter, everyone had longed for summer, to be warm, but now, in September, they were experiencing an Indian summer, and it was too hot for comfort.

Without thinking, she had begun to count the seconds in her head. When twelve had passed, the pain came again, not just a normal pain, but a contraction.

She was in labour.

It would have been easy to panic. She was scared of the more painful contractions that would inevitably follow, the agony of giving birth, scared of Colette, Simone's friend who had come from Reims to deliver her precious baby. She wasn't a properly trained midwife, describing herself as 'self-taught'. What would happen if stitches were needed? She wanted Sam there, and to be in a proper hospital, but had always avoided having anything to do with officialdom since the Germans had taken over Paris; filling in forms with her false name and false nationality, pretending she was Louis's cousin. It was why she hadn't been under the care of a doctor or booked a hospital bed, as she would have preferred – she was thirty-two, not too old to have a baby, but not young, either. Still counting the seconds between pains, she lost track, her brain too muggy to concentrate.

She'd had an awful time giving birth to Jamie, who'd been a huge baby, nine and a half pounds. She'd needed *five* stitches. With Dora, she'd been given some sort of gas to breathe and it had relaxed her. All Colette had to offer in the way of pain relief were tablets similar to Aspro.

Thinking about it, she really *was* beginning to panic.

When Jamie was born, Bertie had accused her of being overly dramatic. He'd actually used that phrase. 'You were being overly dramatic, Jessica,' he'd said when he'd come into the delivery room after Jamie's birth. 'There was no need to have made such a fuss.' Apparently, she had screamed the place down.

The midwife, a stout, red-faced Irishwoman with strong arms and an irascible manner, had asked if he was more interested in criticizing his wife than admiring his beautiful new son.

'Of course not,' Bertie had stammered.

When she'd come out of the maternity hospital, he explained that there'd been two other women having babies at the same time. Jessica was the only one making a scene, and he had felt embarrassed in front of the other fathers.

'I was the only one having a nine-and-a-half-pound baby, that's why,' Jessica had said indignantly. She and the other women had compared notes afterwards.

He had apologized then, and thanked her for giving him such a handsome son.

Jessica groaned as another contraction passed very slowly over her body, a long wave of pure agony. If only she could fall asleep and wake up this time tomorrow when it would all be over.

The groan must have alerted Simone and Colette, who were sleeping together. They appeared in the bedroom, Simone at one side of the bed and Colette at the other, demanding to know what was wrong. They looked like sentinels who had come to carry out some fiendish torture.

'I think I'm in labour,' Jessica had to admit. She felt helpless. Over the next few hours – *hours!* – her wellbeing and that of her baby would be in other people's hands for whatever length of time was necessary.

Both women disappeared, one to boil water, the other to fetch old bedding that had already been put aside for the birth of Jessica's baby.

Frannie crept into the room, her eyes big and round. She must have heard the groan, too. 'Hello, Jessica,' she whispered.

'Hello.' Hopefully, Henri wasn't about to pay her a visit. Even if he had heard the groan, he was more likely to have put his head under the pillow in the hope of not hearing any more.

'How do you feel?' Frannie asked.

'Oh, fine,' Jessica said valiantly. It was important not to put the girl off having children when she grew older by making childbirth out to be some rare form of persecution, though the next contraction raised a very audible squeak. She took a vow not to scream, however painful the contractions became.

Simone and Colette returned. 'Back to bed with you, Frannie,' Simone said grimly.

Jessica reached up, clutched the wooden headboard and closed her eyes. She resolved not to open them again until she'd become a mother for the third time.

She prayed a lot out loud, *very* loud. 'Hail Mary full of grace, our Lord is with thee, blessed art thou amongst women and blessed be the fruit of thy womb, Jesus,' she bellowed over and over again.

The fruit of Jessica's womb came into the world in a violent rush, taking everyone by surprise, Jessica in particular. She opened her eyes and saw the cord was being cut. It was over and hadn't hurt quite as much as expected.

'*C'est un garçon*,' Colette crowed. '*Un garçon magnifique.*' She hung the screaming child by his ankles and slapped his red bottom. 'He came out very fast for a first baby.' She looked meaningfully at Jessica, but didn't say another word.

A magnificent baby for a magnificent liar, Jessica thought, at the same time wondering if he really had to be treated so cruelly in the first few minutes of his life. She held out her arms, and Sam's son was wrapped in a scrap of old sheet and laid against her breast. He was a long, lean baby, without much fat on him, and had a fuzz of pale hair and the most beautifully ugly face she had ever seen. She felt a rush of love that almost choked her.

'Hello, sweetheart,' she murmured. 'I wish your daddy was here to see you.' It wasn't just his daddy who was missing, but his big brother and sister. She wondered if the day would ever come when they would all be together.

Frannie was back in the room. 'What are you going to call him, Jessica?'

'Sammy.' People had asked and she'd said she hadn't made up her mind, but it had always been her intention to call the baby Sammy if he was a boy. Her cup ran over when Colette said there was no need for stitches.

When Sammy was six weeks old and thriving, Colette, who'd brought him into the world, returned to Reims, promising to come back and see them in the not-too-distant future. Life in the house acquired a feeling of normality – as much normality as possible for a woman who'd lost her son, a girl who'd lost her father, and a boy who had no idea whether his family were still alive. And if they weren't, then what sort of horrendous deaths had they suffered? Jessica was the only one for whom something good had occurred.

Henri no longer went to school. It would have been both

mad and dangerous to advertise the fact he was still around. He sat in Marie's old room studying the books on French military history that Frannie had borrowed for him from the library. They were a clever pair, playing tricky word games together and having quizzes. Henri adored Sammy and told him long, complicated fairy stories that were made up as he went along. The baby, not understanding a word, just beat him on the face with his tiny fists or pulled his ears. Henri smiled delightedly and didn't mind a bit.

Now Jessica had a child to look after, Simone took over the cooking and cleaning. It was over a year since she'd lost her son, but she seemed happy enough. Sometimes, she could be caught singing as she rolled out pastry or mixed a cake. Martin from the Café Edgar called regularly with pieces of cheese and slices of cake.

For some reason, Jessica felt safer strolling around Paris with a baby in a pram. It was less likely she would be stopped. She began to go shopping again, wandering far and wide, marvelling for a second time at the wonders of Paris, the sparkling river, the majestic buildings, the interior of Notre-Dame where she often attended Mass with the baby on her knee.

Very occasionally, people, either singly or in pairs, would come to the theatre in the dead of night seeking shelter. They would ask for Louis, whose name and address must still be remembered by individuals unaware that he was dead.

Despite the danger, Jessica, with Simone's agreement, always took the people in for a night or two. It would be too cruel for words to turn them away. They stayed in the space under the middle bench in the theatre, and she fed them as best she could and made sure they were kept warm.

It was with a great sense of relief that she eventually sent them on their way, hoping they'd be the last she would see, but this hadn't been the case so far. Weeks would pass until one night there'd be a dull thump on the front door and she or Simone would open it to strangers.

As for the theatre itself, it continued to flourish mainly as a music hall. It had been a brilliant idea, to contact retired jugglers and musicians, dancers and singers, some of whom were very much past their prime, but their acts created a feeling of nostalgia for times gone by, making the audience laugh and cry far louder and more frequently than they would have done had there not been a war on.

Meanwhile, the progress of the war seemed to have reached stalemate. Jessica had expected that the United States joining in the hostilities would have brought victory closer, but nothing seemed to have changed. America was tied up in the Pacific fighting the Japanese, who seemed to win at every turn. The newspapers reported Germany was making great strides in Russia, but rumour had it their advance had tailed off.

Good news could only be obtained from rumours. In the desert, the German troops were said to be advancing rapidly, but in the shops and on the streets it was muttered that the British Eighth Army was driving the great General Rommel back.

Jessica heard the rumours when she went shopping, Frannie heard them at school and Simone from Martin, who seemed to have access to all sorts of information that might or might not be true.

And now another Christmas approached, the fourth of the war. Jessica had arranged for a week of carol concerts. On Christmas Eve, something happened, something so odd, that she knew she would never make sense of it, no matter how long she lived.

The theatre was full for the final carol concert. Jessica hadn't done much organizing apart from making a list of carols to sing. A woman with the bearing of a formidable sergeant-major was standing in the middle of the stage, having appointed herself choir-mistress. A friend of Martin's, she had been there every night. She waved her arms furiously at the audience, which responded by singing at the tops of their voices. Everyone was obviously enjoying themselves.

'*Vive le Vent*,' 'Jingle Bells', they sang, and '*Mon Beau Sapin*,' 'O Christmas Tree'. Jessica had listed all the Christmas songs and carols she could think of, to be sung in French. Pretty soon it would be time for an interval and the list was nearly finished. It would just have to be sung again for the second half. It had happened every night and no one had minded. Frannie's voice could be heard, higher and sweeter than the others.

The audience had started on 'Silent Night', the last song before the interval. '*Douce nuit*,' they sang, '*douce nuit*.'

'Silent night . . .' Jessica sang with them. She preferred her carols in English.

The woman onstage was swinging her arms higher and higher as the singing approached an emotional conclusion. Simone pressed her foot on the piano's loud pedal.

The singing stopped, the music ceased, but outside the carol continued. Male voices provided a joyful rendition of 'Silent Night' – in German. No one in the room moved, not a word was spoken, until someone whispered, 'See who it is, Jessica.'

Jessica crept downstairs. It was obvious who it was: German soldiers who happened to be passing and had heard the carols being sung. The question was, did she want to let them in? If she didn't, they might bang on the door and *demand* to come in. Though she doubted if they would want to examine people's papers or ask questions. They sounded too cheerful to be officious.

Swallowing hard, she opened the door. Four young German soldiers were standing in the street, singing their hearts out. They grinned when they saw her and came into the theatre, rifles slung over their shoulders, in the best of moods.

Seeing the foyer empty, one ventured up the stairs while

continuing to sing '*Stille Nacht*'. When he didn't return, the others followed, Jessica at the rear.

The audience looked dumfounded. The young men stoppped singing for a minute then began to laugh. They shook hands, squeezed shoulders, and patted the heads of children. They were wide-eyed, fresh-faced, and so very, very nice. Had any been in the firing squad that killed Louis, Jessica wondered, or helped take Henri's family away?

Before long, the entire room, Jessica apart, and possibly Simone, who could only be seen from the back, were singing carols, and the atmosphere was full of friendliness and good cheer.

The soldiers stayed until the concert was over, and left blowing kisses and wishing people a Happy New Year, leaving Jessica to wonder if she'd imagined the whole thing.

In February Sammy was six months old. He was a very advanced baby – Jessica supposed every mother thought the same – but compared with her other children, Sammy could do all sorts of things that they couldn't until they were months older. She suspected it might be her own fault that Jamie and Dora were so unadventurous. They'd been confined to the pram or the playpen, encouraged to sleep a lot, fed at regular times of the day, and left to cry if they woke too early or during the night. It had broken Jessica's heart to hear them, but it was the way the matron in the hospital had advised the mothers to bring up their children.

'Don't give in to their demands,' she had told them in her steely voice, 'or you will do them great harm. They will grow up spoilt and selfish, always expecting their own way. Being fed at regular intervals will instil in them a sense of order and they will willingly respond to discipline when it is applied.'

What a load of nonsense, Jessica thought now. It was really stupid of her to have complied. She felt ashamed that her children had been subjected to such a harsh, stultifying regime that had almost certainly held them back, turning them into good, well-behaved little citizens who would never rebel.

Sammy only had to open his mouth and food would be shoved into it, or he would be picked up and cuddled, or played with, or his napkin changed. One day, Jessica found him standing up in his pram hollering for company and for someone to tell him what a clever little boy he was.

He kept their spirits up, made them laugh. Even the youngsters, Frannie and Henri, were sick to death of the war that people were beginning to think would go on for ever. But 1943 was gradually becoming a significant turning point in the hostilities.

The most heartening news of all came in July, when it was learned that Allied troops had landed in Sicily and not long afterwards in Italy itself. The hated Mussolini was deposed, and the country surrendered and shortly afterwards declared itself at war with Germany, until recently its great ally.

The fact that British troops, as well as others, were fighting in a neighbouring country was reassuring, even if it made no difference to the attitude of their own occupiers, who only became more cruel and oppressive with the awareness that their long-anticipated victory seemed likely to turn into defeat.

She was never sure whether it was Sammy's cough that woke her, or the subdued banging on the theatre door. She sat up and listened. Sammy didn't cough again, but the banging persisted, still subdued, but without a pause.

Groaning inwardly, she got out of bed and put on slippers and a dressing gown. She entered the theatre and opened the front door. A man stood there smiling at her pleasantly.

'I'm looking for Louis Cotillard,' he said in French.

'I'm afraid Louis no longer lives here.'

The man's face didn't register any emotion. He was about

thirty, tall and slim, good-looking in a refined sort of way. 'I was told I could get a bed here for the night.'

'Who told you?' He wasn't like their usual visitors. He was clean and well-dressed, obviously not tired. There was nothing wretched or pathetic about him.

'I was told by Jean Leclerc in Brussels. I am on my way to London with urgent messages for General de Gaulle. Jean said if I failed to get a lift when I was in the Paris area, I would be given a bed here.' He pulled his collar up and shivered. 'I find it rather cold for September, madame, and would appreciate being invited inside. *Je suis Claud Petrou.*'

'*Et je suis Jessica Deveraux.*' Afterwards she realized, when it was much too late, that she should have given in to her instincts and slammed the door in Claud Petrou's face. She neither believed nor trusted him, yet his story sounded genuine. Louis had had contacts in Brussels, but she hadn't known their names.

She said in French, 'I'll show you where you can sleep.' She led the way up to the theatre and lifted the wooden seat, indicating the hidden room beneath. 'You'll find bedding in there and a lavatory in the yard. I'll make you a warm drink. Are you likely to leave early in the morning?'

The man nodded. 'Very early.' He removed his hat and a rather fine black overcoat and laid them on a bench. The coat had red quilted lining and looked well warm enough for September. She resolved to wake Simone when she went next door and ask her to come back with her when she brought the drink; there was strength in numbers.

'Good.' She didn't want him around any longer than necessary. She turned to leave the room, when a hand fell heavily on to her shoulder and she was spun round. 'It doesn't matter about the drink,' Claud Petrou said. He laughed. 'What I prefer is a little light relief and all the money you have on the premises. Afterwards, I'll call in the Gestapo. There'll be a hefty reward for reporting people like you.'

Jessica was about to scream, but was prevented by a punch to the jaw that propelled her backwards against the wall. She was sliding down, stunned, when her attacker grabbed the top of her nightdress with both hands and ripped the thin material in two. Underneath, she was completely naked. She tried to scream, but had no breath left.

Somewhere at the back of Jessica's confused brain was not fear for what was about to happen, but for what would happen afterwards. All she could think about was Sammy. What would happen to Sammy?

The man was supporting her limp body with one hand and struggling with the buttons on his trousers with the other. He was preparing to enter her, when there was an enormous, deafening bang, and he fell to the floor. Jessica could feel something warm on her face and her ears began to buzz.

'Are you all right, Jessica?' a shaky voice enquired. Henri was standing over her, a small gun in his hand.

Jessica swallowed hard. She nodded, but didn't speak. The sound of the gun had been very loud. She was waiting for a knock on the door or the wall, someone wanting to know what the noise was. She had no idea how long she waited to see if they'd heared, five minutes perhaps, but maybe people had become used to hearing shots in the night and had taken no notice.

'Where did you get the gun?' she stammered.

'I brought it from home the night I found everyone gone,' Henry said. 'It belonged to my grandfather. I thought I might need it one day.'

'And you did!' Jessica gasped. 'What are we going to do with him?' She waved her hand at the body. Blood was seeping out of the hole in the man's head.

Henri appeared dazed, as if all his willpower and courage had been used in firing the bullet that had killed another human being. He hung his head. '*Je ne sais pas.*'

With an effort, Jessica managed to stand up. She wrapped her dressing gown round her as best she could. Despite all that had gone on, she found she was still wearing her slippers. 'He can't be left here,' she said.

She went down into the foyer and opened the theatre door. She had no idea what time it was, but the street outside was black and deserted. It would have been easy to believe that everyone who lived there had died, so quiet was it. There was no moon, either, which was a good thing.

Stepping outside, she scanned the nearby buildings, a mixture of private houses and businesses that merged with the black sky: the Café Edgar opposite, the house next door, the *pharmacie* on the other side of the café and beside that the *cordonnier* where shoes were repaired. She recalled that the building next to the theatre had housed Monsieur Dumas, the funeral director, who had passed away the previous month at the age of ninety-three. There was still a vase of wax lilies in the window, but the property was empty, waiting for a new tenant. The front door was set back a few feet, leaving a decent enough space to dump a body.

She returned to the theatre and found Henri searching through the dead man's pockets. While she'd been gone, he seemed to have pulled himself together. 'He's got a French identity card,' he said. 'His name is Claud Petrou.'

'He said he was going to report us to the Gestapo.' Jessica shuddered.

'There's just a receipt for a hotel in Brussels and a few francs in his wallet.' Henri turned the scrap of paper over. 'It's got the address of the theatre scribbled on the back. We should burn it, and the identity card.'

'I wish we could take the bugger's body to the Seine and throw it in,' she grumbled, 'but we couldn't carry him that far between us. Anyway, we'd be bound to be seen. We'll just have to leave him in a doorway outside. Hopefully, the police

will think it's an ordinary crime. At least he's a Frenchman.'
Whenever the Germans discovered one of their own had been
killed, they would shoot half a dozen or more Frenchmen or
women, even children, in retaliation.

It was as if Henri had been able to hear her thoughts. 'If he's
important, if it turns out he means something to the Boche,
then I shall give myself up.' He looked at Jessica, his young
forehead creased in fervor. 'I promise that I will not reveal
the name of anyone in this house. You have my word on that,
Jessica.'

'Henri, love.' She leaned over the dead body of Claud
Petrou and squeezed the boy's shoulder. What a terrible thing
for him to say. 'Let's pray that nothing like that will happen. This person must somehow have discovered we'd been
sheltering fugitives. He knew about Louis. He said something
about getting a reward for finding us.'

An hour later, Jessica, her heart still racing uncommonly fast
and unnaturally loud, sat up in bed nursing a cup of coffee.
Sammy remained fast asleep, undisturbed by recent events, as
were Simone and Frannie. The body of Claud Petrou now lay
in the doorway of the old funeral director's and would be
discovered first thing in the morning. Martin would come
bursting in with the news. Madame Vierny would tell Jessica
all about it when she went to buy the bread. The police were
bound to call and ask if anyone knew the identity of the
man in the funeral director's doorway. Simone would deny all
knowledge of him and she would be speaking the truth, for
Henri and Jessica had sworn to keep the events of the night a
secret between them for ever.

'Don't forget to wash the blood off your face,' Henri had
reminded her when she was about to go to bed. 'And there's a
bruise on your chin.'

Jessica wiped her face with a flannel in front of the mirror in
the bathroom. The blood from the wound in Claud Petrou's

head had dried and was difficult to wash off, and she imagined the red stain staying for ever, like the secret. As for the bruise, she'd think of a reason for it in the morning.

Chapter 20

It was impossible to get Claud Petrou out of her mind. He had nearly raped her, was about to when his brains had been blown out. She and Henri had carried his dead body into the street.

It was like waking from a bad dream, but without the relief of realizing it had been a dream. In her imagination, she visualized the scene not stopping when it had, but continuing; the rape followed by the Gestapo, Sammy being taken away . . . Some nights, she would lie awake engulfed in a nightmare.

For Henri, it was different, she could tell. Perhaps after asserting himself and killing a man, he felt less of a victim than before. He had proven something, done something that was, in a way, revenge for the loss of his family. He seemed older, wiser, more forceful than before.

As for the murdered man, the French police had taken his body away. He was identified and turned out to have a criminal record, though his crimes had been minor – but not minor enough for someone to want to kill him, the police reckoned.

The residents of the rue de la Grand Truanderie were questioned. Simone, who answered the door, invited the policeman inside and expressed her total ignorance of the corpse. Jessica, with Sammy on her knee, remained silent throughout the interview, the bruise on her chin buried in her little boy's shoulder. The policeman jokily shook the child's hand before he left.

Early in 1944, once again someone knocked on the theatre door in the middle of the night. Simone was the person to hear it first. When she realized what it was, Jessica raced downstairs.

But by the time she caught up, Simone had closed the door after admitting an extraordinarily handsome young man with blond curly hair and intense blue eyes whom she was embracing affectionately. His right arm was in a sling that appeared to be made out of a dirty, tattered towel. Simone's face lit up when Jessica appeared.

'Jessica,' she said excitedly, 'this is Nicky Costigan, Louis's friend from London. They met at drama school and were in plays together. Now he is a captain in the Royal Air Force, but his plane was shot down. What happened then, *cheri*?' She took hold of his good arm. 'Let's go into the kitchen first and you can tell us. We'll make coffee, give you something to eat. Oh, it is so good to see you, but not under such awful circumstances.'

Jessica went ahead to put on the water. The newcomer could barely walk, she saw when Simone brought him into the room. Despite the brightness of his eyes and his broad smile, the young man occasionally grimaced with pain.

'Hurt my ankle, too,' he explained as he sank thankfully on to a chair. 'Plane came down in Metz, just inside the French border. It took a few bullets underneath. The Maquis were there within minutes and we were whisked to safety.' The Maquis was the French underground movement.

'Thank the Lord, *cheri*,' Simone said emotionally. 'How did you manage to get this far?'

'Felix, one of those who rescued us, brought me in his van. He's a farmer. I don't know his other name. He dropped me off a few doors away from here and waited to make sure I was let in. By now he'll be on his way back to Metz. My crew are still there and will make their own way home.' He reached for Simone's hand. 'I heard about Louis some time ago, Simone. I'm so sorry. He was the best friend I've ever had – ever will have.'

There was silence that must have lasted a good minute. Jessica wouldn't have broken it for the world. In the end, Simone shrugged and smiled bleakly.

'Where's Sara?' Nicky asked.

'In Liverpool with two of the children,' Simone said. 'I haven't introduced you properly yet. This is Jessica, Sara's friend.'

The young man held out his left hand. 'How do you do, Jessica?'

Jessica shook his hand carefully and said, 'Sara probably doesn't know about Louis.' It worried her sometimes that it might eventually fall upon her to tell Sara that Louis was dead. 'Have you met the children?'

'Years ago, yes. Two little girls, Marie and Frannie. In fact, I thought that's all there were.'

'Now there are three. Joseph was born . . .' Simone looked at Jessica. 'How many years ago? My mind has gone blank.'

'Five years,' Jessica said.

'Is that all? It seems like for ever. Anyway, Nicky, Frannie is still with us and Henri also lives here. He's seventeen. There's a long story attached to all this. We'll tell it to you another time.'

According to Nicky, the Royal Air Force was dropping tons of bombs on German factories every night, Berlin in particular. 'But,' he told them gravely after he'd been there a few days, 'the loss of life on both sides is horrendous. As far as the RAF is concerned, a hundred planes – sometimes double that many – are shot down during a raid and the entire crew of each are killed. I count myself and my crew as exceptionally lucky. I was able to crash-land my plane when it was still all in one piece.'

Jessica thought yet again about Sam, who had badly wanted to join the RAF, and wondered if he could possibly still be alive. The heavy bombing of Germany had been going on for more than a year. A new bomb weighing over four thousand pounds had recently been introduced.

She went down to the kitchen where she could think in peace. The parlour, where Nicky slept, had replaced the kitchen as the place where everyone in the house congregated. He was a gregarious, outgoing young man, very likeable, and, at thirty-four, not as young as Jessica had first thought. Simone spent all her spare time there, as did a surprisingly besotted Frannie and a forlorn Henri, whose nose had been pushed out of joint since Nicky's arrival.

Henri followed Jessica into the kitchen. 'Will Nicky be here for much longer?' he asked glumly.

'Only until his arm is better. His sprained ankle has much improved.' Colette had come all the way from Reims for a few days to put his arm in a splint and check on Sammy, who was now one and a half.

Henri kicked the table leg. 'He doesn't like me.'

'Nicky? Why on earth should he not like you? You are without doubt the finest young man I have ever known.' She patted a chair. 'Come and sit down, you silly sausage. He's probably jealous of your good looks and charming manner.'

'No, he isn't, Jessica. The reason is that he doesn't like Jews.'

Jessica looked at him sharply. 'Has he said anything?'

'No, but I can see it in his eyes, in his expression.' The boy sat disconsolately on a chair.

Jessica seized his head with both hands and kissed his black curls. She owed this young man so much. 'Well, *I* like you, so to hell with Nicky. He'll be gone soon.' Henri was just as much a hero as Nicky; it was just that neither Simone nor Frannie knew it.

About six weeks later, at the dawn of another spring, an invigorated Nicky, his arm and ankle healed, left the house in the dead of night, promising to return one fine day when the world was free again. He also promised to write to Sara and tell her about Louis.

A fresh rumour said the Allies were preparing to invade France from somewhere along the south coast of England. Such news gave heart to the people of Paris while they shivered and starved after four years of curfews, blackouts and occupation. At least half the supposed rations were impossible to find, as was fuel. March was at an end before Jessica and Simone were able to stop deciding which of the furniture to burn next. The supply of gas and electricity could no longer be relied on. The *Métro* only ran spasmodically and so did buses. The war had gone on for far too long and it was easy to feel despair that it would never end.

What deepened the despair was learning of the acts of utter savagery, such out and out barbarism, that were being enacted upon innocent civilians all over Europe, upon Jews in particular. Small children, babies, were being slaughtered without a second thought. Jessica wondered if the world would ever be able to live with itself again, knowing the depths to which some people could sink; not in defence of anything, nor in support of something else, but on the whim of a mad man who had turned his country into a killing machine.

Despite everything, the *Petit Théâtre* continued to flourish with full houses every night no matter what was showing: a choir, a musical hall, a play, a silly review, a retired school-teacher, Gerald Mansart, reading Charles Dickens's novels translated into French, in his beautiful, melodic voice, an act that was particularly popular. The audiences sat silent and rapt as they listened to tales set in Victorian England. Their favourite novel was *The Pickwick Papers*. Occasionally, some of the audience were seen to be in tears.

It was early in June, on a gentle, sunny day, when Martin burst into the house, shouting, 'The Allies have landed in Normandy. The Allies have landed.' He grabbed Simone by the waist and danced her around the room.

'The Allies have landed,' echoed Sammy, running after them. To his mother's dismay, his French was much better than his English. 'Is the war over, Maman?'

'Not yet, sweetheart,' Jessica cried jubilantly. 'But it soon will be.'

Over the next few months, barricades were erected, small battles took place here and there, explosions and gunfire could be heard. German tanks roamed around the city and were showered with weapons: street cobbles or homemade fire bombs. Lorryloads of German troops were glimpsed returning home; collaborators were savagely attacked or murdered.

It was late in August when the Free French Army was able to enter Paris to an ecstatic reception from its citizens, though it took days before it was safe to go out. Sniper-fire could be heard. The Army was targeted, members of the French Resistance and sometimes bystanders who'd survived the war, only to be killed when nearing its end.

Days later, Jessica and Simone left the house in the rue de le Grande Truanderie, accompanied by Frannie and Henri, with Sammy running excitedly in front. Even the little boy was aware of the heady atmosphere, the happiness of the crowds, the laughter and the singing that could be heard everywhere.

For Henri, it was the first time he'd felt free to walk the streets since the night his mother and father and little sister, Delphine, had been taken away. He knew there was a good chance they all would be dead by now and he might never know where they had died or how.

That night, at the end of the show, the Marseillaise was sung with such spirit and enthusiasm, the voices loud and firm, that the building actually did respond with a chorus of creaking and groaning of its own. Jessica briefly worried that the structure was about to fall apart.

The triumphant voices floated outside where it was still light and warm, and the doors and windows of the Café Edgar were wide open. The customers poured outside and joined in the singing. When the anthem finished, they raised their glasses.

'*Vive la France*!' they shouted. '*Vive la France.*'

Jessica was searching Paris for a length of material. At some time in the near future, she would return to England – to Liverpool – and wanted to look her best. Apart from the blue dress she'd made years ago, all her clothes were old and out of fashion. The big shops stocked only expensive materials – pure silk, taffeta and velvet – but she wanted something lightweight; cotton gingham, maybe, or linen. She gave up on the big shops and caught the *Métro* to Barbès Rochechouart where there were tables of material set up on the pavements.

She managed to buy four metres of apple-green knobbly cotton and another four of pink-and-white check from the stall of a tall black woman, who wore flowered satin robes and a matching turban at least a foot high, as well as an assortment of necklaces, earrings and bracelets.

'Oh, it is so good to see you,' Jessica said impulsively.

She had no idea if the woman understood, but her broad smile was wondrous to behold.

Nursing her parcel, Jessica returned to the boulevard Barbès, took a seat outside the first café she came to, and ordered coffee. She sipped the drink, closing her eyes rapturously when she caught a whiff of Gauloise cigarettes from the next table. Gauloise had been her favourite brand when she'd come to live in France. She reminded herself that she'd vowed never to smoke again.

On the road, a few feet away, a jeep stopped with a screech of brakes, the driver leaped out, and, to her total amazement, pulled her off the chair and virtually flung her into the air. A pair of strong arms caught her on the way down.

'Hello, ducky,' said Harvey Cope.

'Harve!' She almost fainted in his arms. He put her back in the chair and drew up another. He had three stripes on the arms of his jacket.

'You're a sergeant,' she gasped. 'What are you doing in Paris?'

'Well, you see, *I* joined the Army.' His eyes sparkled in the lovely way they'd done when they'd met in Liverpool a lifetime ago. 'What are *you* doing in Paris? I'm sure that answer's more interesting than mine.'

'I've been here since before the war.'

'Is Paris where you were off to when you wrote me that letter?'

She blushed and lowered her head, remembering that he knew everything about her. 'Yes. I had a friend here – oh, it's a long story, Harve.'

He took both her hands in his and squeezed them. 'Did you ever get your kids back, Jess?' he asked gently.

'No. I still miss them, but it probably sounds awful, I don't miss them nearly as much nowadays. I have another little boy you see, Sammy. His father went to England to join the RAF, but I don't know if he managed it.' She sighed. 'How about you, Harve?' He'd made her feel happy during one of the most difficult times of her life.

'I married a girl I went to school with – Eileen. We've got kids, a girl and a boy. Joey's three and Jessie's two.'

'Jessie?' She raised her eyebrows.

He looked straight at her, right into her eyes. 'Eileen picked the boy's name and me, I picked the girl's. I called her Jessica because I'd known a Jessica once and she was the love of me life.'

A waiter came out and broke the spell. 'Monsieur?' he said to Harve.

'*Une bière, s'il vous plaît.* See, I can speak French already,' he said when the waiter had gone.

'I always knew you were a clever lad, Harve.'

'And I know I'll always love you, Jess,' he said sombrely. 'Getting that letter of yours darn near killed me. I'm not kidding, but I felt like topping meself at first.' He grinned his old, mischievous grin. 'Glad I didn't, though, else I'd've missed having me kids.'

The waiter came with his beer, but waved away the money when Harve went to pay. '*Non, non, monsieur. Pour vous, la bière est gratuite.*'

Harve picked up his beer. 'Thank you, mate. I mean, *merci*!'

'No, monsieur.' The waiter, a very old man, gave a half-salute. 'Thank *you*.'

He was on a recce, Harve told her, booking rooms in the best hotels and tables at the best restaurants for the senior officers of his unit who were expected to arrive in Paris later that day and wanted to celebrate.

She invited him to dinner that night at the Café Edgar, and told him how to get there. When they parted, she went to kiss his cheek, but he pulled her close to him and kissed her on the lips instead. It was the kiss of a lover, not a friend.

He didn't turn up at the Café Edgar. Although she'd been looking forward to seeing him, in a way she was glad. He'd made no secret of the fact that he was still in love with her, and the less they saw of each other the better.

But meeting Harve had brought home to her that it really was time she made plans to return to Liverpool. She had no idea if the ferries had started to run again. Even if they had, they would still be at the mercy of German bombs.

She sat alone in the Café Edgar, listening to the laughter

coming from the little theatre across the street, while Martin fussed around, worried she was upset about being let down, bringing her too many glasses of wine to compensate. She felt pleasantly dizzy by the time she went home.

Liverpool! She wanted to be there as much as she wanted to stay in Paris. Simone, Frannie and Henri were her family now as well as Sammy. Sometimes, she almost forgot she had another family back at home. Nowadays, when she thought about Jamie and Dora, they seemed like phantom children, just memories who were no longer flesh and blood, but ghosts she could no longer touch, hold or hear. She would have to shake herself to make everything real again.

She remembered that Frannie would come with her to Liverpool to be reunited with her mother and sisters. Simone would stay and continue to manage the theatre – it had belonged to Louis, her son, who'd wanted Jessica to look after it. For his mother to take over would be perfect.

But what about Henri? Where would he go?

She asked him one day when Simone and Frannie were out shopping.

'Where am I to go?' He looked terribly lost and not a little frightened. 'I don't know,' he confessed. He'd expected to have his family around him for at least half his life, to be present at his wedding and other important events. There were aunts and uncles, he told her, distant cousins, but they were all in a little village in northern Russia. The grandparents who'd made their way to Paris half a century before were long dead. In truth, he had no one.

'Would you like to come to Liverpool with me and Frannie – and Sammy, too, of course?' Frannie had confirmed she would go back to her family, but didn't seem all that keen on the idea – 'I might well come back to Paris again very soon,' she'd added darkly.

'Frannie's mother might not want me there,' Henri said

now. From time to time, Frannie made uncomplimentary remarks about her mother.

'It's nothing to do with Frannie's mother, it's to do with me. *I* want you there.' She smiled and tried to make light of it. She didn't want to suggest things like becoming his mother or his big sister, anything to do with family. 'I'd like to adopt you as my friend,' she said eventually. 'Not just an ordinary friend, but a permanent one.'

His dark eyes were moist behind his round glasses, which probably needed changing after all these years. 'I'd like to be your permanent friend, Jessica,' he said shyly.

Frannie had returned to school, Simone was shopping, and Henri wandering around Paris, perhaps wondering what to do with the rest of his life once he was living in Liverpool.

The front door of the house was wide open to the September sunshine, as it had always used to be in the good weather before the Germans had invaded. Jessica was sitting at the table, blissfully conscious of the new, changed atmosphere. Sammy played with the coloured bricks that Frannie had played with when she was the same age.

'Excuse me? Are you Simone Cotillard?' A soldier was standing in the doorway, an officer who looked slightly familiar.

Jessica felt too lazy to get to her feet. 'She's gone shopping,' she called.

'In that case, you must be Jessica Deveraux.'

'Yes, that's me.' She leaned forward, but still didn't get up. 'Would you like to come in.' She waved at a chair on the other side of the table. 'Sit down.'

'Thank you.' The soldier half-saluted, letting his hand fall when he realized there was no need. He obediently sat down. 'I'm Nicky Costigan's cousin, Roger,' he announced.

Jessica smiled. 'How do you do, Roger?'

'Very well, thank you.' He looked uncomfortable, as if he

found her relaxed attitude off-putting. 'Finding Paris pretty impressive.'

'It's remarkably impressive.'

'Nicky's back in Blighty. He sent a message. I'll read it to you, shall I?' He drew a piece of paper out of his pocket, unfolded it, coughed, and began to read. 'There is an RAF transport plane taking off from Roissy Airport for England on Saturday afternoon at fourteen-thirty hours that has room for passengers.' He looked up. 'Nicky said if you want seats reserving to let him know straight away.'

'Seats!' she said faintly. 'Saturday!' Today was Tuesday. Saturday was only four days away. But she needed more time than that to get ready and even more time to *think* about it. 'Can you come tomorrow and I'll let you know what I've decided then?' she said to Roger.

He looked faintly indignant. 'I've got to know *now*,' he impressed upon her. 'I have to contact Nicky as soon as I get back to base.'

'Oh, Lord!' Jessica got to her feet at last. 'Would you like some coffee? I'll let you know my answer by the time you finish it.'

Roger considered this, seemed to find it to his liking, and agreed. 'Is this Sammy?'

Sammy looked up. 'Me Sammy,' he said, nodding furiously.

'What are you building there?'

'The Fifle tower.'

'Can I help?'

'Yes, please. They keep falling over.'

The young soldier sat on the floor. 'Perhaps if we put more blocks at the base we can build them higher.'

Jessica was thinking frantically as she made the coffee. *Four* days. Yet she had little to pack. The clothes she'd brought with her six years before were hardly worth taking. Everything she and Sammy owned would fit into a medium-sized suitcase. There hadn't been much to buy in the shops during the war. At sixteen, Frannie was slightly more interested in clothes than she'd been at ten, but she hadn't many and her most important possessions were books, which it would be perfectly safe to leave behind with her grandmother. Henri had arrived with nothing except the clothes he stood up in and a gun. He had been told to take what he liked out of Louis's wardrobe, but his possessions would probably fit in a carrier bag.

She had plenty of money. Ever since Louis had suggested it years and years ago, she'd been putting aside ten per cent of the theatre takings for her own use. She'd earned it, she deserved it. It was in the wardrobe drawer in her bedroom covered with bedding, at least a hundred pounds in French francs, she reckoned. It was ages since it had been counted.

So, there was nothing to stop her from leaving for England in four days' time. It would be perfectly possible to leave tomorrow if she wanted. Whether Frannie and Henri felt the same, she wouldn't know until they came home and she could ask them. She just had to hope that they would agree to go with her.

The coffee made, she called Roger to the table. 'I'll go on Saturday,' she told him. 'Tell Nicky there'll be four of us, including Sammy.'

Chapter 21

The plane roared and rattled all the way across the Channel. The metal seats were cold and uncomfortable, and Jessica had acquired a splitting headache by the time they landed in the wilds of Lincolnshire, where it was virtually dusk – they'd been late leaving France – and a cold wind blew. The only building in sight was a small wooden hut barely visible in the dimness.

A young man in blue overalls opened the passenger door and waited at the foot of a ladder to help them down. He introduced himself as Private Heath and pointed to the hut, promising to be with them in a minute.

Sammy began to cry. 'Maman, I don't like England.'

Neither did Jessica at that moment. It was somewhat of an anti-climax to have left behind her busy, cheery little street for this wasteland. Right now, the theatre would be nearing the end of a Feydeau farce, the Café Edgar would be crowded, full of chatter and cigarette smoke. If she'd had the power, she would have ordered the pilot to take them back.

Inside, the hut was bigger than expected. A light was on and the orange curtains were tightly drawn. With a sigh, Jessica threw herself into one of the easy chairs in a row against the wall, pulling Sammy on to her knee. Without saying a word, Frannie and Henri sat on each side of her. Sammy hiccupped tearfully. An electric kettle on the floor in the corner was just beginning to boil, a welcome sight.

Private Heath came in rubbing his hands and accompanied by the pilot, Tim Haggard, plump and fortyish, who had spoken to them before take-off. The younger man made the tea and a cup had never been more welcome to Jessica, if not the others, who rarely drank tea.

Tim Haggard told them that Private Heath would shortly take them somewhere local to spend the night. 'Tomorrow, after breakfast, he'll drive you to London. There our responsibility for you will end,' he said, slapping his knees with the satisfied air of a man knowing an important job was over.

'But the RAF doesn't owe us anything,' Jessica protested. 'You have no responsibility for us.' They'd been the only passengers in the plane, as if it had been laid on especially for them. There'd been no need to reserve seats.

'You sheltered one of our chaps, Nicky Costigan, for six whole weeks at considerable danger to yourselves,' the captain said. 'It was Costigan's idea that we bring you back to Blighty. The plane was due to return today anyway, so it was no skin off our nose, as it were.'

'It's very kind of you,' Jessica murmured.

Private Heath took them to a pub called the Lamb and Flag. It appeared to be the only building for miles and was packed with servicemen, many of them American, all of them singing as loudly as it was possible for a human being to sing. Somewhere, far away in another bar, a faintly audible piano was being played. The only thing louder than the singing were the occasional bursts of laughter, which were almost deafening.

Private Heath told them to wait just inside the entrance while he fetched someone. The 'someone' turned out to be a middle-aged woman called Bridget, who asked in a broad Irish accent if they'd like something to eat: 'As long as it's sandwiches – we've got cheese and tomato, ham and beetroot, and egg and cress.'

Everyone chose cheese. Bridget showed them to their

rooms and said she'd bring the sandwiches in a minute and did they want tea or coffee?

Their escort had gone, having promised to collect them in the morning. 'Nineish,' he'd suggested.

'Nineish will do,' Jessica agreed.

She looked around the low-ceilinged room with its thick, black beams and dark tapestry curtains. Had she felt a bit more cheerful it would probably have looked charming rather than dull. Still, it was only for one night.

Henri knocked on the door and Frannie shouted at him to come in, just as Bridget appeared with the food and they all tucked in.

'Maman, birdy. *Bonjour*, birdy. Maman, come and see birdies.'

Jessica woke. She lifted her head and saw Sammy at the window, everything apart from his little fat legs hidden behind the closed curtains.

'It's the crack of dawn,' she grumbled, throwing back the clothes and stumbling towards the window. She pulled back the curtains and gasped with surprise. Outside was a different world from the night before. The blue sky shimmered and the early-morning sun cast a golden light over what was obviously an orchard. The upper branches were almost within touching distance, and within the leaves nestled dozens of bright red apples, the sort that made a lovely crisp sound when they were bitten. Tiny birds, very much like sparrows, were hopping jerkily from branch to branch, undeterred by the twitching curtains. They rose in a loud flutter when Sammy reached for one and knocked on the window.

'Don't go 'way, birds,' the little boy said sternly.

Jessica lifted him up and opened the window, and he made a valiant attempt to fall out. She put him on the floor, dressed him, then dressed herself. Looking at her watch, she discovered it was well past the crack of dawn – nearly half past seven.

Sammy climbed on top of Frannie in her single bed and bounced up and down on her stomach. 'Frannie, birdies,' he sang. 'Birdies outside.' There hadn't been much in the way of birds in the rue de la Grand Truanderie or he might not have been so taken with them.

Frannie opened her eyes. 'It's sunny,' she announced, as if Jessica hadn't noticed. She sat up and pulled Sammy on to her knee. '*Bonjour, cheri.*' She kissed his rosy cheek.

Jessica combed her hair and powdered her nose; she'd clean her teeth later. 'I'm going downstairs in search of a drink.' Kitchen noises could be heard, dishes rattling, the clink of pans, the jingle-jangle of cutlery.

Downstairs, it was like an old-fashioned painting the way the sun shone through the open back door on to the black-and-red tiled floor. Sammy ran right through the door on to the grass outside. He looked up and spread his arms, 'Birdies,' he cried triumphantly.

'Ye'll never catch one, darlin'.' Bridget appeared. 'I've set a table in the snug, Mrs Deveraux. Would you like coffee or tea wicha breakfast?'

'Coffee, please. Is it all right if we have a look around the garden while you make it?'

'Of course, but mind you and the little fella don't get your feet all wet. There's a really heavy dew out there this morning.'

The dew hung from the thick grass like jewels, running down the blades and disappearing into the ground. Sammy stamped around, squealing with excitement as the long grass touched his bare legs. She'd have to change him before they left. Her own shoes were soaking. Thankfully, he'd forgotten about the birds.

Frannie and Henri joined them. It was a beautiful, exceptionally warm day for September. She had never noticed before how pale Henri was. He'd spent so many months – no *years* indoors. She'd make sure that very soon he'd have some colour in his cheeks. Who could he play tennis with? Would he be interested in watching football? The first free Sunday, she'd take them all to Southport.

She forgot that the first free Sunday Frannie would no longer be living with her, but with Sara, her mother. She was still dreading coming face to face with her old friend, and felt more than a little nervous at the thought that they might meet before the day was out. She had no idea how long it would take to drive to London then catch a train to Liverpool. Sara had wanted her daughter sent home, but Frannie had refused to go, and Jessica hadn't been prepared to take her against her will. Anyway, not only had the war started by then and the journey been dangerous, but Sam was living with them and Jessica had wanted to stay in Paris with him.

Henri was leaping into the air, trying to dislodge some of the highest apples, when Bridget came out and announced breakfast was ready. 'With your coffee, like. We never used to make much coffee until the Americans came. I didn't realize they drank it in France an' all.' She nodded at the apples. 'I'll give you a bag o' them when you leave.'

Jessica had revised her opinion of Lincolnshire. 'It's beautiful here,' she said. 'I'd like to come back on holiday one day.'

'Come back in spring when the tulips are out,' Bridget told her. 'It's more than beautiful then.'

'We're entering Norfolk now,' Private Heath said. He'd said to call him Johnny.

One of the first things Jessica had noticed after they'd been travelling a few miles was that there were no road signs. Or at least the signs were there, but they'd been painted over and pointed nowhere.

'It's because of the Germans,' Johnny explained when Jessica asked him why. 'Say if a spy lands, he wouldn't know which way to go.'

'How would a spy get here?' Henri asked. His English was heavily accented, but understandable. She remembered his father had spoken excellent English, and wondered about the fate of that awfully nice man with a star on his jacket.

'By boat, mate; U-boat, probably. The Channel ain't far over there.' Johnny jerked his head to the left. 'Mrs Deveraux, what time would you like us to stop for something to eat?'

'About midday, I suppose, though if you see somewhere suitable, I wouldn't mind stopping for a drink quite soon.'

'You're a woman after me own heart, ma'am. I wouldn't say "no" to a cuppa, either. Out of interest,' he continued, 'what part of London are you making for? Meself, I'm from Fulham. I was wondering if I'd have time to call in on me old ma.'

'Euston Station, where the trains leave for Liverpool.'

To Jessica's surprise, the car stopped with a screech of brakes. Johnny turned and looked at her in astonishment. 'You're going to Liverpool?'

'Yes. Didn't Captain Haggard tell you?'

Johnny was making a three-point turn in the middle of the deserted road. 'If I turn down the next main road on the left, I'll have you in Liverpool in half the time it'd take to get to London. And you won't have to catch a train, either.' He sniffed indignantly. 'I know I was ordered to take you to London, but there are times when it's only a bleedin' idiot who would do as they was told.'

It was much too warm in the car with the windows closed, and much too noisy with them open. Fortunately, after a while, everyone fell asleep, leaving Johnny with no one to talk to. Jessica half woke every now and then to hear him whistling, and wondered what she would say when he asked where in Liverpool did she want to be dropped off.

Before meeting Sara, she would like to have a good wash and change her clothes, perhaps iron something. As it was, she felt hot and sticky, and suspected she might smell a bit. Sammy had dropped food on the front of his Aertex shirt – maybe the smell came from him. She was sure that Frannie, nowadays quite particular with how she looked, would want to look her best before meeting her mother again after a gap of more than five years.

Oh, Lord! She, Jessica, was wearing Sara's hat – the white halo one that she'd got married in. Knowing Sara, she would recognize it straight away and not be all that pleased to see another woman wearing it.

'Where would you like to be dropped off, Mrs Deveraux?' Johnny eventually asked.

'Lime Street station,' she said. The George Hotel, where Will and Lena had gone for a meal after their wedding, was directly opposite. She could leave their luggage there when she took Frannie back to her mother in Kirkby.

'Bleedin' hell!' Johnny said in a choked voice. 'What the hell's happened here?'

Jessica looked up and discovered they seemed to be driving through a war zone. Where once there'd been streets, there were heaps of rubble. As they drove further into the city, there was scarcely a street left that hadn't a gap in it where houses had been destroyed. And she'd thought it dangerous living in Paris!

'Jessica, what's happened?' Frannie sounded frightened.

'It's the bombing, darling. Someone told me Liverpool was badly bombed.' Was her mother still alive? And what about Jamie and Dora? Jessica closed her eyes and inwardly began to panic – Sammy's arrival had slightly reduced the hurt – but it took very little for them to come to the surface. Since Roger Costigan had offered a flight home, one of her first thoughts had been whether she would soon discover her children's whereabouts, if not the children themselves.

'We're here, ma'am.' Johnny's voice cut through her thoughts. The car had stopped. 'Lime Street station.' Frannie and Henri were already getting out of the car, but Jessica had to wake Sammy from a deep, deep sleep before she could move.

Johnny had already said goodbye and shaken hands with the others. He shook Jessica's hand last. 'Good luck, Mrs Deveraux.'

'The same to you, Johnny.' He was a nice young man and had been very helpful. Had he not used his initiative, they would still be on the way to London.

'Oh, I hope the Jew boy gets on all right, poor bloke. What a helluva thing to happen. Someone told me last night about him losing his whole family.'

Jessica looked at him, stunned, but he continued to smile at her cheerfully. She realized he'd just said the words naturally, not as an insult.

She sighed and picked up her suitcase. By now, Sammy was wide awake. He insisted on carrying something, so she gave him her handbag, and the small party set off across the road to the hotel.

Lime Street was as full of people and traffic as it had ever been. It was as lovely a day in Liverpool as it had been in Lincolnshire. The solid white pillars of St George's Hall, said to be the most elegant building in all of Europe, glistened in the brilliant sunshine. From here at least, there was no sign of the destruction she'd witnessed on the way into the city.

Jessica's heart swelled. Although she knew it wouldn't last for long, her only sensation just then was one of pure happiness.

'*Bonjour*, Liverpool,' she said aloud.

In the hotel Jessica explained she only wanted a room for the afternoon. 'So we can get washed and change our clothes. We've come all the way from Paris,' she added when the young man behind the desk looked inclined to refuse. Instead, at the mention of Paris he was greatly impressed, and even

282

suggested she use the laundry room when she enquired about ironing. 'It's not in use today, being Sunday, like.'

It was only then that she remembered it was Sunday and she hadn't been to Mass.

Two hours later, after a good wash, a change of clothes, some of them ironed, and a pot of coffee between them in the bar, they were ready to go and see Sara. Jessica had pressed a white cotton frock that was old, but she had always felt she looked her best in it. Hatless, she wore a blue ribbon in her hair and was quite pleased with her appearance when she checked in the mirror before leaving.

She asked Henri if he would prefer to stay behind, have a look around Liverpool while they were gone, but he said he wanted to meet Frannie's mother. He took Frannie's hand and squeezed it. The girl raised his hand to her lips and kissed it. It was the first romantic gesture between them that Jessica had ever seen.

Kirkby station was some way from Kirkby Castle where Jessica had worked. The only buildings to be seen when they emerged from the station were two public houses, both closed, and a newsagent's that was closed, too.

A woman walking her dog informed them that South Park Road was a mere minute's walk away. 'Just go along beside the railway line and turn right at the first road you come to.'

The top half of the road was unmade, already liberally scattered with red and gold leaves, and consisted of spacious semi-detached houses with room to park a car at the side. Further down, the road surface changed to bright new concrete, and the houses either side were newly built. These were for the people who'd come from all over the country to work at Kirkby Castle. She was glad that Sara's house was one of the older properties; they were much more attractive.

A pretty blonde girl of about fourteen was cutting the grass in a very desultory manner in the garden of the nearest house. The shears appeared to be blunt, judging by the way she had to tug at the grass rather than clip it. She didn't look exactly happy with her task.

'Marie,' Frannie said loudly.

The girl stopped work and looked blankly at her sister. 'Hello,' she said hesitantly.

'Oh, Marie, it's Frannie.' Frannie jumped over the small hedge and threw her arms round her sister.

Marie responded by bursting into tears. 'Frannie! I've missed you so much. When did you get home? Are you back for good? It's lovely to see you.'

'I'm not *home*,' Frannie said bluntly. 'This isn't *home*. Home is Paris, but I'm here for now.' She turned and extended her hand to Henri, who stepped over the hedge and took it. This is Henri,' she said proudly. 'We're getting married one day.'

'Over my dead body,' said a voice that was much sharper than the shears, and could possibly have felled a tree. Sara had emerged from the side of the house, a thunderous expression on her face. She gave Jessica a disgusted look. 'Thank you for looking after my daughter so well, Jessica, that she is planning to get married when she's barely sixteen. And how old are you?' she asked Henri.

'Eighteen,' Henri stammered.

Jessica groaned audibly. The reunion couldn't have got off to a worse start. She'd had no idea Frannie and Henri had even discussed marriage. If only they'd kept the news until later! She wondered if Sara knew about Louis.

Sara's fiery gaze had fallen upon Sammy. 'And who's this?' she growled.

'This is Sammy,' Jessica said quickly, giving no time for Sara to suggest that Louis might be his father. 'Remember Sam Deveraux? He and I got married.'

A small boy, though not as small as Sammy, had appeared at Sara's side. This must be Joseph, who was going on for six.

Sammy recognized one of his own species. ' 'Allo,' he said loudly.

Joseph, taking after his mother, responded with a scowl. 'I go to school,' he announced.

'*I* don't,' Sammy responded.

'You will one day.' Joseph spoke as if a terrible fate awaited Sammy in the not-too-distant future.

'Is Josef here?' Jessica asked desperately. 'I mean, your father.'

'He went back to live with Ruth, his sister.' Sara shrugged. 'It must be years ago now.'

Jessica could only guess why. Poor Josef. He hadn't got on with his sister, but perhaps she was easier to live with than his daughter.

She had no idea what to do or what to say next. Did Sara intend to ask them inside or offer them a cup of tea? Should Jessica suggest it? Did she *want* to go inside? Well, no, not really, except civility called for it – if they were invited, that was. If she returned to town without being offered tea, then a rule, an unwritten law of basic politeness would have been broken, and she would never be able to speak to Sara again. They could no longer be friends. Did she care? Probably not.

She was trying to think of something to say while Sara's scowl grew deeper. It was the other woman who spoke first. 'You needn't think you're getting married, Frannie.' She shook her head emphatically. 'At your age, you need my permission and I've no intention of giving it, no matter how many times you ask.'

Frannie merely shrugged. 'Please yourself. Just don't complain in February when I give birth to an illegitimate baby.'

Jessica grabbed Sammy's hand, turned on her heel, and began to walk back to the station. She could still hear Sara's screams when they reached the booking hall.

'I don't like England,' Sammy said, a touch angrily.

'You'll like it better when you meet your grandma,' Jessica

told him, but she recalled her mother had never been all that fond of children, even her own. What was more, she might not even be alive. And if she *was* still alive, she still might not want anything to do with her daughter.

Frannie and Henri arrived at the station at the same time as the Liverpool train came puffing in wreathed in smoke. Sammy hid behind his mother's skirt and had to be carried on board.

It wasn't until they were approaching the next station that anyone spoke.

'I'm not expecting a baby,' Frannie said. 'Just in case you thought I was.'

Jessica folded her arms and stared out of the window. 'I didn't think it for one moment.' She wasn't in the mood to be nice or smile at anyone apart from Sammy.

'Henri and I intend to get married, but not for ages yet. We'd both like to go to university before we settle down and have children, wouldn't we, Henri?'

Henri had blushed deep scarlet. 'That's right,' he gulped.

'Then why did you have to rile your mother like that?'

'Why did she have to jump to the conclusion that we wanted to get married straight away when all I said was "one day"? She's horrible. I wish we'd stayed in Paris with Simone.'

Jessica was beginning to wish the same. The remainder of the journey was made more or less in silence. Sammy seemed to think it was some sort of game. He kept looking from one person to the other saying, 'Shush!' and giggling madly.

Chapter 22

Jessica had always considered Tom McGrath's sparkling white house in the most frightful taste. 'It's like a wedding cake,' her brother Will had said the first time he'd seen it.

It still looked like a wedding cake when the taxi drew up outside later on that Sunday, though the effect was spoiled rather by the shabby caravan parked on the drive. Smoke was coming out of a little pipe in the roof that was presumably a chimney. At least the road had survived the air raids. Every house was still intact, unlike Toxteth and Allerton, which they'd just driven through. Some of the streets there had been bombed unmercifully.

'Nice place your mam's got,' the taxi driver remarked. On the way, he'd listed all the notable buildings that had been demolished or damaged in the raids.

She paid him and began to wonder if her mother still lived there, as she walked up the drive and noticed there wasn't a single flower to be seen in the once-beautiful front garden. Instead, there were rows and rows of rather dreary-looking plants that she suspected might be vegetables.

Sammy demanded to be lifted so he could use the door knocker. Henri picked him up, and the little boy was still banging away when the door was opened almost straight away by a grey-haired woman wearing a white blouse with the sleeves rolled up, black slacks and a pair of black lace-up pumps.

'Oh, my God!' the woman cried. 'Oh, my God. Jessica, my darling girl. How wonderful to see you. Come in.' She ushered them inside. 'Everyone come in. The more the merrier. And what a beautiful little boy. What's your name, sweetheart?'

'Sammy,' Sammy said proudly.

'Mother?' Could this possibly be her mother, with grey hair and her *sleeves rolled up*? And wearing those shoes, the sort the girls wore for gym at school. And on a Sunday, too, when she'd used to be dressed up to the nines.

'Jessica,' her mother cooed, embracing her warmly. 'And who does Sammy belong to?'

'Me,' she said, weakly.

Her mother laughed. 'What a surprise you turned out to be, darling.' She turned to Frannie and Henri. 'And who are you?'

Frannie almost curtsied. 'I am Françoise Cotillard and this is Henri Brun. We are engaged to be married, but have not yet bought a ring.'

'Well, you'll make a lovely couple, that's for sure.' She kissed them both. 'I do hope you invite me to your wedding. Shall we go into the kitchen? You must all be aching for a drink.'

A woman was washing the dishes in the kitchen. It was Mrs Black, who had been the housekeeper years ago. 'That'll do for now, Ivy,' her mother said. 'I'll finish that lot. You have a rest and we'll start on the laundry later.'

'Actually, Ethel, I'd sooner sort out the dining room than rest. It hasn't been touched all weekend and it's in a hell of a mess, with toys all over the place.'

Jessica was beginning to wonder if she'd entered some sort of wonderland where nothing was real. The housekeeper had called her mother 'Ethel'. Why were toys 'all over the place' in the terribly elegant dining room? Even stranger, 'Ethel', who'd always gone out of her way to avoid housework, intended doing laundry on a *Sunday*, which was supposed to be a day of rest.

She sat at the big kitchen table, badly wanting to talk to her mother alone. Had her children been located? She longed to know. Sam had promised to write to her care of this address. Had his letters been received? How was Will, her brother? The questions tumbled over each other in her brain.

There were more people in the house. She could hear talking in another room, the excited cries of children in the garden, a wireless on somewhere. The sun was beginning to set, casting dark shadows over the white kitchen. Birds tweeted dully, as if they were encased in cotton wool. Jessica swayed and the table came to meet her, but she jerked awake just in time.

'You must call me Ethel,' her mother was saying. 'These days, everyone calls me Ethel. Not Eth, never Eth. If anyone calls me Eth, I shall explode into little pieces.' She tapped Sammy on the nose. 'Say "Ethel", young man.'

'Effel,' Sammy said obediently.

'Very good. Jessica, darling,' Jessica was aware of the voice changing direction, 'you are falling asleep in front of our eyes. Would you like to lie down for a little while? I will look after Sammy and this gorgeous young couple you have brought with you. While you are gone, they can tell me exactly who they are.'

'Yes, please, Mother.'

'Ethel, from now on, please, even though you're my daughter. Or Effel. It sounds even better. Come along, and I'll find you a bed.'

There was a double bed in the room and two singles. The full-length windows were slightly ajar, making the room feel cool. None of the beds had been made. Ethel said to sleep on top of the coverlet for now and she'd put on fresh linen later. The bedroom was at the back of the house and the childish voices sounded louder. Through the window, a long way away at the bottom of the garden, Jessica could see a number of youngsters throwing a ball to each other.

'Whose children are they?' she asked.

Her mother glanced through the window. 'Two of them are yours,' she said as she left, closing the door behind her.

Jessica's heart seemed to have dropped to her stomach and was thumping noisily, almost painfully. She walked unsteadily to the window and studied the children outside. It was six years since she'd seen them, six long years, and from here they looked awfully small and a little bit misty, as if they were ghosts. She rubbed her aching eyes – she was finding it hard to keep them open. Jamie had been seven, but now he would be thirteen, a teenager. His voice might have started to break – or was thirteen too young for that? Dora would be eleven.

There were two boys playing in the garden who could have been thirteen, and three smaller girls whose ages she wasn't able to gauge. One might have been eleven or they all might have been.

Now tears were running down her cheeks at the thought that she was unable to recognize her own children. She stepped outside. More vegetables had been planted at the back of the house, rows and rows of them. There were two apple trees full of fruit, fruit bushes, loads of rhubarb plants, little green shoots that looked as if they might turn into cabbages or lettuces. A small greenhouse was chock-a-block with climbing plants. Beyond all the vegetation was a big square of worn grass where the children were playing. There were also two iron benches, a matching table, a swing and a tiny wooden hut.

Jessica walked along the narrow paved path towards the children. She wanted to ask them to stop playing and stand still so she could inspect them because they were moving too quickly for her to see their faces, throwing themselves around, leaping up and down, twisting, turning . . . It made her feel dizzy to watch.

Then one of the boys collapsed on top of the ball. He got up, clutching it, and caught sight of Jessica, so near, so still. She was petrified that he might not recognize her, or that he might recognize her, or that he might not be Jamie but some other boy.

He turned away, the boy, but only to put his arm round the shoulder of one of the girls, a girl of about eleven. They stared at Jessica, a look of puzzlement on their faces. She had never seen such beautiful children.

'Mum?' the boy said questioningly, and Jessica nodded.

'Jamie.' She held out her arms. 'Dora.'

She woke up when it was barely light, wide awake immediately, not gradually coming to. Sammy was fast asleep beside her, and Frannie was dead to the world in one of the single beds. Jamie and Dora were elsewhere in the house. Her mother – Ethel – had advised her not to overwhelm her children.

She'd said this last night when, unable to sleep for all the excitement, despite being totally exhausted, Jessica had got up to look for a drink and found her mother alone in the kitchen, smoking a cigarette and ready to offer all sorts of advice.

'Dora sleeps with May and Heather, who are twins,' she'd said, 'and Jamie shares a room with their brother, Ian. All three have lived here since their mother was killed in an air raid. Their father, Dillon, is one of Tom's very best friends and does important work for the Admiralty in London. He comes to see the children most weekends. You must let your own children adjust in their own way to having you back.'

Jessica wouldn't have dreamed of doing anything else. She had thought about today's reunion so many times and had always known she couldn't just walk back into their lives and expect things to return seamlessly to the way they'd been before. For one thing, she didn't want to upset Sammy and make him jealous of his brother and sister, and she didn't want to upset Henri, either. He was entitled to as much attention as her real children.

'When did Jamie and Dora come to live here?' she asked. 'Where had they been living before?'

'You'll never guess.' Her mother – Ethel, she'd get used to it one day – smiled. 'They'd only been living over the water in Secombe.'

'Had they always been there?'

'Ever since they left Atlas Road. Bertie went into the Army just before Christmas, 1940. He asked if I'd look after Jamie and Dora. What a nerve, I thought, considering the way he'd behaved with you. By then, France had been invaded and I couldn't let you know. He's in Colchester, loathsome man, a second lieutenant. I can't abide him.' Her lip curled. 'He wasn't sent abroad to fight or anything nasty like that, but is in charge of transport or something. His equally loathsome mother went to live with relatives in Wales. They had a tiff, or something.'

Jessica thought of all the money she'd paid the detective to find her children. He'd cast the net far too wide.

'I remember that Will had an artist friend in Secombe,' she said. 'He was best man at his wedding. How is Will? I really should have asked before.'

A dark cloud passed over her mother's face. 'Will's dead, I'm afraid, darling. He drowned. There've been so many tragedies.' She shrugged hopelessly. 'His ship went down in the middle of the Atlantic not long after your children came to live here.'

Jessica burst into tears. She couldn't imagine having had a nicer, kinder brother than Will. 'I was really looking forward to seeing him again.'

'The children – *your* children – were terribly upset. They truly loved their Uncle Will. Lena was devastated, and Calum, her little nephew. Daniel, the baby, had seen little of his dad. Lena had already realized she was pregnant for the second time before Will died. Six months later, she had a little girl, Rose. They were living here at the time, but,' here her voice took on a tone of disapproval, 'Will had been dead for less than a year when Lena started going out with a soldier. His name's Kevin and he's in Burma at the moment.' Her lips pursed once again. 'I asked her to leave. I couldn't stand seeing her look at the soldier in the same way she'd looked at my son. Soon afterwards, she and Kevin got married.'

'She was only very young, Lena,' Jessica said, though she too couldn't help feeling upset with the girl. 'Perhaps she felt she needed someone to provide for her and the children.'

'Tom and I were already doing that,' her mother said sharply. 'I don't blame her for wanting to get married again. After all, I did myself, didn't I? But she could have left a decent interval between husbands, not be making eyes at another man quite so soon. I found her a nice place near Penny Lane to live – after all, Daniel and Rose are my grand-children.'

Jessica sniffed, wiped her eyes on the sleeve of her night-dress and yawned. She was getting tired again. 'How is Tom?' she enquired.

Ethel made a shooing gesture with her hands. 'Go to bed,' she commanded. 'Go to bed now before something happens and you wake up again. If we stay up any longer I'll smoke another cigarette and I've only got one left for in the morning. We'll talk about Tom then. There's just one other person you haven't asked about – your grandma. She has passed on, I'm afraid. I was sorry to lose her, but Gladys was going on for ninety and had had a good innings, as they say.'

Jessica would shed tears tomorrow for her grandma, but not as many as she would shed for Will. She sighed. 'Have any letters come for me?'

'Yes, dear, a few. I'd forgotten all about them.' She

disappeared and came back with three letters. 'There's a name on the back, S. Deveraux, but each one has a different address. I suppose you intend to read them now, in which case I'm off to bed. Oh, and tomorrow we must arrange for ration books for you all, apart from Frannie. Her mother will have to get hers.'

The next morning, Jessica slipped quietly out of bed and went straight into the sunny garden still in her nightie, Sam's letters in her hand. The grass already felt warm and dry beneath her bare feet. She found it almost impossible to accept that it wasn't quite twenty-four hours since she had walked on the dew-soaked grass in the garden of the Lamb and Flag in Lincolnshire.

Despite the early hour, Ethel and Mrs Black could be seen at work in the kitchen; they waved to her through the window and she waved back. She felt disinclined to help with household tasks just yet, but would muck in and do her share as soon as she'd settled in. She sat gingerly in an old deckchair – she'd never felt safe in deckchairs – and read Sam's letters again. The first was dated June 1942, just before his son was born in Paris:

My dearest, darling Jess,

I have joined the British Royal Air Force and had to do a few months' training before they will let me fly a plane, even though I've had a pilot's licence since I was seventeen. Once I am able to fly a Lancaster bomber, I will be transferred to a camp on the east coast.

I think of you all day long and dream about you at night. I would write to you every week – every day – until your mother's house would have room for nothing but my letters. But you won't be there to read them, will you? At least, not until the war is over and you're back again in England.

With all my love and all my heart,
Sam

Jessica sighed and pressed the letter against her breast. The other two were shorter and less emotional. One came from Norfolk, the other Kent. The Kent one was dated December 1942. So many airmen had been killed in the war that wasn't over yet. It wouldn't be at all surprising for Sam to have been one.

The thought of Sam being dead made her feel sick. She leaned back in the chair and tried to concentrate on the garden, which smelled lovely and fresh.

Her gloomy thoughts were distracted by the sight of a very old, bent gentleman coming out of the greenhouse – it was Oswald, the gardener, she learned later. He was followed by a ginger and white collie dog. The dog became aware of the strange person in the garden and came trotting towards her, wagging its great plume of a tail. It flopped at her feet and began to lick them. She patted its head, introduced herself, and it licked her feet with greater enthusiasm.

Mrs Black came out of the kitchen with tea in a mug. She was about forty now, a slim, attractive woman with small, neat features. 'Do you take sugar?' she enquired.

'No, thank you.'

'Good, hardly anybody does since the war began. At least, women don't; most men can't get out of the habit.'

'It was rationed in France,' Jessica said.

'It's rationed here, too.' She turned to leave. 'I'd better go back and help get breakfast ready for the kids.'

'You mean Jamie, Dora and the others?' It was rather early for them to have breakfast.

'No, I mean the ones that don't live here, about a dozen altogether,' Mrs Black explained. 'Their mothers work at Rootes Securities in Speke, a munitions factory. After breakfast, I take the seven older ones to St Anthony de Padua's school and the little ones stay till their mothers have finished their shifts and come to collect them.'

'Tell me,' Jessica said, deeply impressed by this amazing news, 'what on earth has got into my mother? I never thought I'd see her with grey hair and no make-up until she was at least ninety.'

The woman smiled. 'The war had hardly started when she joined the Women's Voluntary Service. She put her whole heart and soul into it.' The smile faded. 'But then your brother got killed, you were in Occupied France and she had no idea if and when she'd ever see you again, and there seemed no point in "tarting herself up", as she put it. You just wouldn't believe how hard she works.' She began to edge towards the kitchen door. 'I'm sorry, Mrs Collins, but I really must be getting back.'

'Please call me Jessica – or just Jess.' She couldn't remember when she had last been Mrs Collins.

'And you must call me Ivy.' She disappeared inside the kitchen.

Frannie must have been waiting for Ivy to leave. She came out of the bedroom as soon as the kitchen door had closed, and knelt on the grass beside the deckchair. She began to stroke the dog.

'Her name's Daisy, it's engraved on her collar,' she said after a while, burying her head in the dog's furry neck. 'When I was little, we had a kitten called Snow White – Papa called her that because she was as black as coal. Marie and me really loved her, but all Mama did was moan because she left hairs on the divan and scratched the stool in the kitchen. One day, we came home from school and she'd given Snow White away. She wouldn't tell us who to, and we never saw her again. I got terribly upset. I told Mama that I wished it was the other way round and Snow White had given *her* away instead.' She looked up at Jessica, her expression desperately tragic. 'Why is she the way she is, Jess? I mean, fancy speaking to me like that yesterday when she hadn't seen me for so long.'

'I don't know what's wrong with her, *cherie*,' Jessica confessed. 'We all have different personalities.'

'Your mother was really thrilled to see you,' the girl said sulkily.

'When I was a child my mother was of the opinion that children should be seen and not heard. She hasn't always been so friendly.' She couldn't remember exactly what her mother had said before Jessica had been about to leave with the children, but it was something to do with it being a long time before they should see each other again.

The conversation might have continued, had not Sammy appeared, demanding to know where he was. 'Where will we sleep tomorrow?' He seemed to think that from now on they would be sleeping in different places every night for the rest of his life. Without waiting for an answer, he spied Daisy and threw himself on to the grass beside her. She began to lick his face.

It's not very hygienic, Jessica thought uneasily. 'Let's go inside and have a good wash,' she suggested. The last time she'd washed her feet properly had been in Paris.

She wondered whether to look for Jamie and Dora to say goodbye before they left for school, or wait for them to find her? She was still wondering when they knocked on the bedroom door where she was drying Sammy after giving him a bath. They came in with satchels over their shoulders. Sammy was pretending to be terrified of his mother wielding the towel, and Jessica was obliged to chase him around the room.

The two older children looked benignly at their little brother. Sammy calmed down and let Jessica put on his underpants, smiling sweetly.

'Was I like that when I was little?' Dora asked.

'Not a bit, no. Nor was Jamie. You were very well

behaved. Sammy's spoilt. Back in Paris there were too many people making a fuss of him. Are you both off to school?'

'In a minute.' Jamie's voice hadn't quite broken, but it was deep, almost manly. 'We have school dinners so I won't be home until nearly four o'clock. Dora's school finishes a bit earlier.'

'Which schools do you go to?' Jessica asked. It seemed an awfully strange question to ask your children.

Dora answered first. 'I'm at St Anthony de Padua's. I go with May and Heather; it's our final year. Jamie goes to Quarry Bank Grammar – he passed the scholarship,' Dora finished a trifle pompously.

'Maybe you and the other girls can sit the scholarship this year?' Jessica suggested. Dora wasn't nearly as shy as she used to be.

'Oh, I don't know.' The girl seemed to shrink a little.

'I'll coach you,' Jessica promised. 'Mind you, I sat the scholarship but didn't pass.'

Henri came in and Jamie's eyes lit up. 'Will you help me with my French homework tonight?' he enquired.

'*Mais oui*,' Henri replied.

'It's the grammar I get stuck on, not translating the words.'

'I'll explain it to you,' Henri promised.

Sara arrived later that morning as Jessica had guessed she might – it wouldn't have been sensible to keep her vow never to see her friend again. Sara had got the address from her father, whom she'd gone to see as soon as she'd delivered Joseph to school. Frannie and Henri had gone for a walk in Calderstones Park and weren't expected back for a while.

The Women's Voluntary Service was holding a meeting in the parlour; small children, Sammy included, were in the dining room playing with plasticine and crayons on the oak table that had cost a mint, and a man whose identity she had yet to learn was using a typewriter in Tom's study. Tom was in London at the moment working on a case. His chambers in Castle Street had been bombed during something called the 'May Blitz', when Hitler had attempted to bomb Liverpool to destruction. He had a temporary office in town and he, or one of his assistants, sometimes worked from the office in the house. The lovely red sitting room had been turned into a bedroom.

The only other empty room Jessica could find was small and contained a folding bed, two folding chairs, and a portable sewing machine on a table along with various lengths of material and a box of cotton reels in assorted colours. She opened the chairs, sat down, and indicated Sara do the same.

'I'm sorry about yesterday,' was the first thing Sara said. Jessica noted her tired eyes and discontented face. She tried to feel sorry for her friend, but it was hard. 'Is Frannie here?'

'She's out with Henri at the moment. I'm not sure when they'll be back.'

Sara made a face. 'They're not serious about getting married, are they?'

'They probably are at the moment, but they're only young and things can change with time.' Jessica picked up a scrap of material and began to pull it to bits. She had a feeling Sara was about to become difficult. 'Yesterday, Frannie didn't say they were getting married there and then, did she? I think the best thing to do is just go along with it. The more you disapprove, the more determined they will be to get married. Left alone, they could well go off each other.'

'Oh, you!' Sara said belligerently. 'You're always the soul of patience. Never arguing, never refusing anybody, always wanting people to like you, whereas me, I make my views known and don't care if people like me or not.'

Jessica stared at her patiently and didn't say a word. Perhaps some of what Sara had said about her was true; it was just that she preferred a quiet life to one full of rows and ill-temper.

After a while, Sara began to cry. 'I want Frannie back,' she sobbed. 'I've really missed her, particularly when I got the letter from Nicky Costigan saying Louis was dead. Did the Gestapo really execute him?'

'Yes.' Jessica nodded. 'I spoke to him the day before. He said, "Tell Sara how much I loved and missed her."' He'd also said, 'If Sara was here now, she'd kill me.' But she wouldn't tell Sara that; she might not see the joke.

'I loved him,' Sara wept. 'I know it wasn't obvious, but I really did love him.'

It had never been even faintly obvious, but Jessica had always taken for granted that deep down Sara genuinely loved her husband. 'Will you go back to Paris when the war is over?' she asked. 'Another thing Louis said was to keep the theatre going. Simone, Frannie and me all made sure it never closed apart from Sundays. Now Simone is looking after the place all on her own.'

'Simone!' Sara's lips twisted. 'I could never stand that woman.'

'I found her extremely nice. We worked together very well. There was never any unpleasantness between us.'

Sara tossed her head contemptuously. 'Oh, you would say that!'

'Frannie will say the same if you ask her. She really loves her grandmother. So does Sammy, even though she's no relation.' Jessica was having a job keeping her temper. She said reasonably, 'Why have you come? To insult me or persuade Frannie to go back with you?'

Sara dissolved into tears again. 'Like I said, I want Frannie back.' She began to list all the things that were wrong with her life. She hated Kirkby; she hated the house in which she lived. 'It's so big, so cold, not at all like our house in Paris. Oh, Jessica, I loved that house so much, and the theatre.'

Jessica blinked. Although that was nothing but a big fat lie, it was how Sara saw things so it was no use arguing with her.

She continued to moan, appearing to think the war was being fought solely to spite her.

Concerned that Frannie and Henri would return soon, Jessica cut short the litany of complaints. 'I want to tell you about Henri,' she said bluntly. 'He's Jewish and the Germans took his parents and his sister away; they're probably all dead by now. I have adopted him. I regard him as my son, though there's nothing official about it. If you hurt him, or offend him in any way, then I shall never speak to you again. I hope you're listening, Sara, because I mean it.' This time she really did.

Sara waited for the young couple to return. It wasn't long before Frannie had packed her clothes and gone home with her mother.

'I'm going to hate it,' she hissed when she was saying goodbye.

'Don't let her bully you,' Jessica hissed back. 'If it's unbearable, you can always come here.'

'Neither my mother nor father could stand their mothers-in-law,' Henri remarked after Frannie had gone. He didn't look as upset as Jessica had expected, probably because he'd arranged to see her the next day. 'Maybe it's one of the rules of marriage.' He disappeared, saying he was going to sit in the garden with a book. 'An *English* book. It will help me get used to the language.'

The meeting in the parlour came to an end and the women went home. Not long afterwards, the mothers finished their shifts in Rootes Securities and collected their children. With no one to entertain him, Sammy came in search of his mother. The typing had stopped. All of a sudden, the house was unnaturally quiet, the only sounds coming from the kitchen where Ethel and Ivy were washing dishes.

'We made aeroplanes with sticky stuff, and danced,' Sammy said.

'Danced!' Jessica exclaimed. 'Let me see you dance.'

The little boy commenced to lumber around the large square hall with all the grace of a miniature elephant. Jessica clapped her hands and ran into the parlour where the radiogram was the very latest design. She sorted through the records and, to her delight, found Al Bowlly with the Lew Stone Orchestra.

'You'll love this,' she said to Sammy. 'It will bring out your romantic side.'

Al Bowlly's haunting voice began to sing, 'Is it a sin, is it a crime, loving you, dear like I do . . . oo . . .'

She picked up her son and danced with him around the room while singing along to the music. Sammy squealed with delight.

'I love you, *cheri*,' Jessica cried. 'I love you, love you, love you . . .'

There was a cough, and a voice said, 'You're very beautiful, Jessica. More beautiful than ever.'

Jessica stopped dancing. A man was standing in the doorway, very handsome, very blond, wearing the uniform of an officer in the Army.

'Bertie!' she gasped.

Chapter 23

'Hello, Jessica.' He strolled into the room. 'So you're back.'

She retreated a few steps. 'So I am.'

'Don't worry, I'm not going to attack you.' He laughed.

'I know you're not. Sammy would floor you if you did.'

'Is that his name, Sammy? How do you do, Sammy?' He shook her son's small hand.

Sammy hid his face in Jessica's shoulder. She explained that he wasn't used to men. 'We had an all-female household in Paris.' Apart from Henri, that was.

Bertie raised his eyebrows and nodded at Sammy. 'It couldn't have always been an *all*-female household.'

She didn't know what to say to that, so changed the subject. 'I thought you were based in Colchester?'

'I am, but last night Jamie told me you were home and that he and Dora had a little brother. I had a few days' leave due, so thought I'd drive over and renew my acquaintance with my wife.' Jessica noticed through the window that a khaki saloon car was parked outside. He was in charge of transport, her mother had said.

'*Jamie* told you?' Sammy was falling asleep in her arms. She laid him on the velvet cushions of the settee. He rolled on to his side and began to suck his thumb. She put a protective hand on his shoulder.

'I ring Jamie and Dora every Sunday night without fail.'

'I see.' There was no doubt about how much he loved his

children. 'After you took them away, did you tell them I was dead?' He had threatened to.

'You mean after I took them away before you took them away from me?' He smiled sardonically. 'No, I told them that you were ill and we'd all be together again when you felt better. I had always meant for that to happen.' He shook his head regretfully as he sank into a chair. 'You needed to be punished, darling, after what you did. So, a year passed and I went to the house in Bootle, but was told you'd gone. "I think she might have married that boyfriend of hers," said the landlady. Apparently, the boyfriend, whose name was Harvey, spent so many nights there the relationship must have been serious.'

Jessica shrugged. 'It *was* serious.'

His cheeks flushed angrily. She knew she'd hurt him and wished she hadn't said that. But how dare he decide to 'punish' her. 'It was then,' he went on, 'that I realized you were nothing but a whore. I thought it odd you'd shown no sign of it while you were married to me – though we're still married, aren't we? I may yet find out.' He looked at Sammy. 'Well, we know what it makes that little chap.'

'That's a really ugly thing to say, Bertie,' she said coldly, furious, not just because of what he'd said about Sammy, but for suggesting there was a chance they'd get together again. Yet despite that, she couldn't bring herself to tell him how useless he was in bed. He had to have some pride left.

'I suppose Harvey is Sammy's father?'

'He isn't, actually.'

Bertie winced. He looked at his watch and abruptly got to his feet. 'I think I'll meet Jamie and Dora coming out of school.' He laughed ironically. 'Don't worry; I won't go off with them again.'

'I know you won't. I don't think they'd go so easily a second time, Bertie, not now they're old enough to know their own minds and realize when their father is telling lies.'

He left without another word. Jessica found herself

trembling. It hadn't been a very agreeable conversation and she wasn't sure if it was his fault or her own. She feared one day he would do her harm.

Her mother came in. 'Are you expecting any more visitors today?' She sat down and lit a cigarette, smoking in the same urgent way that Jessica used to.

'I hope not.' She felt desperately tired. It was hard being in Liverpool after Paris. And she was mourning the death of Will. The house itself was making her head ache. It was so big and airy and white. The house in Paris was small, dark and cramped, but it was what she'd grown used to.

'He's still in love with you, Bertie,' her mother said. 'Once Will told us you were in Paris, he asked after you regularly. He pretended not to care, but I could tell he was anxious to know if you were all right. His hatred for Tom is palpable, but he has to be polite if he wants his children to stay in Tom's house.'

Bertie's hatred was understandable. Tom McGrath had committed adultery with his wife. He was also her mother's husband. Jessica shifted uncomfortably at the thought, at the same time feeling relieved that her mother showed no trace of animosity towards her. 'How is Tom?' she asked.

'Brought down,' her mother said dramatically, almost gleefully. 'Brought down by his own arrogance. He had a case once, years ago, when he managed to get a "not guilty" verdict for a young woman who'd been accused of murdering her employer. It was something to do with fingerprints. It was in all the papers, feted as a breakthrough, and Tom was the hero of the hour. A year later a lawyer, half Tom's age, who was defending another woman accused of the crime discovered the whole thing had been a sham and it had been Tom's bad luck to be taken in. The young woman, I can't remember her name . . .'

'Mary Anne Donovan,' Jessica said. She remembered the case well. The verdict had come the day she'd been in The

Temple hotel and Tom had turned up triumphant, later carrying her off to bed.

'Well, Mary Anne was much cleverer than Tom. She got off scot-free, can't be tried again, and Tom was made to look like a fool. He's never recovered, poor lamb.' She winked at Jessica. 'I still love him, but I'm not quite as smitten as I used to be.' She stretched and announced she was going for 'a little lie-down'. 'Ivy's making the children's tea. Then she can have a rest and I'll prepare dinner. It's scouse and only needs warming up. I do hope Bertie doesn't intend staying. He can't stand scouse.'

Jessica was amused at the idea of her mother making scouse. But war was a great leveller. No matter how rich a person was, they could only buy what was available in the shops. 'Before you go,' she said, 'is there a London telephone directory in the house?' It was the sort of thing Tom might have. 'I want to telephone the headquarters of the Royal Air Force and try to find out where Sam is.' If no one could tell her, they might at least give her an address to write to.

'Darling,' her mother cried, 'Dillon will find that out for you, Dillon Reilly, Ian and the twins' father. He's in Intelligence and knows absolutely everyone. Write down Sam's details, his full name and date of birth, and I'll telephone him this instant.'

Moving from a liberated Paris to Liverpool where air raids were a thing of the past, it would have been easy to regard the war as virtually over, but on the wireless and in the newspapers, the news was grim.

In the Dutch town of Arnhem where a bridgehead was planned that would speed the war to a rapid end, 36,000 troops were parachuted in to where the enemy were secretly waiting, resulting in 6,000 men being captured and 1,400 killed.

The Germans had at last crushed the Polish uprising in Warsaw, resulting in a total of 200,000 Poles killed.

In Occupied Paris, this information had been mostly hidden. The general public had to guess what was going on. But now all they had to do was pass a newsagent's and see the placards outside with headlines bearing the latest news, though it wasn't always bad. The German Army was being driven back on every front and the forecast was that Allied troops would be on German soil within a matter of weeks.

Dillon Reilly was an attractive man going on for fifty. He had a magnificent head of brown, curly hair, with the odd grey curl here and there, small, sparkling eyes, a snub nose and a wide, laughing mouth. All in all, his face was attractively ugly. Jessica liked him straight away.

He arrived by taxi on Saturday morning, having caught the first train from London. 'I thought I'd rather give you the info in person,' he said in his pleasant voice with a slight Irish accent, 'rather than on the telephone. Anyway, it's a good excuse to see my kids.'

'What info?'

'Let's wait until Ethel brings us the promised coffee.'

Her mother came in with a tray containing a beautiful willow pattern coffee pot and crockery to match. She left with a promise that they wouldn't be disturbed.

Jessica poured the coffee. Dillon Reilly was no longer smiling and she felt sure that the news he'd brought could only be bad.

'Samuel Deveraux joined the Royal Air Force in April 1942,' he said in a flat voice devoid of expression, as if he were reading the news on the wireless. 'He was already a qualified pilot, but required further training. He spent time in several different counties. Once fully trained, he began to fly Lancaster bombers in raids over Germany. In January 1943, he took off from Mildenhall in Suffolk as part of a bombing raid on Berlin.' He looked at Jessica and his tone softened. 'His plane was witnessed flying over Berlin, but at some point it vanished. Nothing has been seen or heard of it since, nor its crew of eight. Sam's parents in Quebec received a telegram some months later informing them that their son was "Missing, Presumed Dead". He reached for her hand and squeezed it. 'I'm sorry, Jessica, to have brought such bad news.'

Christmas came, the sixth of the war so far but generally reckoned to be the last. In the week beforehand, a day didn't pass without a party being held in some part of the house. People brought their own food, a loaf perhaps, a tin of sardines, a pound of flour, cakes they'd made themselves . . .

The Women's Voluntary Service had their party one afternoon in the parlour, another day the small children had one in the kitchen, while after school the bigger ones played hide and seek and other games, their cries audible in every room of the house. The women from Rootes Securities came to collect their children and stayed for sherry and mince pies.

Old friends of her mother and Tom came in the evenings: mayors and councillors, managers of this and chairmen of that. New friends turned out to be air raid wardens, fire-watchers, members of the Home Guard, and the elderly woman who'd been delivering the post ever since the war began. Oswald, the gardener, who lived in the caravan at the front, insisted on bringing Daisy, his dog.

Her mother appeared in the parlour one night wearing a long, electric-blue velvet dress with a short train. She had diamonds in her ears and round her neck. That morning she'd had her hair set, as well as something called a facial. She and Tom were going to a dinner dance in the Adelphi Hotel.

'You look beautiful, Mother,' Jessica said reverently.

'You look beautiful, *Ethel*,' her mother emphasized.

'You look beautiful, Ethel.'

Her mother giggled. 'What do you think of the diamonds? They cost twenty-five shillings from Owen Owen's.'

'They're lovely. I thought they were real.'

'People are supposed to think that.' She looked in a mirror and patted the necklace approvingly. 'I sold all my proper jewels the minute the air raids started. I thought that if the house got a direct hit, there'd be precious stones scattered all over Calderstones and the poor birds would end up choking on them.'

'You could have put them in the bank,' Jessica said.

'Yes, but say the bank got a direct hit? Even the strongest safe might not be able to stand up to the blast.'

'Are you ready, Ethel?' Tom had come into the room behind her. He half-smiled at Jessica and she dipped her head in response. The incident in The Temple that afternoon so many years ago had never been mentioned or acknowledged in any way, which suited her right down to the ground. He was no longer the charismatic charmer who had taken her to bed that afternoon and done wonderful things to her, but a smaller, greyer person with a diminishing career.

Dillon Reilly had come to stay a few days. That afternoon, the day before Christmas Eve, he had taken Jamie, Dora and his own three children to see *Going My Way* with Bing Crosby. Afterwards, they had gone for a meal. They came in just after Ethel and Tom had left.

'I can't stand an entire evening ahead with these tiresome children,' Dillon complained in a loud voice. 'Not Jamie and Dora, who are perfectly well behaved, but the three horrors that belong to me.'

One of the girls, Heather, threw a cushion at him. 'You are a truly horrible daddy,' she told him, grinning.

Dillon made a face. 'You have no idea how horrible I really can be. If you sing "Would You Like to Swing on a Star" again, then I shall go berserk. They sang it in the restaurant and all the way home on the tram,' he complained to Jessica. 'It was desperately embarrassing.'

The children stopped taking any notice of their father and disappeared into their bedrooms. 'Would you like a cup of tea?' Jessica asked. She'd not seen much of Dillon, but whenever she did, apart from their first meeting, he never failed to cheer her up.

'No, I would not like a cup of tea,' Dillon said emphatically. 'I would prefer something alcoholic drunk in a childfree environment. Let's go to a pub, Jessica, where no singing is allowed and we can talk about really important things that children don't understand.'

'I couldn't possibly,' Jessica said, upset that he should ask when he knew her circumstances, that Sam was almost certainly dead, and the last thing she wanted to do was go out with another man.

'We'd be going out as friends,' he said quietly. 'Nothing else. It's three years since Eithne, my wife, was killed, and I have no desire to have a relationship with another woman except as a friend.'

'I'm sorry,' Jessica said uncomfortably. 'Of course I'll go out with you as a friend. But I'm not sure if I'm willing to leave Sammy with that lot the mood they're in.' Blood-curdling screams were coming from other parts of the house. 'I think Jamie and Ian are pretending to be ghosts again.' She rushed out of the room. 'They'll wake Sammy.'

She calmed the children down and remembered Henri was somewhere in the house with Frannie, who had come to see him earlier. She was staying overnight, sleeping in the girls' room. The pair were discovered in the dining room absorbed in a giant Christmas crossword.

'What was Scrooge's first name?' Henri asked when Jessica entered.

'I have no idea.'

'Ebenezer,' Dillon shouted. He came into the room. 'Have

you read any Dickens, Henri? In my view, he's the very best English writer. I'll fetch you a copy of *A Christmas Carol* from London next time I come back.'

Jessica requested that they keep an eye on the children, who were acting as if they had inhaled laughing gas while they'd been out that afternoon, and look after Sammy if he woke. She went into the bedroom to make sure Sammy was still asleep. He now slept in a single bed on his own. With his rosy cheeks and pale golden hair, her little boy was doing a pretty good impersonation of an angel. She blew him a kiss, put on her new sage-green coat with a velvet collar and matching hat, and joined Dillon in the hall where he was waiting.

In the pub, a log fire burned and the atmosphere was joyful but quiet, apart from the buzz of conversation and polite laughter. There was no piano and no one sang, but Dillon didn't talk about anything important as Jessica had expected. Instead, he told her loads of Irish jokes and recited funny poems, which, it turned out, he had written himself.

'In peacetime, I'm an accountant by trade and I write silly poetry to keep me sane. The minute I retire, I shall grow my hair long and do nothing but write poetry. I might even try to have it published.' His eyes lit up. 'Have you ever read the poems of Ogden Nash?'

Jessica had never heard of him. 'No,' she said.

Dillon got to his feet and assumed a dramatic pose, ' "Celery raw" ', he quoted, ' "develops the jaw, Celery stewed is more quietly chewed." ' He collapsed into helpless laughter. 'Don't you think that's brilliant? That poem is called "Celery", as you will have guessed. Would you like to hear another called "Fleas"?'

'Yes, please.' His laughter was catching.

' "Adam had'm." ' He laughed so much that his face turned red and she thought he was about to have a heart attack. She suspected he was more than a bit tipsy, though he hadn't drunk much.

He continued to narrate Ogden Nash poems until their part of the bar had stopped talking to listen. Eventually, she had to insist they went home. A sprinkling of applause followed them out of the pub. She was worried about Sammy. Despite knowing Henri and Frannie were thoroughly responsible young people, she still felt uneasy.

Dillon insisted on singing as they walked home, arms linked. ' "Would you like to swing on a star," ' he warbled in an excellent baritone voice, ' "and carry moonbeams home in a jar?" ' He only seemed to know the one song, and then only the first two lines.

'Shush!' she whispered as she opened the front door. They stumbled inside where it was pitch-dark and unnaturally silent. The door closed, she felt for the light and switched it on.

A curt voice said, 'Have you had a nice time?'

She turned and saw Bertie standing in the doorway of the bedroom where she and Sammy slept. His face was flushed and his eyes feverishly bright.

'Yes, thank you. What are you doing there?' She went into the room, feeling panicky for some reason. Sammy was still fast asleep, breathing evenly. How else did she expect him to be? Did she seriously think that Bertie would harm him?

'If he had woken, I was going to tell him a story,' Bertie said. 'Remember the one I used to tell Jamie, the one about the dragon and the snail?'

'I do remember, yes.' She touched his arm and led him into the hall. He had been drinking, something strong like whiskey; she could smell it on him. 'Have all the children gone to bed?'

'They must have done. I've only just got here. That boy Henri and the girl are somewhere.'

Dillon was still by the front door. He looked very alert, as if he could feel danger in the air. She suspected he hadn't been tipsy. He hadn't exactly been pretending, just enjoying himself, letting go. She'd felt a bit the same herself, just sitting in a pub listening to silly poetry and forgetting all about the war and Sam being missing and everything else unpleasant.

As Bertie spoke, Dillon went into the dining room. She heard Henri say, 'Did you have a nice time?' though in a completely different way than Bertie. Dillon said something and Henri laughed. 'They began falling asleep all over the place. Frannie and I had to wake them and show them where their beds were.'

'It was really funny,' Frannie said.

'Well, I'll say goodnight now.'

'Before you go, do you know who discovered something called penicillin? There are a few clues here that we can't manage.'

'Penicillin is a really clever drug; it was discovered by a man called Alexander Fleming.'

'Thank you.'

Dillon emerged, smiling. 'They're a pair of brain boxes! I'm off now,' he said to Jessica. Turning to Bertie, who was standing, hands in pockets, swaying slightly, he asked, 'Are you all right, old man?'

Bertie scowled. 'Why shouldn't I be?'

Dillon shrugged. 'No reason.' He looked at Jessica. 'I'm sleeping in the sewing room. OK?'

'OK.' The atmosphere was strange, almost threatening. Dillon had gone. She asked Bertie where he was sleeping.

'In the study,' he said sulkily. 'There's a camp bed there.'

'Goodnight, then. I hope you have a nice sleep. Turn the hall light off, won't you? It's usually left on all night, but not until everyone is home.' Her mother and Tom were still at the Adelphi.

She hurried into her own room, got undressed, and was under the clothes in no time and fast asleep in even less.

★

She was woken by someone smelling strongly of whiskey trying to climb on top of her. Bertie!

She did her utmost to push him off, but he was too strong for her. Within a minute, he had his knee between her legs, her nightie round her waist; she could feel him hard against her. She was pinned to the bed by one of his hands, which was over her mouth, and he was trying to force himself inside her with the other. Her arms were trapped.

Strangely, she wasn't a bit frightened, unlike when the same thing was about to happen in Paris with Claud Petrou. This time, the house was full of people. She wondered if her mother and Tom had come home. What was more, it was a stupid reaction, but she actually wanted to giggle at the idea of being raped by Bertie. Across the room, Sammy uttered a little cry and she badly wanted to go to him, to soothe him.

With a huge effort she tried to twist her body and throw Bertie off, to lift her knees and kick him away, but nothing worked. He was a leaden weight on top of her, and she was completely helpless.

But suddenly, the door opened and seconds later Bertie was pulled away and thrown to the floor. He uttered a terrified yelp.

'Get out!' Dillon Reilly said quietly.

'But she's my wife,' Bertie gasped.

Jessica adjusted her nightdress, pushed herself to a sitting position on the bed, and switched on the bedside light. Bertie crouched on all fours. He wore only a pyjama jacket buttoned to the neck. She wanted to laugh and cry at the same time. He looked so downright silly, yet at the same time terribly pathetic. He scrambled to his feet and ran from the room. She heard the door to the study close.

Dillon was still fully dressed. He said in a low voice, 'I didn't like the look of him. I thought he was likely to do something mad before long. I sat and listened. It was the

314

creaking of the bed that alerted me.' He looked at her with concern. 'Would you like a drink to calm your nerves?'

'I'd love a glass of sherry.' She got out of bed – her night-dress was winceyette and not at all revealing – and glanced at Sammy, who was fast asleep, oblivious to the attack on his mother.

'I'd like me whistle wetting after all that fuss,' Dillon said. 'Is the stuff in the kitchen or the parlour?'

'Once a bottle is opened, it's left in the kitchen.'

'The opened bottles are exactly what we want.'

Frannie stuck her head out of the dining-room door. 'Is everything all right?'

'Everything's fine, darlin'. Are you two eggheads going to stay up all night doing that bloody crossword?'

Frannie grinned. 'Yes, Mr Reilly.'

In the kitchen, Jessica had poured a glass of sherry and was sipping it slowly. She left the cupboard open for Dillon to choose a drink for himself.

'I'll have rum for a change,' he said when he came in. 'I don't suppose you realize how brave I was just then. By the look of him, Bertie is a strong, healthy young man, whereas I am much older as well as being a craven coward.'

'I haven't thanked you yet.' Jessica sighed. Something had to be done about Bertie, but she had no idea what. As for herself, she'd have to learn self-defence. That was the second time in her life that she'd almost been raped, and needed a man to rescue her.

Chapter 24

The next morning, Christmas Eve, when Jessica got up, she found a piece of paper had been shoved under the bedroom door.

'I'm sorry' was all it said.

'Oh, Bertie,' she said. In the hall, she saw the door to the office was open, and the camp bed was folded. There was no sign of her husband.

'He's gone.' Frannie came out of the girls' bedroom. 'I heard him leave. He drove away about three o'clock this morning.'

Jessica was able to breathe more easily, knowing that Bertie wouldn't be there to spoil the day, though he'd been much too drunk to drive. 'What time did he arrive last night?' she enquired.

'About nine. He burst in on Henri and me and wanted to know where you were. I told him you were out with Mr Reilly, but Henri said I shouldn't have done because he was your husband.' She wrinkled her brow. 'I'm sorry, Jessica, but I must say you are a very confusing person. I thought Sam was your husband. Not only that, until recently, I had no idea you'd been married before and already had Jamie and Dora when you came to Paris. Since Maman found out, she's not stopped going on about it.'

'I did tell your mother, but she was too absorbed in herself to listen.'

People began to arrive bearing gifts. She had never thought her mother would become so popular for her good works and kind heart.

The children disappeared into their bedrooms and emerged with presents wrapped in red crêpe paper that had been used in previous years and looked distinctly the worse for wear – it was impossible to buy it now. Parcels appeared beneath the imitation tree – the grown-ups weren't opening their presents until before lunch on Christmas Day. Jamie and Ian went into town to buy last-minute gifts and see John Wayne in *Flying Tigers*.

That afternoon, Jessica left Sammy with her mother and went to see Lena, her late brother's wife. One of Jessica's favourite memories was of Christmas in the house in Bootle when Lena and Will had met and Will had fallen in love straight away.

Lena now lived in a three-storey red-brick terraced house close to Penny Lane. For a present, Jessica took a flowered silk scarf that someone had given her mother as a Christmas present but she didn't want, and a bag of sweets for the children. Because it was Christmas, for one week only, the sweet ration had been doubled. Also, there was an extra eight ounces of meat and the same of sugar.

She had thought Lena might be alone with just the children for company over the holiday, but found Kevin's mother and one of his sisters there – he had four and Audrey was the youngest. The mother's name was Tess. They and Lena were clearly fond of each other.

Lena was delighted to see her. 'I didn't realize you were home from Paris,' she cried.

Jessica was introduced to Will's children: Daniel, four, who was the image of his father and had the same happy personality, and Rose, two, a little firebrand of a girl, who was even prettier than her mother. There was also Calum, now nine, who claimed to remember Jessica from when they'd lived in the same house. She felt desperately sad to think her brother wouldn't be around to see Daniel and Rose grow up. She recalled him saying he wouldn't want to be married if there was a war on and he had to leave his family behind.

'They're all lovely children,' she said to Lena. Kevin's mother and sister had gone, but were returning that night with other members of his family for a party.

Lena smiled. 'Well, I think so. Kevin really loves them.' She looked keenly at Jessica, who'd once been her good friend. 'Your mother really disapproves of me. She thought it was much too soon for me to get married again. I hope you don't feel the same.'

'I'm not sure how I feel,' Jessica admitted. 'We loved Will so much, everybody did. I can't imagine wanting to marry another man after him, at least not for a long time.'

Lena clasped both of Jessica's hands in her own and squeezed them. 'Oh, Jessica, I *adored* Will. I was broken-hearted when he died, but I don't think I ever really *loved* him. I was too much in awe of him for that. He was so special it was like being married to a prince or a god. I could never understand what he saw in me.' Rose began to cry and Lena picked her up. 'What's the matter, sweetheart?' She jigged the little girl up and down until she'd stopped crying and began to play with her mother's hair.

'Anyway,' she continued, 'about six months after he died I met Kevin. I was out with the children in the pram – Rose had only just been born – and it started to rain. I couldn't get the hood up. Kevin helped me. He wasn't in the Army then; he'd been deferred until he finished his apprenticeship. He's a motor mechanic,' she explained. 'He walked me home and when I said I was a widow, he asked me out. I hope you don't mind me saying this, but I only went because it made a change from being in your mother's house. I felt stifled there. Before I knew it, Kevin and I were in love. It felt completely different from how it had been with Will, easier. I didn't feel as if I had to be on my best behaviour. I'm afraid it really upset your mother and she asked me to leave, but not before finding me this lovely house. I hope I haven't upset you, Jessica,' she said fervently.

'Not in the slightest.' Jessica threw her arms round the girl. What right had she to be upset or disapprove of how Lena behaved, when she herself had behaved dreadfully over the years? She wished Lena and her family a Merry Christmas and promised to come and see her again in the New Year.

'Oh, and by the way,' Lena said as Jessica was leaving, 'I never got that compensation I was expecting.'

When she got home, Henri had already left with Frannie to spend Christmas Day with Sara. He hadn't exactly been looking forward to it. 'But I suppose I'll have to go for Frannie's sake,' he'd said gloomily.

'I suppose you will.' It would do him good to get involved with the ups and downs of family life, even if it wasn't his own. 'If Sara is rude, take no notice. She's rude to everyone.'

'I'd sooner be here with you and Sammy and everyone on Christmas Day.'

'And we'd sooner you were here – Jamie will miss you.'

'Ethel said Frannie could stay here, but she doesn't like letting her mother down.'

'That's because Frannie is a really nice person. And so are you, Henri. You and Frannie deserve each other.'

The rest of Christmas Eve was spent in relative quietness. Tom and Dillon Reilly listened to the wireless and drank whiskey in the parlour, while in another room the children played cards for halfpennies with only the occasional cross voice raised. Ethel and Ivy stayed in the kitchen preparing food for tomorrow's dinner. Jessica sat on the bed and told Sammy stories, making them up as she went along. He'd been cantankerous earlier, announcing that he wanted Simone.

'Where is she?' he sobbed. 'Where Simone?'

'In Paris, darling. We'll see Simone again one day.' Just then, she wouldn't have minded seeing Simone herself.

'Want her now!' Sammy bawled. He eventually fell asleep, his cheeks streaked with tears.

Around midnight, the children fast asleep – or pretending to be – the grown-ups crept around, placing presents beside beds and hanging socks from bedposts. There'd been little in the way of children's presents to be found in the shops. Books and a few toys had been bought second-hand, jumpers, hats and scarves had been knitted from wool that had once been a completely different garment, undone, washed and knitted again, not just into more clothes, but a Humpty Dumpty and a fat pink pig for Sammy, and dolly bags for the girls for which they were much too old.

Jessica couldn't sleep. Her experience the previous night had deeply disturbed her. She lay buried under the clothes and visualized being unable to escape from Bertie, who seemed to think he was entitled to his marital rights after all these years. Say he refused to divorce her and she was stuck with him for ever?

How could her brain feel so wide awake yet so terribly muddled? Horrible, really horrible thoughts chased each other through her mind, like Bertie taking Jamie and Dora away again, but this time to the other side of the world where she would never find them. She imagined him taking Sammy, too, secretly, when she was out, as he'd done with the others all those years before.

But hadn't she tried to do the same thing to him? 'I wouldn't have dreamed of doing such a thing,' she told herself, 'if he hadn't threatened I could only see the children for two hours a week.' Her 'crime' hadn't deserved such fierce punishment.

She tried to distract herself by reliving the last night that she and Sam had slept together in Paris. It almost worked. If she stayed quite still and didn't move, then she could almost feel his arms round her, hear the things he said, recall the passion of them making love. But then Bertie said in a loud, rasping voice, 'But you're *my wife*, Jessica,' and she came to with a start. She sat up, but there was no sign of Bertie. And no sign of Sam, either. The awful thing was that Bertie was still around to torment her, but it seemed likely that she would never see her darling Sam again.

When she woke, feeling as if she'd spent the night running a marathon, she found Ethel, Tom and the children had gone to Mass, but Dillon Reilly was waiting for her. Sammy had woken up and was playing with Humpty Dumpty and the fat pink pig, which, along with other presents, had mysteriously appeared beside his bed during the night. They wished each other Merry Christmas.

'There's just time for tea and toast before we set off for the ten o'clock service,' Dillon advised her.

Jessica said she could neither eat nor drink as she intended to take Holy Communion, and he confessed he'd broken his fast with a glass of whiskey and two mince pies consumed after midnight.

'Tom did the same. Ethel is really cross with us.' He edged towards the kitchen. 'I think I'll have that tea and toast.'

Jessica followed. It would be all right to have a glass of water, and breakfast was Sammy's favourite meal – he loved cornflakes. He climbed on to a chair and plonked the pig on the table to share the meal while Jessica emptied cornflakes in a bowl.

'How are you feeling?' Dillon asked as he lit the gas under the kettle. 'I didn't have the opportunity to speak to you yesterday. I understand that husband of yours went back to Colchester during the night. You really need to see a solicitor about him. Why not ask Tom for his advice?'

'I'll think about it.' As Tom was the person who had caused the rift with Bertie and the upheaval that had followed, he was the last person in the world she would ask for advice.

Counting the children, eighteen people sat down to Christmas dinner. The table was extended as far as it would go and the food was served buffet-style in the kitchen where people helped themselves. Ivy Black had gone to Bootle to have dinner with her sister where she would be waited on for a change.

Tom's relatives were all living in Ireland, but Jessica's Aunt Mildred and Uncle Fred and their son, Peter, were there. Peter had brought his new wife Irene – as an aeronautical draughtsman, he was in a reserved occupation and had never been called upon to join the Forces, much to his bitter disappointment.

'But not mine,' Irene pointed out.

'Our Lydia badly wanted to come home for Christmas,' Aunt Mildred said, 'but she just couldn't manage it.'

Lydia had joined the Wrens and was stationed in Portsmouth. They hadn't seen each other since Jessica had returned from Paris, and she wasn't exactly looking forward to it. Last time they'd met, her cousin had appeared to be in the middle of a nervous breakdown.

The couple who lived next door had been invited and two of Tom's colleagues at work, one a bachelor and another who had recently lost his wife.

Considering there was a war on and food was rationed, the meal was more than adequate. The family never went short of vegetables and fruit from the garden. Some of the fruit had been bottled during the summer months, and today there was a mouth-watering plum pie.

The bachelor, whose name was Francis, monopolized Jessica throughout the meal, but she didn't mind. All he wanted to talk about was himself, so there was no need to think of things to say. Throughout the meal she kept expecting the door to be flung open and Bertie to come in and make a scene.

Halfway through the afternoon, Sammy started to fall asleep, so she took him into the bedroom and stayed there herself, looking out of the window at the dreary garden and thinking about Sam and how much she missed him.

It wasn't until she heard the sound of carols being sung that she woke Sammy and they joined everyone in the parlour where they were now singing 'Silent Night', reminding her of the night in the *Petit Théâtre*, when the young Germans had joined in singing the same carol. The rest of the day she did her best to think only nice things, but at times found it very hard.

On Boxing Day, Dillon Reilly returned to London on the train. 'Will you come out with me for a drink next time I'm home?' he asked before he left. He wore the scarf she'd knitted him for Christmas, and she the amber bracelet he'd bought her. 'Only as friends, of course.'

Jessica nodded dutifully. 'Of course.'

Dillon had not long gone when Henri arrived home with some startling news: Sara had a boyfriend. 'Well, a manfriend; he's really old. She's been seeing him for over two years, before she found out that Louis was dead,' he said indignantly. 'Frannie knew nothing about it and she's really upset.'

'I'm not surprised, *I'm* upset.' Not only was Louis one of the nicest men she'd ever known, but also the best-looking. And to think Sara had actually been two-timing him! Just like you two-timed Bertie, a little voice reminded her.

Christmas over, Jessica decided it was time she got a job. She'd brought enough money back from Paris not to need to work for a while, but it was time she got out of the house more. Mornings, Sammy seemed happy to stay with Ethel and the children she looked after, but early in the afternoon he would invariably come looking for his mother.

She registered at the Labour Exchange and in January started work at the infant and junior school in the centre of the city where Lydia had used to teach, something she chose not to mention at interview in case Lydia had spoken of her immoral cousin to her fellow teachers.

'Most of the pupils are from wretchedly poor homes,' Mrs Milton the headmistress told her, 'which is why we give them a glass of warm milk and a thick slice of bread and margarine first thing in the morning, which will be your job, as well as helping to prepare the midday meal. If it weren't for that little snack, some kids would have nothing to eat from one school dinner to the next.'

'But don't they have ration books like everybody else?' Jessica queried.

'If you come and work for us you will quickly learn how the other half live.' Mrs Milton glanced meaningfully at Jessica's smart green coat and hat, which had cost an impressive amount of clothes coupons. 'Not everyone makes use of their ration books in the way we do ourselves. Did you know you can sell meat coupons for enough to buy twenty cigarettes? Milk, butter and eggs will purchase an entire night's beer. And the well-off will pay the earth for clothing coupons.'

Jessica didn't exactly love the work, but she did it willingly. She had always known poor people existed, but in the past had kept her distance. Seeing these children shivering in their thin clothes, with pinched little faces, she just wished she had the power to change the world so no one would be poor again and there would never be another war.

★

324

Henri was doing well at St David's. He spoke of going to university the year after next. 'Oxford or Cambridge, the teacher said,' he told Jessica. 'History, I'm not sure what period.'

'I didn't have a bar mitzvah,' he said one night. It was late March and Jessica was sitting in the garden for the first time that year, though it wasn't exactly warm. Sammy was chasing Daisy, who was determined not to be caught, while Jessica looked after the pig of which he was excessively fond. Henri leaned against a wall with his hands in his pockets, looking worried.

'What's that?' she asked.

'A bar mitzvah? It's a ceremony Jewish boys go through when they're thirteen. They become responsible for following Jewish law and the Torah – that's the first part of the Hebrew Bible.'

'Is it too late to have one now?'

He shrugged. 'I don't know.'

'Can't you ask someone at school?'

'I don't like to.' He shrugged again. 'I'd sooner other people didn't know.'

'Do you *want* a bar mitzvah?'

Unexpectedly, he burst out laughing. 'I don't know that, either. You see my parents were secular Jews who were also Communists.' He blushed slightly. 'They didn't have me circumcised and there was no question of me having a bar mitzvah, but I'm pretty certain everyone at school who is over thirteen has had theirs.'

'And I don't suppose you like the idea of being left out.' Jessica spoke half to herself. This was the first time he'd ever talked openly about his family and she felt glad. 'This is probably a silly question, but who would you sooner please – the boys at school or your parents?'

Henri gave up the wall and began to walk in a circle round

325

her. 'I suppose it depends on what sort of Jew I want to be,' he said eventually.

'Then perhaps it would be best to wait to make any decisions until you find that out.'

'Thank you, Jessica.' He beamed at her. 'I just knew you'd come up with the right answer.'

Jessica was surprised she'd come up with any answer at all. She hadn't heard of a bar mitzvah until today and had no idea what the word 'secular' meant.

On Easter Saturday, Sara married Victor Ford, a 48-year-old widower. Victor couldn't have been more different from her first husband, Louis, the blond, dazzling patriot and hero. Victor was amiably dull, which is perhaps what Sara wanted. He had no ambitions to be an actor, write plays or run a theatre, but worked as a clerk for the Liverpool–Victoria insurance company and his hobby was going to football matches. Though that might not last for long if Sara preferred he went shopping with her on Saturdays or demanded help making the dinner.

Frannie made a very reluctant bridesmaid and Marie re-membered her father enough to prefer him on every count to Victor.

It was a very low-key wedding. Jessica was happy for Sara, naturally, but couldn't get her dear friend Louis out of her mind as the priest in St Kentigern's church joined Sara and Victor together in Holy Matrimony.

'They're moving into Victor's house in Walton Vale, thank goodness,' Josef, Sara's long-suffering father, told Jessica when the ceremony was over. 'It means I will get my own house back. I only took it on for Sara to live in when she returned from Paris. I thought I could also live there and escape from my sister, Ruth, but my daughter drove me out with her bad temper and never-ending complaints, and I was forced to escape back to Ruth.'

As promised, Dillon Reilly came home once a month to see his children as well as Jessica. He brought her a small gift each time: a box of lace-trimmed handkerchiefs, a bottle of Shalimar perfume, a pair of lilac suede gloves. On Easter Sunday, he brought her a marcasite brooch in the shape of a J.

'Thank you,' she murmured when she opened the box. 'It's lovely.' The presents embarrassed her. She felt that, by accepting them, she was making some sort of commitment. At Christmas he had claimed to be still in love with his wife, that he and Jessica were only going out together as friends, but she sensed the relationship changing, at least on his part. The presents were becoming more and more expensive, and she imagined him searching the shops, looking for something suitable. And he had a look in his eyes that he probably didn't realize was there. He was falling in love with her, she could tell. But she felt nothing for him other than friendship.

Since Christmas, Allied troops had been approaching Germany from every front. Jessica read the papers eagerly and listened to the news on the BBC. Countries, cities and towns, places she had never heard of had been freed and the enemy vanquished, though not before they had slaughtered thousands of innocent prisoners and the pitiful occupants of concentration camps. The Royal Air Force continued to bomb Germany to destruction. The beautiful city of Dresden was bombed until there was hardly a building left standing.

But German rocket bombs were still falling on London, killing hundreds of people. The final bomb didn't fall until the end of March, by which time the Americans had crossed the Rhine and were already on German soil. Victory had begun.

Months ago, Jessica had written to Sam's parents in Canada. The letter had taken ages to compose because she didn't know what to say, but felt his family were entitled to know how happy he'd been in Paris where he'd had a girlfriend who loved him dearly. She didn't mention the pretend wedding or Sammy.

As German U-boats still prowled the Atlantic, she couldn't be sure if her letter would arrive. However, a highly emotional reply did come many weeks later from Sam's mother.

'My dearest Jessica,' the letter began, 'how wonderful to hear from you . . .' The letter went on to say that Sam's three brothers had served in the Forces, but as of now were safe and sound, 'though there is still time to go before this terrible war is over.'

Sam's father had been hit hard when the telegram had come to say his eldest son was Missing, Presumed Dead, and was recovering from a subsequent heart attack. He was still frail but would write to Jessica as soon as he felt better: 'And you must come and visit us, my dear girl, as soon as the world is at peace again. Your friend, Monica Devereaux.'

Jessica wrote back with a promise that she would. She had only written out of a sense of duty. She didn't want to visit Canada and publicly mourn Sam's death along with his parents and his brothers. She might go in a few years' time, but not yet.

Now it was April, almost May. The Allied armies were in Germany, closing in on Berlin from every direction. A sense of anticipation was in the air. It made people breathe more quickly because they knew something of worldwide importance was about to happen and it would be a day the like of which they would never experience again. A terrible war was about to end.

On 1 May Hitler killed himself in his bunker in Berlin. On the second day of the month, the Germans in Italy and Denmark surrendered. By the time Berlin fell, British people had already started to celebrate, though they were still waiting for an announcement that the long fight was finally over and peace had been declared. Flags were erected, bunting washed, Christmas lights unearthed to be hung in windows.

The day dawned at last. Jessica opened her eyes, half expecting there to be church bells ringing, trumpets blowing and the sky to be full of rainbows. But the sky looked quite ordinary, though she could hear the children calling to each other, and in the kitchen her mother and Ivy were laughing almost hysterically. The wireless was on and an organist was playing 'Roll Out the Barrel'.

On hearing the interesting sounds coming from outside the bedroom, Sammy climbed out of bed, clutching his pig, and left in search of entertainment.

'What shall I do today?' Jessica asked herself. The day had been declared a Bank Holiday and the schools were closed. Sara and her family were coming in the afternoon, except for Frannie, who was expected this morning. She and Henri were going to St George's Hall where it was rumoured a band was to play outside. Jamie, Dora and Dillon's children just intended to wander around Calderstones and the neighbouring areas to see what was going on, joining in if it took their fancy. Dillon himself was expected, though no one knew when; it depended if the trains were running. Bertie hadn't been seen since Christmas, but still telephoned Jamie and Dora on Sundays. He hadn't said if he was coming today.

Mid-afternoon, Larch Avenue was throwing a party and the ultra-respectable residents intended to dance in the streets. Tom was in charge of the music. He had rigged up a loudspeaker system and attached it to the radiogram.

Jessica got out of bed and opened the wardrobe to look for something to put on, something special for a special day. She caught her breath when she noticed, right at the end of the rack, almost hidden, the blue frock she'd worn when she and Sam were married. She put it on, smoothing the thin woollen material over her hips as she had done three, or was it four years ago? It felt like a million. She left in search of Sammy, who was still in his pyjamas. She found him in the kitchen eating cornflakes.

'That's a nice frock, Jessica,' her mother said. 'Did you buy it in Paris?'

'I made it myself, Mother – *Ethel*!'

Her mother grinned. 'You'll never get used to it, will you? What do you intend doing with yourself today?'

'If the trams are running, I thought I'd go to the Pier Head. I used to go a lot with Jamie and Dora when they were small. They loved watching the ferries sail in and out. I've never been with Sammy since I came home. I'll take his pushchair and walk back into town.' There might be somewhere open selling ice cream.

'Oh, my dear girl.' To Jessica's amazement, her mother came and cupped her face in her hands. 'You look so pale and wan, darling. Why don't you stay at home with us?'

She would sooner be alone with her son, who had the pig's nose buried in his cornflakes, urging it to eat the last few. When it didn't, he ate them himself. 'I feel like going out,' she said. 'Sammy could do with the fresh air. We'll be back in time for the party. Come along, Sammy, let's get you dressed and we'll be off.'

'I'm worried about her,' Jessica heard her mother say to Ivy later when she and Sammy went out the front door.

The trams were running normally, and she caught the number 8 down to the Pier Head. ' "Wish me luck as you wave me goodbye",' the driver sang when they arrived at the terminus, and the conductor insisted on shaking hands with every passenger when they got off. There were hordes of people about, many of them singing, some dancing, all deliriously happy.

An unexpectedly chill wind blew in from the river. Jessica

wished she'd worn a cardigan and brought a warm coat for Sammy. She lifted him into his pushchair and walked across to the dull pewter-coloured water. Seagulls hovered, squawking angrily. A packed ferry was about to dock at the landing stage and another was halfway across the river, sailing towards Birkenhead.

Sammy began to cry. 'Don't like it, Maman.' He jammed the pink pig over his eyes. 'Don't like it.'

'Sweetheart!' She picked him up and sat on a bench so he had his back to the river. His arms were cold. What an idiot she was. It hadn't crossed her mind that Sammy, used to the narrow confines of the rue de la Grand Truanderie, then Larch Avenue, where she hardly ever took him out, would find the sight of the river terrifying, with its strange colour and shrieking birds, and the giant ships like nothing he'd ever seen before.

'There, there, sweetheart.' She rocked him back and forth, yet still he cried. After a while she began to cry herself, hating herself for being so cruel and insensitive that she had made her baby cry. And because this was Liverpool, in no time at all they were surrounded by well-wishers. Jessica's back was patted, her shoulders squeezed, her arm stroked, while an old man played peekaboo with Sammy over her shoulder.

She was assured, most positively, that everything was going to be all right. The war was over, the lights were on again, Hitler was dead, and all was right with the world.

Another man offered a flask and urged her to 'take a swig, luv', which she did; it tasted horrible and made her choke, but she felt better for it. A woman asked if she would like a lift home, and Jessica gratefully accepted.

'My name's Enid Gray and I'm a midwife,' the woman said when, after thanking everybody profusely, Jessica, with Sammy on her knee and the pushchair in the boot, was being taken back to Calderstones. 'That's why I'm entitled to petrol to run a car.'

'It's really kind of you to give us a lift. I've never known Sammy be in such a state before.' Sammy had stopped crying, but clung to her tightly and still gave the occasional pathetic hiccup.

'You were in a bit of a state yourself,' Enid Gray said sympathetically. 'It's the sort of day when an awful lot of tears will be shed. I shall doubtless cry myself before the sun sets. I lost my sister, Caroline, in an air raid, you see. She was working down in London as a nurse.'

'I'm so sorry, that's awful.' Jessica felt as if she could easily cry again.

Her mother insisted on inviting Enid Gray in for a cup of tea. 'Jamie and Dora are in the parlour,' she told Jessica. 'They want to talk to you. Bertie has been, but he didn't stay long. He preferred not to wait until you got back. Give me Sammy. I'll look after him for a while. Come on, darling,' she cooed when the little boy was put in her arms. 'Has that mummy of yours been horrid to you?'

Her children wanted to talk to her! They hadn't really talked since she'd come back, not properly, not deeply. They hadn't been given an explanation for why she'd gone away because she had no idea what to tell them. She didn't think she could ever tell them what had happened with Tom, not even when they were adults with children of their own and she was an old, old woman.

Her blood curdled at the thought of what Bertie might have said. It would be just like him to turn Jamie and Dora against her. He might be concerned that when the war was over they would want to live with her.

Oh well, there was only one way of finding out. She flung open the parlour door and went in.

Dora jumped to her feet. 'Mummy! Daddy, just told us what happened. He said it wasn't you that left us, but us that left you. He said you and he had a terrible fight and when you went out one day he moved us across the water to Secombe so you wouldn't know where we were. But Mummy,' she said indignantly, 'Jamie and me, we didn't know, did we, Jamie?'

Jamie's face was bright red and Jessica realized it was because he was angry. 'No,' he growled. 'We didn't know.' He looked curiously at his mother. 'Why didn't you look for us?'

'Oh, Jamie, I looked everywhere. I even hired a detective. He searched all over the world. If I'd known you were only in Secombe, I'd've been over there like a shot.'

Dora clutched her hand. 'And Daddy said when he went to look for you, you'd gone to Paris to help Sara and hadn't been there long when the war started and you couldn't come home.'

'That's right.' She sank on to the settee, feeling lightheaded. Jamie sat on one side of her and Dora the other. They sat pressed against each other for quite a long time, not speaking, but knowing something that had been badly damaged had been mended and would never need mending again.

The spell was broken when Dillon burst into the room with his children to announce that tea and sandwiches were ready in the kitchen. 'We're not having a proper meal today because of the party.'

It was the longest, most cheerful and loudest party Jessica had ever known, though she felt too sad to enjoy it to the full. Too many people had died, too many terrible things had happened. She stayed mainly for Jamie and Dora, wanting them to know that from now she would always be there for them.

The lights had been switched on in every window of every house and, before the night was over, neighbours who'd hardly spoken to each other before had become the greatest of friends. People had racked their brains for songs to sing, and not a single one had been sung twice during the entire day.

Tom asked her to dance. Neither said much. When the

dance was over, he shook her hand and Jessica wondered if it was actually possible that he'd forgotten he had once made love to her.

She went indoors at about ten o'clock. Sammy had been in bed for hours being watched over by Ethel, who was badly missing Will.

'I'm a tiny bit drunk,' she confessed when Jessica found her in the kitchen with a cigarette in one hand and a glass of sherry in the other. 'Well, quite a lot drunk if the truth be known. Sometimes, I find it impossible to believe that I'll never see Will again.' She sighed. 'Would you like some sherry, darling?'

'Please, just half a glass.'

'And see that envelope on the bottom shelf of the dresser?' She pointed with a wobbly hand. 'Well, that's for you from Bertie. I forgot to give it to you earlier.'

Tom came in search of beer and Jessica took the sherry into the bedroom. Sammy was fast asleep, but she thought he still looked mournful after his fright that morning. She must be careful where she took him until he felt more settled in Liverpool.

She undressed for bed and propped the pillow against the headboard so she could lean on it while having the drink. First, she switched on the bedside lamp – without having to close the curtains first! – and opened the envelope. A cheque for one thousand pounds fell out and a sheet of blue paper folded in half. She unfolded the letter and began to read:

Dear Jessica,

Enclosed herewith is the money that your father left you. I should never have taken it in the first place. I have given the children what I hope is a satisfactory explanation for what happened between us. We both did some very bad things at that traumatic time, but I can't help but feel that mine were the worst. When I heard what you had done with Tom I wanted to kill

myself. As soon as I am demobbed, I shall go abroad, somewhere
very far away, I think, and not bother you or the children again.

I have always loved you, Jessica, and always will.

Bertie

Silly idiot! Tomorrow, she would write and tell him that under no circumstances was he to disappear out of his children's lives just when they'd got their mother back. They could live near each other, if not in the same house.

There was a knock on the door and Dora whispered, 'Goodnight, Mummy.' Jamie grunted something that might have been 'goodnight'.

'Goodnight, both of you,' Jessica said softly.

There was quiet for a while until she heard Henri ask, 'Is Jessica in?'

'Yes, darling,' said her mother. 'But don't disturb her, she's probably asleep.'

Such a lovely young, man, Henri. If only she'd met him at a less tragic time.

She did feel sleepy, actually, drinking the sherry slowly, sip by sip. So many memories chased each other through her brain. She must visit Simone soon, during the summer holidays perhaps. She'd take Sammy, naturally, and perhaps Jamie and Dora would like to go. She wondered what had been on at the *Petit Théâtre* that night and tears came to her eyes when she imagined Louis's spirit joining in with the audience when they belted out the Marseillaise at the end.

Somewhere, a clock struck midnight. Sam hadn't come, and she knew now that he never would.

She raised her glass and took the final sip. '*Au revoir*, Sam,' she murmured. Then she put the glass on the bedside table and lay down to sleep.

Epilogue

The Liverpool train standing on Euston station was a heaving, puffing, crowded monster. People were hanging out of the windows, and every compartment looked as if it contained at least a dozen passengers when the maximum was eight. The corridors were lined mainly with uniformed troops and just a few civilians. From the sound of it, every single person was jabbering away at the top of their voices, or singing.

It was no use walking further along the train, he realized, in the hope of finding a gap where he could stand for the next four or five hours – he'd given up all hope of a seat. It seemed that the further towards the front he went, the train became fuller. The engine gave a loud grunt and began to belch smoke at a rapid rate. He opened the next door he came to and squeezed inside.

'Breathe in, everyone,' the man next to him in the corridor shouted, an Army sergeant with a bright red face. 'Another passenger aboard. An officer, this time,' the voice continued loudly. 'Not so young, limping a bit, lost two fingers on his left hand, looks a bit the worse for wear.'

'Sit here, sir,' another voice shouted. A man slightly older than himself emerged from the nearest compartment wearing a sports jacket and flannels. 'I have been partying all day. In fact, I didn't go home last night, but stayed with a pal so I would be early for today's end-of-ghastly-war celebrations with friends rather than family. My name is Ronald Wicks, known as Ronnie, and when I get home my wife will kill me. To whom do I have the honour of bestowing my seat, sir?'

'Sam Deveraux.' Sam managed to fit sideways into the vacant space that was just about wide enough to take half an average person. Ronnie Wicks positioned himself in front, their knees touching.

'He's a first lieutenant in the Royal Air Force,' the red-faced sergeant supplied, poking his head in from the corridor.

Sam stifled the desire to hit him. Bloody know-all.

'And where have you come from, Lieutenant?' Ronnie asked. 'Or may I call you Sam?'

'Sam's fine.' Where had he come from? Canada, Paris, England, Poland, Berlin? 'Poland,' he decided. 'I spent most of the war there.'

'Poland!' Ronnie and the sergeant said together. 'What were you doing in Poland?'

'I was shot down there.' That wasn't quite true. He'd been flying over Berlin when both he and his plane had been hit. He'd flown blind, only half conscious, an unknown number of miles, before crash-landing in a Polish forest.

Behind Ronnie, a tiny girl had started to play peekaboo. Her face appeared, grinning, on his left side, his right, then left again. The owner of the knee she must be sitting on was hidden from sight. Sam found it hard to muster the energy to grin back. Eight people were seated and three were standing, including Ronnie. The sergeant was half in the compartment and half out, carrying on two conversations at the same time. In the corridor, someone was playing a mouth organ and songs were being sung.

Could he possibly stand this racket all the way to Liverpool? Of course he could. He'd come out of the plane crash with numerous bones broken; both his legs, his collar bone, several ribs, his left wrist. He'd been unconscious for days, bedridden for weeks, unable to walk for months.

337

If he could come through that alive, then he could stand a few hours of cheerful noise on a train.

Above his head, the sergeant and Ronnie were having an argument about what would be the most horrible way to kill Hitler had he still been alive. Sam closed his tired eyes and pretended to be asleep in case he was asked for his opinion.

In the forest, he'd been rescued by Armia Krajowa, the Polish Resistance. His crew were either dead or had been captured by the Germans that roamed the forest.

It took almost a year before he was able to run. Every new movement desperately hurt some part of his body, but he exercised with such ferocious determination that the time eventually came when he could ignore the hurt.

'Don't disturb him,' a voice said. 'He's asleep.'

The voice was on the train, not in his mind. It was Ronnie protecting him from something or someone. Sam opened his eyes.

'Now see what you've done,' Ronnie said accusingly. 'I told you not to disturb him.'

'I was just wondering if he'd like a cup of tea,' a soft voice said. It was a girl, a pretty blonde, who was offering him a metal cup, the sort that screwed on to the top of a flask. 'It's got sugar in,' she added.

'Thank you.' He took the cup and looked apologetically at Ronnie. 'I really feel like a drink. What's your name?' he asked the girl.

'Rita,' she replied. 'What's yours?'

'Sam.'

'Are you married, Sam?'

'I'm married to Jessica.' The memory of their hilarious wedding day had helped him through the worst of the last few years.

'My wife's name is Gladys,' Ronnie said, as if jealous of being left out.

'Do I really look the worse for wear?' Sam said in a low

338

voice to Rita. Through the window he glimpsed bonfires, fireworks going off, lights on everywhere.

Rita studied his face. 'You look tired,' she admitted, 'but tough. You probably need to convalesce for a few weeks and you'll be fine. Jessica will look after you.'

Ronnie butted in. 'Did you do much fighting in Poland, Sam?'

'A bit.' Along with the Polish AK, he'd lived in the forest and fought the Germans, driven one of their captured tanks, blown up trains. He'd slept in tents, huts, abandoned farm buildings, in the open air, in snow. Once, he'd rescued a baby from a burning house, burning his arms and some of his hair in the process. The fingers he'd lost when a fellow soldier accidentally opened fire on him.

Last Christmas, he'd caught a fever and nearly died. He'd been saved when one of the women with them, Halina, had laid down in the tent with him, holding his shivering body until the warmth from hers had flowed into his. He still hadn't fully recovered when, last week, a rumour reached them that the war was likely to be over any minute. A group of them, all different nationalities, had made their way to Berlin. He'd managed to get the required papers, a uniform, and travel permits, and he'd travelled across Europe by train to London. And now he was on his way to Liverpool to see Jessica.

He opened his eyes. Ronnie and the sergeant had gone. The little girl and her owner had also disappeared, as had half the other occupants of the compartment. Some had been replaced, but it was only half full.

Rita was in the seat opposite and must have noticed his surprise. 'We stopped at Rugby,' she said, 'but you didn't wake up. The chap you were talking to left a note on your knee.'

Sam picked up the scrap of paper. It was a page torn from a diary and said, 'Why not give me a ring sometime? Ronnie

Wicks,' and was followed by a number. He thought he might well do that.

He tucked the number in his pocket and fell asleep again. When next he woke, Rita was shaking him and they were in Liverpool. His legs could hardly support him after sitting for so long, but he managed to stagger towards a taxi. He asked the driver to take him to Larch Avenue and a house that looked like a wedding cake, according to Jess.

The Victory celebrations were still going strong although it was past midnight. Revellers danced in the street, though somewhat tiredly. When they sang, their voices were hoarse. In Larch Avenue, where Jessica lived – where he prayed she still lived – the sound of Glenn Miller playing 'String of Pearls' was coming from a loudspeaker and people were standing in groups on the pavement or in their front gardens. It was a scene you'd expect to see on a Sunday afternoon, not in the middle of the night.

'I think this is the house that you want,' the taxi driver said. He stopped outside a white single-storey building and refused to take the money for the fare. 'Good luck, mate.'

'And the same to you.'

Sam alighted from the taxi. The door to the house was wide open. There was shouting and laughter coming from inside. He rang the bell and a woman came into the hall.

'Hello.' She smiled.

'Hello.' He couldn't think what else to say. 'I'd like to see Jessica,' he stuttered.

'She's in bed. I'll just fetch her mother.'

The door to the room where the noise was coming from opened and Frannie came out. 'Sam!' she screamed. 'Oh, Sam! We thought you were dead.' She leaped upon him and almost brought him to the ground, then began to rain kisses on his face. 'Henri, Henri,' she shrieked, 'come and see who's here!'

Henri appeared and shook Sam's arm so enthusiastically that

Sam worried it would be torn from his shoulder. Henri had grown a foot since he'd last seen him and was now at least six feet tall.

More people came pouring out of the room, children, adults, a dog. They stood and regarded Sam with interest. A capable woman with grey hair came to the fore.

'Am I dreaming?' asked a voice. Sam turned, and there she was; Jessica, rubbing her eyes, looking even more beautiful than he remembered.

'No, no,' a dozen other voices assured her.

'It's Sam, it really is Sam,' Frannie cried.

A little boy wearing striped pyjamas had appeared beside Jessica, clutching a strange stuffed animal to his chest. 'You've woken my pig up,' he said crossly.

Jessica laid her hand on his head. 'Say hello to your daddy, Sammy.'

'Oh, for goodness' sake,' the grey-haired woman said impatiently. 'Let's all get out of the way and leave Jessica, Sam and Sammy to themselves.'

Everyone shuffled silently back into the room they'd just come from, and the door closed.

Sam picked up his son and put his arm round Jessica. He ushered them into the bedroom, and that door closed, too.

MAUREEN LEE

MAUREEN LEE IS ONE OF THE BEST-LOVED SAGA WRITERS AROUND. All her novels are set in Liverpool and the world she evokes is always peopled with characters you'll never forget. Her familiarity with Liverpool and its people brings the terraced streets and tight-knit communities vividly to life in her books. Maureen is a born story-teller and her many fans love her for her powerful tales of love and life, tragedy and joy in Liverpool.

The Girl from Bootle

Born into a working-class family in Bootle, Liverpool, Maureen Lee spent her early years in a terraced house near the docks – an area that was relentlessly bombed during the Second World War. As a child she was bombed out of the house in Bootle and the family were forced to move.

Maureen left her convent school at fifteen and wanted to become an actress. However, her shocked mother, who said that it was 'as bad as selling your body on the streets', put her foot down and Maureen had to give up her dreams and go to secretarial college instead.

As a child, Maureen
was bombed out of
her terraced house
in Bootle

Family Life

A regular theme in her books is the fact that apparently happy homes often conceal pain and resentment and she sometimes draws on her own early life for inspiration. 'My mother always seemed to disapprove of me – she never said "well done" to me. My brother was the favourite,' Maureen says.

> 'I know she would never have approved of my books'

As she and her brother grew up they grew apart. 'We just see things differently in every way,' says Maureen. This, and a falling out during the difficult time when her mother was dying, led to an estrangement that has lasted 24 years. 'Despite the fact that I didn't see eye-to-eye with my mum, I loved her very much. I deserted my own family and lived in her flat in Liverpool after she went into hospital for the final time. My brother, who she thought the world of, never went near. Towards the end when she was fading, she kept asking where he was. To comfort her, I had to pretend that he'd been to see her the day before, which was awful. I found it hard to get past that.'

Freedom – Moving on to a Family of Her Own

Maureen is well known for writing with realism about subjects like motherhood: 'I had a painful time giving birth to my children – the middle one was born in the back of a two-door car. So I know things don't always go as planned.'

'My middle son was born in the back of a two-door car'

The twists and turns of Maureen's life have been as interesting as the plots of her books. When she met her husband, Richard, he was getting divorced, and despite falling instantly in love and getting engaged after only two weeks, the pair couldn't marry. Keen that Maureen should escape her strict family home, they moved to London and lived together before marrying. 'Had she known, my mother would never have forgiven me. She never knew that Richard had been married before.' The Lees had to pretend they were married even to their landlord. Of course, they did marry as soon as possible and have had a very happy family life.

Success at Last

Despite leaving school at fifteen, Maureen was determined to succeed as a writer. Like Kitty in *Kitty and Her Sisters* and Millie in *Dancing in the Dark*, she went to night school and ended up getting two A levels. 'I think it's good to "better yourself". It gives you confidence,' she says. After her sons grew up she had the time to pursue her dream, but it took several years and a lot of disappointment before she was successful. 'I was *determined* to succeed. My husband was one hundred per cent supportive. I wrote lots of

'I think it's good to "better yourself". It gives you confidence'

articles and short stories. I also started a saga which was eventually called *Stepping Stones*. Then Orion commissioned me to finish it, it was published – and you know the rest.'

*What are your memories of your early
years in Bootle?*

Of being poor, but not poverty-stricken. Of
women wearing shawls instead of coats. Of
knowing everybody in the street. Of crowds
gathering outside houses in the case of a
funeral or a wedding, or if an ambulance
came to collect a patient, who was carried out
in a red blanket. I longed to be such a patient,
but when I had diptheria and an ambulance
came for me, I was too sick to be aware of the
crowds. There were street parties, swings on
lamp-posts, hardly any traffic, loads of children playing in the street, dogs without leads.
Even though we didn't have much money,
Christmas as a child was fun. I'm sure we
appreciated our few presents more than children do now.

*What was it like being young in Liverpool
in the fifties?*

The late fifties were a wonderful time for my
friends and me. We had so many places to go:
numerous dance halls, The Philharmonic
Hall, The Cavern Club, theatres, including
The Playhouse where you could buy tickets
for ninepence. We were crushed together on

benches at the very back. As a teenager I loved the theatre – I was in a dramatic society. I also used to make my own clothes, which meant I could have the latest fashions in just the right sizes, which I loved. Sometimes we'd go on boat trips across the water to New Brighton or on the train to Southport. We'd go for the day and visit the fairground and then go to the dance hall in the evening.

> 'We clicked instantly and got engaged two weeks later'

I met Richard at a dance when he asked my friend Margaret up. When she came back she said, 'Oh, he was nice.' And then somebody else asked her to dance – she was very glamorous, with blonde hair – still is, as it happens. So Richard asked me to dance because she had gone! We clicked instantly and got engaged two weeks later. I'm not impulsive generally, but I just knew that he was the one.

*Do you consider yourself independent
and adventurous like Annemarie in* The
Leaving of Liverpool *or Kitty in* Kitty
and her Sisters?

In some ways. In the late fifties, when I was
sixteen, Margaret and I hitchhiked to the
Continent. It was really, really exciting. We
got a lift from London to Dover on the back
of a lorry. We sat on top of stacks of beer
crates – we didn't half get cold! We ended up
sleeping on the side of the road in Calais
because we hadn't found a hotel. We travelled
on to Switzerland and got jobs in the United
Nations in Geneva as secretaries. It was a
great way to see the world. I've no idea what
inspired us to go. I think we just wanted some
adventure, like lots of my heroines.

*Your books often look at the difficult side
of family relationships. What experiences do
you draw on when you write about that?*

I didn't always find it easy to get on with my
mother because she held very rigid views.
She was terribly ashamed when I went to
Europe. She said, 'If you leave this house
you're not coming back!' But when we got to
Switzerland we got fantastic wages at the
United Nations – about four times as much as

we got at home. When I wrote and told her she suddenly forgave me and went around telling everybody, 'Our Maureen's working at the United Nations in Geneva.'

> 'If you leave this house you're not coming back!'

She was very much the kind of woman who worried what the neighbours would think. When we moved to Kirkby, our neighbours were a bit posher than us and at first she even hung our curtains round the wrong way, so it was the neighbours who would see the pattern and we just had the inside to look at. It seems unbelievable now, but it wasn't unusual then – my mother-in-law was even worse. When she bought a new three-piece she covered every bit of it with odd bits of curtaining so it wouldn't wear out – it looked horrible.

My mother-in-law was a strange woman. She hated the world and everyone in it. We had a wary sort of relationship. She gave Richard's brother an awful life – she was very controlling and he never left home. She died in the early nineties and for the next few years my kind, gentle brother-in-law had a relation-ship with a wonderful woman who ran an animal sanctuary. People tend to keep their family problems private but you don't have to look further than your immediate neighbours to see how things really are and I try to reflect that in my books.

'You don't have to look further than your immediate neighbours to see how things really are'

Is there anything you'd change about your life?

I don't feel nostalgic for my youth, but I do feel nostalgic for the years when I was a young mum. I didn't anticipate how I'd feel when the boys left home. I just couldn't believe they'd gone and I still miss them being around although I'm very happy that they're happy.

Are friendships important to you?

Vastly important. I always stay with Margaret when I visit Liverpool and we email each other two or three times a week. Old friends are the best sort as you have shared with them the ups and downs of your life. I have other friends in Liverpool that I have known all my adult life. I have also made many new ones who send me things that they think will be useful when I write my books.

Have you ever shared an experience with one of your characters?

Richard's son from his first marriage recently got in touch with us. It was quite a shock as he's been in Australia for most of his life and we've never known him. He turned out to be a charming person with a lovely family. I've written about long-lost family members returning in *Kitty and Her Sisters* and *The Leaving of Liverpool* so it was strange for me to find my life reflecting the plot of one of my books.

Describe an average writing day for you.

Wake up, Richard brings me tea in bed and I watch breakfast television for a bit. Go downstairs at around 8 o'clock with the intention of doing housework. Sit and argue with Richard about politics until it's midday and time to go to my shed and start writing. Come in from time to time to make drinks and do the crossword. If I'm stuck, we might drive to Sainsbury's for a coffee and read all the newspapers we refuse to have in the house. Back in my shed, I stay till about half seven and return to the house in time to see *EastEnders*.

Don't miss Maureen's bestselling novels:

Stepping Stones
Lights Out Liverpool
Put Out the Fires
Through the Storm
Liverpool Annie
Dancing in the Dark
The Girl from Barefoot House
Laceys of Liverpool
The House by Princes Park
Lime Street Blues
Queen of the Mersey
The Old House on the Corner
The September Girls
Kitty and Her Sisters
The Leaving of Liverpool
Mother of Pearl
Nothing Lasts Forever
Martha's Journey
Au Revoir Liverpool